The Ritual

Adam L. G. Nevill was born in Birmingham, England, in 1969 and grew up in England and New Zealand. He is the author of the horror novels: *Banquet for the Damned, Apartment 16, The Ritual, Last Days, House of Small Shadows, No One Gets Out Alive, Lost Girl* and *Under a Watchful Eye*. His first short story collection, *Some Will Not Sleep: Selected Horrors*, was published on Halloween, 2016.

His novels *The Ritual, Last Days* and *No One Gets Out Alive* were the winners of The August Derleth Award for Best Horror Novel. *The Ritual* and *Last Days* were also awarded Best in Category: Horror, by R.U.S.A. Many of his novels are currently in development for film and television, and in 2017 Imaginarium adapted *The Ritual* into a feature film.

Adam lives in Devon, England.

By Adam Nevill

Novels

Banquet for the Damned

Apartment 16

The Ritual

Last Days

House of Small Shadows

No One Gets Out Alive

Lost Girl

Under a Watchful Eye

Short Story Collections

Some Will Not Sleep

Cries from the Crypt

ADAM NEVILL

The Ritual

PAN BOOKS

First published 2011 by Macmillan

First published in paperback 2011 by Pan Books

This edition first published 2017 by Pan Books
an imprint of Pan Macmillan
20 New Wharf Road, London N1 9RR
Associated companies throughout the world
www.panmacmillan.com

ISBN 978-1-5098-8344-8

1 3 5 7 9 8 6 4 2

A CIP catalogue record for this book is available from the British Library.

Typeset by Ellipsis, Glasgow
Printed and bound by CPI Group (UK) Ltd, Croydon, CR0 4YY

Visit **www.panmacmillan.com** to read more about all our books
and to buy them. You will also find features, author interviews and
news of any author events, and you can sign up for e-newsletters
so that you're always first to hear about our new releases.

For Anne and our cub,
for making me and my life less beastly.

ACKNOWLEDGEMENTS

Tired, bedraggled and wretched is the writer who walks alone. So many thanks to Hugh 'Hershey' Simmons for not only reading this book so thoroughly (and more than once at that), but for the expeditions he has led; especially the one that gave birth to this idea, that saw us forced to make camp in the snow, shortly after finding two dead sheep hanging from trees. I've carried the recollection for nineteen years until it found a home in this story.

The deepest affection to Anne for her love, support, patience and advice, and to my dad for his careful readings again.

National Parks in Sweden: Europe's Last Wilderness by Claes Grundsten; *The Dolmens and Early Passage Graves of Sweden* by Christopher Tilley; *Early Norrland 10: Lapps and Scandinavians: Archeological Finds from Northern Sweden* by Ingrar Zachrissan; *The Land of the Midnight Sun* by Paul Belloni Du Chailu, were all essential to my research. And I owe much to that insightful and fascinating book, *Lords of Chaos: The Rise of the Satanic Metal Underground* by Didrik Soderland and Michael Moynihan, without which Blood Frenzy would never have formed. I have taken a liberty with the concept of 'a fist in the face of God' created in the lyrics of Darkthrone's 'To Walk the Infernal Fields', and amended

ACKNOWLEDGEMENTS

the idea into a notion of 'spitting in the face of God' on page 349, to affect Blood Frenzy's emulation of early Black Metal revolutionary ideas. The chilling true stories of John Krakauer, Simon Yates, Joe Simpson and Nick Heil, and the fiction of Algernon Blackwood, Arthur Machen, Scott Smith, Cormac McCarthy and James Dickey all made me want to write about life and death in the wilderness.

Very special thanks to my agent John Jarrold and my editor Julie Crisp for their support and advice. Much gratitude also goes out to Chloe Healy, Amy Lines and Liz Johnson, and the team at Pan Macmillan for giving me a chance, and then spreading the word.

Cheers to Steve Saville and his wife for checking my Swedish incantation. And I want to raise my claws in tribute to the bloggers, reviewers and readers of *Apartment 16*, who really opened the door for that book and for its author. A final long salute to Horror Reanimated, Mathew Riley, Joseph Delacey, Peter Tennant, Andrew Cox, and *Black Static* for their continued interest and support.

The Gods are here, if they are anywhere at all in the world.

Algernon Blackwood,
from *The Willows*

I

BENEATH THE REMAINS

PROLOGUE

And on the second day things did not get better. The rain fell hard and cold, the white sun never broke through the low grey cloud, and they were lost. But it was the dead thing they found hanging from a tree that changed the trip beyond recognition. All four of them saw it at the same time.

Right after they clambered over another fallen tree to stumble into more of the scratching bracken, they came across it. Breathing hard, damp with sweat and rain, speechless with fatigue, they came to a halt. Bent from the weight of the rucksacks, bedding and wet tents, they stood under it. Looked up.

Above them, beyond the reach of a man standing upright, the dead thing sagged. Between the limbs of a spruce tree it was displayed, but in such a tattered state they could not tell what it had once been.

From the large rib cage drooped the gut, wet and blue in the light seeping through the canopy of leaves. The pelt was spread out across surrounding branches, holed but stretched taut in places. A ragged hem about a crumpled centre suggested the skin had been torn from the back in one quick ripping motion. And at first no head could be seen in the mess of blood and flesh. Until, in the violent red and yellow suddenness of hung meat, the bony grin of a jaw bone was picked out by them all. Just above it was an eye, big as a snooker ball but glazed and dull. Around it a long skull in profile.

Hutch turned to face the others. He always led the group as it staggered through the forest looking for the new trail. It was his idea to come through here. His face was pale and he did not speak. Somehow the shock of this sight made him look younger. Vulnerable, because this mutilated statement up above their heads was the only thing on the camping holiday he did not have an answer for. Didn't have a clue about.

Phil couldn't keep the tremor from his voice. 'What is it?' No one answered him.

'Why?' Dom said. 'Why would you put it up there?'

The sound of these voices reassured three of them enough to start talking over each other. Sometimes answering questions. Sometimes just voicing new ideas. Only Luke said nothing. But as the others talked they moved away from the thing in the tree more quickly than they had approached it. And soon they were all silent again, but their feet made more noise than at any other time during the hike of the last two days. Because there was no smell coming from the corpse. It was a fresh kill.

ONE

FOUR HOURS EARLIER

At midday, Hutch stopped walking and turned to look back at the others; three colourful figures appearing insignificant upon the misty vastness of the rocky landscape they meandered across. They were spread apart along a plain of flat grey rock, smoothed like a footpath by the retreating ice a few million years before. Every set of shoulders on his companions was hunched, every head was bowed to observe the monotony of one foot before the other.

In hindsight, only he and Luke were fit enough for the three-day hike. Phil and Dom were carrying too much weight and the blisters on the heels of Phil's feet were now raw meat. Of more concern, Dom had twisted his knee on the first day in a vast boulder field, and after walking on it for a day and a half he now limped and winced with every step.

Through their discomforts Dom and Phil were missing everything of interest: the sudden strip marshes, the faces in the rock formations, the perfect lakes, the awesome Måskoskårså valley grooved into the earth during the Ice Age, the golden eagle circling above it, and the views of a landscape it was impossible to believe existed in Europe. Even in the rain and bad light the country could be astonishing.

But by the afternoon of the very first day, Dom and Phil had their heads down and eyes half closed.

'Take a load off, guys.' Hutch called back to the other three. Luke looked up and Hutch beckoned with his head for Luke to catch up to him.

Hutch eased his pack off his back, sat down, and pulled the map from the side pocket of his rucksack. His back was aching from walking so slowly at the pace set by Dom and Phil. He could feel his irritation evolving into anger, manifesting as a tightening across his chest; it seemed to bustle behind his teeth too, as if his jaws were clamping down on a long hot monologue of curses he wished to rain down upon the two men who were turning this trip into what now felt like a death march.

'What's up?' Luke asked, squinting through the fine drizzle that made his square features shiny. The rain and his sweat created a froth around his unshaven mouth and upon his blond eyebrows.

'Judgement call. Change of plan.'

Squatting beside him, Luke offered Hutch a cigarette. Then lit his own with hands red as raw beef.

'Cheers, buddy.' Hutch spread the map across his thighs. He issued a long sigh that came from a deep place and hissed around the cigarette filter clamped between his teeth. 'This ain't working.'

'This is my surprised face,' Luke said, deadpan. Then turned his head and spat. 'Ten bloody miles a day. That was all we asked of them. I know there's been some rough ground, but they were done for day one.'

'Agreed. So we need a new route. Got to cut this short now or we'll end up carrying them. One each.'

'Fuck's sake.'

Hutch rolled his eyes in conspiratorial agreement, but realized in this moment of weakness, he was probably only encouraging a similar tirade he'd sensed rising in Luke since they met at his flat five days ago. Luke just wasn't clicking with Dom and Phil at all, and the physical hardship and terrible weather had added a whole new element of corrosive tension and sniping into the mix. Something Hutch had been doing his best to limit by remaining enthusiastic, patient, and with his sporadic optimistic outbursts about the weather changing. He could not take sides; could not allow division. This was no longer a matter of salvaging a reunion holiday, but one of safety.

Luke's mouth went all tight and his eyes narrowed. 'New shoes. Wrong socks. Phil's even wearing jeans today. What did you tell him? Jesus Christ Almighty!'

'Ssh. I know, I know. But breaking their balls is only going to make things worse at this moment in time. Much worse. So we need to put the safety catch back on. Me included. OK?'

'Understood.'

'Anyway, I reckon I got it figured out.'

Luke swatted the khaki hood off his head; lowered his face to the map. 'Show me.'

Hutch pressed a finger to an approximation of where he believed them to now be floundering, and behind schedule, on the map. 'Another afternoon and a full day in the rain up here is going to ruin things beyond repair. So forget Porjus. We're just not going to make it. But if we drop south east. Here. Through this forest, which you can just see in the distance. See it?' Luke nodded at where Hutch was pointing; at a dark spiky strip of distant woodland, half concealed by drifting white vapours. 'If we slip through the section where it's narrow, here, we should come out near the Stora Luleälven River by early evening, maybe earlier. We can follow a trail along it eastwards. And downriver there's a couple of tourist huts at Skaite. Bit of luck and we'll be at the river by nightfall. If we shift it. We can walk downriver to Skaite tonight. Or, worse-case scenario, we camp by the river and hit the huts tomorrow morning. We can put our feet up for a day at Skaite and demolish Dom's Jack Daniel's before an open fire. Smoke some cigarettes. Then I'll look at arranging some transport back to Gällivare the day after. And in the forest this afternoon we'll be less exposed to the rain, which is showing no signs of stopping.' Hutch looked at the sky, squinted, then turned his gaze upon Dom and Phil; the twin huddled lumps, coated in Gore-Tex, seated and silent, just out of earshot. 'Not much walking left for this pair. So I'm afraid, buddy, that the expedition is over today, more or less.'

Luke gritted his teeth. His whole face tensed hard. He dropped his head when he realized Hutch was studying him.

Hutch was shocked at how much anger Luke had in him these days. Their regular phone calls, that Luke tended to initiate, often deteriorated into rants. It was like his friend could no longer internalize his rage and deal with it. 'Hey, anger management.'

Luke looked startled. Hutch winked at him. 'Can I ask a huge favour?'

Luke nodded, but looked wary.

'Like I said, cut the Slim Fast Massive some slack.'

'I will.'

'I know there's some attitude there. Especially Dom. But they're both feeling the strain right now. Not just this. Other shit too.'

'Like what? They never said anything to me.'

Hutch shrugged; could see how disappointed Luke was to be in the dark about Dom and Phil's domestic situations. 'Well . . . kids and stuff. You know Dom's youngest lad has a few problems. And Phil's wife is a permanent state of ball-ache for the guy. There's some trouble at both mills, if you follow. So go easy, is all I'm saying.'

'Sure. No worries.'

'On the bright side,' Hutch said, trying to change the conversation, 'we cut this crap in half today, then we get more time in Stockholm before we head back. You love that town.'

'I guess,' Luke said.

'But?'

Luke shrugged. Blew smoke out through his nose. 'At least here, we are on a trail we can see on the map. The forest is new ground. It's off piste, mate. There are no trails marked.'

'It'll be a treat. Trust me. Wait until you get inside. It's National Park. Completely untampered with. Virgin forest.'

Luke's index finger tapped the map. 'Maybe . . . but you don't know what the ground is like in there. At least this rock is flat. There's marshes in there, H. Look. Here. And here.'

'We won't go near them. We'll just weave through the thinnest band of the trees, here, for a couple of hours, and *voilà* . . . pop out the other side.'

Luke raised his eyebrows. 'You sure? No one will know we're down there.'

'Makes no difference. The Environment office was closed

9

when we left, and I never called ahead to the Porjus branch. It'll be fine though. That's only a precaution for winter. It's hardly even autumn. There won't be any snow or ice. We might even see some wildlife in there. And the fat men couldn't walk on sponge for another two days, let alone rock. This short cut will halve the distance. We're still looking down the barrel at walking through the second half of today. And we'd need another whole day and evening to reach Porjus tomorrow. Look at them. They're done, mate.'

Luke nodded, exhaled long twin plumes of smoke down his nostrils. 'You're the boss.'

TWO

FOUR HOURS, TWENTY MINUTES LATER

Dead wood snapped under their soles and broken pieces were kicked away. Branches forced aside snapped back into those walking behind. Phil fell and crashed into the nettles, but stood up without a murmur and jogged to catch up with the others who were almost running by this time. Their heads were down and their shoulders were stooped. Twigs whipped faces and laces were pulled undone, but they kept going. Forward, until Hutch stopped and sighed and put his hands on his knees in a tiny clearing. A brown place where the dead wood and leaf mould was shallow and the thorny vines no longer ripped into socks or left burrs, impossibly, inside shirts and trousers.

Luke spoke for the first time since they'd stumbled across the dead animal. He was breathless but still managed to get a cigarette into his mouth. Only he couldn't light it. Four attempts he made with his Zippo until he was blowing smoke out of his nose. 'Hunter I reckon.'

'You can't hunt here,' Hutch said.

'Farmer then.'

'But why put it up there?' Dom asked again.

Hutch took his pack off. 'Who knows. There's nothing

cultivated in the whole park. It's wilderness. That's the whole point of it. I could use a smoke.'

Luke wiped at his eyes. Tears streamed down his cheeks. Bits of powdery bark kept getting under his eyelids. 'A wolf killed it. It was an elk, or deer. And . . . something put it in the tree.' He threw the packet of Camel cigarettes at Hutch.

Hutch picked the cigarette packet from the ground.

Phil frowned, stared at his feet. 'A forest has wardens. Rangers. Would they . . .'

Hutch shrugged, lit up. 'I wouldn't be surprised if we were the first people to walk through this bit. Seriously. Think of the size of the county. Twenty-seven thousand square kilometres. Most of it untouched. We're at least five kilometres from the last trail, and that's hardly ever used.'

Luke exhaled. He tried again. 'A bear. Maybe a bear put it up there. To stop things eating it. You know, on the ground.'

Hutch looked at the end of his cigarette, frowned. 'Maybe. Are they that big in Sweden?'

Dom and Phil sat down. Phil rolled a sleeve up a chubby white forearm to his elbow. 'I'm scratched to buggery.'

Dom's face was white. Even his lips. 'Hutch! I'll ram that map up your useless Yorkshire arse.' He often spoke to Hutch like this. Luke was always surprised at the outbursts, at the violence of the language. But there was no genuine hate in these exchanges, just familiarity. It meant Dom and Hutch were closer these days than he and Hutch. And he'd always considered Hutch to be his best friend. It made him envious because Dom and Hutch were better friends. They'd all known each other for fifteen years, but Dom and Hutch were just as close as they had been back at university. They even shared a tent. Both Luke and Phil felt short-changed by the arrangement; Luke could tell Phil felt the same way, even though it would be impossible for them to admit it without offending each other.

Dom pulled a boot off. 'Some holiday, you tosser. We're lost. You haven't got a clue where we are, have you, you mincing fruit?'

'Dom, cool your boots. Just about a click that way' – Hutch pointed in the direction they had been scrambling towards – 'you'll be eating hot beans and sausage beside a river. There's a quartet of Swedish beauties pitching their tent right about now, and getting the camp fire ready. Relax.'

Phil laughed. Luke smiled. Dom felt obliged to join in, but in seconds his laughter was genuine. And then they were all laughing. At themselves, at their fear, at the thing up in the tree. Now they were away from it laughter was good. It felt necessary.

THREE

They never found the river, and the mouth-watering dream of Swedish girls and hot beans with sausage dimmed like the September light, and then vanished along with any expectation of finding the end of the forest that day.

While the other three squatted in silence – Luke sitting apart from Dom and Phil, who wolfed energy bars – Hutch glared at the map again, for what must have been the fifth time in an hour. With a dirty finger, he traced the intended short cut between the Sörstubba trail they had abandoned at midday and the river trail. He swallowed again at the frisson of panic that had appeared in his throat as the light started to dim.

In the morning he had known exactly where they were on the map, where they were in the Gällivare municipality, where they were in Norrbotten County, and where they were in Sweden. By late afternoon, with the glimpses of sky through the treetops changing from a thin grey to a thicker grey, he was no longer certain where they were in the forest that intersected the two trails. And he never anticipated so much broken ground or the impenetrable thickets when he chose this route.

Which wasn't making any sense at all. They were no longer even following an approximation of a direct course; the sense of moving in the right direction stopped for him over two hours before. The forest was leading them. They needed to move south west, but once they were four kilometres deep it was as if they were being pulled due west, and sometimes even northwards again. They could only move where the foliage was thin, or where spaces occurred naturally between the ancient trees, so they were never moving in the right direction for very long. He should have compensated for that. *Shit*.

He glanced over his shoulder at the others. Maybe it was time for another judgement call: to go back the way they had come in. But if he could even find the haphazard route now, it would be dark by the time they returned to the place from where they had started at midday. And it would mean going past that tree again, with the animal hanging from it. He could not see the idea going over well with Dom and Phil. Luke would be cool with it. The forest made him uneasy too; he could tell. Luke's lips moved as he talked to himself; always a sign. And since they had been so deep among the trees he'd been smoking constantly; another bad sign.

At least the exertion was limiting the speculation on how the corpse came to be hanging from the tree. Hutch had never seen, read, or heard of anything like it; not in twenty years engaged in outdoor pursuits. It had confounded Luke too; he could tell his friend was still struggling with the mystery in silence. And also thinking exactly what he was thinking: *what the hell could do that to a large animal?* In his mind Hutch ran through images of bears, lynx, wolverine, wolves. No fits, but it was one of those. Had to be. Maybe even a man. Which seemed even more disturbing than an animal performing such a slaughter. But whatever had done that much damage to a body, wasn't far away.

'On your feet, men.'

Luke tossed his butt and stood up.

'Piss off,' Dom said.

'Here, here,' Phil added.

Dom looked up at Hutch. The lines at the side of Dom's mouth cut deep furrows through the filth on his face; his eyes were full of pain. 'I'm waiting for the stretcher, H. I can hardly bend my leg. I'm not joking. It's gone all stiff.'

'It's not far now, mate,' Hutch said. 'River's got to be close.'

FOUR

Four kilometres due east from the thing in the tree, they found a house.

But this was only after another four kilometres of wading through ivy, nettles, broken branches, oceans of wet leaves, and the impenetrable naked spikes formed by the limbs of smaller trees. Like everywhere else, the seasons were confused. Autumn had come late after the wettest summer since records began in Sweden and the mighty forest was only now beginning to shuck its dead parts to the ground with fury. And as they had all remarked, it was so 'bloody dark'. The thick ceiling of the trees let little daylight fall below to the tangled floor. To Hutch, the forest canopy left an incremental impression of going deeper inside something that narrowed around them; while looking for the light and space of an open sky they were actually descending into an environment that was only getting darker and more disorientating, step by step.

During the late afternoon and into the early evening, when they were too tired to do anything but stagger about and swear at the things that poked and scratched their faces, the forest had become so dense it was impossible to move in any single direction for more than a few metres. So they had moved backwards and forwards, to circle the larger obstacles, like the giant prehistoric trunks that had crashed down years before and been consumed by slippery lichen; and they had zigzagged to all points of the compass to avoid the endless wooden spears of the branches, and the snares of the small roots and thorny bushes, that now filled every space between the trees. The upper branches ratcheted up their misery by funnelling down upon them the deafening fall of rain in the world above, creating an incessant barrage of cold droplets the size of marbles.

But just before seven they suddenly fell across something they were sure they would never see again. A trail. Narrow, but wide enough for them to walk upright in single file, without lurching about or being tugged backwards by a sleeping roll or backpack snagged on a branch.

By this time Hutch knew that none of them even cared where the trail led, and they would have followed it north, just for the luxury of being able to walk upright and in a straight line. Even though the trail would lead them either due east or even further out west, instead of southwards, the forest had cut them their first break. He could sort out exactly where they were later and chose the eastern direction to try and compensate for the north-westward course the forest had thus far enforced. Someone had been here before them and the path suggested it went somewhere worth going. Somewhere out of this dark and choking nowhere.

It led to a house.

Their packs were soaked. Rivulets of water ran from their coats and soaked the thighs of their trousers, and Phil's jeans were sodden and black; the jeans Hutch told him in Kiruna not to take in case it rained. From the cuffs of their sleeves the rain poured onto their scratched and red hands. And it was impossible to tell if the rain had saturated and then seeped into the fleeces and clothes they wore underneath their Gore-Tex coats, or if the moisture was sweat soaking outwards from their hot skin. They were dirty and dripping and exhausted and no one had the nerve to ask Hutch out loud where they could pitch a tent in the forest. But that was what they had all been thinking; he knew it. On either side of the trail, the undergrowth was as high as a man's waist. And it was during that time, when the fear in Hutch's own belly began to turn into a shivery panic reminding him of childhood, and when the realization of the fact that he had made a terrible misjudgement and was now endangering the lives of his three friends hit him, that they found the house.

A dark and sunken building that slouched at the rear of an overgrown paddock. The ground was covered to the height of their knees with nettles and sopping weeds. A wall of the impenetrable forest they were lost inside bordered the grounds.

'It's empty. Let's get in there,' Phil said, his voice wheezy with asthma.

FIVE

'We can't just break in,' Luke said.

Phil bumped Luke's shoulder as he walked past. 'You can have the tent to yourself, mate. I'm spending the night in there.'

But Phil never took more than a few steps through the paddock. Whatever instinct made the other three hesitant caught up with Phil and he eventually stopped with a sigh.

They had seen hundreds of these *Stugas* on the train journey north from Mora to Gällivare, and then again around Jokkmokk. Outside of the cities and towns of northern Sweden there were tens of thousands of these simple wooden houses; the original homes of those who lived in the countryside before the migration to the cities over the last century. Luke knew they were now used for recreation during the long summer months by Swedish families when they renewed their bond with the land. Second homes. A national tradition; the *fritidshus*. But not this one.

It lacked the bright red, yellow, white or pastel walls they were accustomed to seeing on these fairy-tale houses. There was no neat white fence or lawn mowed flat as a bowling green. Nothing cute or quaint or homely about it. No sharp right angles or neat windows about its two storeys. Where there should have been symmetry it sagged. Tiles had detached and slid away. The bulging sides were blackened as if there had once been a fire and the place had not seen any attention since. Boards sprung loose near the foundations. The windows were still shuttered fast against winters that had come and gone. Nothing about it seemed to catch or reflect the watery light that fell into the clearing, and it suggested to Luke that the interior would be just as wet and cold as the darkening wood they were lost inside.

'What now, Hutch?' Within the confines of his glistening orange hood, Dom's round face was tight with irritation, but his eyes flicked about. 'Any more bright ideas?'

Hutch's eyes narrowed; they were pale green with long inky lashes and almost too pretty for a man. He took a deep breath, but didn't look at Dom. He spoke as if he hadn't heard his friend. 'It's got a chimney. Looks solid enough. We can get a fire going. We'll be as warm as toast in no time.' Hutch walked to the small porch, built around a door so black it lacked all definition within the front of the house.

'Hutch. I don't know. Better not,' Luke said. This wasn't right. Neither the house nor breaking into it. 'Let's get moving. It won't be dark until eight. We've got another hour and could be out of the forest by then.'

Around Luke the tension from Dom and Phil gathered until it felt like it was squeezing him to a standstill. Phil turned his bulk quickly with a rustle of wet blue Gore-Tex. His doughy face was dark red. 'What's wrong with you, Luke? You want to go back into that? Don't be a stupid arse.'

Dom joined in. As he spoke a drop of spit hit Luke's cheek. 'I can't walk any more. It's all right for you, your knee isn't the size of a rugby ball. You're as bad as the Yorkshire twat who got us into this.'

Luke went dizzy and hot. They would be forced to stay here for a night because Phil was so fat his feet were ruined merely by walking outdoors. His feet were ruined the first morning. That's when he started bitching about them. Even in London he drove everywhere. He'd lived there fifteen years and never used the Underground once. How was that possible? Dom was no better. He looked about fifty these days, not thirty-four. And every time he swore, it made Luke grind his teeth. Dom was a marketing director for a big bank with a mouth like a hooligan; what had gone wrong? He used to be a superb fast bowler who came close to county cricket, a guy who travelled across South America, and a friend you could stay up with all night, smoking joints. Now he was one of these married men with children, and a forty-six-inch waist, dressed from head to toe in Officers Club casuals, who tutted and sniggered and dismissed him whenever he mentioned some new girl he'd been seeing, or a crazy bar he'd visited back in London.

He recalled his shock when he'd struggled to continue a conversation with either Dom or Phil on the first day of the reunion, when they all met in London the night before the flight. They had laughed at his shared flat in Finsbury Park before they and Hutch fell to the usual banter, as if the three of them had been seeing each other every week for the last fifteen years. Perhaps they had. Right from the start he'd felt left out. A lump formed in his throat.

Hutch must have seen his face. 'Chieftain,' he said, and winked at Luke, conspiratorially, like a grown-up coming to the rescue of a boy being picked on in a playground. It just made Luke's face flush hotter, but his anger immediately switched to himself and against his own poisonous thoughts.

Hutch followed the wink with a warm smile. 'I don't think we have much choice, buddy. We have to get dry. We'll never do it in a tent. We've been pissed on all day.'

'Knock knock, we're coming in,' Phil called out and joined Hutch before the front door with more purpose than he'd shown all day while floundering and wheezing in the undergrowth. Suddenly, Luke couldn't stop himself glaring, all over again, at Phil's rounded shoulders and pointy head in the blue hood. He actually hated the sight of him right now, so he made a decision: once he was back in London, he'd even avoid their one drink a year.

'You can stay outside with the wolf that gave that moose a good seeing-to,' Dom said with a half-smile on his face.

Luke refused to meet Dom's eye, but found his voice; a tight, aggressive, sarcastic thing that slightly shocked him when he heard it come out of his own mouth. But he didn't care what he said, just wanted the others to know how he was feeling. 'Or we could feed you and your useless knee to him, and while he's busy stoving you in, we'll head to Skaite.'

Dom paused as he walked after Hutch and Phil. Disappointment and surprise softened his features for a moment before anger tightened them. 'Spoken with all the petulance of arrested development. Stay outside you silly arse and you can freeze to death. Who's going to miss you but some tart. This is for bloody real, if you hadn't noticed. I'd like to get home in one piece. People depend on me back there.'

Hutch snapped away from the door again, realizing the irritation behind him had turned to provocation. 'Time gentlemen, please. If you don't cool it, I'll fetch me a long piece of green cedar and stripe your arses.'

Phil burst into his dirty laugh that sounded unpleasant

near the house, but didn't bother to turn around. He banged and pushed at the door.

Too angry to move or breathe, Luke stared ahead, meeting no one's eye. As if the exchange had meant nothing to him, Dom followed Hutch back to the house. He even laughed. 'You'd enjoy that. Beating the buttocks of a fine young man in the woods.'

'I would. And I wouldn't check my swing either. You'd get it backhand.'

'There's no lock. But it's stuck,' Phil said.

Hutch removed his pack. 'Not for long. Step aside.'

Luke took the cigarette packet from the side pocket of his wet combat trousers. His hands were shaking. This was not the time to be analysing the situation, but he couldn't help it. Could not stop himself thinking about the four of them. Because the trip had been such a disappointment. Not because of the weather; he'd have come out here even if he had known it would rain every day. He had been so excited about hanging out with them all again and looked forward to it for the six months following Hutch's wedding, when the idea was first mooted. But the trip had been so wretched because he recognized so little of the others now. Which made him wonder if he had ever really known them at all. Fifteen years was a long time, but part of him had still clung to the notion that they were his best friends.

But he was truly on his own out here. They had nothing in common any more.

SIX

Once the door was open, Dom, Phil and Hutch rooted through their packs for torches. Nothing could be seen through the space Hutch had created by directing the stamping sole of his boot around the iron door handle.

With each bang of Hutch's foot on the shuddering wood, Luke had winced. The idea of it opening made him nervous. Reluctance to join the others at the door was worsened by his sulking after the confrontation with Dom, which now made him feel foolish, again. But he was also ashamed by this vandalism. He remained in the paddock in the rain while the others crowded around the door egging each other on.

Like the other three, he was dead on his feet. And wet and hungry and thoroughly miserable. He just wanted it all to end – the tortuous walking, the rain, the dark unpleasant forest – but they should not be reduced to this: breaking into private property. A place that just wasn't right. And had they really thought it through? This was a place no more than a few miles from the carcass in the tree. Something they could make no sense of, but should get as far away from as possible before nightfall.

Everyone's judgement was impaired. Nothing said or done now could be trusted. But somehow it wouldn't be forgotten or forgiven.

Slowly, Luke walked towards the black house. To the sound of their voices. The others were inside now, all talking at the same time. Someone was laughing. Phil. Luke threw his cigarette into the weeds and considered joining them and forcing himself back into the camaraderie.

A crash erupted behind him. A tremendous splintering of wood. From out of the trees.

He turned around and stared at the wall of dark wood they had just walked out of. Beside the silvery rain falling past the trees and the chaos of bracken between the thick trunks, nothing moved. But the terrific sound of strong fresh wood being snapped still rang through his ears. A trace of an echo, like the hollow sound made by a stone bouncing off tree trunks, seemed to pass away, deep into the forest.

What could possibly have broken a tree like that? Somewhere inside there, not too far back, he could almost see the pale sappy fibres and spikes breaking from the bark of a thick limb. Ripped from a blackened trunk like an arm from a torso.

Swallowing, and suddenly feeling weaker and more insignificant than he could ever remember, Luke couldn't move. Pulse up between his ears, he stood still, disorientated with fear, like he was waiting for something to smash out of the wood and rush towards him. He briefly imagined a terrific rage and strength, a terrible intent, out there. Imagined it until he almost accepted it.

Thunder rolled across the sky, over the treetops and into the wet murk above the house. The sound of the rain against the wood changed from a pattering to a sky-fall of stones.

'Buddy!' It was Hutch. 'Get in here. You have to see this.'
Luke snapped out of his trance. Wondered at himself.

Exhaustion overwhelmed you. Played tricks with your mind. The dark trees they had been amongst all afternoon and evening had left a stain inside him; a taint upon every thought and feeling if he allowed his mind to drift.

He needed to keep active. Focused. He moved to the door. Just inside the frame he could see Hutch's pale face peering out. He'd taken his hat off.

'Did you hear that?'

Hutch looked at the sky. 'I know. Thunder and a cloud burst. We couldn't have found this place any sooner. I think a storm would've finished off the fatties. We'd have been forced to lose them.'

'Piss off, Yorkshire!' Dom called from inside the dark hovel.

Despite his unease, Luke couldn't stop the nervous giggle that came down his nose. Stupidly, he was smiling too. Hutch turned around to go back inside the house, where torch beams flashed across indistinct walls.

'No. Not that. The trees. In the trees. Did you not hear it?'

But Hutch wasn't listening. He was back inside with the other two. 'What you got there, Domja?'

Luke heard Dom say, 'More of that evil Christian shit.' He took one look back at the woods then passed through the doorway to join the others.

SEVEN

It was impossible to tell how long the place had been unin-habited. Or what kind of people once lived there.

Uncovered by yellow torchlight, that struggled to reach far into the cramped hovel, the first thing Luke noticed were the skulls. And then the crucifixes.

From small birds to what could have been squirrels and stoats, small mottled heads had been fixed with rusted nails to the timber walls of the large room on the ground floor. Larger skulls of lynx and deer and elk had mostly fallen from the walls and cracked against the floorboards. One or two still grinned from near the low ceiling, where their porous bones managed to hang on.

Between the skulls still mounted upon the walls were at least a dozen crosses. By the look of them, though no one looked for too long, they had been handcrafted from bun-dles of twigs tied with twine, and were mostly tilting now, or even hanging upside down. From the ceiling beams that brushed the tops of their uncovered heads, two empty and corroded oil lamps creaked irritably on their hooks if touched.

Under the floor, mice scampered. In this place they sounded angry at being disturbed, though something far too confident and unafraid was also suggested in their rustlings.

Hutch came back from an annex joined to the main room. 'Tools and stuff. A nasty-looking scythe in there. I'd hazard a guess this place could be a hundred years old.' He went to the little iron stove in the hearth. He patted his dirty hands around its round belly. 'Bugger's rusted shut, but it feels dry-ish.'

Phil was testing the sawbuck table, which creaked under the pressure of his two hands pressing down. Dom had claimed the one seat – a crudely fashioned wooden stool at the head of the table – and was wincing as he tried to remove his boots. 'Hutch. Get your mittens on these. I can't undo the laces. I'm actually scared to see what's inside. And my knee feels like a water-skin full of nails. I want the magic spray you had this morning. Then you can get the fire going.'

From where he was crouching, Hutch grimaced at Dom over his shoulder. 'I'm seriously thinking of leaving you here in the morning.'

Around them the house creaked and shifted like a wooden ship trapped in the ice. 'Is this even safe?' Phil asked.

Hutch swore at the stove. And then, without moving his head, he said to Phil, 'I wouldn't put it to the test.'

Luke flashed his torch over the walls and ceiling again. He was the tallest of the four and as he warned himself to watch the low beams, he cracked the side of his head against one of the iron lamps.

Phil, Dom and Hutch laughed. 'You all right, mate?' Hutch then asked as an afterthought. 'That sounded nasty.'

'Fine.' Luke shone his torch at the narrow staircase that led to the second storey. 'Anyone been up there yet?'

'With this knee,' Dom said, 'I'm not moving again until Hutch fetches help and the Swedish air force lands a helicopter in the garden. Ain't that right, you hopeless York-shire arse? And you can use that map to get the fire going for all the use it's been.'

At this, they all laughed. Even Luke who couldn't help himself, or stop himself from warming to Dom all over again. He was being too sensitive. It was the dreadful forest and the desperate walking. His thighs still seemed to be moving as if they continued to clamber up and down rocky slopes and stretch over deadwood. They were just tired. That was all. 'I don't want to sound like a fool—'

'That could be a challenge,' Dom muttered, as he removed his second boot. 'Where's the spray, Hutch?'

Luke looked at Dom. 'Piss off.' Then turned to Hutch. 'But I definitely heard something out there. In the trees.'

Dom grimaced at him. 'Don't start with that crap. Things are bad enough in here without you giving me the shits.'

'I'm not messing around. It was like . . .' He couldn't describe it. 'A crash.'

No one was listening.

'I want new feet.' Phil stood up in his socks. 'Think I might go and check out the bedrooms.'

'I'll take the one with the en suite,' Hutch said. He was digging at the door of the stove with the penknife he had bought in Stockholm from the outdoor adventure store. Like everything else in the country, it hadn't been cheap. Luke bought one too because he liked the idea of having a knife in the wilderness. Dom dismissed them as being too expen-sive and said he would use Hutch's if he needed it. Phil lost his knife on the first day. He'd left it at the first camp-site.

Outside, the thunder ground iron hulls against granite. A

vivid flash of lightning followed and seemed far too close to the house. It lit up the dusty wooden floor by the open door.

Phil paused on the first of the stairs on his way up, and fingered a dark crucifix. As if to himself, he said, 'You'd think they'd make you feel safe. But they don't.'

EIGHT

Phil came down the stairs so quickly it sounded like a fall. If the bangs of his feet didn't get their attention, his gasps for air did.

Downstairs, three pairs of eyes went round and white. Three torch beams flashed to the foot of the staircase.

Through which Phil burst, then fell to his knees. He turned on to his backside and shuffled away from the whole idea of the stairs.

Inside Hutch's mind came the image of meat dripping from a tree.

Dom dropped his feet from the table to the floor. 'What the hell?'

Luke stood up from where he had been sitting close to the door, still peering out at the rain as if unable to accept that they intended to spend a night here. He kept his shoulders bent forward as if expecting a blow; opened his mouth but couldn't speak.

Stupidly, in his fright, Hutch felt a yawn rise through him.

Phil tried to shout but it came out a yelp. 'Something's' – he swallowed – 'up there!'

Hutch looked at the ceiling. He dropped his voice to a whisper. 'You are kidding me.'

'Let's go,' Dom said.

Hutch held a hand up. 'Ssh.'

Around the table, Dom and Phil scrabbled for their boots. Heads close, Dom asked Phil something in a whisper. Phil turned his head quickly towards Dom's face. 'I don't know! I saw it. In the bed.' It was a preposterous statement, but no one laughed or could even swallow. The very idea of a bed in this place should have cut the tension, but somehow it made everything worse.

Hutch held up two hands, palm outwards. They were filthy. 'Quiet! Cool it. Just cool it. There can't be anyone here. Look at the dust. There were no footprints when we came in. It's not possible.'

Plump face bloodless and quivering, Phil struggled to speak. 'It's in there. Up there.'

'What?' Dom demanded.

'An animal?' Luke asked.

Hutch looked at Luke. 'Get your shank out.'

Luke frowned.

'Knife,' Hutch said, then held up his own.

Dom had one boot on and was stabbing his naked toes at the other wet boot which scooted across the floor. 'This is getting stupid. Bloody stupid.'

Hutch strained his neck forward. 'Can't be an animal. Listen.'

Dom pulled the second boot back on and winced. 'Fuck this. I'm off.'

'Dom, shut it! Listen.' Hutch walked slowly to the foot of the stairs.

Luke moved away from the door to let Phil and Dom pass on their way out. 'Easy H. Could be a bear.'

Hutch shook his head. 'It would be down here with us by

now.' He looked at Phil and Dom who stood together on the porch, peering back inside. A gust of wet air and the smell of damp wood grew stronger indoors, as if eager to replace their presence inside. 'Phil. Was there a hole or something up there?'

'Eh?'

'A hole? In the roof? A window busted? Was it an animal?'

Phil swallowed. 'It was sitting up. Staring at me.'

'What?' Dom asked.

'I don't know. I saw some eyes in my torchlight. And something black. Something big. But it didn't move. It just sat there and stared at me.'

Dom threw his head back. 'Jesus Christ. I can't believe this!'

Hutch glared at him. 'Dom. Cool it. We'd have heard anything alive in here long before now. You can hear mice under here and they're the size of your thumb.'

Hutch looked at Luke, hoping to prompt an idea. But Luke's expression told him that it didn't look like he was convincing anyone about an absence of life in the building. Around them, the sound of rain pelting the walls like hail threatened to engulf the shuffling of their feet.

Hutch looked at the ceiling. 'We can't go back out in this. The temperature will drop like a stone in an hour. We're already soaked. We'll freeze.' For a few seconds no one spoke, but glances were exchanged back and forth.

Luke suddenly grinned at him. 'You first then.'

NINE

It was not possible to creep up the stairs soundlessly, as they would have wished. The planks moved under their feet. They cracked and even boomed with every careful and reluctant footstep taken. Hutch went first holding his torch in one hand, his knife in the other. Luke stayed close behind him, but not too close that he couldn't turn and bolt down the stairs if Hutch so much as flinched. The tiny knife handle hurt his fingers. He relaxed his grip.

'Anything?' Luke whispered, looking up through the narrow, black wooden tunnel they squeezed clumsily through; a thin passage that reeked of the old sheds in an allotment he'd explored as a kid, fragrant with cat urine and clotted with dross.

'Nah,' Hutch said, his voice tight like he was holding his breath.

Luke's pulse threatened to jump out of his mouth and ears at the things his torchlight revealed around Hutch. The old dark wood was crowded with long bearded faces that were nothing more than the patterns in the discoloured grain of ancient timber. It was museum-old, museum-black. It should have been behind glass, not around them in the darkness. He suddenly respected Phil for going upstairs on his own.

The thought of people once living here with no electric

light or power in the foul wood, filled Luke with such a sense of wretchedness he felt like his soul was being pulled down and through his feet. They had been simple and they were old and they wanted comfort from the cross. One would have died first, the other would have lived alone in such despair that just to know it for a moment would make your heart burst.

He tried to shake the terrible feeling from himself. It jostled with his fear. This was never a place for a man to be, ever. He felt that instinctively. You got mixed up with the kind of madness that nailed skulls to walls. Even the cold black air seemed to move about them and through them with a sense of its own purpose. It was stupid, irrational to think so, but his imagination suspected the house was inhabited with something he didn't need eyes to see. They were small and fragile here. They were defenceless. They were not welcome.

Hutch peered around the bend in the staircase. Luke caught his face in profile with the light from his torch. He'd never seen Hutch with that face before. Pale and drawn like he'd received bad news. His eyes were big and doleful. And watering. 'OK,' Hutch whispered. 'There's a few more steps and it opens into a room. Like an attic. I can see the underside of the roof. It's pretty wet up here.'

'Real slow, H. Slow,' Luke whispered back. As they groaned under Hutch's boots, Luke briefly wondered if he would be able to take those last few stairs. Holding his breath, he forced himself to follow.

Hutch was three footsteps ahead of him when he stopped moving. Shoulders down, head cocked forward, Hutch stared at something ahead of him, in the upstairs room, out of

Luke's sight from where he was standing on the last two stairs. Hutch swallowed. He'd seen it too then; he was looking at what sent Phil crazy.

'What?' Luke whispered. 'Hutch. What?'

Hutch shook his head. He winced. It looked like he might cry. He shook his head again, and sighed.

Now Luke didn't want to see it either, but felt his feet shuffle him upwards. 'Is it OK? Is it OK? Is it OK?' he whispered, then realized he had said it three times. He could not take the sight of any more blood today.

'This is wrong,' Hutch said in a little-boy voice. Luke stared at the side of Hutch's face. He climbed the last step and stood beside his friend, then turned his whole body to face the room. At what both of their torches were now directed at.

TEN

It rose from shadow and became shadow again.

At the far end of the attic the silhouette sat upright and completely still between the two sides of the angled roof. Crowded and lightless, the place it occupied pooled with darkness above and below the moving torch beams, which seemed frail in here, powdery at their furthest reach but strong enough to pick out the dust and silvery webs on an old black hide. In the patches of hair moistened by drops of rain from the roof beams, it glistened.

One beam of torchlight dropped to the area from which the figure emerged. A small wooden casket the size of an infant's cradle revealed itself in the dusty yellow underwater light. A coffin possibly, built from wood and dark with age, or painted black.

The other torch – Luke's – lit up the horns that rose from above two dark eye sockets. Brownish bone, long and thick.

Two thin rear legs, ending in hooves, jutted out from the body then bent at the bony knee joints. The hooves looked as if they were poised upon the sides of the casket in readiness of the horned thing rising out of its box.

Black lips were pulled back above long yellow teeth; a grimace to last for all time beneath nostrils that still appeared curiously wet. Up and down the chest, small pink teats parted the fur. This was the most unpleasant thing of all, worse than the ivory mouth which Luke imagined was about to open and then snap shut with a *clacking* sound.

The thin black forelegs, or arms, were raised to shoulder height and bent at the elbow. Blackened hands were up-turned, the palms facing the ceiling, as if it were commanding all before it to rise, or as if the figure had once been holding objects that were now long gone.

Luke could not speak. Did not know how to react or what to think. He just existed before it and within the terrible presence that filled the cramped space of the attic.

Hutch only spoke after he began picking out the pale objects on the floor with his torch beam. 'Bones.'

Looking down, Luke saw the dead things, scattered about the wooden casket, as if dropped after the flesh had been eaten from their tiny bones. Rabbits perhaps, and large birds with broken wings and papery skulls. Some of them were still covered with a hairless grey parchment of skin.

'Over there.' Hutch shone his torch at the scratch marks on the timber roof. Cut deep into the wood were childlike symbols and circles, like on the rune stones they had seen in Gammelstad. The inscriptions appeared randomly, at different heights on some beams, in long lines like Chinese script.

'What . . .' Luke could not finish the sentence. Questions seemed foolish. How would any of them know what this meant or why it was here?

Hutch walked forward. Luke flinched at every step his friend made, as if he were provoking something terrible and sudden to happen just by moving. Things crunched under Hutch's feet. Holding his torch higher, Hutch then cast light onto the torso and the face of the upright thing in the box. 'If it moved, my heart would stop.'

'Goat?'

'Looks like it.'

'Jesus.'

'Quite the opposite.'

'I don't get it.'

'Who would? It was some kind of temple. Effigy and sacrifice. I reckon it's supposed to be the Goat of Mendes.'

'The what?'

'This thing is stuffed. At the back here' – Hutch leaned inwards and Luke held his breath – 'the mice have had a go.'

Luke shook his head. 'What do we do?'

'Madness.' Hutch was talking to himself. 'Just imagine the craziness of the fuckers.'

Luke wasn't sure what Hutch meant.

'The little hands are human. Mummified. Stitched on.' Hutch turned to Luke. In the illumination from Luke's torch Hutch's eyes shone. 'Just as mad as hatters. Crosses on the walls downstairs and a bloody goat in the loft. A dead man's hands sown on. Mixing metaphors. Lunacy. Swedish lunacy. It's the darkness and the long nights. Send anyone mad.'

Luke turned. 'Let's go down.'

'Phil was right. It is a bed.'

'You're messing with me.'

Hutch shook his head. 'I've seen them in the housing museum at Skansen. The first time I came over. And in Norway. They used to build these little wooden box beds into the rooms, then fill them with hay. You put a lid on and it becomes a bench during the day. The people must have been tiny back then.'

'Who'd want to lie in that?'

'This guy.' Hutch grinned and shone his torch right into the goat's leering face.

'H!' It was Dom calling out from the foot of the stairs. 'H!'

Hutch nodded at the staircase. 'Come on. Let's split.'

Luke resisted the temptation to take the stairs to the ground floor in two bounds.

Behind him, the flash of Hutch's camera lit up his retreat.

ELEVEN

'You couldn't make this up,' Dom said; his words were slurred after drinking the lion's share of the Jack Daniel's. Supped from their plastic mugs after they'd eaten half of the remaining food: the last four tins of sausage and beans, preceded by a first course of powdered chicken soup with noodles. Two chocolate and oat cereal bars each completed the meal. But it wasn't enough. Despite gulping at the soup and then stuffing the steaming beans into their mouths, even licking the bowls clean, which they had never done before, they remained hungry. This had been the most demanding day so far, even though a shorter distance had been covered than on the previous day.

Phil's feet were bare and glistening with antiseptic. Dom's swollen knee was raised and supported under Hutch's rucksack. All of their thighs were stiff with slowly pumping aches and their lungs were flat with exhaustion. A coma of tiredness had swept through all of them the minute their sleeping bags were unrolled. Luke had never felt so beaten. Had not known it was possible to become so heavy in body and so listless. He could take about one more day of this. Phil and Dom looked like this had been their last.

Enough food for one more day outdoors remained. And only a tea-coloured trickle was left in the small whiskey bottle

Dom had lugged around since leaving Gällivare. It was to have been a treat, opened beside some lake of an astonishing Nordic blue, around an open fire, with the sky turning pink as the darkness of night approached. That had been the plan.

Luke watched Hutch push the last leg of the stool through the door of the iron stove they were huddled around. A shower of sparks erupted inside as he rooted the ancient wooden spoke around the hearth. They coughed in the acrid smoke that belched out. The chimney was almost totally closed. Smouldering remnants of the seat formed the base to the red ashes inside the little oven that only heated part of the ground floor, before the draughts from the door and between the floorboards took over with a night chill, a tang of damp earth, and the ferment of rotten wood.

Phil and Dom had smashed the stool to firewood earlier, against Luke's wishes. *Aren't we in enough trouble?* And he'd been unable to watch Hutch start the fire using four of the crucifixes as tinder. By not watching Hutch snap and twist them into small bundles, he quietly hoped he was exempt from the further misfortune this act of desecration might evoke.

Hutch frowned at Dom, then leaned back against his friend's knees. 'Go easy on the sauce Domja. It's got to go four ways. That's your last tot. I've barely had a mouthful.'

Phil smiled to himself. 'We should save one last swig for when we leave the forest.'

'I'd see it off tonight. It's the worst thing you can drink if you're wet and cold.' Hutch seemed to stop himself from saying anything further, as if what he had suggested might befall them the following day.

Sitting and leaning forward on top of their unrolled

sleeping bags, which in turn were placed on their foam mats on the filthy floor of the hovel, they consumed the hot red air that belched from the tiny door. Even when they got too close and it burned their faces and seared their heavy eyes, they welcomed it. It was the first heat they had felt in two whole days.

Above the stove, hung from a tent's guy rope fixed between four of the nails that had once held animal skulls in place, sodden clothes gradually steamed and smoked dry in the darkness: four bedraggled fleeces and four pairs of grimy trousers. Their waterproof coats were hanging behind them on the nails of the far wall. Everything else gone damp inside their packs, was haphazardly suspended from other nails about the room. Dom had taken all of the skulls and cruci-fixes down. Something else that made Luke uneasy. Though he wasn't sure why.

He felt the warmth of the whiskey rise from his belly and numb his mind. It was worn out anyway and grateful for this cushion of temporary oblivion, or at least the promise of it.

In the swimming gloom where the backdrop of ancient blackened timbers disappeared beyond the reassuring glow of the flames, Luke was struck by the wear on the three faces around him, lit up by the reddish flicker. His own must look the same.

Patches of Dom's unshaven jaw shone silver in the glow from the fire. He was going grey. Even his fringe was salt and pepper now. Deep shadows gathered under his eyes too. They looked too old for his face. He had three kids to look after, and a big mortgage to pay. He'd not mentioned anything in any detail about his current circumstances, but said, 'Great.

Never been better,' when Luke asked him 'How's things?' during the small talk of that first evening together in London. But the absence of specifics might be the clue. Other than a brief conversation about schools he exchanged with Phil on their first afternoon in Stockholm, Dom had not mentioned Gayle, his wife, once: the bone-thin and unhappy woman Luke had met for the first time at Hutch's wedding.

Something was up. He could feel it. Dom had been blind drunk the day Hutch got married, and the night before they left for Sweden, again in Stockholm, and then in Gällivare before the hike. In fact, at any opportunity he coerced the others to start drinking heavily. Something Luke didn't have the wallet for in London, let alone Sweden. He barely scraped enough together to cover his share of the walking holiday, and secretly suspected Hutch suggested camping in the first place so he could be included in the reunion. But despite his bluster and boisterous approach to everything, Dom was acutely sensitive. Luke wasn't fooled. He remembered how quickly he fell to pieces after romantic setbacks when they were students. All living together at number 3, Hazelwell Terrace in Birmingham. The best days of his life. Of all their lives, he liked to think.

And before this trip, he couldn't ever remember Phil's face looking anything other than pink and shiny, like it had just been scrubbed. But his cheeks looked jowly now and his usually florid face was blackened with dirt. An inflamed scratch arched above an eyebrow. Occasionally Phil would reach up and touch it with a neat fingernail. His white-blond mop of hair had lost its boyish lustre too. It was still thick, but had plastered itself to his scalp with sweat and rain and not revived itself indoors. Around his mouth and eyes, Luke noted the deep lines that looked like slices cut into fresh pastry.

It had taken Phil most of the evening to warm up when they met in London. He'd shown up with a long face and a voice both deep and muttery. He'd hardly spoken until they were all drunk at around ten. But it had been his girth – the middle-aged spread – that had given Luke a brief shock when seeing him at Hutch's wedding for the first time in twelve months. It was something he still had not got used to when they all hooked up in London before the trip. Stretching his blue work shirt taut, Phil's hairy white stomach had been visible. And his arse looked bulbous enough to suggest the feminine. They were all supposed to have exercised before the trip. Phil and Dom hadn't made any effort at all.

But Phil had really let himself go. Once the biggest peacock of them all, the man's style had completely gone now. His jeans were pulled far too high these days and his socks were visible to the anklebone. He didn't care any more. But why? Phil was loaded. Had made a killing as a property developer in West London. He'd won the career lottery, so why the long face? His wife, Michelle, that was why. Luke was certain. Michelle was nuts. They all knew it.

She'd been high-maintenance when Phil met her in their final year at university. Great-looking but difficult. Eating disorders, a maniac pissed, and violently jealous. Luke remembered her as a tall, difficult creature with long bony feet and hands. What had Phil been thinking? But he'd still gone ahead and married her after graduation. And now they had two daughters and a big house in Wimbledon. Private-school fees, two cars to run, an apartment in Cyprus, practically a second mortgage in council tax, and according to Hutch they hated each other.

Luke had never been to their house. Never been invited in the ten years he'd lived in London. Michelle didn't like him. Didn't like what he represented, or so he assumed. Single and still living like a student; a man with no clear goals or purpose as she perceived him; a dreamer; a loser. Everything Phil's wife despised, but maybe feared too as a source of temptation to her husband. Some of her disapproval must have rubbed off on Phil. He was harder on Luke's lifestyle, and more disparaging about his patchy work history than the others. Phil always made a point of making him feel small when money was involved. He'd been listening to his wife too much. A hypocritical stance it was anyway, as Phil never stood his round, or chipped in for cab fare whenever they met. He'd even stiffed them on three rounds in Sweden since they arrived. The other two didn't seem to notice, or if they did they weren't bothered. But it stung him. With all his money Phil still wouldn't buy his mates a drink, and seemed to take every opportunity to joke about Luke's parlous finances.

Or did Phil know that Luke had slept with Michelle, a year before he met Phil? In fact, he seemed to remember introducing them to each other. But he'd been intimate with the girl who was now Phil's wife. And decided against seeing her again the morning after the Easter Ball. Sixteen years ago, but he could still recall her hissing beneath him, like a cat, not to mention the way she rolled her eyes back until they were white when she came. Shamefully, after he ejaculated, he had not only struggled to find anything to like about her, but realized he actually disliked her.

Only Hutch still seemed to be in great shape and he was the eldest. He climbed, scuba-dived on sunken wrecks in the North Sea, and mountain-biked everywhere back home. He was ranked nationally in the Masters mountain-biking league and ran his own bike shop out of Helmsley. Last year he'd run the Paris marathon.

But even though he'd found his friends shelter, built them a fire, and promised to lead them out of this godforsaken place by noon the following day, Luke could tell Hutch was troubled. He'd kept up the banter and camaraderie since they returned from the room upstairs. Made sure his humour and enthusiasm for adventure and adversity rubbed off on nervous Luke and the two fat men. But if Luke wasn't mistaken, Hutch was anxious. If not afraid. And that worried Luke more than his own suspicions of the house and forest.

Phil shuffled about on his sleeping bag. 'I'm so tired I can't see straight, but I don't imagine I'll get a minute's sleep here. My arse is already bruised.'

'There's a bed upstairs if you want it, Phil,' Hutch suggested, then took a sip from his mug.

To which they all grunted their approval at the display of sick humour.

Dom stared into the fire. 'Do you think anyone will believe us? About this?'

'I have photos,' Hutch said. 'Got a smoke on ya, Lukers?'

'Not of the thing in the tree,' Dom said with such a serious facial expression, Luke began to laugh as he lengthened an arm with a cigarette pinched between two fingers. Which set Phil off too, chortling and wheezing.

Hutch smiled and accepted the cigarette from Luke. 'We

can go back in the morning if you like.' He winked. 'I'm sure your kids would like to see it from all angles.'

'You could frame it,' Phil said, his face relaxing into a smirk and his eyes twinkling by the light of the red flames.

'Do you think it's connected to here?' Luke looked at the floor as he asked all of them the question.

'I'm trying not to connect the two,' Phil said. 'Especially as we have to spend the night in one of the places under consideration.'

As they all laughed at this, Luke suddenly felt his body suffuse with a warmth of good feeling for his friends. Maybe even love. He winced at his vow to never see Phil again, and at his outburst at Dom. It was just the situation. It had made them all emotional, irrational.

'What do you think?' Dom asked.

Luke looked up at him, his eyes narrowed to meet what he felt was a sarcastic challenge.

Dom smiled. 'No messing. What do you really think?'

Luke shrugged and raised his eyebrows. 'I don't know. I mean, I cannot think of any reasonable explanation as to how an animal, completely eviscerated, because that's what it was . . .' The three faces around him grew grim, so he altered the tone of his voice and made it sound more confidential and lighter, 'Got to be hanging from a tree. So high up. I don't know anything about this area, or the wilderness of Sweden, other than what I've read online, or in the travel guide. H is the expert there.'

Hutch sighed. 'I wouldn't say expert.'

Dom rubbed his hands up and down Hutch's head from both sides. 'Neither would I. Yorkshire bastard.'

'But,' Luke said. 'Don't you have the feeling . . .'

'What?' Dom asked.

'That it's all just wrong.'

Phil laughed. 'No shit, Sherlock.'

'Just imagine you weren't lost and were just walking through this wood, on a day trip.'

Dom burped. 'A nice, but cruel idea at this point in time.'

'It would strike you as wrong. It would make you uneasy. Don't you think?' Luke noticed Hutch was watching him intently as he spoke, but couldn't read his expression. 'The actual environment. The trees. The darkness. It's not like any forest I've ever been inside, and I've been in a few. I've been camping with H in Wales, in Scotland and Norway. And nothing has ever felt like this. The other forest we saw the first day up here wasn't the same either. Wasn't so . . . rotten. And lightless.'

The others all watched him in silence.

'Apparently we're all programmed at a primal level, in the reptilian brain, to fear the woods. But it's more than that. I've felt, since we entered this forest, that this fear isn't unjustified.' Luke took a final long pull on his cigarette and then threw the butt through the tiny door of the stove.

'Shot,' Hutch said.

'Shot,' Dom murmured.

'Shot,' Phil said through a yawn.

Luke leaned back onto the palms of his hands and his head was immediately swathed in the colder air that pooled beyond their tight circle about the stove. He looked up at the ceiling. 'And now this. The forest made these people crazy. Because I don't think people are supposed to come here.'

'And usually they don't,' Dom murmured, his eyes closed. 'That's why there's no paths, aye Yorkshire?'

Hutch sighed and rubbed at his filthy face. 'I have to say, I've never seen anything like it before. It just suddenly changed. It wasn't dense enough at first to ward you off. But then it just kind of swallowed us and there was no going back the way we came in.' He yawned. 'And I really don't want to be here any more.'

'That's good to know. Thanks for sharing.' Dom pushed Hutch off his legs and stretched his body out lengthways, in readiness for sleep.

'The blasted heath,' Luke said, smiling. 'The cursed wood.'

Phil stood up. 'I need a piss.' He stumbled away, his feet booming on the floor. He disappeared into the annex where the rusty tools were stored.

'No. Please,' Luke said, more horrified than he sounded.

'Phillers, you weasel,' Hutch cried out, through his giggles.

'Outside for a shit,' Dom added.

'I'm not taking a shit,' Phil said, his voice muffled in the darkness. 'Yet.'

Hutch and Dom exploded into laughter.

Luke shook his head, fighting a smile that ached around his mouth. 'I cannot believe you are my friends. Burning furniture and crucifixes, and now pissing indoors. Totally unacceptable behaviour for fathers and husbands.'

Dom sat up to unzip his sleeping bag. 'Tell me where you've done it. I need to go too. We might as well piss on the same spot.'

When Phil and Dom were lying down inside their sleeping bags, Dom snoring within minutes, Phil wheezy but motionless, Luke remained awake and propped up on one elbow inside his own sleeping bag. Hutch lay concealed in a funnel of red nylon that tapered down to his feet, but stared wide-eyed at the fire he'd replenished with as much dry wood as he could shave from the walls before they all turned in.

'H?'

'Mmm?'

'Forgive me for speaking out loud, but what is the plan?'

Hutch turned his head and grinned. 'Haven't got a clue.'

Luke laughed quietly. 'It's not been without merit. This trip. We can dine out on it for years. This place is off the scale.'

'Which is no exaggeration. But if the sun had been shining and it hadn't been raining, I have to ask myself if it would look half as terrifying as it does.'

Luke nodded. 'I still think it would.'

Hutch yawned around a smile. 'Me too.'

Bunching up his last set of unworn and dry clothes inside his pack, Luke fashioned a pillow behind his head. He tried to shuffle closer to the stove without disturbing Phil, but ended up in a foetal position. 'I had this freaky idea earlier. When we were upstairs.' Luke knew the idea would be unwelcome to the ears of anyone still awake, but could not stop himself thinking out loud. 'If that thing upstairs was a representation of the thing that threw the carcass into the tree.'

'I heard that,' Phil said, sleepily.

Hutch sniggered. 'It was a shocker to be sure. But we all know,' he winked at Luke, 'that things like that don't exist. More's the pity. But it's amazing what mountaineers think they've seen when they're oxygen deprived. And sailors lost at sea. Exhausted soldiers. Same deal. We become detached from the familiar and our ancestral imagination tries to work shit out. Isolation. Long winter darkness. That's what did this.' He looked at the ceiling. 'Someone lost their mind for sure out here.'

'Think I would too. This place has put an end to my long-held fantasy about living alone, in a cabin in the woods. But the thing in the tree . . .'

Hutch yawned, his eyes half closed. 'Animal. We're not wildlife experts. For all we know, it is something bears do. Larder or something, like you suggested. Anyway, I better turn in. We can embellish to our heart's content once we're in that tourist hut by the river tomorrow.'

Luke nodded. 'Sure. Sweet dreams.'

TWELVE

Sticks. Spiking cheeks. Looking for eyes. Poking the throat. Sticks. Bristling phalanxes needling from branches and erupting from the ground. Sticks everywhere.

Into the dark. Throwing your weight forward. Head down to protect your face. Arms flung out, fingers grasping for purchase, to seize handfuls of the sharp sticks and tug them aside. But down sleeves, inside your collar, and into your socks to catch like barbs, go the sticks and they bring you to a thrashing suspension, your feet never finding the ground. Because you cannot feel the earth, the dark clay from which all of it springs. Down through cracking bracken, sharp brown thorns and crunching dead wood, your feet plunge. Buried to the knee in small crevasses from which you cannot haul slow spent legs.

And there you hang. Gulping at the air like a man drowning. Dizzy with exhaustion, weary like the dying, you hang between the bindings of vine and the scaffolding of sticks. And wait. Wait for *it*.

Loping through complete darkness that begins a foot from your eyes, its stride covers thickets you could not even crawl through. Sweat cools from your neck down to your waist and turns to shivers.

Will it be quick? The end?

The Ritual

You haven't even seen it, but the darkness transmits images at you, composites from a thing you have seen elsewhere, at another time. So maybe the horns will go through you. A puncturing thrust to the dense meat of torso before a furious shaking. Before the teeth get busy. Sharp yellow teeth. Old ivory snapping shut with a woody sound. Some teeth long for ripping, gleaming wet from black dog gums.

So keep your eyes closed at the end. You don't want to see such a mouth up close. Before the bite, before its oblivion in the goring of your soft parts, the speckled lips will curl back in a whinny of excitement. You just know it.

It comes. You can hear it. The bellow of a bullock slowing to a nasal whine. A puff of air, shot through wet nostrils. A doggish grumble, and you can almost see the jaws part before the growl soars through the octaves to become the devilish *yip yip yip* that has circled you for hours. In the solitary hunt, driven wild by the salty minerals of your fear hanging in the cold air, and the expectation of gouting blood – the hot rush to bathe a black snout – you sense it tensing into a final stalk.

Now you scream. Into the darkness. Above, behind, forward and below. Scream until your throat rubs to rust. Scream at the futility because there is no one to hear.

The air about you stills, or even disappears into a vacuum of anticipation. In your imagination, behind closed eyes, its flanks and haunches are hardening to muscle, tough as ship's rope. Forward comes the long neck, through the dark, through your mind. Out go two mottled spears of bone. Black horn. Stained and flaking from the last kill.

A final rasp of foetid air, bestial and hot with spoilt meat, engulfs you from behind. Air that comes from a shape so long and powerful, the terrible unseen presence sets fire to every one of your nerves in limb and spine, one more time. To fuel your last thrashing plunge into the sticks. The skewers. Arrows of wood. Hard as bone. Sticks everywhere.

Awake. Into the darkness with a whimper. Shuddering as if you've just climbed from cold water. Your lungs pumping, sucking down the kind of air that gathers for decades beneath old houses, tainted by mildew-softened wood and the dunes of dust in lightless spaces.

Where are you? The air moves above your face, or does it?

Bruised. Your back and shoulders hurt against the wooden floor on which you lie looking up into the dark. Moving your arms, you make a rustling sound. The sleeping bag. It's the sleeping bag that has rolled from the foam mat to the dirty wooden floorboards and ruffled around your knees. Gasping, you sit up. The palms of your hands touch the gritty wood beneath your body.

Luke. My name is Luke and I am on the floor. Of the house. The one we found in the black wood.

His breathing slows down. He stops panting. The sticks are gone. And he's not being chased. It was just a dream, nothing more. But his skin feels sore all over, like it has been scratched from so many brambles, thorns and trees with bark like the barnacled hulls of old boats. Must be from yesterday. From the long, delirious and exhausting trek through the wet forest that never ends.

He looks about the room and sees a ruddy glow from inside the stove and remembers Hutch lighting it the evening before. Hard to tell what time it is with the windows shuttered tight, the door closed and no light filtering down the staircase from that windowless attic. Where is his watch?

The Ritual

And where are the others?

About him in the thin ruby light he can see three empty sleeping bags, all strewn about and open beside backpacks and the debris that has spilled from them.

Staying still, too afraid to move, he listens. Strains his ears and sends his hearing out and into the darkness.

And there it is. A sound, so faint but still distinguishable from the patter of rain upon the walls and the occasional creak coming out of this broken home in a wet world. Sobbing. Someone is crying. Upstairs. He looks to the indistinct ceiling and swallows the fear that is tightening his throat.

THIRTEEN

On your knees you weep. Sobs wrack your chest and your eyes are cried dry. Parched heaving comes out of your raw throat and sounds strange to your own ears. You cry because this is the end. Your life closes this way, in this dark and stinking place that makes no sense. There is no justice in this and no way to escape. But your anguish does not penetrate *it* at all. Sitting there on its haunches, on that wretched wooden throne, the long horns rising majestically to the ceiling like some crown, as it watches you, without mercy, empowered by your disgrace on these dirty planks. Its arms are flung to the ceiling in hideous triumph.

Your underwear is wet through, your thighs sticky.

Someone calls to you. From behind.

'Hutch. Hutch. Mate. What? What is it? Where are the others?'

The voice sounds familiar, but Hutch cannot respond because it is too late and he must wait here for his end. Not long now.

A hand on his shoulder, shaking. 'Wake up. Hutch, wake up. It's a dream. Mate, a dream. You don't know where you are. Wake up now. It's over. Come on, mate.'

Hutch raises his head, keeping his eyes down and away from that awful black shape before him. He looks up and towards the voice, feels the dry salt crack on his dusty cheeks. Luke.

The recognition of a familiar face makes his own face screw up and tears would have fallen if there were any left. His mouth tastes hot and briny from sobbing. But why? Why is he here, in his boxer shorts, shivering in the darkness with a wet lap, weeping? He was going to die. After being scared for a very long time. Hutch squeezes his eyes shut, and forces his recollection of the dream from his thoughts.

Foolishness creeps through him, warming his cheeks and skin. 'What the hell?' He turns to look at what terrified him. In the gloom, faintly lit from some chinks in the ceiling, he sees its outline. Long limbs and horns, the body taut with expectation.

But it's not alive. No, it is an animal. Stuffed and mouse-eaten. Some remnant of lunacy abandoned in a decrepit attic of a forgotten house. He looks up at Luke and shakes his head.

Luke looks down at him; his eyes full of confusion and fear. 'We need to get out of here. Now.'

Hutch nods and reaches out to steady himself against his friend, who holds him beneath an arm and pulls him to his feet.

'The others,' Luke says. 'We've got to find the others.'

FOURTEEN

They found Dom outside, kneeling in the long wet grass, wearing just his underwear and a T-shirt. Watching the trees with glassy eyes. His whole body shivered in the dawn chill.

Neither of them could touch him. Hutch and Luke had never seen him look this way. Lips dark in a dirt-streaked face, bleached of colour beneath the filth by the cold and by what he had seen, or dreamed of, like them. Dom's face was oddly pink too, at the sides of his eyes, where his tears had cleansed a hot and salty path down his unshaven cheeks. He was unaware of them. Was just motionless and mumbling to himself with the other two shivering beside him, coming down from their own shock and trying to keep it together.

Tousle-headed and wild of eye, Hutch and Luke could not help but follow Dom's stare to see what it was he had found out there in the dark trees. But they saw nothing but black wood, dripping greenery and the whitish glimmer of birch bark, all struggling from the choked forest floor.

Hutch spoke first. 'Domja. Domja.'

He must have heard Hutch, because without turning his head, he said, 'It's going to put us up there, in the trees.'

It could have just been gibberish that Dom had brought with him from sleep, but for a while no one spoke. Until Luke turned to face the house. 'We've got to find Phil.'

FIFTEEN

Phil was found in the larder, standing up but cowering naked in a corner of the filthy cramped space. Almost luminous in the shadows, his heavy body had withdrawn itself away from their presence in the doorway. His eyes were locked on to something that was not there, as if *it* was behind them and slightly above them at the same time. But as his expression was rigid with such an intensity, they were all still tempted to look up, and behind themselves, to see what it was that their friend saw. Both of Phil's arms were raised. But there was something indecisive about the position of his hands. Perhaps he had lifted them to ward something away, but the supporting limbs had become weak as the hopeless idea of defence struck him.

'Phil. Mate. Come on. Let's get you sorted.' Hutch had recovered enough from his own trauma upstairs to approach Phil; wary, slow, but confident.

Phil's lips trembled like a child's in the middle of a fright. His voice was too low for words to be heard. When Hutch touched the fingers of one hand, Phil whimpered and dropped his head between tensed shoulders.

'It's all right, mate.' Hutch held Phil's hand and gently led him from the annex. The smell of stale urine on damp wood came out with him.

He was covered in his blue waterproof by Dom, huddled out the door of the hovel by Hutch, and taken into the dull aluminium light of early morning.

The forest around the wild paddock looked exhausted after the lightning storm, even relieved. Long wet grass and the cold fresh air revived Phil. He came back to them, to the world, with three powerful heaving sobs that sounded incongruous, strange, unlike any sound they had heard Phil make in their presence before. And then he was standing before them, blinking, with only the top half of his indignity covered. His forlorn eyes questioned each of them, but he received no answer, no understanding. The other three just returned a sense of awkwardness and mystification to him. And they could not hold his intense stare for long.

Hutch turned back to the hovel. 'Come on. Let's get packed up.'

Luke moved ahead of him. 'Amen to that.'

'Wait,' Dom said. 'What the fuck?'

Luke nodded at the hovel. 'I told you it was a bad idea. Who knows what we stirred up.' He was about to elaborate, but thought better of it. Phil and Dom stared at Luke, their faces stricken with a desperation to comprehend what he had just suggested.

Hutch paused on the threshold, looked over his shoulder, his face grimed with smoke and dirt. His eyes appeared too big for his dirty face. 'There'll be time to talk about it when we're tear-arsing out of here.'

SIXTEEN

'How about here?' Dom leaned forward, his arms hurriedly pulling at the undergrowth, trying to move saplings and nettles aside to find a section of the dreary silent forest clear enough for them to walk through.

The remnants of the path that brought them here continued out of the clearing due north, in the opposite direction they needed to take. The tension among the others, their very desperation to get away from the house fast, seemed to bustle all about Hutch's body and get inside his thoughts. Mostly, he just avoided their eyes as he scratched about for a solution in silence.

Again, they were thwarted. Needed to move out in a south-westerly direction, to correct the easterly drift along the path the evening before. The edge of the forest in the thinnest band of trees on the map could not be more than six, maybe seven kilometres away, but only if they followed a south-westerly route, then turned due south at some point. There was no way he was going to start the day by leading them north; he reckoned Dom had half a day's limited mobility left in his bad leg.

'Hand me the machete and we'll make a start,' Hutch said, at the south side of the paddock, further along the treeline from Dom.

'Then where?' Dom's voice broke into a shriek. 'How the bloody hell do we get out of here?'

From the western side of the clearing, Luke jogged over and stood behind Hutch. 'Anything?'

Hutch pulled his torso back from behind a dead spruce tree. 'Nothing over here. It's all debris. Full of snags and logs. Even the standing trees are dead. I can't see further than fifteen feet. It's worse than anything we saw yesterday.' *Like it built up overnight*, he was tempted to say out loud in the spirit of the paranoid frustration they were all directing into him. 'We'll never force a path through. We could try, but we'd move about ten feet an hour.'

Dom seized a handful of dwarf willow and yanked at it, his teeth set in a grimace. 'Why? Why is it like this?' A branch bent to him, and then stopped moving, burning his hands and greening them with a watery sap. Dom dropped the branch, but kicked uselessly at it with his good leg. Then winced in pain. 'Shit! What about that right to roam bullshit-line you sold us back home? Who can roam through this crap?'

'It's virgin forest.'

'What? It's bloody dead, H. There's nothing virginal about it.'

Hutch looked at Luke's tired face. 'Lukers, toss us a fag.'

Luke handed Hutch his packet of Camels. Hutch leaned into the flame of the Zippo. Took a long drag and then wiped at the sweat on his forehead, before inspecting the back of his hand and wincing. 'Some little shit just bit me. Gnats.'

'If it wasn't so wet I'd set fire to the bitch,' Dom said, his hands on his knees, his face a picture of hopelessness. 'Burn our way out. The whole bloody place should be scorched earth.'

Hutch sighed through a cloud of fragrant smoke. He looked at his hands; the tips of his fingers were still trembling. He swallowed. 'It's never been managed. There's never been any clear-cutting. That's the point.'

Under the dirt, in the rivulets his tears cut below his eyes the night before, Dom's face whitened with anger. None of them had washed their hands and faces for two days. 'Then why the hell did you bring us in here, if we can't bloody walk through it?'

'I never planned for us to get stuck in it. I just wanted to see a bit of it. This far north. Something original on the short cut.'

'It's bloody original all right. So original, no fucker in their right mind would come up here for a holiday.'

'And few do. Not in this part. Only scientists and conservationists would usually go this deep, I reckon. We're only here by accident. Because of the short cut. We were only supposed to quickly cut through it.'

'Cut through my ass! We're stuck, H! Trapped like rats!'

Hutch sighed; looked to Luke for support, which he had done rarely on the trip so as not to create the clique he sensed that Luke wanted. Hutch's voice sounded weak, insubstantial, when it came out of his mouth again. 'These national reserves are here to protect the last bit of real biodiversity, Dom. For the future. It's just about gone everywhere else.'

Luke looked about himself, as if seeing it for the first time. Hutch took another drag on his cigarette. He talked himself down from the urgent instinctive need to just start crashing out, southwards. A dark silhouette from his dream reared up in his mind; an unpleasant reminder of something he was committing every ounce of mental discipline to suppress. He took a deep breath. 'This is one of the last parts of the Boreal coniferous belt. Goes all the way from Norway to Russia. It's what grew after the Ice Age. This. It's been around for that long. A Norwegian spruce can even live for five hundred years. A Scots pine for six. Can you imagine it? It shrunk by ninety per cent in the last century. All cut down and cleared. But they left parts like this, in the national parks, so fungi and lichen can grow in all this shit we can't get through. To preserve the habitats. For birds and insects. Wildlife. This whole place is chock-full of rare species. All of that forest we saw from the train on the way up is managed. Probably no more than a hundred years old. They don't let forests get this old any more.'

Momentarily, Luke looked grateful; at least he always appreciated how much thought went into where Hutch took them. Because he always invested himself wholly into anything he organized. Always wanted his companions to see something wonderful. It was his fault they were lost. But even though they were lost, he reminded himself, at least they were stranded inside something so few people, even most Swedes, would ever see. Something this old and undisturbed. He thought of reminding Dom of this, then decided against it. Because it no longer served as a source of compensation for him either, if he were honest with himself.

'It's on all of the trees.' They heard Phil's voice, coming to them across the small clearing about the black hovel they were still trying to escape from. It had been twenty minutes since they had dressed in their grubby, smoky clothes and packed up. 'Goes in a circle. Round the house.'

Luke, Hutch and Dom all turned to look at Phil on the far northern side of the clearing. He was standing near the thin track that wound outwards into the darkness. They all exchanged glances with tight-lipped faces.

'What's that, mate?' Hutch called out.

'On the old ones. The ones with the dead branches.'

'What's he going on about?' Dom asked.

Hutch shrugged. 'Guy's really shaken up.'

'You think he's lost it?'

'I think we all did last night. If Luke hadn't woken me up, I'd still be up in that attic. Kneeling before the goat.'

Laughter burst from Luke. It sounded too high in the still air and in the enclosure of the trees around the hovel. It sounded inappropriate, like laughing out loud in church.

Hutch smiled. 'Jesus, boys. How are we going to P.R. this when we get home?'

Dom slapped the back of Hutch's head, his face expanding into a tight and forced grin. 'We gotta get there first, you useless Yorkshire bastard. Never mind virgin forests and Ice Age fungus. I want to put me feet back on concrete.'

Hutch side-stepped the second swat. 'Come on. Let's go see what the fat man wants.'

SEVENTEEN

'What is it, mate?' Hutch asked Phil, who was leaning forward with one dirty hand spread on the dark bark of a thick tree trunk. Phil hadn't said much to anyone since they woke him, and he'd shrugged off any attempt to speak of how he came to be naked in that tiny sordid space that they had all used as a urinal at some point the night before, except for Luke who had gone outside. Luke, Hutch and Dom were all too tired and shaken to talk of their own experiences in any detail either, each acknowledging in an unspoken way it was the sort of thing you only discussed once you were at a safe distance from the source. But the night seemed to have affected Phil worse than the others.

'Here. See it? And it's on all of the other trees on this side.' Where the bark had been sheared away or smoothed down in a band about the tree at waist-height, Phil's red fingers pointed at a series of marks or scratches, cut deep into the wood, which had then darkened with age but not become entirely invisible.

Hutch bent over and traced a finger around the marks.

'What is it?' Luke asked.

Dom sighed with irritation and looked up at the sky.

'Runes,' Hutch said. 'Remember those runes on the stones we saw in Gammelstad?' He glanced over his shoulder at

Dom and Phil. 'Me and Luke saw some in Skansen and Lund too, a couple of years back.'

'No way,' Phil said, his face stricken, as if this observation by Hutch was evidence to him of something far worse than their current dilemma.

'Yes way. Good spot, Phillers. I bet these are real old too. Vikings used them about a thousand years ago.'

'They can't be that old,' Luke said, leaning down beside Hutch.

'No shit. But someone still knew how to use them after the Vikings.'

Luke placed an index finger on one. 'Looks like a B. The trees get how old?'

'This is a Scots pine. A big one too. Dead as a door nail, but they can live for about six hundred years.'

Dom threw both hands into the air, his waterproof swishing as he moved. 'OK. OK. So what's the plan, Time Team? I'd say runes on old bastard trees are at the bastard bottom on our list of priorities, boys.'

Hutch and Luke moved away from the tree.

'It's all wrong,' Phil said to himself. 'Wrong.'

'Yessum,' Hutch said. Then looked at the sky, so pale and white, the sun itself could have been white. Rain began to patter against their coats and rucksacks. 'Great.'

From the breast pocket of his coat, Hutch pulled out the plastic wallet with condensation on it. The map was sealed inside. He knelt down and removed the map from its sheath. He unfolded it by one half and put the compass against it. 'Chaps. I reckon we're about here. A fair way inside the tip of this band of woodland. I was trying to get us down to here yesterday, so we can pick up the Käppoape trail. A morning's walk on that and we'd be beside the Stora Luleälven River. Following that east to Skaite for a few hours would put us by the overnight cabins there. And a branch office for the Environment Protection Board. But we can't make it any further south through the scrub here. This place is so old, if there was ever another path going south out of this clearing, it's gone now. And if the undergrowth doesn't clear up, there is still the best part of a day between us and the end of the forest.'

'So what?' Dom said.

Hutch wrinkled his eyes and gritted his teeth in a wince. 'Well, we can't risk following that track north.'

Phil said nothing. He stood apart from them and stared at the house.

'Hang on. Hang on. Gimme the map,' Dom demanded.

Hutch pulled it away from Dom's grasp. 'What are you going to do with it hobble-horse?'

'Let me see, you Yorkshire ring-piece.' Dom snatched the map from Hutch's hands and then held it a few feet from his face.

Luke hung his head and pulled his fingers down his cheeks. 'Maybe we should go back the way we came in.'

Dom shook his head. 'No. If we go back the way we came in, it'll take a whole day just to get back to where we started from yesterday at noon.'

'As long as we don't get lost again,' Luke said. No one else took him up on the observation. Hutch and Dom stared at each other with tense faces.

Dom's jaw trembled. 'And then another day to get back to the STF cabin we left two days ago!'

'Agreed,' Hutch said to Dom. 'Or the same amount of time

again to get to Porjus on your bad leg. So I think we should see where the track we used to get here goes, in the opposite direction. Then see if we can cut down south from it at some point.'

Dom frowned. 'Well, it ran from west to east in a straight line. It'll take us straight back out west. What's west?'

'Norway,' Luke said.

Dom slapped the map down against his thighs. 'We need to get south, H, to come out on the other side of this blasted heath.'

'You don't say. But we can't get through, dufus. There is no way we can move south from here. And we've enough food for one more day, tops. Considering how many calories we're going to be expending walking on this terrain today, we'll need every crumb of it. For argument's sake, if it takes us all day to get out, we'll have to camp tonight above the river. Tomorrow, on the outside of the blasted heath, our army will be marching on an empty stomach for about half a day. And that's the worst-case scenario we are facing. So there is no need to panic, but we have to make the right choice now. No indecision. I'm confident that if we just retrace the path it'll lead us, more or less, above a good point to make an exit. With any luck, the trail might naturally turn south at some point. Skaite can't be that far. A day, day and a half tops at a very limited pace.'

Luke lit another cigarette. 'We cannot . . . cannot risk staying lost in this wood for much longer, H.'

'Spark us one up, mate,' Hutch said. Luke placed his cigarette between Hutch's lips. He took another out of the packet for himself. Hutch squinted through the smoke at Luke. 'The trail must go somewhere. It was cut out of this wood a long time ago. We didn't follow it from its source, we just kind of happened across it yesterday and followed it east. We originally came in on the far westerly side of a narrow band of forest. I brought us east to correct our position. Out west it gets really thick again. About thirty kilometres deep, I'd say. But if we stay on the track we came in on for as long as we dare, we'll move faster and avoid all of the fallen logs and shit that made Domja bitch like a baby yesterday. If we can then cut south at some point, we could be out by late afternoon.'

'But then . . .' Luke rested the tip of his tongue between his teeth.

Hutch looked at him, surprised Luke would object to his idea, again. 'What?' He heard the irritation hardening his tone.

'That's if the woods south of the track clear up at all. And following the track further west will mean new ground again. The unknown. Going somewhere else in this wood that might not be an exit. Our precise downfall yesterday.'

'Why would you make a track that just endlessly snaked around inside a wood?' Hutch asked. 'It has to be the vestige of a way in and out. There's no sensible alternative, Chief.'

'I think there is. It's total ball-ache, but we go back in the direction we came in, then try and pick up from where we crashed through yesterday. Or take that track north and hope it leads to the top edge of the forest.'

'Oh, fuck off!' Dom cried out. 'We've been through this! We'd have another day walking across those pissing boulders to get to where we started from. Or another day's walk to Porjus in the opposite direction.'

'But we know the way we came in leads out of here for certain. This path might just stop two miles deeper inside this shit. Or run in a straight line to Norway. As soon as we put one foot on it, it's already leading us in totally the wrong direction.'

Hutch blew out another geyser of grey smoke, and winced. 'We got so turned around in there, mate. I honestly cannot say whether we will pick up our tracks again. And these two won't make it back through that crap. We have to stay on the level as much as possible. Phil, how're your feets?'

'Not good,' he said, without turning his head. He'd put his hood up.

'Fucking fucked up is what they are, like my knee,' Dom snapped.

Luke turned to face Dom. 'Well, if you'd hit the gym like we agreed, Dom.'

'Oh, listen to the gentleman of leisure. I've got three kids, mate. Try hitting the gym when you work sixty hours a week and have a family to support.'

Hutch raised both hands. 'Boys. Boys. We're wasting time here and we're getting pissed on. At least on the path we'll have a bit of purpose. If it goes nowhere, we make a judgement call. And either break south through the crap again or we try and find our way back the way we came in yesterday, like Luke says. But that's got to be a last resort, considering the condition some of us are in and how difficult it is to even move across that terrain.'

Phil finally spoke, but kept his back to them. 'The last thing we want is to be in here again at night.'

EIGHTEEN

The very thought of which was exactly why Hutch could not prevent the unnaturally vivid images of the dream from recurring as he walked slowly away from the hovel, with one of Dom's arms around his shoulders. He'd never sleep walked in his life before.

He could still visualize the details of the dream as if it were a film he had seen the previous evening in a cinema. His mind clawed through the dim and grubby recollections for some kind of sign; some sense that would explain exactly why he had risen from his sleeping bag and climbed the stairs to the attic and then been found kneeling before a hideous rotten effigy.

Two figures had been standing beside him in the dark downstairs of the house. That was how the dream began. Old faces with dirty teeth told him to climb the stairs. Had told him that *someone* was waiting. *Don't keep him waiting*, they had said. *Your clothes are in the fire.*

And up he had gone. Up, up, up the black wooden stairs. He desperately didn't want to climb them, but the will of the dream would permit no turning around or going back down. He'd tried to stop his ascent, but remembered going numb and being unable to breathe. So up he went. And to think he had even been physically climbing the stairs at the same time.

'Not so fast, H!' Dom called out beside him.

'Mmm? Sorry.' Hutch slowed down.

His feet had been bare, the soles black with the filth on the old wooden stairs. Hands out, he'd steadied himself against the dark wood that had felt wet underfoot. He was naked. His body thin and pale and shivery; he'd felt like a little boy tottering for his bath. Yes, he had been smaller, and younger in the dream. He'd desperately wanted to be covered, protected.

There were no windows in the house, just a faint reddish light coming down from *up there*. Around the corner of the staircase he'd then staggered into the attic, and opened his mouth to call for help. But no sound had come out of his mouth. There was no air inside him, like he was winded.

Inside the red place he'd kept his head down and his eyes fixed on his dirty feet. Dirty and wet. Wet from the piss that had tickled warm against his thighs and dripped down his calves.

He'd tried not to look up, because something was in there with him. Snorting with excitement because it could smell his piss and fear.

Bones. There were bones on the floor. They made it all worse. Especially the ones with the grey bits attached. And some of the little bodies had gone so black he could not tell what they had once been. On the stained planks he'd stepped around the bones, but some had still crunched under his blackened soles and slid around his grimy toes. The bones got bigger as he moved closer to the snorting sound.

And then he could smell *it*. Dung in straw, cattle sweat and sulphur stink; it made his eyes water. A goaty breath panted over his head and bare chest and made him cough.

The taint had still been inside his mouth when Luke woke him.

In the dream, the knocking began when he smelled *it*. Near him. Sounded like wood banging against wood. In front of him. And he could not prevent a peek at what made the hollow knocking noise.

Black hooves. Once again they reared up in his mind. Big and sharp with yellowish bone at the tip. Wide as a horse's feet, snapping down against the wooden box it sat inside. Banged them with excitement it did. The black rim of the wooden box was chipped and grooved.

Its glee grew as his soft white body came closer. So close. Coming out of a big head he had heard wet snorts and deep whinnies. *Clack, clack, snap* went its hot mouth with the yellow teeth inside, like a trap.

Before him, below him, cut smooth into the front of the box had been a small circular gap to rest his throat. So that his head would hang into the unbreatheable musk of devil and animal. His head was to hang below its teat-pocked belly, pinkish under the longer black hairs. Then those hooves would smash down like a hammer onto a dinner plate.

Bits of skull littered the dirty straw between the black stick legs of the thing. The forelegs were long and down they came again and again to make the imbecile rhythm of hoof on wood.

Its body had been so tall, like it had long outgrown its little cradle. And he knew the horns on the terrible head were scratching the beam in the middle of the ceiling.

And over he had gone against his will. Into the blinding stink, and the sound of his own cries were obscured by the knocking. Speeding up. Drumming with no rhythm on the scarred black wood. He still seemed to hear the echoes of it now, which is why he could not stop his hands from shaking.

Into the worn circular slot, in the front of the little box, he'd rested his throat. And up, up, up went the thin black forelegs. Up towards the ceiling together. And paused for half a second before they came back down. So fast.

And then Luke had been beside him, shaking him, waking him.

'Look! Through there. And there. Two of them!' Luke's voice broke his reverie. Hutch looked up and squinted at where Luke crouched down, further along the trail, pointing off into the trees.

Hutch's stomach contracted.

NINETEEN

They had been travelling for two hours westward on the increasingly overgrown track when Luke noticed the two buildings engulfed by the undergrowth.

When no one answered him, he turned his head and looked at the other three coming up the narrow trail, their elbows out, fending back the stiff wet branches that hung from the enclosing treeline and draped belligerently across most of the open space. Dom and Phil were both limping. Hutch was hanging back to help Dom over the fallen logs that had begun to present themselves with an alarming frequency beyond the place they had joined the trail the night before.

Luke walked point all morning. It was better to go first; you would be the one to see the way out and by walking out front, all the time yearning for the trees to clear and for a vista of escape to present itself, you were better motivated to keep going.

'Look!' Luke called louder this time to be heard over the din of rain scattering through the canopy of leaves above them. He pointed in the direction of the dark sides of two indistinct buildings.

The wooden planks of the visible walls bulged with damp and were black up to the dim windows; though it was hard to tell if they were shuttered or not. A suggestion of a stone chimney jutted from the end of one building before becoming obscured by a mesh of foliage.

'What's that, Chief?' Hutch called back. 'A nice little café?'

'Or some big bastard wolverine,' Dom added.

Luke waited for the others to draw level with him. 'Another two houses.'

Hutch was breathing hard from supporting Dom's weight over the last fallen log. He looked at where Luke was pointing.

Between their position and the two buildings, grew a thick bed of nettles with black thorny stems. Above the nettles the bare branches of dwarf birches and willows formed a twenty-metre portcullis of criss-crossing sticks, choking the spaces between the larger trees. It was impenetrable.

'Just keep moving,' Dom said. 'Don't know what's inside them.'

Luke nodded. 'I genuinely hate to think. Wonder why they're here.'

Hutch rested a hand on Luke's shoulder. 'Bum a fag off you?'

'Sure.' Luke reached for the side pocket on his waterproof trousers.

Hutch put the cigarette between his lips. 'Must be an abandoned settlement.'

'Where more of them mad fuckers lived,' Dom said.

'No one's been here for a while.' Hutch looked down at his feet. 'This track must have joined them up with the other place. See this' – he prodded his foot under a blanket of bracken and lifted it – 'ruts from a cart wheel under there. You can still see them at the sides of the track.'

Luke rose back to his full height. A knee joint cracked. He

visualized the unwelcoming interior of the two buildings; wet, lightless, spoiled with rot and animal spore. He imagined the despair they would feel in the comfortless air, in the desolate age of the place.

'How's it looking ahead?' Hutch asked, breaking Luke's absorption that made his thoughts sluggish.

'More of the same,' he said.

Hutch moaned and rubbed his hands over his face. 'We're not making great progress guys.'

'Piss off,' Dom said. Bent double, he pushed at the sides of his injured knee with both filthy hands. Raising the foot off the ground like a lame horse, he grimaced. Phil said nothing, but stood and stared in the direction of the abandoned buildings.

Luke took a deep breath and then exhaled. 'Why don't you guys take a breather. I'll scoot ahead and see what's what further down. It might open up.'

'And try and clear some of this shit off the path before I get down there. On me hands and knees at this rate,' Dom said.

Luke smiled. 'With what, a camping spoon?'

Hutch cackled. 'Make sure you keep the edges neat.'

Luke moved ahead, more quickly than he had walked all morning. The slow pace set by Dom was reviving his backache and his impatience was fast turning to irritation and a total flattening of his spirits. At times it seemed as if the path had actually come to an end. When he met a blockage now, of which there were many, at least he could turn about and just force his way through backwards, with his arms held across his face to protect his eyes against the whipping branches that scored his cheeks and forehead. It was all difficult ground, and one of his ears was bleeding, but he didn't have to keep stopping while Hutch held the branches up for Dom and Phil to shuffle through; nor was he subjected to Dom's constant moaning.

Phil still hadn't said much. He was either mute from the pain in his blistered heels, or so dead on his feet he couldn't think straight enough to form a sentence. Or he was still in shock from the night before. Maybe all three.

Twenty minutes out of earshot of the others and the path stopped moving in a straight line; it began twisting about the ancient trunks, sometimes rising and sometimes falling away.

It became exhausting and hard on the joints to haul himself up a tangled incline, festooned with slippery tree roots, to then suddenly descend over uneven ground on the other side. A tree seemed to have fallen about every twenty feet.

He couldn't believe how much his chest hurt. He thought he was fit. Despite the smoking he worked out three times a week and ran at the weekend, but it was no preparation for this kind of exertion. He tried not to imagine how Dom and Phil felt.

They were all pathetic; getting lost like a bunch of amateurs. The kind of idiots who attempted to climb a mountain without proper training or the right gear; or those wankers who tried crossings of treacherous water and ended up diverting the ocean's shipping in a search and rescue. People who were lauded as heroes of survival upon rescue. Why? They were nuisances. He could not believe they were fast becoming one and the same.

He put his head down and smashed through the bracken. Gritted his teeth and forced through the pain barrier in his chest and thighs. Refused to be defeated. *Enough now.* Some sky; that's what he wanted. A bit of sky and some open ground, soft with leaves, so they could weave effortlessly through the trees.

A branch dug into the loose cloth under his arm and propelled him backwards and onto his backside. He snatched at the branch and tried to snap it, but the supple strength of the wood resisted and made his arms feel like water.

He remained seated, and panted to get his breath back. Hutch insisted they were beginning to angle south west, 'more or less'. But Luke had instinctively felt himself being led back north west on this trail, and no nearer to the edge of the forest than they were the previous night when they made camp.

He could not stand much more of the suffocating wet wood, forcing him into a crouch, knocking him about, tearing his skin. His throat burned. Dried sweat was producing salt on his skin and chafing the inside of his thighs and beneath his belt all the way around his waist. He wanted to tear his clothes off.

Thick with pain, the muscles in his legs began to cramp. They had to get out of the heavy stuff. If the undergrowth didn't clear very soon, he would walk back and find the others. Then he would retrace their steps back to where they had come onto the trail the day before. Alone if necessary. And he'd go for help. Whether Hutch agreed or not, his instincts were telling him they were approaching *that time*. The time for drastic action. Of one of them going for help.

He cursed Hutch's decisions again, his ridiculous baseless optimism. 'Jesus Hutch! What were you thinking?' Grinding his teeth, he ran through everything Hutch had said that led them into this mess. His lips began to move and he said things about his best friend he knew would make him cold with guilt and warm with shame later.

Luke closed his eyes. Tried to calm down, to think straight. Slowly, the intense heat of the sudden rage drained away and left him shivering.

It was so dark where he sat in the wet verdure. Little light was descending to the forest floor, but the rain found its way down. The entire wood was sodden. He felt dizzy and took an energy bar from his coat pocket. His hollow stomach ached. Did they even have enough food remaining for one proper meal?

He began to imagine what would happen if he never moved from this spot. Would his body ever be found, concealed beneath these bushes and weeds and nettles? Or would his bones be picked clean by teeming insects and foraging rodents? A too clear image of the remnants of his dirty camping clothes, a faded rucksack and his browned bones grinning from the dark leaves, propelled him into a squat. His lower back ached from where the damp seeped up through the seat of his trousers. The black soil sucked the warmth out of a body.

Back on his feet, he pushed on, driven by the desperate hope that somehow, miraculously, the end of the trees would present itself at any moment. But when he had long passed out of shouting distance with the others, he began to worry he had left the path and was crashing off through the under-growth in entirely new directions, being led by the forest into the places the thickets were more sparse. At times he would stop and reassure himself that he was following the faint out-line of the manmade track. Because if he wasn't he would never find the others again. There were no landmarks here; it was all the same and then more of the same, stretching into forever.

Thirst burned out of his stomach, up and into his dry mouth; the last of his water had gone over an hour ago. Save sucking rainwater off the leaves from where it dripped all around them, they would need to find running water before the day was out. He doubted any of the others were carrying anything but empty canteens either.

After thirty minutes alone, he blundered into a granite plinth. A standing stone concealed by ivy.

TWENTY

It was the silence Hutch gradually became aware of, though he decided against sharing the observation with the other two, who hobbled beside and behind him on the rapidly narrowing trail. About him, he imagined the forest holding its breath, in anticipation.

Since they had moved away from the derelict buildings, the birds had stopped their sporadic chatter. There was no breeze. Beyond the scuffling of their feet, the almost inaudible patter of rain, and the whipping of leaves against waterproof fabric, the forest had fallen completely silent around them.

It was a stillness that provoked a reaction, a response. He found himself looking with uneasy eyes into the thickets on either side of the diminishing trail. And had they just changed direction again? He wasn't sure. In places, the trail now seemed to have disintegrated into deceptive-looking shadowy hollows. Areas that promised easier passage through the choking obstacles pushing them to either side of the faint trail; a vague path he often had to stare at hard to even recognize amongst the tangles of briars and pale green ferns.

The light had dropped; the canopy was so thick here. *Again.* He worried about Luke becoming lost. Stopped and wiped the sweat from his eyes. Was suddenly furious at himself for letting Luke just tear off on his own. 'Stop.'

'Eh?' Dom asked, between his heavy breaths.

Phil stopped; his breath wheezed in and out of his bulk. Hutch heard him suck hard on his inhaler.

'What is it?' Dom whispered.

Hutch held up his compass, angled it away from Dom's wet red face. *North west.* He wanted to scream. They were shuffling off course again. They were slanting up and back into the forest. Going deeper, not down and outwards. They had been turned around too incrementally for it to feel like a definite change of direction. But when? How had that happened? He would have noticed. Were he not so encumbered with Dom's heaving uncoordinated bulk against his left side, he might have been more alert.

'No good.' He shook his head.

'What isn't?'

'This direction.' He let go of Dom and slapped his hands against his hips. 'Shit.'

TWENTY-ONE

At first Luke thought it a natural outcrop of rock. They had seen plenty of boulders and even cliff faces on the first day of the hike, which suddenly reared up from the green earth. But once he'd pulled himself around the stone and torn some of the wet ivy from an inclined side, he saw the worn runes. They covered one complete side of the rock, and were ringed by an oval border, thick with petrified lichen.

He turned about, lowering and raising himself on his ankles to peer through the surrounding thicket that had overrun the rock. Between the mesh of dead wood and the thigh-high weeds that coated it, he saw another of the standing stones about twelve feet away from where he was crouching, and then another beyond it.

Breaking away from the face of the stone and lowering himself even further, he rediscovered the path that wound about the three stones but was now impossible to walk upright upon.

He tried to move forward, but his pack became immediately stuck in a branch and held him fast. Swearing through his clenched teeth, he reversed his body. Then removed his pack, groaning when the hot weight of it fell behind him, into the leaf mulch and dirt.

Against the ground, he crawled forward along a natural

tunnel that had formed over the surface of the trail. Was it the trail? Yes. He stretched out an arm and followed the cart-wheel rut with his fingertips. Small animals must have worn the tunnel through with their scurrying. Face down, he squirmed about and felt the cold damp soil embrace his chest and stomach.

He would move as far as he was able, to see if the foliage cleared from the path ahead. But this was the very last effort he would make in this direction. They'd already been trav-elling for four hours since sunrise and were no closer to getting out. Once he'd ascertained he had reached the end of the stretch of the track beside the standing stones, he would go back and tell the others it was time for the last resort. His plan. His idea. They could have been four hours into it by now. And it would take the very last of them to get out before nightfall, if they could even find the route they had come through the day before.

After twenty feet on his stomach the steely light suddenly brightened and the range of his visibility increased. He had reached the end of the natural tunnel, and could even look up above ground level.

He pushed his wet and bedraggled body on to its feet and broke through the lighter saplings about the exit. Lifting his legs high, to clear the thorns and nettles, he took a step for-ward into an area where the forest cleared of the thicker trees and presented an airier space of thigh-deep undergrowth and dwarf birch, with little growing higher.

The rain came down in silvery spikes. The jagged pieces of exposed sky he could see through the upper reaches of the wet spruce bordering and overhanging the clearing were bleak and dark with rain. A bit of white sky was all you got up here at about 5 a.m., then it just went grey. The path was somewhere beneath the undergrowth. It must have been, because it had once led to a building.

Luke stood still and stared across the clearing at what presented itself to him on the other side. A church. And what he had just crawled through was a cemetery. A very old one too if the graves had been marked by standing stones.

TWENTY-TWO

None of them said anything when Luke reappeared, without his rucksack. He'd been careless rushing back to find them; a deep scratch was hot and inflamed down his left cheek. It had bled along his jaw line and coagulated. And he was unaware that the tree branch that had lashed into his mouth had cut his top lip and painted his teeth with a scarlet film. Dom and Hutch just stared at his wild eyes, breathless attempts to speak, and at his wet and cut face.

On his way back from the cemetery, he had been gripped with an urgency that made him feel hot and loose and angry inside. He'd begun punching branches that hung across his return path; had even stopped to smash flat some small toadstools. Because getting back to the others had been harder than his leaving of them, as if the forest forbade it. He was reminded of his dream and was not grateful at all for the recollection. He'd stopped a dozen times and unhooked the sharp ends of broken branches from his jacket. It was now torn under one arm. He could not remember the undergrowth being that bad coming the other way. The constant hampering and snagging of the foliage, and his uncoordinated stumbling through it, made him hot and dizzy with a rage familiar to him, and always unhealthy. He had cursed the wood, cursed Hutch, cursed Dom, cursed this world and his reduced position in it. He'd boiled. And every step of the way back to the others, his thoughts had been dark with the image of the decrepit broken church in the dismal wet world.

And when he found them again, he could not believe how slowly the other three had been moving, how little ground they had covered since he had been away. He felt as if he'd had to retrace his steps all the way back to the same place where he had left them.

Luke straightened up from where he had been bent over to catch his breath. 'I thought I'd lost you.'

'What happened?' Hutch asked.

'Eh?'

'Your gear? Where is it?'

'I dumped it. Was slowing me down.'

Dom looked at Hutch and frowned, as if this act of madness confirmed a belief he had long held about Luke. 'What the fuck you going to sleep in then?'

'Not permanently. Just so's I could get back to you guys faster.'

'Why?' Hutch said, with a nonchalance that annoyed Luke. 'You find something?'

'Because . . .'

'Because what?' Dom asked.

What the hell was wrong with them, ambling down the path like this? Dom and Hutch had been smiling about something when he reappeared. He even thought he had heard them laughing from a distance. 'Are you even taking this seriously?' he asked and immediately wished he hadn't when he saw Dom and Hutch's surprised faces. Phil stood behind them. He had more colour in his cheeks now, but looked at Luke with a mixture of disappointment and caution. The hood of his coat was half off his head and made him look ridiculous.

''Course we are, you silly arse,' Dom barked. 'Think I'm enjoying this?'

Hutch said, 'Dom,' quietly. But there was something in that rebuke, something about Dom's flat, stolid, scowling face; and something in Hutch's supporting grin, that made Luke think his vision had lightened, as if the terrible pressure of rage that suddenly filled his body again had forced the darkness out of his eyes. He felt weightless and could hear nothing but a hot rushing through his ears. His voice seemed to originate from somewhere outside of his head. He didn't recognize himself in his own voice, as if it was a recording played back to him, to his embarrassment. 'You call me that again and I'll put you on your fucking arse.'

He watched his own progress, as if disembodied, as he walked three steps up to Dom, whose face went pale and stiff as if he'd been forced to look at something unpleasant.

A remote part of Luke remained conscious of what the other bigger part of himself was now doing on instinct. It was the rage he brought back to them from the trees; the endless wet trees that would never let them go. And it demanded an eruption from him. 'Did you hear me, bitch?' he shouted into Dom's face and watched a droplet of froth from his own shouting mouth hit Dom's cheekbone.

'Luke!' Hutch shouted from beside him. 'Woah!'

But he was not to be brought out of this trembling mad place until something snapped him out of it. With both hands, he shoved Dom backwards, hard. Dom lost his balance and dropped his weight onto his bad knee and then fell sideways into the undergrowth. Something swished behind Luke and hard fingers clamped around his biceps. He was pulled back and away from Dom, his feet clearing the ground at one point. All the strength seemed to leave his body for a moment. He scrabbled to find his feet when Hutch let him go a few feet down the trail.

'You fuck!' Dom struggled to his feet; all chubby arse, shirt pulled out, and clumsy stiff movements. Then Dom was coming at him, the limp gone. Hutch was knocked aside. The whites of Dom's eyes were going pink to red. His freckled knuckles moved slowly then made a wet slap sound against Luke's mouth that he felt like a push, not a blow, but it made his top lip instantly go numb. Is that it, he thought. Is that all a punch feels like?

They seemed to stare at each other for a long time, until the idea that he had been struck mingled with the supporting notion that this was a contact that stated he should just continue to accept Dom's jibes, criticisms, bullish rants, and his disregard for anything Luke had said since they had met the night before the trip. But this role assigned to him in their little group hierarchy was not one he would accept any longer.

When he swung his fist from the left, he'd taken his arm back enough to make his shoulder go tight, lock and then release his hand like a spring. Dom's arm didn't rise quickly enough to defer the strike, and Luke's knuckles impacted with a loud smack under Dom's right eye.

Dom's head snapped back, and his expression was one of bewilderment and distaste. Luke's second fist came in from the other side. He watched his own arm, in its wet khaki sleeve, whip about quickly to make his hard fist strike Dom again, this time on the jaw. He had been aiming for the jaw.

Dom went down quickly, and didn't get his arms out to break his fall, because his hands were still clutching at his face.

Hutch and Phil took a step away from Luke, almost cowering. They looked at him like he was a dangerous stranger. They were shocked. Frightened of him. But he wanted to keep on punching. He wished Dom had not gone down so fast. Then he could feel the satisfaction of hitting his face really hard again, and again, with clenched fists.

It had not hurt his hands at all and the sudden release of energy, twinned with Dom's fall, gave him a sudden lunatic rush of euphoria. His body seemed to re-form itself again into a tight, stable and defined frame; his whited-out vision rushed back into his head, and returned to full colour; his hearing cleared as if a blockage of warm bath water had just drained out. He realized he was panting so hard he had started to wheeze.

Dom sat up with his legs splayed and his head dipped over his chest. Both of his hands were clutched around his mouth. No one could see his face.

Dom was crying. He was so angry, he was actually crying. 'I'll not spend another fucking minute with that bastard!' From where he sat on the fallen log, Luke could hear Dom's voice penetrating through the trees. It was high-pitched now and squealing.

'He can piss off in the opposite direction . . . No I fucking won't . . . It's not you who's had that bastard have a pop at you . . . That loser's a headcase. He always has been. That's why he can't hold a job down for five minutes. And why he's always single. Makes sense doesn't it? He's a twat. I don't

94

have the patience for him any more. Who does? He needs to fucking grow up. I've no time for the stupid bastard.'

Then the terrible heat was back inside Luke's body and he was suddenly crashing and stumbling back to where Hutch and Phil were holding Dom, out of sight. His teeth were gritted so hard Luke regained enough control of himself to know that a tooth could snap at any moment and fill his head with a white lightning of agony. He unlocked his jaw.

'Keep it up, you fat fuck!' he bellowed as he came into view and watched Phil and Hutch scrabble aside. Dom put two hands up and shouted, 'Piss off!'

This time he was punching so quickly between Dom's raised palms, he immediately felt something rip at the base of his neck, then go tight and hot. Three punches littered across Dom's face and Luke felt a nose slide and then snap under his knuckles, like the wishbone at a Sunday roast. The fourth and fifth blows struck the top and back of Dom's head as Dom collapsed into the undergrowth. He curled himself into a ball on the floor and pulled both arms over his head. The last punch hurt Luke's little finger, the knuckle above it, and the bone behind the knuckle. He put the hand under his armpit and stepped away from Dom.

'Another word. Another word . . .' He tried to speak but was breathing too hard to get it out, and his voice was trembling with emotion.

'Jesus Christ. Jesus Christ. Take it easy. Shit.' Hutch was talking quickly and holding Luke's shoulders now with iron fingers, leading him away.

'Any more from him, and I'll put him out of the game. I swear.'

*

They walked together, away from the other two; Hutch's hand around his elbow. Dom had not uncurled himself from the ball. Phil was crouched down, talking to Dom in a low voice, but Luke could not hear what he was saying.

'Jesus, Luke. Listen to yourself. You're talking like a binton. A chav. This isn't you. What the hell?'

Luke sat down on the fallen log where he had been a few moments before. His hands were shaking so badly Hutch had to take the packet out of his hands and light two cigarettes. One for each of them.

'Calm down. Take it easy. Just relax. Cool your boots. Man, what has got into you?'

Luke didn't speak, just smoked the cigarette in quick inhalations until he felt sick. So much cortisone and adrenaline had leaked into his empty stomach along with phlegm and cigarette tar, he thought he might throw up. He unzipped his coat down to the waist, and bent over. Sucked in the cold wet air in great heaving lungfuls. He'd never felt so drained in his life. He started to shudder.

'Well, I guess that is the official end to the holiday,' Hutch said after a few minutes' silence.

Luke started to smile, felt ashamed, and then found himself laughing in silence. Hutch was smiling too, but only as part of a thin and pained expression. He shook his head. 'Didn't know you had it in you, Chief. God knows I've thought of giving Dom a shoeing over the years, but people like us just don't do things this way. What were you thinking?'

Luke looked at Hutch and saw the disappointment in his friend's eyes, the permanent estrangement. You could never come back from an event like this. Nothing would ever be the same again. He knew his friendship was over with all three of them.

'Shit,' he said and shook his head. He had to take a moment and swallow hard several times, otherwise his eyes would well up and he'd start crying. A lump closed his throat down. It would be impossible to speak for a while. He stood up and walked away from the dead and fallen tree.

'What am I doing here?' Luke said, further down the path. Hutch had followed him, his head bowed, his face pale and long with the strain of dealing with them all, on top of the situation they were in. They were forcing him to be a parent, to make every decision.

'I couldn't even afford to come. But I won't have him call me a loser.' His chest was going tight and he wanted to say so much to justify what he had just done, because of how Dom made him feel, but it wasn't coming.

Hutch looked at the sky and blinked as the rain hit his face. 'I better get back to the walking wounded.'

'He doesn't know anything about me any more. Nothing. None of you do.'

'He doesn't mean anything by it. No one does.'

'Am I being a prick?'

Hutch looked at his feet and sighed.

'You think so too. It's OK. Say it. I don't give a shit any more. I'm happy to take off now, Hutch.'

'Don't be so free with the crazy talk. We've had enough of that.'

'I meant to get help.'

'We're not there yet. Not by a long chalk. This is just a

setback. And I do wish you'd all just chill out a bit. This really isn't helping.'

'I'm sorry. I just lost it.'

'You don't say.'

They couldn't look each other in the eye. They looked at the earth, at the sky, at the endless trees and bracken all around them that were all utterly indifferent to them.

'Man. I went for miles, H. I reached the end of the line and got scratched to buggery. To find a way out. And when I came back . . . I just got so angry. I lost it. Because . . . you'd hardly moved. Like there was no urgency.'

'That's crap, and you know it.'

'I meant—'

'They can't walk. They're both broken. I was just trying to keep their spirits up. Keeping them talking and trying to take their minds off the situation.'

'And I fucked it.'

'Totally.'

Luke sighed. Touched his face where Dom had hit him. It wasn't even sore, just puffy. 'I had so much to tell you.'

Hutch turned his head to the side. 'See a way out?'

Luke shook his head. 'Nah. And it just gets worse. All of this shit.' He kicked at a bush.

Hutch closed his eyes and made a groaning noise. Then opened his eyes and sighed. 'Next year, we're renting a caravan.'

'I was just about to throw the towel in and come back when I found a cemetery.'

Now he had Hutch's attention again.

Luke nodded. 'Tors, standing stones, whatever you call them.'

'Rune stones.'

'Rune stones. All overgrown. In a big thicket that I crawled under. But on the other side of it is a church.'

'You are shitting me.'

'I'm not. A really old church. Like one of those buildings we saw in Skansen. In the housing museum. And the forest clears up a bit around it.'

Hutch's face brightened. 'Let's go.'

They walked back along the track towards the others, who were still out of sight. Luke slowed down. 'I'll keep a low profile and walk out front.'

'Good idea. But it means I'm now stuck in the rear with the fear again. Cheers.'

Luke was about to laugh, but Hutch wasn't smiling as he turned and walked away.

TWENTY-THREE

'Strange. Real strange, fella,' Hutch said to Luke, who walked so close to him in the scrub, he felt like a child behind an older boy, seeking guidance.

'What?'

Hutch stopped by a pile of rocks tumbled about a slight rise in the tangled earth of the cemetery; the rocks were engulfed in waist-deep foliage, right up to the flattish but tilting stone at the top. 'It's a cromlech. Bronze Age.'

Luke squinted at Hutch, pulling aggressively on the filter of his cigarette with lips he could only half feel.

'This was the roof.' Hutch tapped the flat tilting rock on top of the stone pile. 'All these stones are on a mound. A burial mound. That's why the stones are raised like this. The rocks underneath this big flat one were the sides, but they've fallen in. And back over there' – Hutch pointed his stick at another small hill behind the mound – 'another one. Cromlech. Or dolmen. Old, old graves, mate.'

He turned suddenly and pointed his stick at the tangle of white-trunked silver birch trees and brambles that engulfed an outcrop of large rounded stones, grey with reindeer moss, at the far side of the clearing. They had walked around it earlier trying to find more of the rune stones. 'And that's a partially collapsed passage grave. Big one. Sure of it. Would have been about twenty feet long. You can see the two upright stones where the entrance would have been. It's the giveaway that it's a passage grave. They're all over Sweden. Dolmens too. But not usually in the same place. Passage graves are Iron Age.'

He turned about, his face intense. 'And if you look around, the long flat stones we keep tripping over are bits of upright stone coffins. Built much later still. I reckon we can only see a few of the rune stones too. Rest are hidden out there in the trees. But I'll bet they form a circle. A perimeter around a much older site holding the cromlechs and passage grave.

'Look at the trees too. There's a chestnut. Oaks. Mountain ash, as well as the birch. Like an enclosure. A boundary to create repose inside. Christian cemeteries have them. So these trees were planted even later. Probably when this church was built in the last few centuries. It's amazing. What a find.'

Luke stayed quiet; just watching Hutch's tense, committed face.

'The Stone Age graves must have been built, I reckon, about three thousand years BC. They're so old they just look like piles of rocks now. I'd have walked right past them if we hadn't seen the rune stones and the church. The cromlechs and passage grave should all be completely covered over by now. Or had the boulders removed. Only bits of it still visible, you know? But this has all been preserved at some point. Not recently, but at some time in the past few centuries. They're not this intact unless they are cared for. Someone has been looking after this site for about four thousand years. Must have been, until that church was abandoned and the stone graves toppled over out here.'

Luke looked at him closely, awaiting a final summation

that would shed some light on how this would lead to them escaping from the forest. Because he didn't want Hutch's enthusiasm ending on the refrain that they were currently lost inside a forest that contained an undiscovered 4,000-year-old burial site. And that they had spent six hours that day following an old path to it; a trail grooved with cart wheels from the terrible houses abandoned amongst the trees.

Hutch winked at him, his eyes wide. 'Come on, let's get into that chapel.'

The tier of stone at the foundations had slumped into the black soil, and the next tier had slipped down to pull the entire structure gradually earthwards. Its right angles and straight lines had become concave; it sagged. The roof was gone. Some beams with slate tiles attached remained, exposed like the bones of a blackened rib cage. The three window casements on either side were empty of glass. Vestiges of a rotten wooden shutter hung from an iron fitting on one side. Any other visible metal was either black with rust or had corroded to a stain on the dark stone.

Twenty feet from the ruined porch of the chapel, Phil and Dom were sitting down on their rucksacks in a demoralized and exhausted silence. Dom had his trouser leg pulled up again and was pressing at the sides of the grubby bandage Hutch had fastened around his swollen knee for support. His mouth was bruised and his bottom lip was split and still bleeding into the dirt on his chin. The top of his nose was purple and fat, his top lip stained crimson. Two pieces of white toilet paper hung from each nostril.

As Luke stood before the porch of the chapel he realized

with discomfort that it was the first time he and Dom had been this close, and fully in sight of each other, since the fight. Something he could hardly believe had happened now. An event that made him restless with shame and anxious about his sanity. He was exhausted, his blood sugar was low, he'd hardly had any sleep in three days . . . but still. It was Dom he had attacked. Dom: his friend.

Luke had stayed so far down the track on his way back to the cemetery; making sure he turned and walked ahead the moment the others broke through the foliage and saw enough of him to know they were heading in the right direction. Occasionally, Hutch would shout, 'Chief! Where are you?' or 'Chief, show yourself!'

But now they were all gathered in one place and he and Hutch had completed their tramp around the accessible cemetery grounds and had turned their attention to the ruined church, it was harder for Luke to keep his distance from Dom.

The sight of what he had done to Dom's face made him feel sick. Guilt replayed the shock and fear on Dom's face the second time he attacked him, over and over again in his imagination, and he could think of little else now. It was throttling him. He would have to see someone; get help, when he got home. Because he knew only too well that this was not the first time this blinding suspension of self-control had occurred, and recently too.

He desperately wanted to apologize, but couldn't face another confrontation. It would come. Dom had to vent at some point. The best thing he could do, he kept telling himself, was to atone by getting them all out of this mess. By finding an escape route. Water first. Then a path out. He would do this for these men he had once loved like brothers, even if they weren't his friends any more.

Hutch peered at the weathered stone arch around the doorway. He bent in close and gently scraped his penknife against the stone. Luke stood behind him. If Dom hadn't been mute with smouldering anger, he would have been shouting right now, and demanding Hutch explain what he was doing looking at old bits of stone when he was hungry and wet and lost. At least it was good not to hear that voice encroaching again on the stillness and limited space they had managed to find here amongst the endless thickets.

Hutch slapped his hand against the arch, as if to indicate that when the rest of the building collapsed to rubble the arch would still be standing.

Upon the two stone pillars of the arch, markings depicted what could have been figures of men or animals, but they were so spongy with the lichen that Hutch scraped at with his penknife, it was hard to be certain what they had once represented. Runic inscriptions and other indecipherable carvings framed the characters and leaping figures in the centre of each pillar. Wheels with angular markings were carved into the worn limestone arch above the granite pillars. Above it, a wooden apex must once have completed the doorway, but it had rotted down to dark wet stumps.

Inside, the walls had once been covered in plaster; almost all of it had fallen away to reveal rough granite blocks beneath. The exposed stone was speckled with a milky green lichen. Rotten with damp and spored with black fungus, the remains of two rows of sagging wooden benches, or pews, still faced forward to a pulpit that looked like a lump of stone hewn roughly from a quarry. The top of the altar was covered with dead bits of forest. The floor was knee-deep with leaf mulch and dead branches that had fallen through the holed roof.

'A small congregation,' Hutch said. 'Probably held about twenty.'

Luke could not bring himself to speak. He was too uncomfortable with Dom's presence somewhere behind him; it glared against his back, all molten with rage and salted by grief.

'Odd though. Really odd.' Hutch stepped through the arch and onto the floor of the church. Luke followed him. The floor felt spongy, almost mobile, beneath his feet, like he was walking on a mattress. The floor sloped.

And then Hutch was suddenly down on his side, his legs buried to mid-thigh in the leaves behind the first row of pews. 'Shit.' Hutch didn't move. 'I've gone right through the floor.'

Luke looked down at his own feet. 'You OK?'

Hutch didn't answer and didn't move anything but his head. He looked down at what his legs had disappeared into, then propped himself up on one arm, which he had to bury to the elbow in fallen leaves to find something solid enough to support his upper body.

'Hutch. You all right?'

'Think so. But I'm scared to look.'

'Here. Let me give you a hand.'

'Careful,' Hutch said. 'It's rotten through.'

Luke stopped, then inched towards the interior wall on his left, instinctively feeling that the floor at the base of the walls would be a safer option.

Hutch stood up fully inside the hole he had made. 'Just as well the wood is soft. Imagine what splinters could have done.'

'Or a rusty nail.'

Hutch leaned his head back between his shoulders and shouted 'Fuck off!' at the remnants of roof. Then raised a foot from the hole and tried to find an adjacent piece of board sturdy enough to take his weight near the bench on his right side.

'I'm on my way over,' Luke said

'Nah. We don't both want to end up in the crypt.'

Luke let out a strangled laugh that sounded aggressive to his own ears. He shut it off and stopped smiling.

The floor was firmer at the side, and Luke carefully worked his way to the last row of the pews. Then he stepped over the first little black bench and into the space between the two end rows. He could barely get the width of one leg between them. 'People must have been tiny. Like children.'

His own observation unnerved him in the faint but perceptible way the interiors of historical buildings always did when he ducked through tiny doorways and saw the little beds and chairs that once serviced the long-dead. Perhaps it was this sudden and unwelcome reminder of his own mortality that made him feel, so acutely, a sense of a frightening loss that was like vertigo. That all things must pass. That anyone who had lived there and used the furniture before it became antique was now dust. The dank oppressive atmosphere of the enclosed and rotten space he was inside added a sense of desolation. Despite the rain, he was glad it had no roof. Even the dull mackerel light was welcome. He felt suddenly grateful for the company of the others. 'The last thing this place feels is holy.' He could not stop himself from just blurting it out.

'I know what you mean.' Hutch had regained his feet and

was standing in the narrow aisle between the pews, testing the floor in front of him, before taking careful steps forward as if he was walking on ice.

Luke stepped over the next row of pews but the section of floor he placed his foot upon was soft and gave way. He withdrew the leg and tried further down until he found a firmer spot. Hutch reached the altar.

'You reckon where you are can take our combined weight?' Luke asked Hutch.

'I reckon.' Hutch wiped the thick mulch of dead leaf mould from the top of the altar, until his bare hand reached stone.

Luke gingerly approached the altar from the side, rubbing his back against the dark wall that was down to stone in most places, the plaster having been dissolved by the rain falling through the roof for . . . for how long he had no idea. But for a long time.

'Anything on it?' he asked.

'Like what, a virgin sacrifice?' Hutch replied without smiling.

'Runes and shit.'

'Nope. Just a weird hollow. See, right in the centre. It's been hollowed out.'

'Baptism font.'

Hutch nodded. 'You could be right, Chief.'

'What did you mean before?'

'Eh?'

'Before. You said it was odd.'

Hutch frowned at Luke, then his grimy forehead smoothed out. He tapped a finger against the top of the stone he stood behind. 'No crucifixes on the stone arch. All the carvings on the stone face are pagan.'

'Really?'

'Old too. And those runes. You know those circular markings on Viking carvings? Serpents? With those long snaky bodies, all swallowing each other at one end?'

'Yeah. Yeah.'

'Well, I think there was once a pair of those on it, with what looks like carvings of' – he wafted his hand towards the door and the wood outside – 'all of this around them. Vines and leaves. The rain has corroded most of it.'

'Cool. I'll take a look.'

'I chipped away a little bit of the dirt with my penknife on the pillars. It's quite intricate, which is odd because the actual building is very basic. Like a shed or croft. But it must have been a Christian church once. Probably the last time it was used. It's weird because there are no Christian symbols in here. No Christian headstones outside either. So no one was interned here in the last . . . millennia. How does that work?'

'The church has just been built over an earlier site?'

'Exactly. A sacred site, I think. And the church must have once been the centre of that . . . settlement we found. Which can't be more than a century old, like this building. So people still came to worship, but stopped burying their dead here. Weird.'

The mention of which did something unpleasant to Luke's empty stomach. In the maelstrom of his confusion and his disorderly thoughts, he wanted to start peppering Hutch with questions but held his tongue. And felt anxious to get moving again; to get away from the place, and quickly.

'And the other crazy thing is,' Hutch said, raising both hands into the air, 'it's still here.'

Luke frowned.

Hutch pointed at the stone plinth. 'No one has carted any of this off to a museum. I don't think there are that many good examples left of the Norse carvings in the wild. They're all uprooted and preserved. Protected from acid rain in display cases in museums down in Lund or Stockholm. That's where I've seen them before.' Hutch lowered his voice. 'So, between me and you, I'd guess that no one knows this is here.'

Luke could not hide his shock at hearing this fact voiced, even though he had privately arrived at the same disconcerting conclusion.

'No one has been through here since this place was abandoned. I'd put money on it, Chief.'

Luke shook his head in disbelief and with a disquiet he hoped did not show.

Hutch's voice lowered even further. 'And if we weren't lost and soaked and hungry, it would be pretty cool to discover it. We'd make the papers.'

'But now it's just freaky and scary.'

'Exactly. And we still might make the papers for another reason.'

They looked at each other and were both beginning to crack mad grins when Phil started shouting outside.

TWENTY-FOUR

Luke burst out of the church. Dom was on his feet, but poised to cringe or run, it was hard to tell. Phil stood knee-deep in undergrowth with his back to the chapel, staring into the overgrown cemetery. When he turned about his face was tight with shock and terror. The same expression he had that morning when they found him naked and incoherent in the hovel. His trousers were undone. He must have been taking a piss. If he had not been so disturbed by what he had just seen, it might have been funny.

Hutch was swearing aloud from somewhere behind him; he had not followed Luke out through the church arch. 'What's wrong?' Luke called to Phil, then looked at Dom when no reaction was forthcoming.

Dom returned his stare. 'I don't fucking know!'

Phil had begun by crying out, like he had been bitten or burnt and was just coming to terms with the pain. But then he had been shouting with more than fear. By the time Luke stumbled over the pews and emerged into the weeds outside the building, Phil was silent and standing still in the rain. It was worse than the shouting.

Luke looked at the back of Phil's head, blue and pointy with the hood of his coat up. 'Phillers? What is it?'

Phil was staring into the trees, towards the two rune stones visible from the rough clearing in front of the church. At the sound of Luke's voice, Phil quickly tucked and then belted himself away. He turned around and stumbled through the undergrowth towards the church like he was wading through seawater in a hurry.

Dom and Luke could not stop themselves exchanging glances, until looking at each other became too awkward. Dom looked over Luke's shoulder and roared, 'Hutch! Get your arse out here. Now!'

Hutch said something from inside the walls of the church. It was muffled and too low for any of them to hear. It was like he was preoccupied with something. But what could have been of more concern than the noise Phil had just made?

'Hutch!' Luke took long strides back to the church building. He looked through the door and saw Hutch bent over in the gloom. Part of the floor had collapsed again around his hips, and the pews on one side had now dipped into the centre aisle which Hutch must have tried to run across. 'You all right, mate?' Luke asked.

Hutch nodded. 'Which is more than I can say for these poor bastards.' He had both of his arms stretched towards his feet and was pulling dead branches and leaves from the floor with both hands. He threw the debris onto the collapsing pews.

'Buddy, something's up with Phil. You better get out here.'

'I know. I looked out the door. But he was just standing there. What was it? He see a snake? I told you guys about the adders. You got to stamp your feet before you go into undergrowth.'

'I don't think it's a snake. What the hell are you doing?'

Hutch looked up at him. Only his teeth and the whites of

his eyes were clean inside his dirty face against the backdrop of the dark and rotten floor. Hutch looked ill. His face was lined and slack with exhaustion. Whatever he had found seemed to have finished off the last dregs of the optimism and humour that had begun to flicker back to life when they explored the cemetery. 'Jesus. Jesus Christ. I don't know what to make of this.'

Luke slid and shuffled his way back inside the building. 'What? What is it?'

'I don't really know if I should touch it.'

Luke leant, gingerly, on the back of the intact pews and peered into the hole Hutch stood inside. Around Hutch's feet were more of the large wet leaves, thickening to a brownish mulch in the poor light. And there were other things down there too that Hutch had partially cleared of foliage. They looked like more of the dead tree branches, black with damp. 'What? What am I looking at, Hutch?'

Hutch raised his face. 'Remains. Human remains.'

'The crypt?' Luke hardly heard his own voice and then had to swallow the nerves that put a tremor in his words.

Hutch shook his head. 'They weren't interned. No coffins. Just dumped in a pile. They're all broken. All the skulls are smashed in.'

'Shit no.'

Hutch bent over and picked something up. Instinctively Luke said, 'Don't touch it.'

Hutch raised it to catch the watery light that fell in on them along with a chilling drizzle that was getting heavier. 'This is from an animal.' It was a long rib he held up. Then dropped it, slapping his hands together noisily in an attempt to clean them. He bent in again, sorted through the black wet dross around his feet. 'A mandible. Three vertebrae. Another pile of ribs. Maybe from a horse. Moose. Dunno.' He bent back into the reliquary. 'But all mixed up with this.' The next thing he held up was a human rib cage. An arm soundlessly popped out of it as he raised it from the leaves. The pale brown colour of it was unnerving; it looked newer than the animal bones. 'And this.' He next raised a human skull, the jaw long gone, the upper row of teeth blackened, half of the small cranium punched through. He dropped it and aggressively wiped his hands against his trousers.

'Human remains and animal remains mixed in together. Bloody weird. They're not all old either. I mean, they've all been here ages, but some have been here longer than others.' He was talking to himself now, oblivious to Luke's tense presence, as if by speaking out loud he would arrive at a satisfactory explanation for what felt so wrong. They were both now shivering inside their wet-weather gear; shivering from more than just the effects of the cold air and the rain.

Luke could not swallow. And what shocked him more than anything he had experienced since they had become lost, was the evidence in this place that the boundary between men and beasts had been scored out.

'Children's bones are in here.'

'Oh, Christ no, Hutch.'

Hutch sighed, and sifted his foot through the wet dark detritus.

TWENTY-FIVE

They all squatted down, around Phil, staring at him. The rain dropped steadily from a darkening sky and made a constant pattering against their coats and packs. Phil looked unhealthily pale and shivered. He'd wrapped his hands under his arms, clutched himself. He glanced over a shoulder. 'It's here. It followed us.'

Hutch and Luke looked at each other, then back at Phil. Luke blew two deep lungfuls of smoke into the wet air. 'What did?'

Dom's eyes were too wide in his stained and scabbing face. 'What the fuck are you talking about?'

Phil swallowed. 'I saw . . .'

Hutch groaned and eased himself down and on to his knees. 'Buddy, buddy, take it easy. Just take it nice and easy. Tell us exactly what you saw.'

'I went for a piss. And I was looking at the ground so I didn't hit my feet. But I started to feel weird. You know, like someone was standing next to me. Like they'd come up to me. Was right next to me. And when I looked up . . . I thought it was a tree or something. Out there. It never moved, but it didn't look right. I stared at it and . . . then it moved.'

Luke squinted through the smoke around his face. 'Eh?'

The other two turned their faces towards the overgrown cemetery.

'In there.' Phil pointed at a copse of trees crowding over the first rune stone they had passed. 'By those trees. At the edge. Something moved out from between them and kind of went backwards really quickly and then it was gone. Never made a sound. It was so fast.'

'An animal?' Hutch asked.

Phil shook his head. 'I thought it was a dead tree. One of those hit by lightning. But then . . . I don't know . . . I thought it was something on two legs. Standing up. Really tall. It's dark in all that scrub. But something was kind of camouflaged in there, because it was standing really still.'

'Fucking stop it,' Dom said. 'It's not funny. Not here.'

'It's no joke, Dom! I saw something. It was in my dream last night. In that house. Coming down the stairs.'

'Enough,' Dom barked. 'I'm doing my best to forget last night. And whatever the fuck was in that tree yesterday.'

Luke looked out at the forest. Then glanced at Hutch, who looked pale under the filth and all jittery around his big eyes.

'You don't believe me?' Phil said.

Dom's face was so tense his lips thinned to nothing and his teeth were showing. 'No we bloody don't! So stop trying to freak us out!'

'Something's gone bad out here,' Luke said quietly, as if to himself.

'What the fuck are you on?' Dom challenged him.

'Nothing, and more's the pity. But that rotten mess' – Luke pointed at the derelict chapel – 'is full of human remains. They're in a right state.'

'What?' Despite the grime, Dom's face still gave the appearance of being pallid.

Hutch shook his head, and looked as if he'd been told some terrible news. 'Something awful happened here. I'd hazard a guess they all came to a bad end.'

'Bad end?'

'Torn up. Heads smashed in, like a war grave.'

Phil's shaking was getting worse. For once, Dom didn't respond.

'How?' Phil asked Hutch, but there was as much pleading as curiosity in the question.

Hutch swallowed. 'Thank Christ we didn't go into those other two buildings. I'd have put money on us finding something just as fucked up in them.'

'What is it, Hutch?' Phil pleaded.

'I don't know, mate. I'm really not sure I want to know either.' He stood up. 'Witchcraft. Black magic. Some old cult. The Swedes are really religious up here. I just don't know. But it's messing with us, chaps. With our heads. Some places are just bad, I reckon. And it's getting on top of us. You saw an animal, Phil. An elk. Moose. Red deer. They're all over this part of the country. That's all. We're just jumpy. Who wouldn't be? But let's chill. Just cool our heels a bit. I mean it.' He looked at Luke, his eyes hard. 'Let's not fall apart any more than we have already, yeah?'

Luke stood up too, and looked out at the trees. 'It's two o'clock. We need to put our foot down if we're going to get out of here before it gets dark. Judgement call. Go back and try to get out the way we came in yesterday?'

'Which means going past that fucking tree,' Dom said, his fear turning to anger.

'And the house,' Phil said, and drew further into himself. He was almost crying; they could hear it in his voice.

'Or,' Luke said, raising his hands, palms out, 'we take our chances on the other side of this clearing and just peg it.'

Dom looked up at him as if he were a congenital idiot. 'How do we "just peg it", in this bloody state?'

'We do the best we can. I'll get you a crutch.'

'I don't want a fucking crutch. I don't want anything from you.'

Hutch put both hands over his face and groaned, and kept on groaning until they all stopped talking. He didn't speak but raised his pack and slipped his arms through the straps.

'New ground?' Luke asked, in a conciliatory tone.

Hutch nodded.

'Cool. And if anyone has any water, I'd sure appreciate a mouthful.'

'I'm all out,' Phil said, and scrabbled for his pack, as if terrified the others were about to leave him behind.

Hutch handed his drinking bottle to Luke. It was half full. The last of it.

TWENTY-SIX

Cramped inside the tiny porch of a tent, Hutch and Luke sat and watched the little gas flame stutter around the stove ring. Rain hazed into drizzle. Grey dusk-light dispersed around the oncoming concussion of night. As every minute passed and they waited to see bubbles appear on the murky surface of the soup, it was becoming harder to see their feet, or where they had put the plates and mugs. The ground was too wet for a fire; sopping, like all of the dead wood around them that could have made kindling.

On the far side of the abandoned churchyard, the dwarf birch and willow were not so thick and the bracken and thorns between them had thinned, but their mobility had still been slowed, first by the acres of ferns that grew out of marshy soil to waist-height, and then by ground made uneven with lichen-slippery, grey rock formations. It had taken nearly an hour at one point to manoeuvre Dom over an outcrop of boulders. From the stony ground they entered more of the thick bracken. And since leaving the church, the canopy overhead had revealed only glimpses of a watery-grey sky.

Hutch had called an end to their slow and hesitant progress through the forest at seven. There was still an hour, maybe even ninety minutes of light left, but Phil and Dom had gone beyond their limit. Twice Dom had sat down in the woods, in silence, and been unable or unwilling to move. Phil's movements had developed an ungainly, uncoordinated aspect, like he was drunk. In a way he was; he was intoxicated with exhaustion.

The darkness in the forest always made it appear later than it actually was. Watches were even checked; held up to ears to detect ticking. Even as early as four in the afternoon, under the ancient leafy canopy it began to feel like night.

They'd barely moved six, maybe seven kilometres all day.

The forest floor about their campsite was so strewn with broken wood, the erection of the two tents in this spot had been nearly impossible. Behind them in the thinning light the tents sagged and fluttered like discarded parachutes. Much ground had to be cleared first and Hutch's fingers were scratched from scraping aside the dead wood and bracken to create a temporary clearing. Now the two tents were up as best he and Luke could manage, crammed together and sagging, with so many roots, nettles and lumps visible beneath the groundsheets it would be impossible to lie down comfortably and sleep inside them.

Hutch anticipated a bad night ahead, sitting up or curled into a corner of the two-man tent. But at least it would be dry inside, or so Hutch promised the others. From the waist down they were all soaked. The chafing inside Phil's jeans was bad. He had managed to slowly peel the wet denim down to his knees, but doubted he would ever get them back on again so left them half down. His inner thighs were now shiny in the faint light with a salve they could smell. Tomorrow, he would have to squeeze into the pair of filthy over-trousers

Dom had worn during the first two days of the hike. Phil lay down inside a tent, on top of his sleeping bag, in silence.

Spread out over Hutch's sleeping-bag cover was the remainder of their food supplies. There was hunger ahead. Dom had demanded a substantial lunch. As a result, in the little metal pot on the camping stove was the last meal they could fashion together out of the two remaining packets of dried soup, a bag of soya mince, some freeze-dried savoury rice and the last tin of hot dog sausages. After that, they were down to four energy bars each and one communal chocolate bar, some boiled sweets and chewing gum. And even tonight's food would amount to little more than a mug of soup each, cooked in pre-boiled marsh water, with two sausages standing upright in each of the four cups surrounded by soya mince. But not one of them could concentrate on anything but the slow advance of the pot's contents to readiness.

At the perimeter of one of the stony outcrops, Luke had found a creek. Water that never grew beyond a brownish trickle in three separate locations. The actual stream seemed to be underground. But at least the murky water ran freely, and was cold and fresh. For ten minutes they had sat in silence and filled themselves, and then the plastic litre canisters and personal canteens. Hutch had felt dizzy and sick afterwards. But there had been no stopping them gorging on the first fresh water they had seen in two days.

At least their pitiful campsite was on the best ground they had seen for hours; out of the chilly breeze that could come through the trees at dusk, and more or less level once the scrub had been removed. With the tents up, Hutch set about preparing the stove and assembling the ingredients. They were all too tired to talk. And didn't even look at each other.

Luke was spent. Aches bruised his thighs and jabbed through his buttocks. Had he taken off by himself, he wondered how far he would have made it alone. At least twice the distance they had covered as a group. Maybe he would even have found the fringe of the forest. Who could say? But once they were clear of that dreadful church, he had just wanted to break free of the others. Every moment of misery endured since fuelled his resentment at Phil and Dom for slowing them down; putting them at risk by being so physically unprepared for the trip. And the rash decision Hutch had made with the short cut still made him smoulder. Much of his anger should have been directed at himself. He was transferring it onto the others. He knew it. Taking the short cut had been against his instincts. As had their continuation on the trail from the house that morning, westwards into the unknown. Taking both routes had been the wrong thing to do; he had known it, but he had followed the others and not raised enough of an objection. Why? Same again with squatting in the hovel last night; his participation had been contrary to his instincts. And look at what it had done to them all. It had been a night they had lacked the energy and inclination to confront since. Something terrible happened to each of them they could later blame on environment or tiredness. But they were not random, those dreams.

He wanted a clean break from it all and from all of them. Tomorrow, he would take off. On his own to get help. He had made the decision earlier that evening. And when he told Hutch in a whispered aside, his old friend had just nodded his assent. Not raising any of his usual enthusiasm for the new strategy, or a single objection, Hutch had just moved his head slowly. Inside his grimy sockets Hutch's eyes had looked too old, dim somehow.

They were *fucked*. Really in trouble now. The day had been a waste of time, exhausting the last of their supplies and what little energy Phil and Dom had left. They had turned that corner, from camping to survival. It had happened sometime during the day. Probably in the early afternoon. Had not been marked by anything specific, but by everything. And only now, once they'd stopped staggering, foot by foot through the debris, had Hutch finally accepted their situation. Just knowing it made Luke's head heavy. But at least it stilled the maelstrom of ideas in his mind, and the sense of choice, that had almost made the morning exciting for them in the way men can get excited outdoors.

There was no choice now, no debate. Someone had to go for help. One of the fitter ones. Him or Hutch. While the other one stayed behind with Phil's terrible blisters and exhausted overweight body, and Dom's painful swollen knee, and the way it too was exasperated by an exhausted over-weight body. Hutch wasn't happy with the arrangement, but Luke's fight with Dom had settled it.

He'd take off at first light. Due south with the second com-pass. After a few hours' sleep. And he was looking forward to it, despite the risks. Those pitfalls he could not allow himself to dwell on in any great detail, like the sudden gaping chasm of solitude that would swallow him up and boom through his ears. He would just have to keep going through the madness of it, the awe and terror, and stay focused. But he wanted to settle a few things before he left the others. 'Dom?'

Inside the mouth of the tent, he could see Dom lying down in silence, with his injured leg raised and propped up on his rucksack to ease the swelling. No answer.

Hutch raised his face and frowned at Luke, then shook his head. He mouthed the words, *Not now*.

Luke nodded and sighed, before looking up at the dark roof of tree branches and heavy wet leaves they had camped below. The individual limbs and branches above merged into an inky ceiling. Tiny segments of paler sky glimmered through the holes. Drizzle settled onto his face. A few heavy drops regularly smacked the earth about him. The water would always find a way down to them.

'Ready chaps,' Hutch said.

The two figures inside the tents stirred. Dom groaned. Then stuck an arm out of the awning of his tent. The hand at the end held a metal dish. 'And don't skimp on the sausages. I don't care if they taste like scrotum.'

Hutch grinned. 'Well I had to thicken the sauce with something.'

Luke didn't have the strength to laugh. Phil turned his torch on inside the tent and looked about himself to find his own tin.

'We'll wash this down with some coffee after.'

Luke's mouth filled with saliva. Even with the milk powder that never fully dissolved and the sugar sachets they had swiped from the hostel in Kiruna, just the idea of it made him stupidly happy.

They ate quickly and noisily, almost weeping into their tins as they licked at the final dregs of liquid around the sides. None of the pans had been washed from the previous night and the dried residue of yesterday's meal could be felt against their tongues as they lapped like starving cats.

'That might have just been the best food I have ever eaten,' Hutch said, when they had all finished, his tone of voice lighter and warmer than it had been since midday.

Luke thought of saying something about losing sight of the simple things that really mattered. But decided against it. He doubted anyone in that camp had any interest in what he had to say any more. They all felt awkward around him now. He sensed it on the few occasions he had spoken since the fight, and intuited a tensing of their bodies when he came close to them as they made the clearing and set up the tents. The majority of both tasks he had performed, but his efforts had gone unacknowledged. He was getting impatient again, at his exclusion, and it was turning to irritation.

He lit a cigarette. And pondered again on why he had been at the very edge of the group since they met in London six days ago. Six days? It seemed much longer. He looked into the packet and squinted. Only eight filter cigarettes left and then he'd be into the emergency ration of roll-up tobacco, 12.5 grams of Drum. Being out of tobacco would make him truly psychotic; he'd take cigarettes over food every time.

He fidgeted. He sighed. If he were honest, something had happened to him in his late twenties that seemed to man-oeuvre him away from other people, not just his friends, but from the normal course of human affairs. He'd begin to catch people exchanging glances whenever he spoke up in group situations; or they would be half smiling when he entered the offices and warehouses he worked in, but he never stayed for very long before he moved on to something else equally unsatisfactory. Invitations to join others lessened, then ceased before he was thirty-two. Only damaged and insecure women seemed to find comfort in his company, though they had little interest in him besides his being a confirming presence. By thirty-four he was lonely. Lonely. Genuinely.

Back in London and Stockholm, before the hike began, unless he was talking to Hutch alone, his every attempt to start a conversation in the group had been treated like an ill-thought-out statement, or just ignored. No one even tried to pick up the threads he started. Most often there would be a silence and then the other three would fall back into whatever natural camaraderie they had rediscovered. A bond he was only interrupting by speaking. At best, he had been humoured from the start of the trip.

How he had become so estranged from his oldest friends puzzled him, and wounded him deeply. It could be down to something that happened to him in London after a few years in the city. He knew how the city changed whoever you were before you lived in it. Or maybe he'd always suffered a fundamental disconnection with other people that had been latent in his youth. He didn't know, and was getting too tired to think about it now, and was sick of analysing it. *Fuck it*, what had he got to lose? 'Dom. Look. This morning . . .' He took a deep breath and sighed.

Inside his tent, Phil turned away, onto his side, his back to the open door. Hutch stayed preoccupied with boiling water for the coffee, but Luke could tell the tension was almost unbearable for him.

'I'm sorry, mate. I mean, really sorry. About this morning. It was just . . . unacceptable.'

Dom did not respond for a while. And each second of

125

silence thickened the chilly air about the campsite. When he did speak, his voice was calm. 'It was. But stuff your apology right up your arse. I don't want it. And unless it's a strict matter of our survival, I don't want to exchange a single word with you until we get home.'

Luke looked at Hutch, who winced and pursed his lips, but continued to busy himself with the coffee preparations.

Luke's temperature rose and warmed his entire sheath of skin. He felt light-headed and choked up with emotion. All over again. Self-pity. Anger. Regret. Every-fucking-thing as usual, thickening his throat like the mumps, blocking his mouth with the taste of iron. 'Fair enough.'

'Too right it's fair enough. And I swear, if you even go for one of us again, you'll get more than you bargained for.'

Had they a strategy to defend themselves against him then? Had he been discussed? Of course he had been; when he was out ahead, walking point. The fight was an event that would have commanded any breath they had left for debate.

'Like you were blameless.' He was speaking on instinct again. That terrible instinct that he could barely control when he felt aggrieved, which if he were honest, was every morning on his way to work on the London Underground and then for the best part of every day at work in a second-hand record shop.

'Eh? I provoked you, did I? Into what you did? I deserved that? You're a bloody psycho.'

'Dom,' Hutch said, his tone stern.

'Leave it, Luke,' Phil said. 'Just leave it. You've done enough for one day.'

'Piss off.' It was out of his mouth before he spared a fraction of a second to consider it.

'Here we go again,' Dom said.

Luke took a deep breath. Paused. Looked at the end of his cigarette. 'You've been on my case since London. You think I'm happy being the butt of all your jokes, mate?'

'Oh poor you. Boo fucking hoo.'

'You're doing it again. Belittling me. Why?'

'Can it, Luke,' Hutch said, his voice sounding tired.

'Why? Why is it whenever I speak, it's too tedious for you all to listen? What do I say that is so inappropriate, or stupid?'

'Maybe it is,' Dom said.

Luke ignored the comment, knowing it was an attempt to get back at him for the humiliation Dom felt about the fight. 'I can't believe any of us used to be friends.'

Dom kept it up. 'We're not any more, so don't strain yourself.'

Suddenly, Luke did not regret a single punch he had landed on Dom's face. 'What the fuck am I doing here, with you? I've been thinking that since you all showed up at my flat.'

Dom propped himself up on his elbow, so Luke could see his tight flat face in the dark entrance of the tent. 'Well maybe you should have said something then and spared us all your company for the last few days.'

Luke laughed out loud. 'Forget what happened this morning, which is seeming more justifiable now, by the way, but just put that aside for one moment, and tell me. Tell me what your problem is? With me? Come on, let's have it.'

'Luke!' Hutch barked.

'No. Piss off.' Luke moved his eyes back to Dom and spoke slowly. 'What is it that I have done? Tell me. You've been breaking my balls non-stop. Everything I say, you contradict.

I'm not entitled to an opinion. Anything I say is rewarded with a sarcastic comment from either you or Phil. Or you look at each other with those pathetic half-smiles. Why? I've done my best to get along here, but no matter what I do, it's like I've committed some cardinal error to provoke this contempt. Because that is what it is. Contempt. But I am goddamned if I know what it is that I have done to deserve it. And this is what I want to know now. So tell me.'

No one spoke.

'Things have changed Luke. We've all moved on,' Hutch said.

'What does that mean? Really mean?'

'We're different people now. People move apart. Time does that. No big deal.'

'It is a big deal if you invite someone on a camping trip and then exclude them and make them feel like shit. And even when everything has gone to shit, you've still kept it up.'

'You're overreacting,' Phil said.

'If we've made you feel that way, I apologize,' Hutch said. 'Now can we drop it?'

'Not you. You've done nothing, H. I'm not talking about you. It's this pair.'

Dom shook his head. 'Ever thought about some of the things you've said that just might piss us off?'

Luke raised both hands. 'Like? An example?'

Dom leaned further out of the tent. 'Who do you actually think you are? You can't help reminding us of what a free spirit you are. No family. No wife. You don't believe in monogamy. You won't take any shit from anyone at work. Don't want to be trapped by responsibility. You're bloody thirty-six, mate. You work in a shop. You are a shop assistant. You are not eighteen. But you never changed and it's hard to take you seriously. Because you still get excited by the fact that Lynyrd Skynyrd have a new record out.'

Phil and Hutch sniggered. Luke looked at all three of them and then dropped his head back to laugh derisively. 'So that's it.'

'Do you think your philosophy impresses anyone with any responsibility in their lives? You said back in Stockholm that you have made other choices. What choices? What have you done with your life? Really? What have you got to show for yourself?'

Luke leaned forward, his voice raised, until he became too conscious of it and lowered it. 'It's not a competition. I don't want what you have. I genuinely don't. And because I haven't bought into it, you try and make me feel like some kind of loser. True enough, I've made my life difficult for myself, with the record shop that went tits-up. With London. But I'm not some aimless loser. I work in a shop now to get by. It's not a career choice. It's an occupation to pay my rent. Something I am doing now. And that's all. It's not *who* I am.'

Phil sniggered and Luke could tell he was looking at Dom. *Would he like a fucking slap too?* He stared at Phil. 'But it bothers you. It pisses you off that I'm not crippled with debt or saddled with some moody bitch. Instead, you P.R. your lives and act like I'm supposed to envy you. Who would want it, boys? Look how bloody old you look. Both of you. Fucking fat and grey and you're not even forty yet. Is this what a family does? And marriage? Am I supposed to aspire to it? Envy it? And if I don't, I should be excluded? Why? I'll tell you why, because I remind you of everything you can't do. Yes, can't do. Because you are not allowed to.'

Dom just shook his head.

Phil quietly said, 'Twat.'

Dom looked up at Luke again, trying to hold his mirth back. 'Which is something you try and rub our noses in every time we see you, because it's all you have. Arrested development is hardly a way of life I aspire to.'

'What?' Following your heart. Not compromising. You can't see it as anything but failure and avoidance.'

'Listen to him,' Phil said, quietly, but it was the most engaged he seemed to have been with anything since his cries of distress chilled them all that afternoon outside the church. 'And he earns two pounds fifty an hour and lives in the sort of shit-hole you were supposed to leave behind in your second year at university.'

'But it still pisses you off,' Luke said. 'It really does. It's all that regret and resentment you carry around. It's not my fault you're both terrified of your own fucking wives.'

Dom snorted. 'Shagging those scabby tarts and living like a bum. Oh, I'd swap places in a heartbeat. And where has selling CDs and that music journalism course got you, eh? Finsbury-fucking-Park.'

'Why is it that any woman I go out with is a scabby tart? Whereas the uptight bitches you got shacked up with are somehow what . . . desirable? Respectable?'

Hutch was shaking his head, but it was too hard to tell in the gloom if he was smiling or nervous. 'Fellas, you're all getting way out of line here.'

But no one was listening to Hutch. Even he was irritating Luke now, trying to protect Dom as usual. Always babying him. Did they know how they looked together? 'Money,'

Luke continued. 'That's the only worth anyone has, is it? What they earn?'

'Well it's a start and better than nothing.'

'The only criteria with which you judge anyone these days. What they own, acquire, have. What a sad fucker you turned into. And don't pretend you're happy, mate. Don't kid yourself because I am not fooled. I saw you at Hutch's wedding. How many arguments did you have with Gayle?' He glared at Phil. 'And you with Michelle? Eh? She had a face on all day, like a bulldog chewing on a wasp. I'd have got shot of the pair of them years ago. Put them out with the fucking bin bags. Let alone married them. I mean, what were you thinking? I'd rather be on the street than have to look at one of their miserable faces for a single night.'

Hutch reached out and grabbed Luke's calf muscle hard. 'Luke. Luke. Luke. Too far. Too far.' Then Hutch stood up quickly and said to them all, 'Fellas, I'm done with you all. Remind me to never ever set foot in a room again when you're together. Like we don't have enough to deal with. I mean, men, get real. We're in some pretty deep shit right now.' He stalked away, into the treeline to urinate.

'And whose fucking fault is that?' Dom shouted after him.

Luke still didn't feel that he had finished, or had said anything right. 'Once we get out of here, we go our separate ways.'

'Well, as far as you are concerned, yes. I won't be looking you up again. You can be sure of that,' Dom said and laughed, a note of triumph in his voice, that made Luke fondly recall smacking his face with both fists.

'Fine by me.'

'We only went camping because you're so skint. Me and

Phillers and H wanted to go somewhere warm, but you couldn't afford it. We were thinking Egypt for some Red Sea diving. So this is what happens when you compromise for a free spirit, who lives by his own rules. Who ended up selling CDs for a living and is always skint.' Dom raised the zipper on the tent flap.

Luke sat still and tried to regulate his breathing. The rage was strangling him again. When he felt like this, he wondered if, one day, he might actually kill someone.

'Best thing for you to do now,' he said to the closed door of the tent, 'is to think of how you are going to get your fat useless arse out of this place tomorrow. Because I won't be here when you wake up.'

'Piss off.'

TWENTY-SEVEN

Phil and Dom were both snoring inside the tents. Phil sounded like an engine, inhuman. It was not a noise Luke could get used to. He and Hutch could hear them as they sat opposite each other in silence, more coffee brewing in the pot between them. As long as they could find water, coffee was the item they had plenty of. They smoked and stared at the little blue ring of fire on the stove. It was the only thing that offered any comfort in a forest that had become as lightless as an ocean floor. The darkness became disorientating if you looked into it and tried to make sense of anything that suggested itself. Rain pattered about them.

Luke had shrunk inside himself and was accompanied by familiar thoughts. Why did some people have everything: careers, money, love, children, and some nothing? He'd not even come close to those things.

Or had he? Again, he revisited the unresolved questions of his existence. If he'd married one of those girls he'd chucked one year after meeting them in his twenties, like Helen or Lorraine or Mel, would he now be just like Dom, or Phil or Hutch?

And the full gravity of the last few years came pressing upon him again, even here, in this place, in these circumstances, after all he'd been through he still wasn't free of himself; whenever he stopped and rested, when the external distractions abated, he always felt worn out, so tired by his life; was forced to acknowledge that he had achieved nothing for his pains, his transience, his changes of direction, or lack of direction, his misfires and mistakes. And he admitted to himself that he had always coveted his friends' families, homes, careers, their seemingly contented lives. Without such, it came to dawn on him a few years ago, you could not even begin to hope to be accepted. Not really; not in this world when you were well past thirty. But he'd always hated himself too, for craving what Hutch, Phil and Dom had; those impenetrable worlds that so many took for granted; he loathed himself for desiring acceptance, when he also knew how thwarted every job and relationship made him feel. But still, he craved it all. It was at the heart of his unhappiness, his despair. He would probably die incomplete, undecided, and disappointed.

'Buddy. There's something I never told you.' Hutch kept his voice low, but it was tense, as if he were about to make a difficult confession. Luke looked at Hutch's face. Light from the flames caught his eyes and jaw, but little else. It was hard to even recognize Hutch from what Luke could see of his face inside the hood and tight woollen beanie hat. He guessed Hutch was going to tell him about something he had found in the church or the hovel. Something he had kept from the others. Either that, or he had made a miscalculation about where they were on the map.

Luke braced himself. 'Give it to me straight. Part of tonight's theme. Instead of sniping and crap. I'm sick of it.'

'I noticed.'

'You think I went too far?'

'Off the scale. You're full of surprises, Chief. I think they were taken aback by how pissed off you are.'

Luke felt the first embers of shame, then took control of himself. 'No. I didn't overreact. No. I had to get it out.'

'Clearly.'

'You just stay on that fence. You've had your moments too. I never noticed anyone stamping on your nads when you were in a slump. Why should it be different for me? I won't stand for it.'

Hutch never spoke for a while. Then said, 'Luke, I'd say you've burnt out a few fuses in London. The ones you can't replace. Done it myself. When I was a benefits adviser. Remember?'

Instead of snapping back with some instinctive defence, he nodded. 'I'm not in a good place right now. To be honest, I've just about had enough, mate. Of everything.'

'But try and target the rage at the right cause, aye?'

'I get so angry. I reckon I might be a psychopath or something.' Luke said this with a face as straight as the belief that issued the statement.

Hutch laughed.

'I mean it. This morning. With Dom. It's not the first time. I did it on the tube going to work.'

'No way.'

'About two months back. Some tosser just pushed onto the carriage before I could get out. You know, they have this announcement, about letting people off first. And there's another one about moving right down inside the carriages. It makes no difference. No one listens. Anyway, I threw down. Pulled this twat off the train by his neck and laid him out. On the platform. In front of about three hundred people.

135

I didn't care. Just wanted the arsehole to know that you do not push onto a train when someone is trying to get off.'

'You get arrested?'

'I pegged it.'

'You're kidding me?'

Luke shook his head. 'I've got to get out. It's driving me nuts. There are no fuses left in my box. It's burnt out, melted plastic and wires, mate. That's me. I've had a dozen confrontations so far this year. In public. Other stuff too.' He stopped himself, spat into the darkness. 'I'm just so angry. All the time now. You ever felt like that?'

'Can't say I have.'

'It's just *me*, *me*, bloody *me* all the time. You know? All around me. I wanted it to stop out here. Just for a bit.'

'It's why I live in the country. Cities don't work.'

'I think you're right.'

'I knows it. Devon calling. Time to go home, Chief.'

Luke nodded, and felt his stare lengthen into nowhere.

Hutch brought him back. 'Anyway. I was going to tell you something. And this goes no further.'

'What?'

'The reason why I was trying to stop you ripping into the fat men about their wives. And this is something I hope will act as a deterrent to future hostilities.'

'Go on.'

Hutch took a long pull on his cigarette and then threw it away. A trail of orange sparks marked its descent into the darkness. 'Michelle kicked Phil out.'

'No shit.'

Hutch nodded. 'He's had to move into a flat. She's got the girls and is going for the house too. The complete shakedown.'

'Why?'

Hutch looked over his shoulder at the tent that contained Phil. When Phil's snoring ended a pause of silence, he turned back to Luke. 'She never liked him. You know that. But he was loaded. Bank of mom and dad, then the property business. That was the only reason she was ever interested in him. Though things aren't so peachy on that front either. His company's been fisted by the recession. Property. No one will buy the luxury flats his company built. He's got massive, and I mean massive, debts. It was all based on loans and borrowing. They've nothing to pay the banks back with. And soon as it all wobbled, Michelle was off. He's lost the place in Cyprus too. Bankrupt.'

'Shit.'

'That's one word for it. And Domja is in the same boat, give or take a few million.'

'No.'

'Ssh.' Hutch looked at both tents again. 'Separated.'

'For real?'

Hutch nodded, reached for the pot. 'Pass your bucket.'

Luke handed him his empty mug.

Hutch concentrated as he poured the coffee from the pot. 'Since before my wedding. They weren't even technically together that day. Gayle's been really depressed for years. Self-image issues. Post-natal stuff after Molly, their last kid. Who knows? And sometime last year she just stopped functioning. And you know what a handful their youngest is, asthma, A.D.D., now they think it's autism. The works. Plus Dom's got the bullet from work. Marketing in a financial services industry. First out. His whole shtick has been flushed.'

'So what's he doing?'

'Looking after the kids, getting pissed, and chasing tail with very little success. Gayle's at her mum's. Heavily medicated.'

Luke put his face in his hands and groaned. 'Shit.'

'And he's come all the way out to Sweden to get pissed on, lost, and to cap it all you give him not one shoeing, but two. So that's why they're both a bit wound-up and spiky and probably not that agreeable to being reminded about how a man without responsibility lives it up.'

'Why the fuck didn't you tell me, H?'

'They didn't want it to intrude on the holiday. Just wanted a total break from it and if you knew, there would have been too many explanations and a whole bunch of soul searching.'

Luke felt his body go cold, from his scalp to the soles of his feet. He shuddered. Felt self-loathing fill him up. 'God, I am a cunt.'

'You weren't to know.'

'If you don't have your mates at times like this.'

'Chief, you've hardly been close. You've been off their radar for years.'

'I knew something was up. Knew it. I should have guessed. Jesus, I am so selfish. So self-involved. I can't see past my own bullshit—'

He was interrupted by a crash. Out there, somewhere in the length and breadth of the countless trees and the oceans of invisible ruin and tangle, a great bow or strong limb had been snapped in half. The sounds of its breaking seemed to shoot in so many directions, it became impossible to guess where the sound originated.

'Jesus. That freaked me.'

Hutch exhaled noisily. 'Me too.'

'I heard it before. Outside the hovel.'

'Just falling wood.'

'You reckon?'

'Diseased branches get waterlogged and just break off.'

But the next series of noises they heard were not caused by a tree, nor could they be passed off as being similar to anything they had heard before in this forest, or in any other forest. It was a mixture of a bovine cough and a jackal's bark, but one so deep and powerful it suggested a chest more expansive and a mouth wider than either of those comparisons. Bestial. Ferocious. To be avoided. Then it was repeated. Downwind of them, about twenty metres deep. But not preceded or followed by the sound of movement.

It was definitely animal, something big, but Luke knew how the dark obscured or amplified nocturnal sounds. Even a small toad could seem gigantic and be heard for miles; a bird call could be mistaken for a human scream, and a mammal's sudden mating cry might even have words inside it. There were no predators they need be afraid of out here, he reminded himself. Plenty of wildlife for sure, but unless they stepped onto an adder or crossed the path of a wolverine with young, they would be fine. They had checked. It was just a case of city ears not accustomed to the cries of the night out here in the wild. Or so he quickly told himself.

And yet, something of significant size, power and savagery had thrown the carcass of a large animal into a tree yesterday. An elk or moose. Stripped it and flung it upwards as if to mark territory or create some outdoor larder.

Hutch broke Luke's train of thought, which seemed to be quickly derailing his attempts at reassuring himself, to say,

'Make sure the soup packets and hot dog tin are buried. Or some long-nosed mutha will be rooting around tonight.'

Luke snorted, but was too tense to laugh. 'What do you think—'

And there it was again. Closer than before, but coming from behind Luke and not Hutch, as if it had soundlessly circled their encampment.

Their torch beams scattered into the trees and then were swallowed by the thick wet walls of foliage that surrounded them.

'Badger or something,' Hutch suggested.

'Wolverine?'

'I have no idea what they sound like.'

'Bear?'

'Possibly. But they're too small to be dangerous up here. Just clap your hands if one comes snuffling around.'

Try as he might, Luke could not picture a small bear.

After ten minutes of silence, Hutch stood up with a groan. He seemed satisfied that there was no danger, which alarmed Luke, who was too anxious to feel foolish, but was stunned to silence by Hutch's confidence as he then said, 'I'm going to turn in, Chief, and try and get some kip. Give me a shake before you take off tomorrow. We need to look at the map and talk tactics.'

'Sure. No problem. Best if I leave soon as it is light,' Luke said, over one shoulder while still flicking his torch about the treeline that any of them could simply reach out and touch from the mouth of a tent, so close was the forest about their ramshackle camp.

Hutch nodded. 'I can't see us lot moving far. I'm beginning to think we might be better off waiting here for a day until Dom's knee goes down a bit. We've got enough water. And at least you'll know where we are. Roughly.'

After discussing this matter of survival almost nonchalantly, Hutch unzipped the fly of the tent he shared with Dom and began fumbling at his laces, as if this situation was suddenly all banal again, some kind of camping formality without terror being involved. But it *was* involved, at least in Luke's thoughts; Hutch was just too exhausted in the cold, strange, pitch-black world to inject much else into the sound of the cries at this hour.

'Night,' he said to Hutch.

'Night,' Hutch replied under the noise of the tent's zipper going back up. Luke watched the tent shake about as Hutch prepared his bedding, saw the bright yellow disc of torchlight skim about the inside of the tent like the luminous eye at a porthole of some submersible craft, with the forest about them a deep black sea.

Luke sat down within the awning of his tent, listened beyond Phil's wheezy breathing and Dom's snoring. In minutes of his torch being clicked off, Hutch was whistling through his nose as he too fell into a heavy sleep.

Luke took out his cigarette packet. His face and skin were burning from exhaustion, his head felt unnaturally heavy, but his mind was still too active to let itself fully rest. At least out here he could smoke.

He lit up. Smoked the cigarette slowly. And silently, he asked himself again, how was it that some people got left behind?

When he finished the cigarette, he wiped at his eyes and climbed into the tent he shared with Phil.

TWENTY-EIGHT

The moon, large and so bright. Is it possible for it to be so near the earth? To arc across the night sky from one end of the horizon to the other?

Silver light frosts the treetops that stretch away forever. Near the ground, the air is bluish-white and gassy as moonlight mingles with the cold. And the wood looks like the bristling surface of an army, with lances, standards and great armoured backs rising out of a dark mass, once seething forward and now frozen as if a terrible march or retreat has been suspended. But it parts around this place. Avoids it. Thick trunks of ancient trees and whipping walls of bracken pull back from the edge of the paddock, from where they uneasily circle the loose, faded and stained tents. Nothing but long weeds and grass dare to mill about the campsite.

And what is that hanging from the treeline? Stretched between the black fringe of the wood like washing blown from a line and caught in the high tiers of forlorn branch and limb, something flutters. They could be shirts, holed and ragged. Discarded things with torn sleeves. Three of them, matched with three sets of frayed leggings, thin as long johns arranged below. And all stained with rust.

Skins. Stripped from dead things. Peeled off and flung

142

upwards to hang like pennants, about the place you sought refuge in.

And now something is moving out there, through the vague and dark spaces behind the treeline. Wood cracks and splinters as it moves, just out of sight.

Pacing the weed-fringed clearing it begins to announce itself more readily with a yipping sound that occasionally breaks into a bark, and soars up to the icy clarity of indigo-black sky. A cry this place has known for a long time before you stood here, shivering and alone.

It's trying to tell you something.

It is letting you know that you can wait for it here and watch it come fast from the trees, or you can try to run on slow and strengthless legs. Flee out there, through the spikes and snares of ungroomed woodland. Into the heaving army that will not let you pass easily through its rows and ranks.

It must be tall, because the branches so far from the ground begin to move straight ahead of you. Some are bent aside and allowed to whip back into place, where they settle and shudder. And through the silvery leaves come the deep guttural grunts. Almost a voice, but not something you can understand. Thick with doggish whines, bull coughs and jackal cries. Its breath turns to fog among the leaves and now you can see no more than the suggestion of something long and black moving swiftly between bush and trunk.

Sinking lower to the ground, it makes ready to appear.

Then the air is filled with screams, but not the cold air here, Luke realizes. But in the air of the world outside his nightmare something even worse was now occurring.

TWENTY-NINE

At first Luke heard the screams from a distance, inside his dream. And then someone's terror was all around him as he lay with his eyes open, staring at the dark roof of the tent he shared with Phil.

Heavy with the thick fugue he had been jerked from, his first thought was to lie still in the dark and to wait for the cries to stop. Only the screams of hysteria, of mindlessness, did not cease. The awful sound of a man shaken apart by panic and fear to the point of extinction, turned the very air into a turbulence in which no clear thought could form or settle within earshot of it.

In the sightless cold he had awoken into, Luke then comprehended, both with shock and a sudden relief, that the noisy commotion was coming from the adjoining tent. It was Dom.

The loose fabric on the ceiling of his own tent rippled from the commotion in the neighbouring tent, from where the screams were issuing. It all brought to his mind the sense of someone being violently yanked from their berth, accompanied by sounds of cloth torn into long strips and a thrashing of bushes.

Luke sat bolt upright and fumbled for the zipper of his sleeping bag. Then snatched about for his torch in the darkness, but his hands could not find it. By the time he gave up on the torch and pawed his shaky fingers across his damp trousers, needing to find the shape of the Swiss Army knife in the front pocket, Phil sat up beside him.

'What is it? What is it? What is it?' Phil repeated in a daze, but within his tone was also an underlying note of acceptance, as if he had been expecting the disturbance and now it had arrived he only wanted to know specific details.

And then their movements and their words stopped, as did Dom's wailing. All was frozen into silence by the sudden roar of pain unleashed by Hutch. A short expulsion of noise from an agony so great it made the listeners feel sick. It was followed by a childlike whimper, and nothing more.

Away from their camp tunnelled the noise of a heavy weight at ground level, rushing into the forest, snapping aside and crushing flat all woody impediments as it retreated at speed into the returning silence that was once again only dimpled with gentle rainfall upon the leaves and the fabric of their half-collapsed tents. Then into this vacuum came several strange bird and animal cries, as if these creatures had also shared the terror of the rout of the camp, out there in their own darkness, and were now calling out nervously to survivors buried in rubble.

Phil's torch clicked alight. Coloured entrails of clothing spilled from his rucksack. Two damp waterproof coats lay dishevelled by the sagging entrance. No inch of groundsheet was free of the clutter Phil had littered about the tent. In the mess, Luke saw his own torch, snatched it up.

Beside them, through the thin material that pressed against Luke's body as he scrambled to his hands and knees, they heard Dom's rhythmic panting in the next tent. He sounded like a man suffocating, or suffering some kind of fit.

Luke kicked free of his sleeping bag. He trod on his cold waterproof trousers, still damp with yesterday's rain, and shivered when the naked parts of his body touched the clammy groundsheet and the interior of the tent's moist fabric. Bent double, shuffling to the entrance, he looked about for his boots. They were still wet inside. He discarded them. Behind him, Phil clutched at his own clothes.

Knife extended, Luke ducked through the unzipped flap. Lost his balance, swore, then righted himself and rose into the night air. It punished his cheeks. Around his startled senses a thousand things dripped into the darkness. Through small apertures in the forest canopy the sky was a black void that quickly swallowed his torch's feeble beam. He could not move his body out of the tent's porch.

When the white light of his torch came down to earth it found the second tent.

There were several things terribly wrong with it.

Luke heaved in his breath and tried not to sob: the tent had completely collapsed into a lumpy mess of nylon and guy ropes and much of one side had been torn away; the ripped white netting of the inner compartment had been revealed, its incongruous appearance utterly shocking against the wet black earth; around the jagged edges of the rent in the outer skin of the tent, a liquid glistened in a series of long streaks and clots, and even pools. Shaking from his hand that held the torch, the beam of weak white light trembled about the heavy stains on the torn nylon. They were bright red in colour: oxygenated blood.

Luke's mind could not be whole, or steady. There was a rushing of incomplete thoughts and notions, some utterly petty, in and out of the space inside him where his mind needed to define itself and focus. He could not move; just stood upright in his underwear and shuddered from the cold, from the emotion, from the sudden surge and ebb of adrenaline in his own blood.

Somewhere inside the punctured rag that was once a two-man tent, Dom lay gasping. Luke did not want to look under the wet green and yellow nylon. Guy ropes lay slack as if the tent cloth was a sail collapsed upon a yacht's deck at night in some black godless sea, with a crew member trapped beneath it.

The articulated fibreglass poles of the dome frame had been pulled apart in some places, and protruded in the disorderly display of fabric. The tent now reminded him of a great kite that had smashed to earth. Inside the crumpled mess was pain and bleeding. Something Luke wanted to run from without seeing.

He turned about where he stood and flashed his torch across the uneven and encroaching perimeter of the clearing. Mossy bark, blackened tree branches, dark sopping leaves, shadows between. Inside himself he cringed and thought of what Phil thought he had seen in the cemetery. He expected to see the limbs of trees suddenly animate and draw his stare to a terrible shape taking form. But nothing moved.

He swallowed noisily, blinked his wide dry eyes. 'Dom! Dom!' he suddenly called at the lumpy remnants beside his own half-collapsed tent. Flashed his torch over the ruin again. 'Are you hurt, mate?' His voice seemed to die before two words were out of his mouth. His chest shuddered like it had just endured a great sob or an intake of icy air.

Got to keep it together.

'Where's Hutch?' Phil said from the ground level beside

Luke's naked legs. He had come pushing, clumsily, through the doorway into the porch of their tent on his hands and knees. His torch beam clashed with Luke's, tried to move it aside while it flicked and probed at the heap beside them.

Luke stepped out of the tent's porch in his underwear. The shock of the cold earth against his pale bare feet punched his breath back inside his chest. Disorientated, he trod on the end of a tent peg, then tripped over one of their tent's few taut guy ropes and fell sideways into the trees. A sudden slap of wet verdure against his soft face, and the poke and snap of a small branch under his weight, forced him to right his position, to get fully to his feet, to gather his bearings. Wakefulness came fully and coldly and shivering right then.

'Domja!' Luke called, resorting to the nickname he used in better times. It drew a reaction. A punching out, a raking of fingers from inside the deflated green and yellow tent.

'Easy. Easy,' Luke said, but then stepped back as Dom came through the rent on his hands and knees. Dom was wearing a purple fleece, boxer shorts and thick grey socks. His sleeping bag followed him through the tear, caught on one foot. He kicked it away and stood up as best he could. The leg with the grubby bandaged knee was hopelessly bent. His dirty streaky face looked like it had just emerged from a coal mine; it shuddered in the light from the two torch beams. He eyes were red and wild.

Phil was on his feet now too, his legs bare, boots unlaced, hair sticking upright in a fan across one side of his head.

'Where the fuck is H?' Dom demanded of them, breathless. He looked at Luke, then at Phil, then Luke again. 'Where the fuck is he?'

THIRTY

They returned to the campsite two hours after waking. Above the forest, where they could see it, the sky was now a dark indigo.

No one spoke from the shock of it all. They were numb with fright and sick at the colossal thought they each tried to comprehend, then accept. Something that would keep rearing up in their minds and hearts when they were too tired to suppress it and were caught off guard. Something impossible, something consuming, something choking.

They had called his name a hundred times; hobbling and shuffling in a nervous pack, torch beams flashing all about them at the dripping impenetrability of the forest; heads whipping back and forth at every meagre sound or far-off screech of a bird in the cold air, until they were dizzy and aching and exhausted by their own skittish fears. No one answered their calls; calls that were strident at first, then desperate, and finally just hoarse and not penetrating much beyond the immediate thickets.

'Hutch!'

'Mate!'

'Hutch!'

'H!'

It had been too dark to see the evidence of his departure.

But Hutch was gone and now they were left alone with his blood that was dark and thickening all about the broken-down tent.

'Can you take the other tent down?' Luke asked them, breaking a long silence with a voice that was flat and distant to his own ears. 'And pack it up. Plus your gear. We need to move the minute the light improves.'

Mystified, Dom and Phil just stared at Luke. Shocked and angry with him too, but also listless and apathetic, they just stared, and stared. He tried to explain himself. 'I'm packed. The map. I need to look at it.' He glanced at the destroyed tent. 'Maybe sort Hutch's things as well.'

It was four in the morning; they had been woken at two. But at least they were all inside their sleeping bags by eleven the night before, so a few hours' sleep were behind them. Not enough to recover from the previous day's exertions, Luke calculated, but enough to give them a few hours of strength this coming morning. The most important hours of the entire trip so far. Luke knew the edge of the forest must be reached in the coming morning, by noon latest. Dom's knee would slow him to a weak shuffle soon after. Once that happened, they would not progress more than a mile or two before nightfall.

'What?' Dom finally said, stupefied.

'His torch. Knife. Stuff we can use. He had energy bars in his bag.'

Dom looked at Phil. Then raised both arms, before clapping them at his sides. 'We're not going anywhere 'til we find him.'

Luke looked at the ground and released a long and tired sigh.

'What are you suggesting? We just take off? Cherry-pick his gear?' Dom barked, his words trembling with emotion.

Phil looked at the ruined tent and the blood that had gone viscous and oily in the thin light of a stray torch's light, idle and unfortunate in its placement. And there was so much of it to be seen, if you angled your torch through the hole as Phil then did.

'Oh God, H.' Phil suddenly crouched down and covered his face with both hands. *Now he understood.*

But at the sound of Phil's distress, a huge lump came into Luke's throat. He stopped listening to Dom, closed his eyes. *H, H, H is gone*; an idiot rhyme chanted through his head. He felt like a child. The urgency of his purpose to get them occupied and then moving dissipated.

Phil was crying. Dom's face crumpled. A long syrup of saliva drooped from his bottom lip. His eyes welled with water. One hand across his brow, as if shielding his face from the sun, his shoulders moved with each sob. Luke felt his jaw loosen. Salt scalded his throat down to his sternum. Hutch's smiling face came into his mind. He almost heard a cackle. The idea he no longer existed was so preposterous it made him lightheaded. Then it was as if he had heartburn and indigestion at the same time.

Luke dropped to his buttocks and groaned through a cage of fingers wrapped about his face. For once he was oblivious to the stinging scratches on his calves and those hot lines etched across his cheeks and ears, was immune to the tugging aches inside his thighs. Beyond his own clasping hands, the other two wept into the darkness.

At one point Luke stood up and immediately bumped into Phil, who seized him, his head down, and he squeezed Luke's biceps so hard Luke thought Phil's long dirty nails had drawn blood inside his waterproof. He had to prise Phil's fingers off his arms. Then hold Dom's shoulders as he too shook from terror or grief or a panic attack; Luke didn't know. And for a long time they were all disorientated and incapable in the darkness and the cold. They blundered. They cried. Until they all sat and stared in silence, shivering in the cold that drew their warmth from out of their fragile bodies and into the dense black earth.

THIRTY-ONE

'You can't stay here.' Luke spoke quietly to Dom, who sat on his pack beside the demolished tent. 'You've a few hours in that knee this morning to make another concerted effort to get out of here. We'll keep going south. We have to. Now. In as straight a line as possible.'

Dom hung his head between his knees. He'd grieved himself to silent exhaustion before they had even taken a step.

Luke took a deep drag on his cigarette and then spoke through the veil of bluish smoke hanging before his face. 'Your knee is shot. It'll seize up before midday. Me and Hutch . . .' he paused and swallowed, 'we talked last night. We were hoping you two would be able to rest up for a day or two here, while I carried on to find a way out and get us help. He wanted you off your knee for a bit. And to give Phil time to get his wind back. There is enough water for a couple of days, and we know where to get more if help is more than two days away. But everything has changed now. We cannot . . . we cannot spend another night in this place. End of story.'

'Don't,' was all Dom said, elbows on his knees, lifting his bruised and puffy face and looking at Luke in such a way as to prevent any reminder of what happened at night out here.

Luke waved a hand as if to knock something away. 'I've just been looking for . . .' He cleared his throat. 'He was taken through there.' Luke pointed at the faint aperture in the wall of scrub on his right side. 'The way it's all been broken down stops about twenty feet in. And the blood.'

'You're not leaving us here. We stick together from now on,' Phil suddenly blurted out from where he was standing at the side of the clearing, looking into the wet darkness.

Luke nodded. 'Of course. Goes without saying.'

Dom looked at him. 'You don't know where the fuck we are, do you?'

'Vaguely.'

Dom laughed mirthlessly. 'Vaguely. Vaguely. Haven't we had enough of vaguely? I mean vaguely is the reason we are sitting here now around a tent full of blood. Any more vague ideas of which way we should be heading are going to get the rest of us killed.'

Phil sucked in his breath.

Luke studied the outline of Dom's face, again suppressing the urge, which came up his throat like panic, to just take off on his own. He took a moment to place his thoughts in a careful row. 'The chance to retrace our steps back out of here is long gone. So we have no choice but to keep going south. We've got to hope we can break out through the closest edge of the forest. What Hutch was aiming for.'

Phil looked at Dom. 'We have to. I'm not staying here, waiting for help.'

Luke looked at his watch. 'Today we should have reached Porjus. Tomorrow night we're supposed to head back to Stockholm. Day after that we're supposed to be back home early.' He looked at the other two and heard a note of hope lighten his tone of voice. 'How long before someone realizes something's gone wrong for us and raises the alarm?

Your folks expecting you guys to call home tonight? Tomorrow?'

Neither Phil nor Dom would meet his eye. Both looked down in a new kind of discomfort that had nothing to do with exhaustion, cold, or a lack of sleep. It was as if they had suddenly realized the consequences of some unfortunate news.

Hutch said they were both separated, but Luke wondered what that really meant. Would they still be in daily contact with their wives because of the kids? Would they be expected to physically reappear and perform fatherly duties at a pre-scribed time? Because no one was expecting him to call. He'd only been seeing Charlotte, casually, for a month. His supervisor at work would call his mobile if he didn't show up on Monday. But that was still four days away. And being absent from work and out of reach for a few days would not result in his colleagues putting in a call to the authorities. He doubted his boss would do anything other than hire someone else to take his job after a week of him not checking in. His parents might be concerned after a couple of months of silence. And his handful of friends in London might wonder why he had gone to ground for a while, but he couldn't imagine them making a prompt and determined effort to track him down either. He often went months these days without seeing any of them. They were all busy with their own lives and lived in different parts of the city. And he was just not that close to anyone any more, if he was really honest with himself. His best bet was his flatmate; they had little in common, and she'd only lived in the flat for six months, but she was looking after his dog while he was away in Sweden. Surely, she'd be the first to try and work out where he was;

maybe a week after he failed to show. But who would she call? Who did she know of to call? She'd leave messages on his mobile and then maybe check in with the record shop, if she could even remember the name of it. And that would only probably be because she was sick of walking the dog twice a day.

These thoughts saddened him, then made him angry at himself. If you had no partner or career then who gave a shit about you at his age? That had been the whole point: to disengage from any responsibility so he could do his own thing. Well he was doing that now for sure. Luke laughed out loud.

'What?' Dom asked. 'What?' his voice eager with curiosity to hear what Luke had just worked out.

Luke tossed his cigarette into the bushes. 'I just ran through a list. It could actually be months before my own family and friends report me missing. I guess my best hope is my flatmate, who I'm not close to. Or . . . hang on . . . maybe the airline. But then . . . damn, people miss flights all the time; they don't call search and rescue. And we've already paid for the seats, so they have our money, so why would they give a damn?' He imagined his name being called out over a public address system at Stockholm airport, by a female Swedish airline official. It would probably be the last time his name was spoken outside of this forest for a while.

'I'm thinking maybe four, five days for me,' Dom said. He must have been referring to his family which ratcheted up Luke's fear. But four days would be too late for them all. 'What about you Phillers?' Dom asked.

Phil didn't even turn round from where he was facing the trees, shining his torch about as if keeping watch. 'What?'

'How long?'

'Mmm?'

'How long before someone gets worried because you are a no-show back home?'

'Michelle wouldn't give a—' He stopped himself. 'Maybe work. I have a meeting next Monday at the bank. Maybe . . .' He seemed to be struggling with his thoughts, whatever they were.

Dom sighed with exasperation, then suddenly raised both hands. 'Hostel. The hostel we should be in tonight. Hutch booked it. Told them where we were coming from too.'

'True,' Luke said, his voice flat. 'They might call his mobile when we don't pitch up. If there is even a signal up there. But people must blow off those places all the time. Change of plan. Better offer. Whatever.'

'The forest wardens?'

'Hutch never called the Porjus branch. Said it was just for winter hikes.'

'Shit!' Dom kicked his good leg at the ground. Phil continued to search about the treeline with his torch.

Luke lit his fourth roll-up cigarette since he'd woken. Squinted through the smoke. 'Hutch's missus. Angie will be expecting him to call as soon as he's near a signal. That's our best bet.'

Dom frowned. 'Makes sense. We'll have to tell her. Jesus.'

'Come on. Forget about that. We've got to move. Now. Just keep going like our lives depend on it. Because they do.'

THIRTY-TWO

And then they found Hutch hanging from the trees in the same way they found the animal two days before.

Luke turned, shouted, 'Don't look! Don't look!' as if he were protecting children in his care, which made Phil and Dom look up like children.

Dom fell against the nearest available tree trunk. 'God! God!' he shouted into the wet air.

Without a sound Phil walked away through the trees, back the way they had just travelled. After twenty feet he stopped and started to shake. Then bent at the waist and vomited. Luke saw something white and runny drop from his mouth, then turned away and heard a splash. He looked up at Hutch.

Stripped naked. No sign of his clothes. Opened down the front of his torso to a groin black with old blood. Pale muscular legs stained brownish. Feet drifting in space at the height of their heads. Eyes open wide, as was his mouth, the latter filled with a swollen tongue. His expression was one of mild surprise in an ashen face not without a suggestion of life, as if he were merely looking out and into the middle distance where something had caught his eye and made him stare, distractedly.

Inside his torso nothing appeared to have survived the

attack and most of one shoulder and the adjoining bicep muscle were gone to the white of bone. Where two branches extended out from the side-by-side pillars of dead spruce trees, he had been wedged fast, his weight supported by the passage of a branch under each armpit.

His body had been arranged as if crucified and positioned to face them as they came stumbling and panting through the trees.

Luke's scalp tingled and the temperature of his body plummeted down to his icy toes. His vision began to judder and some white light flashed at the side of his eyes. He thought he was going to faint. Muscles twitched in his face, mostly around his mouth. He couldn't stop the spasms.

Then his head suddenly cleared of everything but a thought that fell like a blow against his face: how did Hutch's killer know they would pass this way?

For the three hours after breaking camp they had followed the most obvious route southwards, down through the forest, directed by convenience through the spaces between thick towering spruce and the thinnest undergrowth on the forest floor to this very spot. Which would mean they were being watched right now and Hutch's body had been hastily erected and exhibited only minutes before their arrival at this terrible place: a carcass presented to them by something with great strength that could climb.

As soon as Luke endured these thoughts, the air of the old wooded land abounded with a bark that could also have been a cough. The same bestial outburst he and Hutch heard the night before while sitting around the flickering stove flame.

Luke swivelled his entire body about, his vision flickering

and failing to settle on any single point out there in the trees. He dropped his rucksack to the ground and flailed for the knife in his pocket.

Dom leapt back from the tree, then stumbled in agony after thrusting his whole weight onto his angry knee. Through the brownish muck on his bruised face, his complexion was bleached with terror and pain.

Phil crashed back through the undergrowth towards them, stumbled and fell to his hands and knees. Rising with a strangled animal sound in his throat before it formed into, 'Fuck, oh fuck. Fuck.' He then turned about in a circle, dizzy and ungainly, his rucksack hanging from one elbow.

'Knife,' Luke called to Dom, holding his own penknife up high and out from his body. Dom slapped frantically about the pockets of his waterproof.

The bark came again from a new direction, and a position closer to them, somewhere behind where Phil was frantically peering about. The rough challenge of the bark was followed by two hard snorts and then the kind of whinny that jackals make with their black lips pulled high in television documentaries.

Luke moved towards the sound, his breath and blood so loud in his skull he fought to hear anything else. Every muscle buoyant with warmth and a sudden energy, he moved quickly, dodging about the trees, light on the balls of his feet, his knife gripped so tightly his whole arm felt rigid-white.

Somewhere within the mad euphoria that propelled him out there to stab and hack, to slash, to bellow, to not think or care in the reddish place a man can inhabit, he heard his name being called repeatedly by Dom and Phil. Their voices drew him back into himself and he lost momentum, entertained doubt. But then grew hot with rage again and shouted so he could stay within the place he needed to be in to face anything, anything at all. 'Come on! Come on!'

He paused and crouched down. Turned about by increments, staring so hard into the lightening forest his forehead throbbed with pressure. He wanted to see it. To suddenly close with it. His teeth ground. 'Come on!' Then again with his chin raised and shoulders back, 'Come on!'

The forest remained still. No bird sang or called. Life paused.

Somewhere to his right a branch snapped and the sound cracked off every trunk for what sounded like miles.

Luke moved to the sound, keeping his head down and shoulders tense. Then found himself rushing at full speed to the place where the silence had been broken. Unthinking, blind with the red maelstrom that foamed and roared in his ears, he leapt over a slippery log and kicked noisily through the bracken. 'Where are you, bitch?'

He saw nothing. In the distance, their cries rising ever more frantically, Dom and Phil begged him to return to his mind.

'Come on. Come on and find me,' he said in a low voice, every word tighter than the last, speaking to the solemn trees and wet verdure, the dead wood and foot-deep leaf mulch, the fungus and thorns, the shadowy air and distant mist atop the green tinted rocks, to all that hid this terrible and unnatural thing. Because only now, like this, could he face whatever it was that could do such things to a man. And at no other time. So this is a place he told himself he must return to; must save some deep part of himself for when the time came to die out here. And it would not be easy for their hunter.

He would not go quickly or quietly. He swore this to the oldest forest in Europe.

After a long moment of remaining still, he began to take careful steps back towards the others.

THIRTY-THREE

'What did you see, Dom? What did you see?' Luke panted as much as spoke. His whole body shivered as the adrenaline drained from his muscles.

Dom and Phil were wary of him. They stared at the mad stranger with their shocked faces like the people on the underground platform after his fight; those who stared from the open doors of the carriages and through the yellow windows at the maniac who had punched a stranger out cold. Dom and Phil did not know him. How little do we know of anyone, let alone ourselves? Luke thought in the kind of clarity he had experienced no more than a dozen times in his entire life. 'What came in Dom? What was in your tent?'

Dom shook his head. 'I don't fucking know. It was pitch-black.'

'Think. Was it big? Bulky like a bear? On all fours, like a dog?'

Dom looked bewildered, breathless. He was showing too much of his eyes. 'Big. Stank. Like, like a wet animal, but worse.'

'Did it make a sound?'

'I don't . . .' He screwed up his face and slapped both hands over his ears. 'Like when a dog gets something in its mouth. Oh, Jesus. Don't make me . . . It had him in its mouth.'

Luke nodded, straightened his back. Looked over his shoulder as his chest rose and fell, rose and fell.

'A bear. It's a big bear,' Phil said, his whole face shaking, his red eyes full of water. 'Big cat. They escape. Private zoos. A . . . A . . . Wolf.'

'We need to know. Need to know as much about it as possible.' Luke looked at Dom and then at Phil, lowered his voice to a whisper. 'It's been following us all day. It made sure we saw Hutch. Arranged it. Animals . . . wouldn't do that.'

'How?' Phil asked, his voice like his face, aghast at the dreadful impossibility of it all.

'It's hunted us for three days. Maybe as soon as we came into this forest. First day, we were supposed to find that animal in the tree.' Luke lit a cigarette, his movements slow, incongruously calm and deliberate. 'And the house. The effigy in the attic. The goddamned church. What you saw in the cemetery. It's all connected. Somehow.'

Dom and Phil stood close together, their eyes not leaving the forest that stretched forever around them.

'Come on,' Dom said, his voice shaking. 'It's an animal. A fucking wolf or something. Don't start with that crazy shit. It's not the right place or time.'

'How can a wolf, a bear, a wolverine, whatever, put a body up in a tree like that? Eh? Think, man.'

Dom's face made it clear how hard he was struggling with the very idea that what they were dealing with was not just beyond their combined imaginations, but also impossible. He looked ill, pale, haggard, and shuffled his good leg a few inches while the other remained bent at the knee, useless. It needed to be raised and straight, Luke thought inappropriately, and stupidly, and emotionlessly at such a time as this.

'A man. Some kind of maniac,' Dom said.

'Possible,' Luke replied, nodding, hoping. 'Some Swedish hillbilly with a hard-on for tourists. This shit is supposed to happen all the time, in America, Australia. Not in Sweden, but who knows? Maybe it does. We've found a bit of the country not too many people seem to know about. Or if they did, they're not around now to talk about it. That church was full of dead people. Some of the bones . . . They weren't new, but they weren't that old either.'

'Sacrifice,' Phil said in a timid voice.

Luke and Dom looked at him. His pointy blue hood was pulled up again and he stood with his back to them, staring into the trees. Back in the direction Hutch was displayed. From over Phil's shoulder, Luke could see one of the actual trees they had stumbled away from, and a pale foot was visible through the branches. He thought of his own sudden mad charge into the forest and suddenly felt cold and sick down to the soles of his boots. His balance deserted him for a moment, and he swayed until a shuffle of his feet moored him again.

'What are you talking about?' Dom sounded angry.

Luke raised a hand to quieten him; looked at Phil. 'Go on, mate.'

Phil looked at the ground. 'I had a dream. In that house. I remember bits of it. There were people in it.'

'What the fuck are you on about?' Dom demanded.

'Dom,' Luke hissed through his clenched teeth. He turned back to Phil. 'I had one too.'

Phil swivelled towards Luke sharply and stared at him; the eyes in his red and sweating face were wild and so full of fear it was hard to look into them and impossible to look away.

Luke nodded. 'Yes, mate. In the dream I was trapped. Out here. Caught up in the trees. With . . . with that sound. Circling me.'

Dom slid to the ground, his back against a tree, his body slack with despair. He had dreamed too. And Luke wanted to know of what. Wanted every scant clue on offer. Their survival would depend upon it. He'd lived ten years of his life in London amongst people whose entire vocal output was a public relations exercise, who spun the truth of their existences into scenarios designed to provoke envy. People who couldn't face the idea that things weren't going right for them. By not speaking of something negative, or allowing themselves to even think about it, the problem no longer existed. He'd once envied them, then felt contemptuous. But he was not like them. In fact, he was their opposite. He'd always analysed the crap in his life forensically. Perhaps the attitude held him back, ruined any chance of real and sustained happiness; this refusal to delude himself. But there was no place for lunatic optimism out here, or denial of the facts, no matter how preposterous they were. Luke found he had almost accepted the situation, and wondered if it was because he always expected the very worst to befall him, all of the time, in every aspect of his life.

'I was stuck,' Luke said. 'And something was hunting me.' Like a premonition, he wanted to say. 'It was so real. Vivid, you know? And Hutch. I found him in the attic. Sleep walking. And he'd seen something awful too. Something in a dream.' Dom was trying not to listen. Luke raised both hands in the air to add emphasis to what he was saying. 'We all lost it in that place. And were too embarrassed in the light of day to confront it.' He pointed at Dom. 'You wouldn't let us. And you still want to pretend it isn't happening. Well fuck that shit. We'd better open our eyes to this. Now.' Luke stared at Phil and nodded at him.

Phil swallowed. Took a breath. 'They sacrificed people. I think. In that house. To something. A long time ago.'

Luke nodded. 'When that church was open for business and that cemetery wasn't so overgrown. The people in that basement were in a really bad way. Murdered.'

Phil raised his face to look at a portion of sky visible through the canopy. 'They hung them. Strung them up for it. I think it was younger then. But it's still here. They're gone. The old people I saw in my dream. Who . . . fed it. But *it* is still here.'

Dom stared into the trees in silence.

THIRTY-FOUR

'I'll never get across it.' Bright-red skin shone through the patchwork of dirt on Dom's face. He leaned a shoulder against a tree, angling the crutch into the spongy ground to hold himself upright. The crutch was a discarded tree branch at the right length and thick enough to be sturdy; it even had a V-shape crook to slip under an armpit. A third attempt at a walking aid; the first two having been discarded as ineffective. Luke found them all in the undergrowth after they left the dismal place where Hutch still hung from the trees.

Sat on a broad rock at the edge of the gorge, Luke tossed the tent bag to one side and let the two rucksacks he had been carrying drop to the ground with a smack. Phil came to a standstill behind him, hands on his knees, bowed by exhaustion and disappointment. His breath wheezed through his open mouth.

'When will we ever get a break?' Dom said to himself.

'Take a hit off that inhaler, mate,' Luke said to Phil, without looking at him. 'You sound awful.'

Phil rummaged in the pocket of his waterproof.

Clambering in a tight pack, through two miles of undergrowth-tangle on increasingly stony ground that rose uphill, only to emerge through the treeline and be confronted by a valley with steep sides, returned a familiar anxiety to Luke.

The notion that had become an idea, and now felt like an acceptance of a fact that they would die out here, threatened to swallow him again.

Dipping away from their feet, large boulders covered the descent into the ravine; the exposed surfaces of the rocks were yellow and pale green with lichen. In the basin of the gorge, a forest of long-stemmed plants with rubbery umbrella-like leaves stretched for thirty metres to the other side, where a rocky ascent waited to take them back onto a swampy soil dense with fir and pine. A strip marsh. Luke checked his watch: 1 p.m.

A soft quiet light fell into the gorge; the most light they had seen falling from the flat grey sky since the cemetery the day before. The rain came down steadily inside the light, chilling the cleaner air. It had a force to its vertical descent and had become increasingly audible against the surrounding rocks. It would become drenching soon; Luke could feel it, could anticipate it now.

Motivated by a fear that would have become group hysteria had they allowed their tired minds to dwell upon it, they had left poor Hutch behind them at eleven and put their heads down and into a slow but consistent progression upwards to this: a gorge, insurmountable in their condition. It stretched out of sight in both directions, until the sudden crevice turned away through the misty trees.

The fact that Hutch was no longer alive – *alive* – had not completely registered with any of them. It could not; their exhaustion forbade it. Luke welcomed the numbness; such an incomprehensible fact had stunned his emotions. But now and again, the full truth would crash back into his thoughts, and those of the others, and someone would sob, or say, 'Oh,

God no,' to themselves as they all hobbled and staggered through the trees together. It was *inconceivable*. They were living in the inconceivable.

'Water. And some calories,' Luke said, hoping to regain some clarity. Dehydration was making his thoughts vague. Ideas came and went, swimming weakly. His lungs were flat, his speech slurring. He was too tired to do much but pant a few words at the others. 'Take a load off. We've earned it. Never mind this bollocks, we've made good progress this morning. You've done well. Both of you.'

It was the first time he'd really spoken for over an hour. He'd been too tired even to pant monosyllables of encouragement or advice to the others. Carrying the tent, his own rucksack on his back and Dom's pack strapped to his front, the morning's hike on rocky terrain had taken him to the end of his endurance and it was only early afternoon. Between the two straps of the packs, his shoulders had been squeezed into terrible aches he could not relieve by repositioning the weight. He'd bitten down on the discomfort and just pushed on until his vision blurred. And yet he had still needed to stop every few minutes when one of the others called out to tell him to 'hold up' or 'slow down', worried he was pulling too far ahead of them. His neck now throbbed with pain after having to look either side of Dom's rucksack to see where he was placing his feet. A twisted ankle and they might as well all strip naked and wait for the end.

He hated the lack of mobility, especially with his arms. If they had been attacked precious seconds would have been lost while he struggled out of the straps and loops. And their opponent was fast. Fast and silent, unless it chose to taunt them from a distance.

The Ritual

It could have taken any one of them within the last two hours, and Luke knew it. They'd eventually become too tired to continue the furtive vigilance around whatever they had been crashing and stumbling through. Maybe whatever or whoever it was only killed when it was hungry. The thought made Luke feel sick.

But his carrying of the rucksacks and tent was the only solution to increasing Dom's speed on his one good leg. His bad knee was tumescent and discoloured. There was no definition at all around the knee cap. The skin under the bandage was tight and hot to the touch. Just looking at it made Luke's eyes water. To mount even a slight gradient Dom shuffled sideways, using the crutch like an ice axe while dragging his bad leg behind him so as not to place any weight on it at all. The leg needed to be raised and rested, maybe for three or four days before he should move again. The more he stumbled about on the joint the worse it was becoming. All morning Dom's face had been set in a permanent rictus from the pain and the fear of more pain if he slipped or knocked his knee.

At the top of the ravine, Dom and Phil sat on a boulder each and planted their boots into the wet moss between the rocks. They panted beside Luke and stared at their feet without seeing them. Both of their waterproof coats were undone and their hoods were down. Hats were stuffed into trouser pockets. Each red face was coated with a film of grease and old dirt and shone with a sheen of sweat.

Gravity thickened around Luke. Responsibility like a tangible weight made the rock under his buttocks harden. He'd never led anything in his life before and they had all been reliant on Hutch for the entire hike. From deep inside his belly, anger flared up through him, revived him. What had H been thinking, taking these two off piste like this? The entire trip had been far too ambitious for Dom and Phil, even without plunging them into unknown terrain, hoping for a short cut.

Luke took three mouthfuls of water from his bottle. It tasted of rubber and of the forest around them: the cloying of damp wood, rotting leaves and cold air. He detested it. He smelled of it too. They were almost part of it now. Just a few bright colours of the manmade fibres they wore marked them out as any different to the thoughtless, relentless decay of season and nature. It would be so easy now to just sink to the ground and get recycled, to be eaten or to rot away. The endlessness of it, the sheer size of the land and their total insignificance within it nearly shut his mind down.

He spread the map across his thighs before the other two noticed the tremors of panic that must have been visible in his face and in his fingers. He searched the green and brown shapes on the map, but could not comprehend much of what he was looking at because his head was so padded with fatigue and exhaustion. The map indicated it was a national park, that they were in a collective of forest and marsh, but failed to indicate any individual contour or noticeable feature they could identify to orientate from. He was feeling listless, and apathetic too now; it didn't abet concentration. What did that mean? Hypothermia. Not possible. They were wet and became cold when they stopped moving, but were not soaked to the skin or shivering. Not yet.

'Where are we?' Dom shuffled sideways to an adjoining stone.

How the hell did he know? He could not even understand

how much ground they had covered that morning. It felt like they had stumbled for miles, but rough terrain outdoors in a wilderness played tricks on the mind. He and Hutch had been lost together once before, six years ago, while walking back from a beach on an island in the Swedish archipelago, wearing only T-shirts and shorts. The island was barely five miles long and two miles across, but somehow they'd turned themselves around and become scratched all over, eventually arriving back at the exact point they had left two hours earlier. Impossible, as they had been convinced they had moved due east in a straight trajectory. At least here they had a compass, but it still didn't supply the answer to where they actually were, or how far they were moving. Never as far as it seemed; he had enough experience to know that much.

'Problem is,' Luke said, avoiding Dom's eyes as he spoke, 'it's hard to know how much ground we have covered since we first came in, over the best part of three days now.'

Dom sighed and shook his head. It felt like an accusation and made Luke suddenly defensive. 'But we are heading in the right direction.'

'But how long is it going to take? We should have come out of here the day before yesterday, and been on the other side of the forest. This bit is not that thick on the map.' Dom spread his dirty fingers across the paper, his eyes frantically searching the colours and shapes and dotted lines, hoping they might suddenly provide a clue as to where they were now sitting.

But it was hardly only a 'bit' or patch of forest. In some areas the forest was at least fifty kilometres deep and from what they had seen of it, mostly impenetrable or unmanaged virgin forest. It had been Hutch's intention to just cut through a far westerly band, where the forest was at its thinnest. No more than ten kilometres deep according to the map. But Luke wondered if they had blundered off the original trajectory Hutch envisaged them taking, while following the track to the old church. They'd also been repeatedly turned about by the terrain and its impenetrable foliage; had walked due west, due east, north west and south west at various times. They'd spent most of the previous day walking west, and even north west, according to the compass, instead of moving south west before angling directly south and down to what Hutch was sure was the lower edge of the forest on the map, with the river running beneath it. That had been the plan. But now H wasn't with them, Luke had turned them due south that morning so they wouldn't overshoot the narrowest section of forest. Which was fine if they were positioned where he'd guessed they were. But if they had strayed too far west the previous day and entered the adjacent thicker belt of forest they were now looking at thirty kilometres of hard terrain and forest so old and dark, the hours of sunlight barely lightened the earth. If they had continued to walk west, eventually, they would have emerged in Norway. Similar endgame situation again if they hadn't corrected far enough in a south-westerly direction the day before, and the due south course he had set that morning pitched them far into a broader area of eastern wilderness. It would take about three days' walking to get through the bigger and more densely forested areas on either side of the narrow band they hoped they were inside, but only if they were fit; for him, if he were alone, that would mean another two, possibly three nights, without food. But for the other two, who were injured . . . Luke felt sick and lightheaded.

'I mean, what if we get over this fucking hole, and then there's another one, just like it, on the other side?'

He'd not even thought of that, but now Dom had voiced the concern, Luke believed it to be entirely possible. Patterns of terrain often repeated themselves, or sometimes they were just single anomalies. There were marshes all over the map on either side of the narrow band of forest. Like the woodland functioned as a funnel; a trap, if you were foolish enough to take a short cut through it, hoping to avoid the bordering wetlands. The very thought seemed to drain the last of his strength as he imagined a bird's-eye view of a topography revealing long deep ravines parallel to this one, a rib cage stretching for miles. It would be the end of them.

Luke made an energy bar vanish in two bites and immediately thought about ripping into a second. The other two were already chewing the end of their second bars, which meant they should each have three left. Hutch's last four had been divided equally, with one left in reserve that he held on to along with the chocolate bar. To remind the others of the perilous situation he said, 'I reckon we should eat two more bars tonight, with coffee and loads of sugar in it. We have the gas for another night and morning. That'll leave one energy bar each in reserve with the chocolate if needs be.' He didn't say *tomorrow*, but since they had been forced to sit down and face the gorge, the idea of another night together in the open, with two of them keeping watch with knives drawn while the third slept, had begun to fill his chest with a pressure so terrible he could not swallow or exhale with any ease. But the inference, the threat of another night out here, was implicit in his voice.

Each bar contained 183 calories. With two consumed now,

and two eaten later they still would not even scrape 1,000 calories each, and they were still facing hours of extreme exertion ahead, hiking into the cold and wet.

'Those were my last two,' Phil said emotionlessly, and looked at the filthy palms of his hands.

Luke stared at Phil's tousled head and swallowed. 'Tell me you are joking?'

'Mate, we're burning off a lot of fucking calories here,' Dom snapped. Even this tired and he still had energy for attitude.

'So what are you going to eat later?'

'We'll need that chocolate,' Dom said, his face stiffening to a challenge.

'We? You've eaten all yours too?'

Dom nodded, without a trace of shame or regret evident in his expression. 'And I'm still starving.'

Luke turned away and stared across the ravine in silence. He could be across it in twenty minutes, maybe less. The idea excited him. And it was the best possible course of action available after all, he thought, as he resurrected the original strategy he'd discussed with Hutch the night before.

If he dropped both packs and the tent and put everything he had left inside himself into the hike, he could walk steadily until nine before it became too dark to walk any further safely. That would still give him another eight hours unimpeded and unencumbered by this pair. He might even make it out of the forest tonight if he was walking in the right direction. He could leave the others here with the tent, beside a notable feature that would be visible from the air. They had water. No food, but whose fault was that? They would just have to wrap up warm, get into their bags and take it in turns to keep watch, maybe get a fire going.

But if they survived tonight, they'd have to spend another night out here too. Because even if he made it out of the forest later that evening, at least one more day of walking would be necessary to even locate the next minor road or settlement and organize a rescue. Two nights with no food and one of them injured. Would they even get a fire going? They had lighters, but just about everything around them was too wet to burn. This was the fourth day of constant rain or drizzle; it would take hours to get the most service-able wood together to keep a fire going for any length of time. And the gas would be gone by tomorrow morning.

His thoughts sped from one scenario to another, and then slowed to consider the repercussions of each potential choice. But no matter what he considered and then dismissed, he still knew his own best chance of survival was to strike out alone.

'So what now? How the fuck do I get across this?' There was a note of accusation in Dom's tone of voice.

'Maybe . . .' Luke said quietly.

'Maybe what?'

'Maybe we go back to the original plan.'

'Original plan? The original plan was to get the fuck out of here as quickly as possible, by the most direct route. Are we not still following the original plan?'

It was the sarcasm. Always the sarcasm. Would it ever end? Hobbling around on his useless knee, criticizing, always com-plaining. Luke was his only chance of survival and still he was contemptuous. 'You're not going to like what I'm about to suggest.'

'I'll fucking put money on it, eh Phillers?'

Phil looked bewildered. 'What?'

'He's thinking of taking off. Aren't you? And just bloody leaving us here.'

'Look—'

'I can't believe you'd even consider it.'

Luke clenched his jaw. 'If you could walk properly, would you even be here now?'

'What?' Dom shook his head in disgust. 'Well, I never. Though I don't know why I'm surprised. You take over the map and play Hutch all day. Get us even more lost than we were already. And when we reach this crater, you're going to just leave us. When we agreed this morning that we would stick together.'

'You said, Luke. You said,' Phil blurted out with an urgency that filled Luke's head with confusion.

'It's not like that.'

'From where I am sitting it fucking is. Every man for himself now is it? Well go on. Fuck off then. Fuck us.'

'Listen—'

'I'm sick of listening. First Hutch's bright ideas that got himself killed, and now yours. And we're still fucking here. Fucking lost. So fucking lost.' His voice trailed off into a breathy hopelessness that made Luke feel every tired sinew and fibre cry out within his own body for it all to just stop. *Please God, just let it stop now.*

Luke stood up. Dom flinched. Phil's body tensed. They thought he might hit them. Why? He wasn't like that. Or was he? And was he just abandoning them because they were slowing him down, or was he really trying to save them all? Maybe Dom was right and he was only trying to rationalize his own selfish desire to survive. In extreme situations self-preservation did take over. Was it time for him to cut the rope, or go down with them too? He didn't know any more.

He suddenly felt ashamed; visualized himself walking away from these two forlorn figures, sitting beside a half-collapsed tent. Neither of them could even erect one. He and Hutch had put both tents up every night from the beginning of the trip.

Luke pointed down and into the ravine, desperate to displace another confrontation. He glanced at Dom. 'Can you get across that?'

'Yes.'

'For real?'

'Yes for fucking real.'

'OK then. Let's do it.'

Phil rapidly looked at each of them in turn. 'Safety in numbers,' he said, his voice rising to form a question within the statement.

THIRTY-FIVE

'I can't go any further.' Dom stared between his knees, at the ground he had slumped upon. His face was concealed by the hood of his waterproof.

'Me neither,' Phil muttered in solidarity.

Luke turned his head from where they lay and looked back up the hill he wanted them to climb. Just the sight of it defeated them. One obstacle too far.

He groaned and removed the rucksacks, first from his chest and then from his back. Aches burned up and down his torso. Stretching upright, his spine cracked with sudden shocks of pain. The worst of the discomfort was deep within his shoulders; without the weight of the rucksacks acting like tourniquets, his muscles were squeezing themselves into brief contractions of agony. What was wrong with his thighs? They were heavy, but trembling uncontrollably. He checked his watch. 4.25 p.m.

Wiping the sweat from his eyes, he stared at the higher ground. The dark fir trees and spruce thinned into the white trunks of silver birches and dwarf willows about the summit of the hillock; one long spruce tree sprouted incongruously from the peak. The high ground was topped with rock, grey with reindeer moss, and could offer a decent vantage point. Maybe he could climb the spruce too, and see over the surrounding ocean of forest. Get a sense of where they were. Be easier to defend too. Smoke from a fire might carry on the breeze. And the hill could be seen from the air. *It had finally come to that*. This had been his thinking.

He'd become fixated with the hill after glimpsing it periodically in the places the wood broke around the boulders they had stumbled over after crossing the strip marsh. His entire focus had been upon the hill from then onwards. He doubted they had moved more than three miles since crossing the ravine, in three hours. Time had elongated around their perpetual rest stops.

At least the rain had finally petered out to a drizzle after they had suffered nearly two hours of a drenching downpour. During which they'd tried to shelter under trees, but had ended up merely sitting in silence and had become soaked, then started to shiver, their fingers going numb. With no means to dry their clothes, Luke had persuaded the other two that it was better to walk wet, in the rain, to maintain body temperature. The other two had agreed in silence by rising groggily to their feet in unison. And then there was just more of the tramping of their feet on the unforgiving ground until they reached the foot of the stony hill.

They were moving four, maybe five, kilometres a day now. *No good*. No good at all.

Another night out here was unavoidable. If they stayed in a group and continued to shuffle at the pace Dom set, while Luke carried most of the gear, they would never get out. But if they could just climb up there. Make camp. Maybe get a fire going with the dead wood buried in the underbrush on the slopes. Rest until the morning. Then tomorrow he could set off alone and use the last of himself to get out of here and to get help. It would be a good place to leave Phil and Dom. They might feel better about the idea up there too.

How would he tell them? He could explain it to them in the morning, first thing, when they were able to think more clearly, after a long rest. There was nothing more to say about it: he had to go on alone from here.

Luke bent over, standing just ahead of the other two. Squeezed his eyes shut. 'OK. OK.' Then straightened his back again. He gulped at the boggy water in his canteen. 'Up there. We camp. Get a fire going.'

'I can't,' Dom said, and then stretched his body out on the wet rocks of the slope. Closed his eyes against the falling rain.

Luke sighed. 'I'll get the gear up there. Check it out. You guys take a breather. Stay together.'

He struggled to get his arms through the rucksack straps. But once he had them front and back and burning into the deep bruises they had made that day, he could not bend over to pick up the tent bag. Phil shuffled across to him, raised the tent bag and looped the straps over the palm of his right hand. Luke nodded, then set off up the hill.

THIRTY-SIX

Sitting beside the partially erected tent, Luke stared at his cold red hands, and let the wave of nausea dwindle. It left him shivering. His stomach burned. Trying to thread the poles through the canvas sleeves in the correct sequence was almost impossible. His vision kept swimming and then his arms lacked the strength to bend the poles sufficiently to get the ends into the four eyelets at the corners of the groundsheet. Phil would have to help him.

'Phil. Help me with these bloody poles. By Christ, I'm so close to snapping them in half.'

Phil never turned his head from where he squatted and stared down the hill. 'Please don't.'

Luke sipped from his canteen. 'How's he doing?'

'About halfway.'

Dom was pushing himself up the rocky hill backwards, in a sitting position, one little shuffle at a time while Phil kept watch from the summit. It would be the perfect time for an attack. He'd told Phil to stay with Dom. He had not, but had followed Luke closely instead.

Why didn't whatever or whoever had killed H make a move now? They were too tired to defend themselves and the weakest member was separated from him and Phil. Isn't that what predators do, wait for the weakest member to detach from the herd and then strike? Because it was down there somewhere, watching them. He knew it.

Luke groaned and moved onto his knees. With the last of his strength, he made ready to bend the tent poles again. He'd done this scores of times over the years; could get the whole thing erected in twenty minutes. But not now; he'd been fumbling with it for over twenty minutes already and only one of the main supports was in place. Last time though; he wouldn't go through this again. The tent stayed here. Tomorrow he travelled light. He'd even leave his pack with them. Take the compass and knife, a few squares of chocolate, a sleeping bag, and just go.

The rain drizzled speckles across the mess of the tent and over his hunched shoulders. He looked up at the gunmetal sky, so low and dark, but at least they could see sky. They had some natural light up here. Maybe it was brightening. Who could say? It could get so dark down there in the trees, like it was night. A godforsaken place. Nowhere for men to be.

Straining to the point of giving himself a hernia, he bent the tent pole again, for the fourth time, and gritted his teeth, focusing his stare on the little chromed eyelet and the alloy-tipped end of the pole that would hover at maximum stretch just above it, but refuse to reach the last few millimetres to slot inside the corner ring. He went beyond the remaining strength in his shoulders and biceps. Fingers turning blue-white, he cried out. The pole slipped into the ring, and he released it. Slumped back on his heels, his punished hands like claws. Blood slowly seeped back into his fingers. He stared at them. 'Done it. Bloody done it,' he said to himself.

'He's stopped. We might have to drag him the rest of the way,' Phil said. 'His knee is totally fucked. Fucked.'

Dom lay inside the canopy of the tent, motionless, silent. Stripped down to a fleece and underwear, he lay on top of his sleeping bag; his bad leg was naked and stretched out, his foot protruding through the doorway. Beneath his heel Luke had slid a rucksack.

Dom had not said a word since reaching the summit of the hill. Using his crutch he'd risen to his feet at the top and hobbled agonizingly to the erected tent. After the tortuous ascent on his backside was complete, Luke made sure not to meet Dom's eye, but muttered, 'Well done, mate.' They both knew this was the end of the line for him. Dom would have to wait it out here until help arrived. The mere thought of persuading Phil to stay with Dom fatigued Luke even further, if that was possible. Let it wait until the morning. He couldn't take another argument.

One thing at a time. Get the stove going. A hot drink. Get Phil to organize the firewood. As much dry stuff as he could scrape together. He would climb that tree and check out the view. Stick to a plan. Be methodical. Keep your mind busy. Leave no room for anxiety to rush in and bustle.

Setting up camp, finding the stove, the pan, and filling it with water, lighting the stove; Luke shuffled about as if drugged, too worn out to even smoke. A cigarette would kill him now; his lungs were spent, bruised, tattered. Much of the coordination had gone from his legs too and he kept tripping over his feet. Balance was an issue. Dehydration or malnutrition or something. Felt like he'd been doing dead lifts in a gym all day. He wondered if any of the greenery around them was edible. He thought of wild berries and began to drool.

Eventually they were all sitting together in silence, their dirty hands cupping mugs of hot sweet coffee. The smell of it alone nearly made them cry. They stared, glassy-eyed, into its black surface while it cooled. No one could wait to find the creamer. The need for heat inside their bodies was too great. As soon as it had cooled enough to be gulped, it was.

Dom lay back after finishing his coffee, but gripped the mug to extract every last quantum of warmth into his dirty hands. Phil put his elbows on his knees and hung his head right down. After a while Luke thought he might have fallen asleep.

But into Phil's mind had come Hutch. He was quietly crying to himself. And such reflections were contagious. The enormity of what had been lost to them reared up again in their chests and clotted the back of their throats. Exhaustion had staved off thoughts of the tortured spectacle of their best friend, hanging limp from a tree. But now they were resting, Hutch's final image came back to each of them swiftly and mercilessly. Dom lay back inside the tent, covered his face; his shoulders began to twitch, to move with the rhythms of grief. Luke stared off into the trees they had stumbled through that afternoon and slowly felt his eyes burn and his vision blur.

'Phil. Mate.' Luke spoke once the cold and drizzle had become an unbearable addition to their mourning.

Eventually, Phil said, 'What?' but never moved his head.

'I'm going to get up that tree. Take a look around from up there. Maybe I'll see the edge of this. Who knows.'

Phil looked up suddenly at the tree, his eyes bright. Dom sat up too quickly and winced; his eyes were red.

Luke pointed at the tree. 'I think I can build up some of the flat stones into a step, then jump and reach the lowest branch. If I can pull myself up, it'll be like a ladder a bit higher. Halfway up I should be able to see between the branches where they taper.'

Dom nodded. 'Could work.'

'It's why I made for the high ground. It nearly bloody killed us, but it's a good spot. Bit exposed, but we have the tent to keep out the rain. And for once it's not under a tree, so we're not risking the waterproofing again. A fire might be possible too. Phil, I'm going to need you to scout about for some dry stuff. In the undergrowth, right down by the soil. Bark. Loads of small twigs. For kindling. We'll get it going and keep it going all night if possible. But don't go far from the tent.'

Dom looked at Luke with something approaching approval, nodded. 'What about me?'

'I think you need to hit the showers, mate. We'll take it from here. But keep a look out. You hear anything, you start shouting.'

'Roger.'

THIRTY-SEVEN

Luke tried not to look down.

Twice a foot had just slipped from the wet bark on the branch beneath his feet, and his fingers tightened into claws on an upper branch until the hot-cold feeling passed from his skin and his frantic mind stilled. Sweat cooled on his forehead. He breathed out noisily; forced his chest to work in and out at a normal rhythm.

He could go even higher, but was already well above the treetops sloping about the foot of the hill. Once the shaking eased in his legs, he dared to look up and then around his position, peering through the branches of the spruce heavy with wet knots of spiky leaves that reached out from the trunk.

For the first time since they'd entered the forest, he could see for miles. Miles in every direction. And he could see the edge of the forest too. He nearly wept. It looked so close. He was about to shriek the news down to the others, but then imagined himself falling and stayed silent.

He squinted again, straining his eyes into the distance. The perimeter of the forest was hazy through the far-off vapours and too indistinct to reveal individual trees; so it was further away than it looked. But still within reach. Maybe six kilometres away. More like seven. And over to the south west, in the direction Hutch guessed at correctly. But Luke had been leading them due south. That route led into a bulge of green, misted with a heavy white fog of low cloud that he could not see the end of. 'Jesus Christ.' Had they kept on in a straight southerly line they would have plunged back into the thicker belt of virgin forest spilling across the border of Norway. This tree had saved their lives.

To Luke came the recollection of faces and streets and buildings in London that he might see again. An impression of Charlotte's soft skin. Dark fragrant ale. Music from a stereo. Egg and chips with brown sauce in the café at the end of his street. The patient faces of his parents. Even the patched and musty shop where he sold CDs. He'd treasure every precious second spent there when he returned, cling on to the counter and tell his prick of a boss that he was so pleased to see him, every day. His chest heaved with emotion. *Out out out*, a little voice started in his head. He found himself grinning. It seemed like the first time in days. It felt awkward on his face, stiff. 'God. Thank you, God.' They could live. He could be alive for much longer than a few days. A pinhead of light spread to a horizon of thrilling, then choking hope. He closed his eyes.

Maybe he should strike out for it tonight. After a rest, and his last three energy bars. He became giddy with the speed of his new and shining thoughts. He shivered and opened his eyes.

Slowly, he withdrew the compass from inside his coat and held it up in front of his face to asses a precise outward trajectory, out of the trees and on to what looked like a long formation of treeless black rocks breaking through a scrub-covered expanse. Mist hovered over the far clear ground. It was a boulder field or hard rock plain, and some-where inside of it was the Stora Luleälven River, which would run east to Skaite. Nothing would follow him out there; *it* didn't like to be seen, he told himself. *It* crept about the ruins and relics of a former time.

From up so high, at least twenty metres from the ground, he could see Hutch's logic with the short cut. But irre-spective of the fact they were now being hunted, actually completing the short cut would have put Dom on a stretcher. Even he and Hutch, on their own, would have struggled to complete this *shorter* route. If one of them had suffered an accident, it would have been doubtful they both would have survived. 'Stupid, H. Just stupid, mate.'

Carefully, he turned his head, but not his legs, and stared down at the branch that supported his weight to make sure his feet did not move of their own volition again. He caught site of the tiny tent below. Raising his eyes from his feet, he saw the inlet in the vast treeline in which they entered this godforsaken place three days before. Behind it he could see the uneven silhouette of a mountain range. About one third of the distance so far covered still remained before they could leave the southern tip of the forest. But at his pace, not slowed down by Dom and Phil, and after a decent rest and plenty of water, plus the last energy bars, he reckoned he could clear the forest by midnight, which would mean three hours in the dark with a torch. Or maybe tomorrow was better and he'd be out by noon the following day, if he could risk another night in here.

Before he could decide on when to strike out for the closest edge of this wooded hell, the world below him erupted into a loud voice. No, two voices. One inarticulate, the other calling for, 'Phil. Phil. Phil.' Each word gradually ascended in volume, until the voice was shouting. Then it settled for cries of 'Oh God. Oh God.' This second voice came from closer to the tree. It came from the tent.

Up in the spruce, Luke could not move his legs. His fingers closed tighter around the branches he was gripping. The thick rounded wood beneath his feet burned into his soles as if to fuse him into the limb.

It's taking them. Won't see me up here. Don't move, don't move. It's still light, you can run. Wait. Wait here. Wait.

But then his head dipped and rose, dipped and rose, and he looked through the leafy branches below for his companions. Turning to the side, at the waist, he peered through the web of verdure and black bough, down to his left where the sounds of terror and distress called up from the earth.

There was the tent. Where was Dom?

There was Dom, standing up, a few feet away from the green and grey tent, looking down the slope, bent over. But silent now.

Luke began his descent, both legs shaking as his eyes peered between the lines of branches and the crevasses of empty air, disguised by false ceilings of green leaf, until his soles found and gripped the branches he had already traversed on the way up. He tried to keep his focus short, on foot placements and no further; not the distant hard ground that he could fall down to and be broken upon.

'Dom!' he called. 'Dom!' he called again. There was no answer, but he kept on going down, limb by limb. His voice sounded feeble, silly, up in the air. Trembling feet hovered above branches too low to comfortably descend upon, his body clutched to the trunk. He went down like a terrified blind man trying to get down a ladder where the thin air told him he was up high enough to die if he slipped. Descending with his body shaking with fear and tense with adrenaline; going down, branch by branch, until he swung by his hands and dropped to the rocky ground of the hilltop.

Pins of pain shot through his feet and he stumbled sideways, then pitched right over, smacking his face against a gnarly tree root breaking from the stony ground. The sudden pain sobered him, angered him. He got to his knees. Stood up, shaky on legs weakened from exertion.

His eyes darted everywhere, looking for what he did not want to see. A long thing, he imagined. Black, loping. Bright wet colour about its mouth.

But he just saw the inert tent, Dom turning back towards it, but looking over his shoulder. And about the tent was the stony ground and grey-black boulders, the dark moss and pale-yellow lichen, and a few small trees on the summit struggling through for life and for the sky. There was no Phil on their hill. A little pile of firewood thus far collected was scattered near Dom's feet, like he had recently dropped it.

Luke's own breath suddenly deafened him. Sweat joined the drizzle and ran into his eyes; blurred his vision that would not stop jumping and trying to see the worst in every direction. He wanted to scream and run fast, anywhere. Panic swamped his mind. He shouted something to clear his head, and then forced himself to stand still, to slow his jumping eyes.

His vision cleared. His line of sight extended to where it had been before he lost his head. He came back into himself swiftly. Then Dom rushed at him.

And Luke saw that Dom was shaking with eyes too wide

for any face but the face of the witless. His mouth was open and ruddy and gasping out incoherent whimpers mixed with shuddering inhalations.

Like a drowning man, Dom seized him. Snatched handfuls of Luke's waterproof and then slipped sideways and onto his hip, pulling Luke over with him. Until they both kicked and scrabbled and pushed at each other on the hard ground, but could not break apart because Dom's white-knuckled hands were clamped onto his waterproof; the fabric tugged out and into an expanse of stretched and ripping material that Luke felt come further away from the seams under his arms.

'Dom,' he muttered. 'Dom, let go.' But Dom hung on to him like he was a life raft in black drowning water. He didn't want to go under alone and he clutched at the only safe and companionable thing within his reach.

'Let go!' Luke roared next to Dom's face. But Dom only whimpered and said, 'He's gone. Took . . . Took . . .'

Until Luke grasped Dom's dirt- and sweat-streaked head in both hands and squeezed, shouting, 'Get off. Get off me,' crushing that frantic, saucer-eyed face. Which crumpled. The hands on his chest, tangled among his clothes, went limp and dropped away. Dom lay on his side and covered his face with his filthy fingers.

Luke kicked away at the hard ground until he was standing upright and flattening his jacket down at the front. He scrabbled for the little oval shape of the closed penknife in his trouser pocket. He got it out, got it open. A pitiful little blade, dull in the dusk light on the desolate hillock.

He walked away from Dom. Didn't blink once until his eyeballs felt like they had soap rubbed into them. Walked straight to the edge of the summit and looked down the rocky slope they had ascended, down to where Phil had been gathering firewood.

'Phil!' he called at the top of his voice. Called until his lungs squeezed out all of the air and hung spent and exhausted inside his chest. 'Phil! Phil! Phil! Phil!' Then he was coughing, his throat wrenched and painful.

There was no sign of Phil at all, and no response from the eternity of wet trees and dark hollows and eruptions of tangled undergrowth. No bird calls, not a breath of wind; even the rain seemed to have paused in shock at what must have come from those trees to snatch a full-grown man from his feet.

THIRTY-EIGHT

'I . . . I heard him scream. I never let him out of my sight. I swear. He was twenty feet away. It was the stove. I was checking the water. Leaning over to see if it was boiling. Then I heard him scream . . .' Dom talked the quavers out of his voice, until it became flat and quiet. 'He's gone.'

Luke crouched beside him, the knife still clenched in his fist. He looked away from Dom and the tent. Scanned the surrounding rise of boulder and stone to make sure nothing was coming for them.

'Jesus. Jesus Christ.' He could not accept this. That Phil was gone too; being pulled apart down there, somewhere in the shadows . . . He stopped the thought from blossoming into something more sudden and red and wet than it already was.

It wasn't possible. Any of this. Perhaps if he wasn't so tired, with every muscle hurting under his damp skin, and his mind thick and dizzy with fatigue, he would go mad. Three days in this place had blunted his edges. His personality was disappearing, paring itself down to instinct and fear. How a rabbit must think. You didn't need to be sentient out here, just afraid all the time and quick to act when the world suddenly felt wrong around you; too still, too easy. That's when you died out here.

He should go now. Take off on his own. He really should. He stood up and looked to the other side of the hill. *It* was taking them one by one then vanishing. Splitting up might confuse it. He should use the last of the light and the last of his legs and just run and never look back.

But would it change its pattern and kill them both tonight? First Dom up here, alone inside the tent, and then him down there, tangled in the undergrowth and delirious with exhaustion. Easy prey.

The dream. The sticks.

Dom's shivering face looked up at him. The rims of his eyes were bright red. Dirty and bruised and dishevelled and wet, wearing only grimy boxer shorts and a waterproof, he looked pathetic. Something thickened and surged in Luke's chest. He shuddered. Dropped to his knees and put his arms around Dom's shoulders. Squeezed his eyes shut. Dom trembled, but his hands gripped the waterproof around Luke's waist and he clung on like a child after a terrible fright.

In the drizzle and thin light, they held each other for a long time, in silence.

THIRTY-NINE

It was getting dark now and there would be no fire. Just their torches and the little blue whoosh of the camping stove, both resources that would need to be used sparingly until the morning. They sat back to back, in front of the tent after finishing the last energy bars and the rest of the sugar. It settled them for a while. A slender stream of nutrients in their exhausted blood allowed a brief period of calm to take possession of them.

A cold breeze blew constantly from the south west; below the hill it stirred the trees like a great and impatient breath. The rain had petered out, but the air was chilly. Shades of evening were created all about them by the dark weight of the cloud cover above. Darkness would soon overcome them.

They sat on Phil's sleeping bag to save their buttocks freezing against the unforgiving stones, and each took a 180-degree view of the hill, keeping watch, alone, and trying to steer their thoughts away from Phil.

Dom began to laugh, but without any warmth, and broke the long silence that began when their backs first pressed together. 'Everything I wanted to get away from for a week, I'm desperate to see again. Fucking crazy.'

Luke could feel the broad weight of Dom's shoulders easing further into him. He hadn't realized a body could be so heavy, so dense. Luke cleared his throat. 'You're not wrong.' He stared into the distance. 'I've been at my wits' end. With my whole life. For so long.' He smiled with tight trembling lips. 'Being disappointed is normal to me. But why is it only now it doesn't seem so bad? Any of it. Jesus, I wish I could be back there. In my shitty old flat with a cup of tea.'

Dom laughed again, then Luke did too, until Dom stopped and there was a sudden intake of breath from him. 'Christ. I love my kids. I won't see . . .' And then he was weeping soundlessly, his shoulders moving against Luke.

A lump grew inside Luke's throat. He shook his head. Still could not believe for a moment that he was here, sitting like this; there was no more Phil, no more Hutch. He sat mute, and stared out as the light dimmed like his sight was slowly going out. The cold moistened against his face and stiffened his joints.

The true gravity of his friends' loss had been restrained by some inner function inside him. But his thoughts would keep darting back to the sheer wordless enormity of their demise; the inexpressible force of it could shut him down.

Then this cold horror and grief would turn towards that image of three little blonde girls on the screensaver of Phil's phone, and the suspension of his feelings could no longer be maintained.

How would the news be imparted to them? Who could explain such a thing? How was it even done? Hutch had a wife. Luke swallowed. His lips trembled and his eyes burned wide. He tried to swallow it all away, but could not. His legs were shaking, his hands too.

His thoughts flitted to the absence of himself back in England. And his imaginings found his mum and dad, his sister, an aunt. They would hold the weight of grief and memory after his loss. That too would dim in time. But not for a while. Jesus, they'd have to fly out to Sweden and talk to polite officials, wait for search parties to come back in with empty hands and disappointed faces. He could see his mum's face long with worry, his dad's arm around her dipped shoulders. Maybe they would make the news, the four English guys lost up by the arctic circle. A mention in a broadsheet. Maybe. Jesus. Dom had a family. Kids. Hutch had a wife. A wife, goddamnit. Phil had kids.

It was too great a weight for his thoughts to bear. Suddenly he could not breathe as all of those faces from Hutch's wedding, all stricken with shock and bafflement and grief, poured into his mind at the same time, vanished, then came back in again. 'Jesus. Dom. Oh Jesus. Dom,' he said, but softly.

Dom turned his head, sniffed. 'All right?'

But Luke could not calm down. It was like inhaling that massive bong back at uni. He'd never been as frightened until that point; terrified of losing control and not being able to find his old self again, as his memory rewound quickly and seemed to erase itself, as he vomited and suffocated and gasped over a toilet. And now he was swamped by that same icy panic and fear all over again and was consumed with a terror that he would never feel any different again. Heart hammering up inside his throat, sweat popped from his scalp and poured into his woollen hat.

It was natural, he told himself. Go with it again. Let it burn out. Find its own end.

'You OK?' Dom asked.

Luke took three deep lungfuls of air and squeezed his eyes

shut until the panic slowly subsided; he opened them when the rhythm of his heart softened. Then fished for his tobacco, papers and lighter in the top pocket of Hutch's commandeered jacket. He nodded. 'Considering.'

'I know,' Dom said. 'I know.'

Luke struggled to keep his hands still as he tried to roll the paper around the shreds of tobacco. He failed. Tried again. Failed. Tried again. His hands had never been so filthy. Black as pitch under the end of his nails. Would he ever get those fingers clean again?

'Can I have one of those?' Dom asked, his voice thick with phlegm.

'You sure?' he said without thinking.

'In our present circumstances, there are greater risks to be faced than smoking. But can you roll it? I've forgotten how.'

'Yeah. No problem.'

He passed a messy cigarette and his lighter over his shoulder to Dom. Their last little comfort from the other world. When their fingers touched briefly, the tiny contact made Luke quiver with shame when he recalled punching Dom's face. Striking his actual, living, expression-filled face. He remembered the surprise, the shock, the fear, the hurt. Like a child's face. *When we're frightened and hurt are we ever anything else?*

'Man, I'm sorry.' He could barely get the words out.

'Mmm?'

'What I did. I can't believe I did that. I'm just . . . angry. All the time. It's not right. I'm not dealing with things . . . well.'

'I can be an arsehole.'

They sat in silence again, until Dom broke it. 'Do you think anyone is happy?'

'Never can tell.'

'It's like you said, it's all about P.R. these days. Brand management. Social networking. The corporatization of our own experience. We're all our very own communications directors. But what a load of bollocks it all is when you're faced by something like this.'

'Kind of levels the playing field.'

'Sweeps all of that bullshit away. All that really matters is being able to survive. Some do it better than others.'

'I guess.'

'You do. You can do this.'

Luke did not know what to say.

'Out here. You're good out here. Better at this shit than me and Phil. Maybe Hutch too, for all his poncing with stoves and tents. You've still got that instinct.'

Was it a compliment?

'Once Hutch was gone, me and Phil were fucked. We wouldn't have got this far without you. For all the good it's done us. But at least you got us closer to the end of these bastard trees.'

Luke snorted back a laugh. 'It's the other world I can't cope with. I'm hopeless in it.'

'Don't be so hard on yourself.'

Luke nodded, sighed, but had always felt unable to take advice like that.

'I don't think any of us knew how to be happy,' Dom said, his voice deeper than usual, wistful. 'Maybe Hutch got it right. He kept it simple. Kept it real. Didn't overextend himself.

Picked a low-maintenance woman. Looked after himself. But the rest of us haven't done so well, mate, when you look a bit more closely at the ledger. What me and Phil had is gone. All of it. We ended up a pair of fatties, about to be divorced, looking at the prospect of limited access to our kids. A couple of fat bastards who couldn't even manage a walk in the woods.'

Luke laughed. And laughed until his face was warm and running with tears.

'Eh?' Dom continued, smiling through his own tears. 'Phil married a nightmare too. That was his problem. Poor bastard. That bitch will get everything now. What she always wanted. Let's hope she gets the debts too. But Gayle . . .' He paused, and exhaled. When he spoke again his voice was almost a whisper. 'She won't be able to cope with this, and the kids too. That's why I want to get out. I have to. I just have to. Her parents are too old. The nippers won't get over . . .' Dom cleared his throat. Blew air out with all the might of his lungs.

'Now's not the time, Domja. Keep it together. Big fat crying . . .'

They sat in silence again. Against Luke's back, Dom's body felt warmer.

Luke turned his head. 'We'll do it, mate. We'll do it. Tomorrow. And take a word of your own advice, and don't beat yourself up. Not now. Not here. I take my hat off to you guys. I do. I always have done. You've all done good.' He paused. 'What I said. The other night. Was bollocks. I was just transferring. Bad habit.' He blew out a long tired sigh. 'I always envied you guys. You know that?'

'Be careful what you wish for,' Dom said, then cleared his throat of emotion.

'I've always been proud of you lot.'

'And we've always been fascinated by what you were getting up to. At least you had a go. Did things a bit differently. Wanted something else.'

'It came to nothing. That's all I know.'

Dom shrugged, sighed. 'We were all fairly monogamous guys. Got into relationships and stayed in them. Then kids. At least you got to throw the hump a few times.'

Luke smiled.

'And we all went back to our home towns after uni. Stayed put. It made life easier, Luke. Things were cheaper when we all graduated. We got houses. Kept the same jobs, until recently. I've never done anything else but play it safe. And Phil. At least you and Hutch had a go at something else. That's got to count for something? And nothing is really safe. Is it? None of us knew what life would throw at us. Everyone is fucked up, Luke. Damaged. We're all messed up, underneath. Doesn't matter what kind of house you live in.'

They sat in silence again for a while. In which Luke felt awkward and ashamed: after what he'd done to Dom, after what he had said, here was his friend, injured, cold and scared, but still trying to reassure him about his car-wreck of a life. If this wasn't friendship, he didn't know what was. 'I had so much and never learned to appreciate it. And I know now I've never even been tested. Not properly. Until now. Have just handicapped myself and bitched about it.'

But now it was time for him to make his mark. To step up. To get them both out of here. If he could pull it off, it would be the only useful thing he'd ever really achieved. Nothing mattered more than life and death.

Now they were together, sitting against each other, the

very contact of their shoulders pressed together informed him there was no way on earth he could leave Dom alone. Not tonight. Not in the morning. Not out here. The very thought of walking away from the tent with Dom still beside it was unbearable. He imagined looking back at the tent, abandoned on this hill. And he imagined what would come out of the trees and go up there to find his friend. To finish him.

They were thinking about the same thing, again, because Dom suddenly said, 'You better take off.'

'Don't be silly.'

'I mean it. The one thing in our favour this far north, that we haven't used to our advantage because I've been slowing us down all day, every day, is the longer evenings. You could make it out tonight if you put your foot down.'

Luke shook his head. 'No.'

'Don't be an arse. It's your only chance. My leg is finished. I can't bend it at all now. How far could I get tomorrow? Dragging it. Stumbling all over the bloody place with that stick. Not very far, that's how far. So get out of here and get help. I mean it, Luke. I'm not messing around. People have to know what happened here.'

'I can't.' His voice sounded pitiful, tiny, in the cold watery air, before the rock and wood that would not be defied in its almighty and far-reaching indifference, its immensity of permanence.

'What use can I be?' Dom's voice softened, but was older somehow. Luke had never heard this tone from him before; the voice of a father, of a man. 'It was different when there were three of us. Now, it's all changed. You've got to give yourself a chance. I would. If that makes it easier for you. If the situation was reversed, and you were hurt, I would have gone already. Staying with me is a death sentence.'

Luke dropped his face into his hands, clawed at his cheeks. He'd never felt so wretched in his life. His eyes screwed up and he wanted to cry.

Dom lowered his voice to a whisper. He stretched an arm behind him and he gripped Luke's bicep with his broad fingers. Squeezed it. 'Please. Go. It's coming for me next anyway. You can't keep an eye on me and where you're putting your feet. It's not possible. You did your best, but it's not an option now. It'll take us both out. First me when your back is turned. Then you. I couldn't even clear this forest if I put everything into it tomorrow. So it would mean another night after this one. You know it.'

Luke tried to keep the emotion out of his voice, but could not. 'Fuck it. Dom. Fuck it.' He swallowed. 'I don't care how long it takes. I don't. But we leave here together. Tomorrow. In the morning. Your pace. We walk. Rest. Walk. Watch each other's backs. We leave all the stuff here beside the sleeping bags. We do it together, or not at all.'

Dom's fingers squeezed his arm tighter. He was crying and trying to stifle it, but failing and getting angry with himself. 'Shit.'

'It's OK. OK.'

Dom growled and cleared his throat. 'I had it all worked out. Now you've fucking ruined it.'

They both sniffed; it was the closest thing to laughter they could manage.

Dom cleared his throat. 'Now you've given me hope again.'

Luke reached backwards and gripped Dom's shoulder.

And from the foot of the hill, no more than twenty metres

below them, as if rising to a new challenge, a long and terrible sound grew from a hidden mouth and made the hill, and every square foot of land for miles around, tremble from its bellow.

FORTY

A flock of birds heaved themselves into the sky, accelerated, swooped to the south; frantic to put distance between themselves and the sound of what now moved over the face of the earth. It was right below their position on the hill, moving through the trees on the south side, its footfalls silent.

Changing from grey to an Atlantic blue-black, the sky sucked the pitiful remains of the sun's distant glow up and into itself, dissolving visibility to vague shapes of trees and silhouettes of rock with black swathes of the indefinable between. Spaces that could be redefined by frantic minds to resemble anything at all.

Dom never stood up. His face blanched under the filth to make his scabbed lips appear dark as if stained by wine. His wide eyes were filled with madness. It was impossible to speak in the gravity of terror that crushed them both against the rocks and made Luke's left leg shake uncontrollably. He was standing, but only just, and watching the rim of the hillock from where the sound had originated, expecting a long shape to rise at any moment.

He could not breathe, like the surface of his lungs were adhered together, and around his mind swiftly spun idiot words, and quick flashes of the shattered, mottled remains in that wet cavity beneath the derelict church.

Within the pit of his belly he tried to find the heat of anger; the rage that made him go to meet it face-to-face when they found poor Hutch, disembowelled and splashing his innards down his legs and onto the black bark of the hanging trees. But there was nothing inside him but a chaotic space with no room for anything beside the kind of terror that could disengage a mind from anything but imbecilic musings.

And then again, to their left, so suddenly at their side, the bellow opened up the damp and boggy forest that remembered prehistory within its depths of peaty soil and in every single stone. Bestial grunting gave way to a devilish yipping in which words could almost be understood.

From the very core of each of them, their ancestors seemed to cry out in inarticulate voices. Right then, they screamed in alarm from times before symbols and language could depict such things that hunted and meant murder. Luke believed they were returned, in this cold and in this dark, to a place and into the presence of something from earth's dawn. Or another, even older place than that. *It* dominated the land. The boughs and leaves of its territory shuddered, marshy surfaces quivered, and the dank and dripping vales held their breath before its arrival.

Luke walked towards the sound, to the eastern edge of the hill on which they were about to make their final stand. Or maybe an engagement with it would be nothing more than it taking twitching sacrifices from the summit. Snatching with a swiftness and euphoria that comes to the predator whose hot sinuses and moist valves inflame with the scent of warm flesh and gushing salty blood.

Luke imagined a sinewy darkness, depressed to the earth. Moving through the shadows, up and over and under things.

The very obstacles that banged their shins or brought them gasping to a standstill, it merely glided past, able to slip through any natural barrier. Every inch of ground must have been mapped with nostril and tongue for years.

He held the knife against his side, and told himself there would be one strike in him. And he must make it instinct-fast. Rapid as a blink. Quicker than a flinch. At the exact moment it came whipping for his throat, or spearing at his torso. One strike, one chance.

Nearing the edge of the hill, Luke dropped to a crouch and raised his left forearm in the way police dog-handlers do. The hand holding the knife clenched white and readied itself for an upper cut.

Then he turned more quickly than conscious decisions or explanations would allow for, and ran back to where Dom sat prone and watching him. Ran with great jumping strides beyond balance or thought of where his feet fell; ran as fast as he could at Dom, at the tent, the knife ready.

And sure enough, just as the tips of the hairs on the nape of his neck had whispered, and as the tiny vibrations in his inner ear bones had trilled, and as the cooling of the blood through his heart warned, it would come in through the back door. Quick and low after luring one of them out to see it.

Behind the tent, pebbles were disturbed and scattered. There was a snort, as if from a bullock, and then Luke received a sense of a dark shape dropping and melting swiftly away, like the passing shadow of a cloud moving beneath the sun. Obscured by the loose tent and the spruce tree, he imagined, more than he saw, a long, black, nimble presence vanishing down the southern slope of the hill, as fluid as water.

Luke stopped in a skittering, lurching scramble over the

lichen-covered boulders behind the tent, violently expelling his breath in a gust that ended in a cry when he plunged into the miasma something inhuman had left upon the summit. He gathered himself in the very place where it had just been, where it had craned forward to snatch Dom as he sat before the tent, looking the wrong way. Downwind of him.

'Clever bastard.'

Which was why Dom had not detected the heavy animal spore of a coat wet and fouled and ungroomed, or the hot meaty stench of a large mouth, and the livestock reek of air silently exhaled through a great muzzle.

At the edge of the hill, Luke looked down to the distant southern treeline. Nothing. There was nothing there at all any more.

'What? Where is it?' Dom whispered, his voice so tight and high it was unrecognizable.

'Gone. Down there.' Luke glanced over his shoulder and across the roof of the tent. 'Look to your front!'

'What?'

'To the front!' Luke bounded back to where Dom sat, staring up at him, terrified and bemused.

Luke scanned the rocky plateau, the edges of the summit, to the west and the north. Nothing.

He shook his head and bent over, hands on thighs, gulping at the dusky air. 'Jesus.'

'What? Where is it?'

Luke looked at Dom. 'It drew me out. Made me follow the sounds. But it doesn't come from there. But from behind you when you're looking in the wrong direction. It was behind the tent.'

'No.'

Luke nodded. 'I suddenly knew what that fucker was up to. It came up the back way, the south side. For you.'

'Shit.' Dom shuffled to his feet, leaned on his crutch. 'Behind the tent? You see it?'

They looked at each other, so deeply into each other's eyes it hurt. Luke shook his head. 'But I think it's big.'

FORTY-ONE

'It was close again. Did you hear it?'

But when Luke turned his head to see why Dom had not acknowledged that he had heard it too, Dom's eyes were closed and he was gripped by an exhausted and haunted slumber, which was all this forest would allow a man.

He shook Dom's shoulder.

Slowly, Dom opened his eyes. 'Did I sleep?' His voice was thick, slurred.

'You go and sleep first,' Luke said quietly, and shone his torch into the entrance of the tent. It was ten thirty and the first hour of eight hours of darkness had passed.

Sitting back-to-back before the mouth of the tent, they had covered themselves in their sleeping bags, open and spread like blankets, to watch the last of the light fade. Each of them held a torch and a knife.

Both of them going inside the tent was certain death; they would have to take turns resting. Luke had suggested it earlier, but Dom had balked at the idea of being trapped inside the tent and unable to see around himself. Instead, he'd opted to stay up, to stay awake all night, and to keep watch.

'I won't sleep,' Luke said. 'You go first. You have to sleep, Dom. I'll keep watch until midnight. You're no good to us if you fall asleep out here.'

But Dom continued to sit outside the tent, his shoulder pressed into Luke's back, his torch flicking about the rocky summit on his side. 'Sorry. I won't fall asleep again. I promise.'

Another hour passed without any sound or sign of it.

Luke shuddered; his mind was dull. He kept his torch beam trained into the darkness. Already the torchlight was vague, dimming. He would soon have to use the spare torch that had belonged to Phil. But his body was enveloped in the soothing warmth of a winter sleeping bag, and he didn't want to move. Not yet. It was the first time that day he'd felt even a smidgen of comfort.

Dom wheezed; asleep again beside him.

Luke's own mind began to insist on the oblivion of sleep too. No matter the threat of extinction, his head even fell twice before he snapped awake, cold with fear and tightening his grip on the torch.

Without sleep, how could he even think about the trek tomorrow, back down there and into the darkness of *its* realm? His body was spent, every muscle flat but aching, his spine a single column of pain. Dom couldn't be trusted to stay awake if he roused him now to keep a solitary watch while he grabbed an hour's rest. Dom needed sleep more than he did. Needed to rest that knee. Every minute of sleep Dom secured increased their chances of survival the following day because it would make Dom more alert, while he blazed the trail towards the end of this ancient hell.

Luke adjusted his position and knelt up inside his sleeping bag, with Dom's weight against his ribs. Surely he could not fall asleep while kneeling up. Shuddering in the cold, he reached over and took Dom's torch from out of his lap. Then held each of the torches at waist-height, and trained their pale beams onto the ground either side of where they sat before the rippling tent.

He sat like that without moving for twenty minutes; then another fifteen; eventually completed an hour. The rhythm of his companion's breathing lulled him, comforted him. He would not be without it . . . Every second Dom slept would . . .

He flashed open his eyes, after what felt like a moment of them being closed. Luke and Dom were not alone on that hilltop.

Dozing off into a waiting, beckoning, soothing coma of exhaustion, part of him had remained alert; a neglected, but now revived and finely tuned region of his mind that sometimes roused him at home when a noise within the confines of his flat contained more drama than the scurry of a mouse, or creak of a joist, or ambient shudder of a pipe inside a wall. The part of him that responded to the unnatural sounds of night, suddenly clicked his mind alive without the yawning stupor of a normal waking.

In the tired torchlight, he could see no further than ten to fifteen feet across the small summit; even the rim of the hill had long vanished into the murk of the cloudy night. The stones closest to the tent were still visible, appearing bluish beyond the torch's beam as if emitting a strange light, but were bleached like sea shells when directly within it.

'Dom.'

Against his side, Dom's solid weight still rested, shoulder blades pushing out from restful inhalations. To his right, between the tent and the southern edge of the hill, Luke's startled vision told him that the shape, no more than two metres away from the first guy rope, had not been there before he fell asleep.

'Dom.'

It was not moving. Immobile as a boulder, long as a fallen log on a forest floor, it was nothing to a casual glance, or even peripheral vision. A long dark reaching form that only a man petrified by the hyper-alertness of a hunt might investigate with a second look.

Luke was too frightened to shine his torch directly at it. He did not want to see it.

He swallowed. Whimpered, 'Dom.'

Dom murmured in his sleep.

And then the nearest part of the shadow, that defined itself by the thinnest light of the torch that brushed that place, moved. Raised itself no more than a few inches, in the way a stalking cat will engage in the next step towards its prey.

Luke turned his stiff thighs into a crouch, and then roared with all the power of his lungs. He shone a torch beam into the shape, and dropped the other torch to reach for his knife in the mouth of his sleeping bag.

What had come up the side of the hill for them, pressed into the ground, was startled by his cry. Within the juddering white light, a black shape flattened itself beneath the light, then withdrew so quickly it almost vanished. Along what could have been a hairy flank something gleamed like oil.

Luke scrabbled and snatched inside the warm interior of his sleeping bag for the knife. His fingers brushed nylon, a zipper, his own leg, empty air. 'Dom!'

Dom woke. Rigid with fear, he pressed his body into Luke's stomach.

Time paused. The air tensed taut, in the way it does before

the clashing tearing violence of living things coming together to kill.

Some part of *it* scraped like bone across stone, backward and down into the darkness beyond the torchlight. It could have been his imagination, but Luke sensed a long shape had cantered, spiderish, sideways, and disappeared behind the tent; and then must have moved, if not flowed, across to the gaunt silhouette of the spruce. Or had even just reappeared there. Because something was now moving, rising up, behind the tree trunk at the far reaches of the arrival of his torch's beam. And then upward it went some more, behind and seemingly around the trunk, on unseen limbs, that must have been as long as stilts. Or were these merely retreating shadows, created by a torch held in a trembling hand?

Luke stood. The light from his dim torch frosted the tree, and washed weakly across what could have been long thin moving branches, or something else entirely.

Fumbling about for his torch and knife, Dom murmured something inarticulate from beneath Luke.

Above them, before them, the long thin shapes that might have been foliage in raking torchlight moved further upward, spearing through the drizzly air. The briefest visual offering of which liquefied Luke's guts, then made the sense-memory of his stomach vanish altogether into a total absence.

Luke moved around Dom and leapt at the tree; as he moved he dropped his right shoulder and filled his fist with the cold density of a heavy rock from the little cairn that weighted down a guy rope. Landing upon his front foot, with the full range of his arm, his shoulder and his back, he catapulted the stone like a baseball, right into the tree and its shadows.

The Ritual

The terrible *thunk* of stone on flesh was followed by a shriek that deafened them both. Luke recoiled from the throw. But before he could straighten his spine, something whipped out from the howling presence behind the tree and cracked his skull.

His vision flared white with pain before his eyes and mind clicked off into complete darkness.

FORTY-TWO

Silty light seeped through his half-closed eyelids and worsened the pain. Relentless in its encasement of his entire skull the agony made him feel sick, and bewildered, and unsure of where he was. His head and face and neck were wet and cold, dripping.

The shape of his head felt too big, ungainly and misshapen. Something wet hung over one eye and restricted the light.

A rucksack had been slipped like a pillow beneath his head. The angle hurt his neck. He raised himself to one elbow and squinted. Empty of anything but gas, his stomach lurched.

The awning of the tent flapped like a sail in a swift wind. He could see it through one squinting eye. Two sleeping bags covered his body. The little stove was hissing a blue flame under the steel pan not far from his feet. He reached up and gingerly touched the part of his forehead where the pain started its thunder, before it rolled backwards. Something soft and loose was arranged about his head, squashing his ears flat, and tied tighter at the back. He swallowed at a dry and swollen throat. Water. He was desperate for it. He coughed. 'Dom.'

He heard the sound of rocks grinding together under someone's weight. The clack of a stick followed, accompanied by a gasp of exertion. He turned towards the sound, then closed his eyes as the pain threw itself against one side of his head and nearly made him throw up. Skull fracture. *Oh shit, oh shit, oh shit.* Suddenly dizzy, he slipped back down to his former position, resting against the rucksack.

'Mate. Thank fuck. You're awake. Wasn't sure if you were in a coma,' Dom said, close enough for Luke to smell his harsh breath and the pungent oily smell of his dirty clothes.

'Any water left?'

'Last of it is in the pan. I used most of it on your head. I had to wash it before I put the bandage on. Coffee and chocolate for breakfast.'

'What's the time?'

'Eleven.'

'No.'

'You've been out cold. It's made a mess of your face. You need stitches.'

'Is it bad?' he muttered, and felt stupid. How would Dom know?

'Good news is it didn't come back after you hit it. What did you do, get it with a knife? Jesus, that sound. You hurt it. You must have hurt it.'

Luke squinted through the one eye it was easiest to open. 'Threw a rock.'

'Rock?'

'Uh huh.'

'Shot.'

Luke tried to smile, but that made him nauseous too. 'How bad is it? My head. Don't B.S. me.'

Dom paused and looked at his boots, then winced as he returned his gaze to Luke. 'I've never seen so much blood.

But that can be misleading. Doesn't mean it's serious or anything. There's more blood in the head than anywhere else in the body. I think. Which is why head injuries look worse.'

'Shit.' Head injury – the phrase made him tingle, then wash cold all over. It could be really bad: a fractured skull, or a concussion, which would explain the nausea. Maybe something worse; a blood clot, or a head trauma that required immediate surgery to prevent brain damage. Fluid had to be drained. *Now.*

Panic started to lurch through him again, to join the squeezing pain that pushed reddish flashes into his vision. He took a deep breath and shuddered down to his toes.

'You are covered in it, mate. I didn't know it was so bad until the sun came up. I nearly heaved. But we got through it. We made it to morning. Can you believe it?'

'Painkillers. Any of those Nurofen left?'

'Sorry. My knee's been a bit greedy on that front.'

'I don't think I can even stand up.'

Dom stayed silent. 'Then we're fucked,' he eventually said in a voice suddenly empty of any warmth or edge or inquiry. His words were flat and tired; the sound of despair, the voice of yesterday. Dom shuffled back to the stove and looked down at the water in silence. Two tin mugs were lined up beside it, next to the tub of coffee granules. The mugs were stained black inside.

'We need water. Badly. I got to drink something. Then look at my head. I have a shaving mirror.'

'Take it easy.'

'Maybe sterilize the wound with some of that boiled water.'

'Shush. Just—'

'Antiseptic. There was some in the medical kit.'

'All gone. Phil's blisters.'

'Jesus.' His face screwed up. He thought he might cry.

'Just take it easy. Drink this coffee. Get your head straight. It's just a flesh wound. A bump. Looks worse than it is.'

Was Dom only trying to make him feel better, or did what he say make sense? He had no idea, but it reassured him because he had nothing else to believe in but unexamined statements.

Dom began pouring boiling water into a mug. 'Let's just drink this. Then we can think about what the hell we're going to do next.'

It took them half an hour to stumble down the south side of the hill. At the bottom, they paused to get their breath and to wait for their respective agonies to subside enough to raise their chins and look back up at the side of the green and silver tent, rippling in the sudden cool gusts that washed over the hillock.

Except for two sleeping bags, the knives and the torches, they had abandoned everything else they had carried this far. Three rucksacks, an assortment of soiled clothes, an empty first-aid kit, and the empty gas canister and stove that had made them a final mug of bitter coffee, was all still in place up on the rocky summit. On the lonely and dreary place where they were supposed to have met their end, remained the final clues of what befell their hiking trip. Evidence of four friends who took a short cut.

They stood on a thin layer of soil covering the rocks at the foot of the hill and both turned and looked at the dark fir trees, solemn in the soft light, awaiting them. Further inside the dark cool forest, a wall of bracken erupted around the last few willows, before the taller spruce and firs resumed their blanket dominance where the soil was deeper.

As they peered into the woods and prepared to move south west, it was the sight of the uneven ground below them, tumbling up and down through the sentinels of trees, tilting from the sudden rocky crests made slippery with moss, that most disheartened Luke before they even began. Back in there for another day's tortuous scrabbling and crying out with pain at every step and every motion that involved the carriage of a wound. And they would be moving slower today than ever before. Luke closed his eyes and readied himself. He was finished before he'd even begun, and knew it.

Dom's messy bandage had fallen off his head at the first prompt. But at least it had absorbed most of the bleeding, a seeping that continued for the hours he was unconscious. The gash ran from his left eyebrow, up his forehead and into his hair. It was pink and open like a sideways mouth. Using his thin shaving mirror, he thought he had seen a glimmer of bone inside it. The gash was at least five inches long and desperately required stitches.

With the last absorbent pad from the first-aid kit, he had dabbed at the wound with the last dregs of hot water from the pan, trying not to cry out too loudly at every contact. Dom could not even look at him while he attended to his torn flesh. He'd then placed the gauze pad under the wrappings of the soiled bandage and gently retied it around the crown of his head. Dom had fixed the safety pin in place.

The most horrifying thing to Luke had been the sight of his own blood-stained face, barely recognizable when it peered back from the tiny shaving mirror. The water Dom had poured over his head had not washed his face clean; much of the streaky dried blood remained caked on. One side of his face was bruised purple, and further blackened with the grime already coating his skin right down to his throat. His left ear was plugged with dried blood and it was like having that side of his head submerged in a bath. If he ever stumbled out of here, he would be scarred for life. His bloodied face and the thought of a cruel white scar made him more miserable and sorry for himself than anything else.

And now they each held a crutch. Dom had found Luke his own wet branch, so they could both support their wincing, shuffling, wounded bodies with dead limbs from ancient trees.

As they walked, Luke could not talk to Dom. In silence, he would point a hand at gaps in the forest floor, where he thought it best for them to proceed through, in an approximation of the right outward trajectory. Inside his waterproof, he kept the compass close to his heart. More often than was necessary he would withdraw it and make sure they were close to the coordinates he'd mapped from up in the tree.

Talking to each other would waste what little strength they had left. Meeting each other's eyes could vanquish whatever kept the other one going so slowly, and so carefully away from the hill. They stayed close together, but somehow avoided each other at the same time.

Luke kept the knife constantly in one hand, but had so little balance and so much pain throbbing against the walls of his skull, he had no fight left in him. If they were attacked, they were dead.

They just hobbled forward, unthinking and unaware of anything but the next footfall; both of them determined to walk in the direction that would take them out of the trees and on to the plain and towards the river below; or to just keep moving until that time when their pursuer decided to take one of them, and then the other.

When they found Phil hanging from a Scots pine, they didn't linger. His butchery was worse than the condition of Hutch's remains; was more akin to what had befallen the animal they all found together, so long ago.

Dom kept sniffing, mumbling to himself; Luke kept his eyes down. Just once he'd looked up at his friend, so wet and spread about the trees, but he would not look again after he'd seen Phil's face. They'd even held each other's eye for a moment.

Like frightened children, Luke and Dom briefly held each other, arms around necks; each leaning his weight into the other as they staggered under their dead friend's cold pale feet, away from him and deeper into the forest.

FORTY-THREE

And he could think of nothing but water. Daydreamed of cold foresty wetness gushing down his parched throat. Silvery and bubbling across smooth cold pebbles it would rush and foam icy through a clear stream bed and then pour over his dry lips and drench the desert of his mouth. If they found a stream, he would fill his stomach with aching loveliness for hours until every cell in his body was saturated with water. *Water*. The very word burned his whole being with thirst.

In his swimming vision he looked down at his hands and wrists that were pin-pricking and itching with sharp little sensations and he saw bandy-legged herds of insects drinking until their black abdomens were bloated. His hands were gloved with them. His neck too. Maybe they were sand flies as the ground was often marshy. He had no strength or balance to knock them away so he let them feed. *At least someone is getting something to drink*. He smiled, but it hurt the roof of his skull and took him seconds to ease the smile from his face, so that he was only in the rhythmic pain and not the dizzy white agony. He would have liked to share the thought with silent plodding Dom, but speech had become impossible.

He wondered if there was any synaptic fluid left in the ball sockets of his hips. A terrible bony grinding and clicking was felt throughout his body after every ungainly step now. Whitish dots speckled his vision. To turn around and check on Dom involved stopping and turning his whole body about, because the movement of his neck created streak lightning inside his skull. So he stopped turning about and checking on Dom. And when he did pause to ease over a rock, or a fallen dead tree, Dom often banged into him and grunted. They were walking so close together, and at such a slow pace, any pause threatened to topple them both.

Luke was too wretched in body and spirit to think long about dear Hutch any more, and poor Phil, whom they were leaving behind. As for the other thing that was surely following them, he would not allow its presence into his exhaustion and delirium either. If he could help it. *Not that*. They would meet it again soon enough. He knew it. He assumed Dom knew it too.

At 2 p.m. Luke threw away his crutch and sank to all fours. He would continue on his hands and knees. It was better to have his broken head closer to the earth.

Dom said something, but he didn't hear it. Luke just pointed ahead of himself, to correct their passage down a rise and into an incongruously sparse glade, in which the dappling light and dark shadows looked inviting. It was also damp and he wondered if he might extract moisture from the peaty soil.

Behind him Dom's crutch clacked against the stones and tree roots as he made his own teetering descent. Every step made his companion grunt in protest.

At the bottom Luke lay against the cold ground and closed

his eyes. Gingerly, he placed his swollen red hands on the outside of the bandage as if to hold in place the shattered crockery of his skull. The tissues of his brain must be bloated now with a great swelling because he could feel tremors inside the vertebrae of his lower back.

He imagined a doctor saying you shouldn't move at all. *Don't move. It's the worst thing you can do with a head trauma.* But he wondered if there was any truth to the imaginary physician's words. He knew nothing about first aid. Or survival, or how to find water and nutrition if the supermarkets were closed. Or what the direction of the wind could tell him, or what information was held in the colour of the sky. He just reacted to shit that had already happened. He was hopeless and broken and deserved to perish. *I am of the generation of arse*, he mouthed and then laughed silently. *We couldn't find water in a reservoir. When we walk in a forest we all die. We are but baby birds fallen from nests to an unforgiving earth.*

He thought he could hear water and sat up. But it was a breeze. So he sucked at the leaves where the drizzle speckled their bitter waxy blades. Went around the clearing like it was a clock face and he was the minute hand, sucking the leaves. Sometimes a whole drop of rainwater would splash onto his tongue but never reach the back of his throat. He licked the wet bark of a tree. He opened his mouth to the sky, but the rain fell onto his face, not into his gaping maw.

In the corner of his squeezed-shut eyes that were hurt by even the faint light of shadows, he saw the blurred orange shape of Dom in his waterproof, picking up leaves and bits of bark. He tried to swallow water from them like they were oyster shells and he was gulping their slippery flesh down. His face was a dirty grimace covered in beard and shit.

Luke checked the compass and held one red hand against the left side of his head like a singer trying to find a note. Through one eye, which seemed to be filling with brown smoke, he could see that they were crawling in the right direction. And then he thought of the vision he had seen from the tree he climbed. That distant edge of the forest. The defined boundary, and the flat mossy stones beyond it. He thought he'd seen water out there too. Maybe he had. Water must have been collecting in stony bits and basins that he could push his face into.

Flies whined in the moist air and gathered like iron filings against the bloodied turban of bandage on his head.

He stood up. He wanted to get to the end of the trees. The short rest had allowed a pang of desire to motivate him again.

'Let's go. Not far,' he tried to say to Dom, but it sounded like a gargle and made him swallow furiously, and he knew it was the last time he would speak.

Dom hobbled towards him and they left the clearing.

Just before six, he had to stop again and crawl on to a fat boulder, because the dizzy spell was so great his stomach convulsed and his skin froze. Somewhere behind him, Dom made a sudden noise.

Dom's voice seemed unnaturally loud. It wasn't quite a word, but must have been a grunt of relief because Luke was allowing them another break. There had been so many now. They rested as much as they moved. Every few metres. And they needed to constantly suck the stones and engulf the wet leaves with their hot mouths. In the distance, Dom's feet kicked out at something, scuffling up the leaves.

Once the swooping of his head settled, Luke squinted through one eye and stood up to continue his uncoordinated tiptoeing and groaning. He tried to grunt while pointing one arm at a thicket in which he thought he could see a trail winding closer to salvation.

And into the tangle he went, the nettles whisking against his waterproof and snagging at the legs of his trousers. Vines would curl like tentacles and he would take a step back until they released him and then step that leg over the vines into more nettles. A familiar pattern they had followed for days. There were rents in his trousers now. Snags and ladders had become holes into which the thorns and gnats could find him.

Behind him, he sensed Dom's shape. Stepping carefully, in his footsteps. Maybe watching out for him should he suddenly lose his balance and collapse into the stinging morass of vine and spike. Every step he took was followed by one of Dom's. There was even something comforting in the way they moved in synchronicity. And Dom was so close to him now, the presence of his bulk was tangible at Luke's back. But god he stank. Even though his nose and mouth were full of dry blood, Luke could smell Dom's heavy breath and sweat-saturated clothes.

But the thicket worsened and without a machete, they would have to retrace their steps and circumnavigate the ridge of thorns. It's only getting thicker because we are not far from the end, Luke told himself. But we must go back.

He stopped and slowly turned his body about.

Then opened his good eye wide. Among the twenty metres

of bracken and nettles he had waded into, there was no sign of Dom.

He frowned. Then a cold feeling of breath-stopping fright brought his heart beat into his ears and eyes and blurred his vision.

Dom must have gone back already. *Because I heard him following me. Every step of the way in here.*

Luke clenched his mind against the sudden nausea of panic that tried to engulf him.

At the far end of the thicket they had entered, he could see into the dark stony glade where they had just rested. But there was no sign of Dom in there either.

Holding his head tenderly, he swallowed and swallowed until a trace of saliva moistened his throat. He called out for Dom.

What was left of his grunty voice seemed to get lost in the woody space that vaulted above and burrowed into darkness on every side. Again he called out. And again. Then with both throbbing eyes wide open he peered, he scrutinized, he begged every inch of forest in the distance for a sign of Dom's orange waterproof.

Nothing.

Dom was no longer with him.

When had he seen him last?

He took his memory backwards; slowly through the recent minutes. By that rock on which he had so recently slumped, he had last seen Dom. No. He had heard him there, but had not actually laid eyes upon him. Dom had been behind him at the rock. He had made a sound. That's right. A grunt, or cry. A sound of surprise? Then he had shuffled his feet about. Kicked at something on the ground.

Maybe he then walked off in another direction, blind and oblivious with exhaustion and pain from his knee. Stumbled away from Luke and got himself lost.

Could not have done because as Luke so recently walked through the nettles, he had heard Dom close at his heels, almost on top of him. Had not seen him, no. But had heard him and sensed him and you cannot be mistaken about that. They had been close together. Almost touching.

The stench.

Luke raised his knife.

FORTY-FOUR

Loneliness came with a suddenness that made Luke shiver. Then came his struggle with himself to not go hysterical with panic. He could do little more than hold himself together when one of the others was near, but now they were all gone . . .

His mind spoke to itself. Immediately tried to create companions in that painful mess under the bandage. But the pathetic voices stopped as soon as they began, like nervous children falling into an embarrassed silence at the sudden appearance of a stern adult.

He remained motionless in the damp clearing where the last two of them had been together. The trees glared at him, patient but unsympathetic, awaiting his next move. The rain dropped with its usual indifference. He was dying of thirst in his ignorance of where it collected on the ground.

No one answered his croaks. He wondered how long he should wait. Was there anyone to wait for?

He shuddered. Gripped the knife. He wanted it to come for him. Right then. To rush low and quick from the underbrush. To lope from the shadows. He was ready to look right into the bright eyes of a devil's head. He could take the sight and reek of it up close. Would thrust the last of himself at its taut flanks. Rip that sneaky killer a new mouth with a Swiss Army knife.

He thought of a black beard wet with hot gore, a snout red in the thin light from where it had been snatching at the coils and plump offal of his friends. Tearing and scattering. Before carrying off the flopping white figures to make its grotesque installations in the trees.

To what end? Why destroy such complicated and sophisticated creations as his friends? Why demolish all those memories and feelings and thoughts that made them? His mates.

Tears stung Luke's eyes. He shivered.

They had come together when young. Were drawn to each other as curious attractions formed permanent bonds amongst all of those people at university, at a time and in a way that can never happen again. They listened to music together and talked for days without pause. They woke in the morning to see each other. They occupied each other's physical space and head space, and wanted each other's approval and needed to make each other smile. They had been good together until life and women and work and urges for new places pulled them apart. But there was enough of that connection remaining to bring them back together. Out here. Fifteen years later. To find each other all over again.

His friends had been destroyed for no reason he could think of. They had been destroyed like most people were destroyed. By just being in the wrong place. After all of that development and growing and cultivating and caution and survivable self-destruction and failure and regeneration and struggling and coping, they had just walked through the wrong bunch of bloody trees. And that was that.

Come on you bastard.

He growled at the air, and begged madness to take him

away from the paralysing realization of what was lost forever. Because what was the point of reason? You lived briefly, died, were forgotten. Just to glimpse this was enough of a cause to go insane or to put yourself away. Out here you were butchered and then tossed into a sodden crypt. Piled up with the mottled bones of strangers and dead cattle.

They were my mates.

The rain pattered near him and the wind made ocean sounds up in the distant treetops. But no one answered him and nothing came for him now he was ready and unafraid and prepared to let his tortured and tired, so tired, and messed-up consciousness end.

He stood alone and placed his hands on either side of his head. The pain banged from recent exertions. He closed his eyes and he thought of those who were gone, those friends he had lost. Best friends to the end; an end that came too soon, without warning.

As you are, boys, I will be. Soon.

He turned and shuffled away into the trees.

FORTY-FIVE

Lying on his back, Luke looked up into the distant canopy of a million leaves and the endless networks of branches. In places he could see the sky and it was dark. For a moment, he wondered where he was. Then remembered and closed his eyes again.

He passed himself from tree to tree, using the great trunks and lower branches as crutches. The constant swoop and hover of flies became a loud whine when one of them disappeared inside his ear to probe. His hands were wet with lymph from where he had clumsily torn at the great white lumps growing into his cuffs. Some of the bites thickened under his watch strap. The splashes the insects made when he swatted them made him thirstier. He prayed it would rain again so the clouds of flies might go. They weren't supposed to be here; that's the main reason they went hiking in September, because of the interminable stream of mosquitoes. Hutch had not mentioned these sand flies, or gnats.

Was this the right direction? He wondered how far he had staggered since leaving the tent. It felt like a month ago. The previous evening occurred in another lifetime. How far now to the end of the trees? Then he stopped caring and just continued; one step at a time, bracing himself for the migraine-judder before each foot landed upon the forest floor.

After every ten steps he leaned against a tree or sat down in the wet verdure and waited for his vision to settle. His breathing was so heavy that the very act of drawing breath was tiring him as much as pushing his leaden legs forward, time after time.

He became oblivious to every feature he passed. The forest was just a blur he barely saw but clambered about in. Maybe his body was breaking itself down, one fat cell at a time to fuel this death march. It had been so long since he'd eaten. The burning in his gut had turned to a combination of nausea and aches as his stomach clenched upon itself.

To alleviate the terrible fatigue and boredom and bouts of terror, he counted what he'd eaten: five cereal bars and half a Dairy Milk bar in thirty-six hours. He repeated the menu in a silent mantra.

The last time he'd drunk any fluid was in the morning; a cup of thick bitter coffee. The sweat on him turned cold and he stopped again to dry-heave against a tree.

At 10, his vision was down to five feet, but he continued hobbling in a dark and blurry void that was more disorientation than direction.

His head was down. Eyes mostly closed. But he suffered a sudden sense that he was not alone. Luke looked up, certain that the presence of other figures had encroached into his immediate space. And he saw, in the dimming gloom between the trees, a whole host of little white figures. Upright, perfectly still, repeated to the ends of his vision. He screwed up his good eye, blinked.

And all of the . . . children? . . . were gone.

Dwarf willows in thin light; he'd mistaken them for an indistinct crowd of little white people; thin and poised and staring.

Sometime after midnight, he was sure Hutch had begun to walk behind him. Phil was there too. They had come to their senses and realized this complicated and well-orchestrated practical joke had gone too far, now that he was so lonely and hurt and lost. They were too embarrassed to see his reaction to their cruel ingenuity so kept their faces turned away from him. And he was so upset that they had been fooling with him that he ignored them. He felt sulky and betrayed and wanted to sob hard. Eventually they gave up following him.

When Dom caught up with him and fell into step again, Luke was too tired to speak to his friend or to ask him where he had been. But he smiled and hoped Dom could sense, in the lightless depths of the nocturnal forest, that he was pleased to see him again.

When he stopped to rest and slap about for his torch – he was sure he had one earlier – Dom had wandered off again.

Sitting on a stone Luke passed out.

And began a conversation with Charlotte in the Prince of Wales pub in Holland Park back home. It was sunny and they were sitting outside, just like they did on their second date when she had come out of the tube station in a short skirt and leather boots and he had been mute with desire and astonishment because she had been wearing trainers and jeans when they first met, when he had gone home content that a girl had taken his number, though was not that bothered about seeing her again. But then was so pleased to be with her that second time, and had decided right there in the beer garden to make a go of it with her. He told her she was a 'fox' and she smiled. She reached across the table and touched his face, bit her bottom lip and told him he was 'lovely'. They sat together for hours. They kissed and told each other everything about their jobs, their hometowns, their families, their last relationships, all of that stuff that can come out on an early date with someone you immediately care about.

When he awoke, dragged from sleep by the ache in his neck and the throbbing behind the slice in his forehead, he continued to talk to Charlotte until he realized he was alone and leaning against a dead tree in a forest. Moisture had soaked up through his trousers and into his underwear. He was sodden and he shivered. Where was his sleeping bag?

Through the upper branches of the trees he could see the sky was turning the pale blue-grey of early morning. He looked at his watch: 6 a.m. He had slept for three or four hours. Why had it not killed him here? He tried to work this out, but was too tired and in too much pain to investigate the idea much. Was too thirsty to even swallow. His lips were crusted with salt.

On his hands and knees he moved so slowly.

Just another twenty feet then lie down and let the darkness take you.

Pressing the compass to his one good eye, he saw nothing. Dropped the compass but felt the loop of string around his neck go tight, but could not catch the compass as it swung like a pendulum above the dark earth beneath him.

Just go up this incline to that tree.

Down at the bottom of this glade are two stones upon which you can sit.

Through those two spruce trees the nettles seem to clear.

Behind that copse of fir there could be water. It looks like the kind of place where there could be water.

The trees thin at the top of that rise. Let's go up it sideways. Might be easier.

At the summit of a mound of earth, around which the forest parted as if to make room for a place where people might gather under the solitary tree, he sat and felt oddly comfortable. Here his skin and head went warm and the pain in his head settled to a distant scream.

He opened an eye and looked down the slope beyond the grubby toes of his hiking boots. The dawn was red. Or was that his vision? The sunrise blazed through the trees to his left, to the east. He turned his head to see it with the only eye he could keep open. And beyond the scattering of trees down there in the rocky soil he could detect a great whitish space widening out forever, where great black trunks and boughs did not suffocate the red light. He squinted his good eye at the ocean of space and scarlet light beyond the trees. And he wondered if this was the end of the terrible forest, or the beginning of hell, or just the end of his mind. It mattered little because he would not move again. Could not. There was not one more shuffle or dragging lurch left inside him. There was nothing left inside him but the dimming of his parts and the quietening of his wordless thoughts.

But what was that thing standing upright with hell on fire behind its long body? As tall as three grown men standing on each other's shoulders, at the edge of the black wood; what was it that filled the gap between two epic trees? It was nothing. Because when he tried to see it more fully the blurry vision of the figure vanished, leaving only the scarlet sky and trees.

But the bark he heard so close to where he was slumped was not a figment of his imagination. No, that was something he had heard before. That dog-bullock cough, from a thing no trespasser here had ever seen and lived to tell of, was real enough. As real as the ridged bark pressing into his spine and the cold wind that curled around his damp face.

Reaching out in front of his unmoving body, he extended a hand that gripped the knife. Pointed it at the misty treeline with the crimson furnace of dawn burning through the branches and shrubs.

He must have passed out and stopped breathing because he suddenly awoke with the sound of his own shocked inhalation in his ears and wondered if he had just been dreaming. So what brought him back out of that endless sinking into a darkness where he could not breathe? *A voice.* He had heard someone speak.

But he could not care enough and could not stop his head from falling forward again. He felt his chin rest upon his breastbone and closed his useful eye. Still he held the knife, but could not raise his arm at the voice that kept coming towards him. So close now. Calling. Calling. Softly. Calling in the way a loved one summons another, with music in their voice. But it was not coming quickly enough to pull him out of this warm smothering darkness, so complete, into which he sank.

II

SOUTH OF HEAVEN

FORTY-SIX

They were close.

Voices.

Footsteps.

People.

A muttering in Swedish or Norwegian outside the warm heavy darkness that engulfed him. A woman, youngish. And . . . two men, their tones deeper. He sensed their presence above him, over him. The voices of the people then came together, near his feet.

He was lying down; his limbs and back were stiff, but sunken into a soft surface. Under his shoulders and buttocks, his skin burned where it touched . . . bedding.

Something was wrapped around his head; he could feel its touch, its pressure, could sense its size, covering his eyes as well as his skull like a big ill-fitting hat.

When he tried to open his eyes there was resistance from his eyelids. They were gummed shut. One eyelid partially broke apart and a streak of white pain shot backwards through his pupil. He closed the eye again. If he moved his head at all it would hurt, perhaps terribly, and not stop hurting. He knew this without putting it to the test.

He gasped. Tried to speak. But there were no words inside the hot arid place that was his throat. A swishing rustle, as if from long heavy skirts sweeping a wooden floor, came out of the darkness and closed about him. And then a small dry hand touched his cheek, to calm him, to bid him be still. An elderly voice made shushing sounds.

Before he remembered anything from the time before his waking, his being there, he sank away, back into a healing darkness and its blessed warmth.

FORTY-SEVEN

He awoke so thirsty he could not swallow and his lips would tear like rice paper if he forced them to part. It was later than before, much later. A great period of sleep had left the back of his eyes feeling bruised.

This was the same place as before, he assumed with a vague recollection of being half aware of lying in this position, on this same surface, at some other time recently. Though something notable was missing now. But what was it? From inside him, there had been a removal or a raising of something, like a weight. A *something* that had driven him, wasted him, spent him, left him witless, big-eyed and alight with panic for so long.

Fear.

Fear. The choking of it. The flinching and the paralysis. The relentless expectation of its cold jolt. Fear had finally gone from him.

And the time before he slept came back to him then. Like a gush of darkness through his mouth and eyes and ears. It even felt wet and cold, the terrible rushing of recollection through him, and it filled his nose with the stink of mulch and dead wood.

Scratched and bleeding, he'd walked to the end of himself. Lungs had burned and legs had cramped, but were now only warm and tired; ghostly outlines of scolds and scars about his tortured body told him a story he did not want repeated.

Stricken faces were lit up in his mind. Hutch. Phil. Dom. Up in the trees he saw the rags again, the rags and bones. Then he recalled the thin silhouettes of gaunt trees standing before the fire of a red sky. As did something else. It was among the trees, it was of the trees, and it was apart from the trees. Something upright, and watching him before a backdrop of some strange planet ablaze. The electric memory of the smashing of his skull, like a china bowl under a hammer, jolted his whole body. And he was disorientated by the noise of his own shriek in the darkness.

But he was saved and was now lying in a bed. He had been found, attended to. His heart burst.

Wrenching his eyes fully open, he felt the sensation of ripping cloth inside his head. A thud of pain behind his eyes followed. Then there was another and another thump, but these were weaker survivable aftershocks, and were smothered deeper inside his skull.

In this place of his salvation, the air tasted unclean. He thought of used clothes in a charity shop. Thirst burned like salt from a swollen tongue down to his navel. He opened his wooden lips and exposed his gritty mouth to the taste of neglect: moisture in old timber, dust, bed linen so oily it smelled of a hot animal.

He looked into the pale blank space before his face. Eyes contracting, refocusing, he saw the stitches of a bandage. One layer of material, close enough to his eyelashes to hamper a blink. Faint light seeped through the fabric. He recalled a vague sensation of his head being rolled between quick gentle hands while he slept. Caring hands that nearly made him surface from the fathoms of damaged sleep. It had been a long time ago: weeks? Days?

Something heavy and thick was covering him from toes to chin. He was warm under its weight despite the stink. Things inside the coverings bit him repeatedly with pinprick teeth. The back of his thighs itched. New constellations of sharp bites spread around his ribs.

Between his thighs and under his buttocks the bedding was also wet. It alarmed him more than the lice.

Concentrating hard, he moved his hips, his legs, his feet, then bent his knees, then his elbows. His neck he kept still, and he merely looked up, straight ahead, into the grubby fabric hanging over his eyes while his body reacquainted itself with sensation, with definition and with its possibilities.

Slowly, he raised his swollen leaden head from the greasy pillow and the scent of dusty feathers rose with him. Tilting his head forward, he squinted under the bandage and down his body.

And saw rolling hills of ancient eiderdown, patch-worked with colours faded or dark with grime; squares of disparate fabrics reaching to the bumps of his concealed feet. The surface of the coverings were level with the sides of the wooden frame he lay inside. It was like he was inside an old wooden chest or coffin; he had been sunk deep within its inflexible confines and covered over with antique swaddling. It was some kind of bed, but a structure he was immediately afraid there might be a lid for.

Carefully, he twisted his head to the left and in the greyish light saw a cabinet made from dark timber beside the bed. A dark wooden jug stood beside a wooden cup. Without his consent his throat contracted but barely completed a painful swallow.

Carefully, he moved on to his left side then shuffled into a foetal position. Propping his upper body on one elbow, he reached for the mug. It was heavy. Full of dusty warmish water. All of which he swallowed, only tasting it afterwards when his mouth became tangy with rust and sparked steely with minerals. Wild water. Well water.

A bludgeoning ache behind his eyes rolled in waves and brought his eyelids down fast as storm shutters. His limbs turned to liquid with exhaustion after the simple exertions. *Am I that broken?* He eased back into the imprint that his long occupancy of the bed had shaped into the bedding. He seemed to sink deeper down than before, the odiferous cavern of unventilated quilt pressing behind his descent.

Now he was still, the pain inside his skull rang more softly, and the slosh of water in his gut lulled him back to restfulness.

He was saved. 'Saved'. He was saved from the terrible forest and what walked through it. He was alive and saved. Saved. Alive. Saved. His face became wet with tears. He sniffed. And then dropped into sleep.

FORTY-EIGHT

There are people in the room.

Again?

Leaning towards you while you stand in the metal tub, they inspect your white body. They are old. So very old. Every inch of each face is furrowed and wrinkled into clumps of yellowish skin, like under the eyes, which are hard to make out beyond glints within the sunken sockets. But when one of them puts their head through a thin strand of light, you can see a milky-blue cornea surrounded by a discoloured iris.

One of them could be a woman, but there is so little hair on the patchy skull. Just a few white bits around the sides of the head; the skin traversed by blackish veins. The other could be a man, or maybe even the body of a bird without feathers, shrunken and starved into a shape of sticks.

Bent in their loose black garments, like robes hanging from bare bone, they squint and peer at your hips, ribs and shoulders.

Fingers with knuckles the size of peach stones, covered in skin as translucent as the flesh of cold chicken, prod at your freckled belly, as if you are a joint of meat. Dark teeth spike behind the tight grins of lipless mouths, grooved like muzzles.

You try and speak but you can't get your breath. They mutter to each other in words you cannot understand. Lilting, musical voices, that rise up and down in strange cadences.

Tallow candles are lit and placed about the walls, making shadows flicker and rise up and down the dark wood, highlighting the horns and discoloured bones nailed to the planks.

Then from above you, through the ceiling, you hear the knocking. The banging of wood on wood. Mad tappings and rappings without rhythm, like a child with a stick and a saucepan. And maybe it is an animal, a dog or something up there, because something is whining. The sounds are dulled through the smoke-blackened ceiling; this whining and mewling amidst the banging.

You are grateful that this makes the old people in the dirty black wool move away from you. But you are only relieved for a moment, because the figures move towards the door where they seem to suddenly be in a hurry to get out. One of them fumbles with the door latch and the other peers up at the ceiling, with eyes full of glee, and more teeth showing than before, at the sound of hard feet resounding against the floor upstairs; unsteady at first, and then cantering.

You try to follow the old people out of the door, but it's not possible for you to move and step over the edge of the black iron tub. Your ankles are tied together with something thin and painful where it squeezes your skin, and when you look up you can see your hands going purple from where they are bound together at the wrist with a leather strap that loops over a blackened iron hook in the ceiling.

Then the old people are gone and you are alone in the cold metal basin. But something is coming down from the room upstairs. You can hear its bone feet on the wooden steps of a staircase outside this room, and you can hear the sound of something squeezing its body down and through a narrow passage, accompanied by quick gusts of excited breath.

A thick shape fills the doorway of your room. You scream when you realize it is coming through on all fours, with the long horns out front.

Luke woke with a cry.

Panted hard like he had just smashed across the finishing line of a sprint down a running track. He called out for his mother.

The remnant of his waking was swift and the nightmare receded to a sepia blur, then vanished. He was awake and gasping into the old bandage tied about the front of his face, reaching down to the tip of his nose. He blinked rapidly. Moaned. Because for a few disorientating moments, he thought he was hanging from the ceiling, tied by his wrists. But it was nothing more than the gibberish of shock after waking in darkness.

Moist and warm, the moulding of the bedding clung about him and outlined his physical shape; prone, stretched out.

He peered beneath the bandages, his eyes slitted to restrict the scorching of the thin light. He saw the murky outline of the old eiderdown; the sides of the box bed; perhaps a dim dark wall beyond his feet.

Still safe. Still saved.

He'd had a bad dream. No problem there. No surprises. There would be others.

He thought of his open wound; the cracks in his skull. He touched the bandage.

Breathed out, slowly. *Sit tight.* He was safe and help was on its way.

He closed his eyes.

FORTY-NINE

So many violent sounds smashed him from sleep. For a few dazed seconds, he continued to mumble to the thin seated figures of whom he had been dreaming. Then he addressed the origin of the noise erupting from somewhere beneath his feet, 'Please. Who?'

Something or someone was screaming. It was a high-pitched, inhuman cry. Beneath these relentless shrieks, a sound like the plates of the earth grinding together in an earthquake became an impossible rhythm. *Drums.*

The bed vibrated. He felt a thicker thrumming sensation in his hands and feet, and in the pit of his stomach. *Bass.*

Music.

He released his breath. The entire room was not filled with a million insects buzzing against each other, inside some giant smoking hive; these were guitar strings being shredded rapidly and amplified into distortion. Some type of extreme music was erupting from nearby. From out of speakers so worn, damaged, and too small for the task set them, they crackled and snapped like cooking fat.

Luke came up from the stinking eiderdown and slumped onto his elbows; his eyes behind the bandages were stuck between a squint and full closure. He clawed at his face. Shoved the bandage up his forehead. The entire loose arrangement of dressings dropped off his head, as if a cap had been tugged away by an unexpected hand from behind. Cold stale air fell fast and cooled against his scalp. He forced his eyelids wide apart. Focused on the room. And then whimpered.

Three figures stood at the foot of the bed, and the very sight of them made him quite sure that the hell of the Bible was real, and that he had awoken in one of its rooms.

Black horns jutted from the head of the goat-headed figure in the middle. Hard as oak, polished like stone, the horns rose from a bristly forehead; curving outwards along their length, before tilting vertically into sharp points at their conclusion.

The sight of them took his breath away and thrust a snapshot of another dark place that made no sense into his mind; a mind that was now opening and closing its doors and windows like a film speeded to a blur.

The goat's coal-black ears stuck out at ninety degrees from the great motionless skull, as if the creature had just been surprised in a forest glade. The yellow eyes with their large oval pupils were curiously feminine, softened by light-brown eyebrows and long eyelashes. Black fur, as glossy as a horse's tail, dropped from beneath the beast's chin.

Alone, even without the support of its two ghastly companions, the goat seemed to rise and not only fill the dim room to the ceiling, but command the entire space. It was blasphemously majestic, and shocking, and maddening, all at once.

Luke expected its horns to drop, and for it to begin a terrible rooting through the eiderdown. He imagined himself retreating up the bed to the rear wall where he would be gored. Opened, ragged up the front and emptied steaming into the bedclothes. He thought of dear Hutch, of Phil, and his face screwed into an involuntary palsy.

But the goat just stood above him, motionless, almost solemn; towering right up to the brownish ceiling.

Was this their executioner? But if so then why was it wearing a dusty black suit and grubby collarless shirt? The fraying sleeves of the jacket were halfway up its front legs. Or were they forearms? The soiled jacket was so tight across the shoulders, the figure's long front limbs were pinched against its torso. It looked like the creature had taken the suit from a much smaller dead man.

Luke looked at the other two figures.

Like the cast of some degenerate Victorian pantomime, they crowded the upright goat and issued across the bed a scent of disused props, of dusty backstage places, of old sweat.

The hare was too terrible to look upon for long. And the fact that it was diminutive, no taller than five feet, somehow made its visage even worse to behold than the goat with its appalling height.

Tatty brownish fur sprung in clumps from a long face. Mad eyes, fiery with amber but also black with rage at their heart, bulged from bony eye sockets. A pair of tall ears were cocked forward, almost twitching. More similar to tusks than teeth, two long pillars of discoloured bone dropped from its dirty black mouth, guaranteeing its prey a deep and fatal penetration.

With a gasp, Luke raised a hand feebly, as if to ward off the toothy menacing he anticipated, so busy and sharp, about his throat. Tufty, stained and stitched, its long neck bushed and bristled down to a pair of naked milky shoulders, and to a heavy bust, tipped with pink nipples, bright and puckered hard.

Aghast, Luke looked away from it. Demands for his attention were now being made by the lamb. It snorted. The first sound any of the figures had made. He stared into the lamb's dead bluish eyes, fringed with pink rims and bleached eyelashes. It seemed to regard him with a great sadness, like a face from a freak-show daguerreotype. Fur stiff and yellowing with age was close-cropped about the head but still managed to curl like a human child's. Atop its head, a garland of dried flowers had been entwined with a spray of heather. Beneath its little square teeth and small chin, a stiff circular collar of lace jutted out. Brittle with age and watermarked, the gown it wore brought to mind both a burial shroud and an old-fashioned christening dress made for a little girl. But the latter juvenile suggestions of its attire did not soften Luke's shock at seeing the upright lamb at the foot of his bed. Did not soften it at all, but prolonged it.

Amidst the cacophony of the shrieking music, and as his mind struggled to comprehend the surreal horror of this welcoming party, he felt unable to move, or speak, or to even think clearly. And his visitors just stood there, still as mannequins, staring at him, their bright hideously animate eyes unmoving, as if they were waiting in expectation for something from him: a word, a scream, some feeble defence.

Suddenly, the great black head of the goat turned to the lamb and something passed between them. The lamb turned sideways, revealing its pink whisker-filled ear, and bent down towards the floor that Luke could not see. A white human arm shot out of the lace gown, the forearm girlishly pale and thin, but blackened with spiky tattoos above the wrist. The music abruptly ceased. Silence expanded.

Luke sat up fully, backed against the end of his little box and pulled his knees into his stomach. His shock lessened in the sudden quiet, but not by much. Beneath him, his quick movements disrupted the dirty sheepskins from a bed of old hay that filled the little box.

Why am I not in a hospital bed? And he also wondered whether this second unwelcome appearance of a black goat into his life had burned up another of the fuses inside him, and that without the fuse he would remain a very nervous man for the rest of his life.

The goat raised two long-fingered human hands. Which were the first things attached to the creature that Luke was pleased to see, as he had been expecting hooves.

Dirty fingernails atop the slender fingers gripped the furry cheeks of the goat head and pushed upwards, removing the mask, but revealing a face beneath it that Luke at once wished had remained covered.

The face was caked in some kind of white cosmetic. It bleached the skin of all colour save the black lines cutting grooves into the forehead and at each side of the down-turned sullen mouth. The eyes had been made especially hollow-looking with solid patches of black make-up, caked inside the sockets. The lips had been painted black too, but inside the hot mask much of the cosmetics had sweated off the thick vulval mouth of the figure, which sneered at Luke and exposed teeth the yellow-brown of unboiled corn.

Long black hair, clotted with sweat, fell like oily string

about the figure's large mournful face. Dark lines, carved as much as painted from between the bridge of the nose and into the forehead, gave the pallid face a permanent frown. The eyes were a cold bright blue; their expression intense, contemptuous, self-serious. The man's beard was long and matted. Streaks of white greasepaint had run into it, frosting the hair, making Luke think of the foliage of wintry trees glimpsed on the banks of model railways.

Taking in his new surroundings as quickly as possible, Luke looked for a door in the plain but stained walls. Between the hare and the goat he spied one where two of the unadorned walls joined; a narrow aperture. It was closed. And all about him, the ancient plaster bulged from between warped timber, giving the room a misshapen bulbous character that made him even more uneasy. If that were possible, and he found that it was. A small window covered in brownish net curtains emitted a smoky light into the room.

Inside the ancient bed, with the sheepskin so soiled it made his skin feel rubbery, he realized that his body was also still filthy from his ordeal in the forest. The fact that he had not been bathed concerned him so much, he felt that if he dwelled upon it, he would begin to cry with all of his heart.

'Welcome,' the white-faced man said. The voice was extremely deep, but affected. The sudden brief animation of his mouth and the timbre of his voice made the man appear younger than Luke had at first thought when the figure unmasked. He now put the figure in his early twenties, even his late teens.

Luke coughed, to clear his throat of what felt like splinters. Swallowed. 'Where am I?' His voice was a croak, dried out, insubstantial.

'South of heaven,' the unsmiling figure replied in the deep voice that sounded even more absurd on its second airing.

A thin delinquent hyena laugh erupted from inside the lamb's head; the harshest edges of the sound muffled by the confines of the mask. The figure leaned forward to grasp its own woolly horror of a head under the tiny ears and removed it after a twisting struggle. Straightening his spine and snapping his head backwards, the youth whipped his own long black hair from his wet face. Several strands no thicker than shoe laces clung to his moist cheeks.

The lamb's thin face, which struggled between being boyishly pretty and weasel-like, was also plastered with white make-up. But crimson streaks had been daubed down his cheeks as if made by tears of blood, and also crafted to run from each nostril and from the corners of his downturned black-lipped mouth, like newly shed red blood.

Luke swallowed. 'Who are you?'

In response to the question, the lamb issued a horrible sound that was both a bark and a high-pitched screech. Then the youth giggled to himself. Within the black caves of eye make-up, his pale-blue eyes were bright with glee. It sounded as if he had screamed, 'Oscar Ray.'

Luke frowned, swallowed again, and again. 'Oscar Ray?'

'Oskerai!' the figure shrieked again, looking even more damaged as it extended two spindly white arms from the nightgown and thrust them into the air.

'We are the wild hunt,' the tall figure said, his tone pompous, the words heavily accented.

'The final gathering,' a petulant, excitable female voice cried from inside the terrible head of the hare. Despite knowing there was a human being inside the hare head-piece,

Luke knew he would never feel comfortable within the presence of its mad eyes and dirty teeth.

'I don't understand,' Luke said, and hoped they could not read the depth of his fear and alarm; he was old enough to know it was always a mistake to reveal such in the company of the unstable.

Off came the wretched head of the female hare, to reveal the plump head of a young woman in her late teens, possibly younger. She too had painted her face, but where the others had created grotesque expressions resembling imperious grimaces or bloodied scowls, the girl's use of white face-paint and black kohl had been more artful. Her spherical head depicted a permanent expression of spiteful mirth, as if the bright red splashes about her lips and chin were evidence of a recent sadistic act performed with the use of her mouth.

To engage their sympathy, and to put an end to this unnerving game, Luke touched the hot part of his head that felt too big to be healthy. Crusted blood in a thick seam indented his probing fingertips. The wound was still wet and open in the middle. The dressing behind him on the greyish pillow was the same one Dom had clumsily wrapped about his skull when he was out cold on the high ground, on the last night they spent outdoors. The white-faced youths had not even attempted to dress his head with a new bandage, let alone bathe his tormented and filthy body.

Now he was sitting up, the pain deep inside his skull, and the constant swoop of nausea it transmitted, made him horribly aware of his desire for an X-ray. 'Hospital. A doctor. My head.' They continued to watch him without emotion. 'I need help. Please.'

The youth who had been the goat defiantly raised the chin on his mournful grimacing face. 'Soon.' With that, he turned, ducked his head, and strode noisily at the tiny door. He must have been nearly seven feet tall; his height freakish within the dimensions of the room. Steel shin guards flashed upon the giant's biker boots, where they shot out from the too-tight and short trouser legs. The thick heels of his boots were studded with either rivets or small nails.

The hare suddenly shrieked at Luke and stuck out a tongue so incongruously red between its liquorice-black lips, that Luke physically recoiled. On her fat dirty feet, she then skipped after the giant and squeezed herself through the doorway.

Luke looked to the remaining youth, who appeared even more idiotic when alone, dressed in his horrid nightgown, the narrow face daubed with clown paint.

'My friends,' Luke pleaded. 'They were killed. Murdered. You have to call the police. Now. You hear me?'

Head tilted to one side, the youth screwed his face into a quizzical expression. Then, imitating the taller youth by adopting a deep voice and mocking tone, said, 'You must understand, there is no police here. No doctors. You are many miles away from such things. But you are lucky to be alive. Very lucky, my friend. We have no phone. But someone has gone to fetch help for you. Soon it comes.'

Bewildered, Luke gaped from inside the reeking box bed. 'I don't—'

Within the nightgown, the figure puffed out its chest. 'You are fine. Be cool.' Then he turned, picked up the CD player, and followed his companions out the door.

The clunk of a heavy key inside an old iron lock preceded

the heavy booming of three sets of feet through a hollow wooden space, or a corridor, beyond the walls of the room. And for a long time after they had left him alone, Luke stared in mute shock at the locked door.

FIFTY

The clunk of a big key in the old lock of the door roused Luke from where he sat in a daze, on the side of the box bed.

He stood up too quickly, and fell against the cabinet. The wooden mug clanged against the floor, the jug wobbled sideways and jetted its remaining contents across the cabinet surface. The unlocking and opening of the door became hurried.

Before Luke could fully right himself, he caught sight of a small elderly woman in a long dress, moving swiftly from the door towards him. Somewhere under the long black gown, which concealed her body right up to the furrowed chin, her little feet knocked loudly against the wooden floorboards. The sound hurt his head.

With the faintest touch of her small hands, she guided more than moved him back to the bed. Where he sat, squinting through the shuddering waves of pain that surged from the middle of his head before crashing behind his eyes. He thought he would be sick. His vision broke into silvery dots and the back of his neck froze. Then he was sick. A great squeezing inside his stomach forced a trickle of dirty liquid out of his mouth. The elderly woman muttered something in Swedish.

At the furthest reaches of his bilious senses, he detected the presence of another figure in the room. When it spoke, in what reminded Luke of Norwegian more than Swedish, he recognized the voice to be that of the youth who had worn the lamb mask.

The nausea drained from Luke and the walls of the room stilled. He looked again at the old woman. Her face was expressionless, but her small black eyes glimmered in sockets so old the skin around her eyes reminded him of walnut shells. What he could see of them was strange and intense. He could not look into them for long.

Her lips had sunk inside her mouth; the chin below was deeply grooved and whiskered. The bright white hair about the tiny head was very thick but short, and looked like she had cut it herself, with a knife and a fork.

He suddenly wanted to laugh madly at this apparition, but he found her weirdness also filled him with a muting unease. Her skin was grey and also yellowy in places, like the flesh of an ageing smoker. She could not have been an inch taller than four feet. From a distance she would resemble a child in a high-necked dress, which looked homespun. Another notion that contributed to his discomfort. About the front of her black gown was a floor-length apron, once white, but now soiled brown with old water marks.

'I don't come near you if you are going to puke,' the grinning youth said from behind the elderly woman. The childlike lacy gown had gone from his skinny body. Instead he wore a black T-shirt emblazoned with the name Gorgoroth and a photograph of a group of men, their faces horribly disfigured with white, black, and blood-red make-up. The cracked white paint on the youth's face stopped under his chin, leaving his throat clean but still very pale. It was thin and made especially pointy with an Adam's apple. Between his feminine hands he held a tray. 'None of us can cook shit. We burn water! But she is OK. If you like fucking stew every day.'

Luke was not sure whether he should smile, or say thank you. He didn't know why he was here, or who these people were. He said nothing.

On the wooden plate, dark floury vegetables were covered with a brown lumpy gravy.

'We have drink. We make it ourselves, so it is very strong. Er . . . you call it . . . Moonshine. Moonshine! But maybe you puke very quickly if you drink it today, I think. So you get water.'

The tray was lowered and placed on the bed. Luke glanced at the youth's tattooed arms; ink crawled in black vines around circular runes. On the inside of one forearm was a Thor's hammer. A badly drawn inverted crucifix disfigured the back of a slender hand. Tucked inside his bullet belt was a long knife. The knife handle was made of dark bone. The blade was shiny against the dull leather of his trousers. The sight of it dried out Luke's mouth.

'Please,' he said. 'My name is Luke. I am hurt. I need . . . Please, I need for you to get help.'

The youth stood back. 'Luke eh? I am Fenris.' He smiled with pride. 'You know what that means?'

Luke stared blankly at him.

'It means Wolf.' He pronounced it *vulf*. 'Ha! Because I am very like the wolf, you know. As many have found out. And the other guy, his name is Loki. You know what it means?'

When no answer was coming from Luke's stupefied face, he said, 'Devil. Because, let me tell you, he is exactly that, my friend. And the girl with the great tits – though don't tell her I say so – is called Surtr. A pretty name for a demon, eh? It means fire. Her name too, it is the same as she is. You understand me?'

'Yes.' Luke did not want to hear another word from the figure he found baffling, and utterly idiotic.

The old woman continued to stare at him, which unnerved him, even though he still avoided looking directly into her almost imperceptible eyes in that small collapsed face. She did not smile. He imagined she never had done.

'So where you come from, Luke?'

'London. England,' he said automatically.

'Ah, London,' Fenris repeated, emphasizing the second syllable and pronouncing it 'don' not 'dun', like those with English as a second language often did. 'One day, I think, we will play there. At the Camden Underworld maybe. I have never been, but Loki, he has been to London.'

Luke's face felt heavy and almost ached from a lack of expression caused by his bemusement at the irrelevance of the youth's chatter. He could think of nothing to say, and part of him resisted pleading for help; instinctively, he felt it would do him no good.

'And how did you get from London to here, Luke?'

Luke looked at the floor, closed his eyes on the pain of recollection more than from the discomfort caused by the thin light. 'A holiday.'

The youth remained quiet, thinking hard on what Luke had just said. Then suddenly laughed, and laughed, and could not seem to stop. Eventually, he wiped at his eyes, smudging black eye make-up into white face-paint. 'Some fucking holiday, eh?' Then he laughed some more.

If two of his friends had not been butchered so horribly, and the third gone missing, he might have seen the funny side of it too. Instead, the man's giggling made him angry. But the sharpness of rage was welcome compared to the anxiety he could not swallow. And his irritation proved a refreshing respite from the sickish skittering of nerves in his gut, which seemed to have rendered him strengthless. 'My friends died. Out there. In the forest. We got lost. We were attacked. By an . . .'

'You took the wrong path, my friend. Let me tell you that.'

'What do you mean?'

For the first time since they met, the youth stopped grinning, or pulling stupid facial expressions and fooling about. He was suddenly serious. He looked over his shoulder at the open door, then back at Luke. 'What did you see?'

'What do you mean?'

Fenris grinned, shrugged. 'Your friends, how did they die?'

'They were killed . . . by something. Out there. In the trees . . .' Luke was confused; was lost for words. Did the right words even exist to explain what had happened to poor Hutch? And Phil? Dom too? Luke dipped his head, then looked up at Fenris. Why was he grinning?

'What were their names?' Fenris asked, but more to change the subject Luke suspected, than through any genuine interest in his friends.

'Why?'

'No reason.' The youth straightened his face and pulled what he must have imagined was a fierce evil expression. Then seemed to grow bored of that pose, and grinned again instead. 'So what do you do in London, Luke?'

Luke's suspicion flexed. He'd been found with no ID; his

passport and wallet were lost in one of the discarded ruck-sacks. He wondered what he should say, how he should answer the questions the youth had probably been sent to ask him. 'I sell CDs.' Say as little as possible, he decided.

'You like music?' The youth seemed excited by this possibility.

Luke stayed quiet. But looked at the man's shirt.

'You heard Gorgoroth?' Fenris asked.

'Of them.'

'Uh?'

'I have heard *of* them.'

'You know true black metal?'

Luke shrugged.

'Which bands?'

Luke became annoyed at himself for trying to think of the name of bands whose CDs they sold from the tiny black metal section of the shop. 'What does it matter?'

'It doesn't. Which bands?'

Luke sighed. 'Dimmu Borgir.'

The youth spat. 'Poseurs!'

'Cradle of Filth.'

The man shrugged, indifferent, yawned.

'Venom?'

He smiled. 'The masters! Now we are getting somewhere, Luke from London.' Then he lowered his voice into a deep mocking tone and frowned. 'But you clearly need to be edu-cated, my friend. You need to hear Emperor. Dark Throne. Burzum. Satyricon. Bathory. And you will hear them all while you are our guest in this forest of eternal sorrow. And maybe, maybe, if you are a very good boy, we play you Blood Frenzy too.' The youth feigned disappointment at Luke's lack of recognition of the name, and at his continuing bewilderment. 'Blood Frenzy! My band. You work in a CD store, and you have not heard of Blood Frenzy. Luke! Very stupid of you.'

'Fenris.'

At the mention of his name, the youth stopped grinning. 'That is my name.'

'I need to take a piss.'

Fenris barked an order at the old woman, who had done nothing but stare at Luke since her arrival. Slowly, she moved across the room and vanished through the door, her little feet loud against the uneven floorboards.

Luke removed his eyes from the open door, trying to suppress the keen interest in it they had revealed. 'And then I want my clothes, Fenris from Sweden.'

'Norway! I am Norwegian. A Viking!'

'OK, Fenris from Norway. I want to leave here. Thank you for taking me from the forest. I would have died otherwise. But my friends were murdered, and I need to report it. And now you and your friends are making me feel nervous.'

Fenris smiled. 'Then you are a very wise man, Luke from London. Because wolves and devils and fire are to be feared when they are on the wild hunt.'

'I don't understand.'

Fenris grinned his yellow grin.

The elderly woman returned to the room, with a large wooden bucket she could barely carry. A very old one, a museum piece, the sides bound with circular iron bands. Fenris watched her struggle, but made no attempt to help her.

The voice of the second youth suddenly boomed from downstairs. He spoke in what Luke had correctly suspected was Norwegian. Fenris rolled his eyes. 'I must go, Luke. But we will speak again.' He nodded at the chamber pot the old woman had placed at Luke's feet. 'Please, feel free to piss.' He turned and walked to the door. The old woman clip-clopped loudly after him.

Luke heard the key turn in the door lock. 'Why? Why lock it? The door?' he called out.

No one answered him.

FIFTY-ONE

The cutlery was made from either bone or wood; Luke didn't know, nor did he want to touch it. The wooden plate was balanced on the foot of the bed and half filled with stew and boiled root vegetable. He dithered, standing over it, his hands wavering uselessly as the smell tormented him. Hunger burned his stomach right back to his spine and made him dizzy. When was the last time he'd eaten? He didn't know because he did not know how long he had been in the room, in the bed, pissing himself.

The food was lukewarm, had cooled while Fenris chattered. At least it was soft. Luke knelt before it. Lowered his face to the plate.

By the time he had licked every dreg of the bitter salty gravy to the side of the plate, he heard a growing tumult of voices and the banging of busy feet beneath his room, one floor down.

Excitable voices. Shrieking, screaming voices, imitating the vocals in black metal music; growling and gargling, before breaking into cracked falsettos. He wondered if they were communicating with each other in this way, or just trying to outdo each other like children. Fenris was the loudest. Luke doubted the youth's mouth ever stayed closed for long. His oafish noises were being underwritten by Loki's booming baritone. Maybe the girl was doing all the jackal noises, in competition with Fenris. He doubted it was the old woman making such a garbled sound. And why did they wear their shoes inside the house? he thought, then felt foolish for the irrelevance of such a query. But the sound of the continual hollow banging of their feet against the wooden floors was maddening, deafening. It made him flinch, set his nerves on edge. It intimidated him; he was afraid it would rise up the stairs to his room at any moment.

The youths could not use furniture quietly either. Wooden legs of what he guessed were chairs were constantly scraped angrily across the floors. It sounded as if the entire ground floor of the building was being rearranged, or vandalized and things were toppling over and smashing down there. He wondered who the old woman was. Was she related to the band, to this Blood Frenzy? He wanted to know why she allowed them to be so aggressive.

He was suddenly annoyed at himself for not asking why he was here, or who the old woman was, or about so many other things he desperately needed the answers to. His temperature suddenly plummeted. Were these youths their killers? Had these adolescents hunted them? Murdered his friends? This wolf and devil and fire?

No, it didn't fit.

Luke had not seen their pursuer, their killer, but what he knew and sensed of it was too swift, too silent, for human endeavour. He could not imagine these painted youths capable of such bestial cunning. Nor did they exude its unnatural presence that infiltrated dreams. *It.* Luke clutched at his face, and started to pant to ease another panic attack.

The noises of the group banged and screeched outside the

house, then lessened as their boots trod upon grass. Save for the idiotic screams, which continued unabated.

Luke moved across the room to the tiny window. He noted black nails, or tacks, poking from the wall to the right side of the window. Over the bed, sections of the plaster featured rectangles of lighter paint. Pictures and ornaments had been taken down. Not a good sign, though he could not define why. He moved the rag of discoloured netting aside and looked down from the window.

It was getting dark outside, but there was still some bruised light in the sky. He guessed it was around eight. A dim orangey glow was being emitted from an open door, or from the windows directly beneath his feet that he could not see.

Outside his little window, the youths were going to light a pyre.

Dark wooden logs were stacked into a triangular shape, about twenty feet from the house in a wide grassy area that extended to the black trees bordering the property. Coils of briar and dead branches formed another messy layer of kindling around the logs. A red plastic petrol can was visible in the dark grass. Grass that had not been cut for a long time but had been flattened by feet around the pyre in a messy circular patch.

A few small fruit trees grew in the flat grassy area. Across from the house was a smaller building. It looked like an elaborate Wendy house, or a shed with a solitary door and a porch. A black miniature house that made him afraid; it looked like the disused buildings they had found in the forest. This one was also very old. As was the room, and no doubt the house. Everything around here was morbidly aged and neglected. The very smells of the place were alien to him. The house smelled of the forest. Of the dark dripping heart of the terrible wood, that reared up black and still and impenetrable around the grassy paddock.

He was suddenly gripped with a terror that the pyre was for him. That the youths were going to burn him alive.

He forced himself to deny the possibility, to stem the spurt of panic that came into his mouth. They were just young and drunk. They had saved him. They took nothing seriously; they were teenagers. Excitable. That's all. Someone had gone to fetch a doctor.

Then why lock the door? Luke turned his head slowly and looked at the little door. *To . . . to keep him safe.* But from what?

Luke shuffled as fast as he dared across the room to the door, the floor gritty under the soles of his feet. Supposing a time came, when the pain in his head lessened and more mobility returned to his body, he wondered if he would need to free himself from the room, silently. The tiny window was too small to climb through, so he was only left with the door as a method of escape.

He turned the black iron door handle. Locked. He knew it was, but maybe it could be forced open. The house was old, the door narrow, it looked flimsy. But when he shook the handle and pressed his naked shoulder into the wood, the door proved to be more solid and heavy than it appeared, and was also swollen slightly crooked in the doorway. There was little movement of it inside the frame. His brief hope of an easy escape died.

He bent over and waited for the quakes inside his skull to subside to ripples. Returned to the window.

Down below, Fenris and Loki had stripped off their T-shirts and revealed their upper bodies to the cold evening air: pale as grubs around the tattoos, chests smooth, upper arms long and thin and festooned with more of the black spiky tattoos. Swathes of matted black hair formed drapes around their freshly whitened faces. He had not realized how long Loki's hair was until now; it fell past his waist in a tatty curtain. The man's limbs were spindly, but he was a giant. He had some sort of bandolier that crossed his chest; it was made from black leather and studded. Both men's forearms bristled with long silver nails, protruding from leather bands that stretched from wrist to elbow.

Grimaces had been newly depicted on to the young but knowing faces of the two men. They widened their eyes at the dark sky and did more of the idiotic shrieking, with their arms held out from their bodies. Luke could not see the girl.

Black metal music suddenly exploded from the old CD player. The machine was out of sight, and must have been operated by the girl, who suddenly ran into view, naked. Her buttocks and heavy breasts shook as she ran. There were no tattoos visible on her skin and she had small feet. Absurd feet. Her skin was so pale too, almost luminescent. Upon her head she wore the mask; had become the hare again. Her head looked oversized, shaggy, and the vague shadow her head cast before the orangey glow of the house was not pleasant.

Messily, Fenris upended the petrol can over the wood. It splashed silvery. Loki produced a Zippo lighter and Luke suddenly identified one major cause of the unrelenting irritation that had refused to subside inside him since he had eaten. He was in withdrawal. And desperately wanted to smoke. Wondered how long it had been since his last cigarette. He'd rather have tobacco than clothes or fucking steel cutlery. 'Please, please let them have cigarettes,' he whispered.

The Zippo took its time igniting the pyre. And the pyre had to be relit four times, despite the leaping of the fat hare and Fenris's excitable shrieking to urge the flames into existence. They were all drunk.

He watched more of the youths' drunken dancing. The two men were gulping something from horns fashioned into cups. Moonshine. The ungainly hare fell to its knees twice. Against the windowpane the light and heat from the fire seemed to beat, and push him further back inside the room.

Tiredness from his exertions made his body suddenly feel old and wretched. He felt faint and nauseous. This was no time to try anything clever.

He made his way back to the bed. Lay upon the eiderdown, unable to face the urine-damp sheepskins and soiled hay beneath. Closed his eyes, shivered. Tried to make sense of what was happening to him. He found it hard to think clearly now. The gargling vocals and machine-gun drumming beneath his window interfered with his thoughts, and even his breathing. He wanted the silence and darkness of sleep again; felt its presence swaying at the back of his mind.

The situation was preposterous. But his acceptance of it seemed too easy. Because he was in shock. Maybe still in shock from what had happened to Dom and Phil and Hutch, out there in the forest he could see from his window.

He wasn't safe at all, and was still within reach of whatever it was, *out there*. There had not been enough time to process his predicament, because he had been running for his life, for days, and was broken by it. Then he was here, in this madness. He struggled to connect the two situations.

He desperately wanted the noise of the youths to cease. He wanted total silence around him. Because noise would carry for miles and miles. It might attract something else to the house.

But the music played and the drunken youths screamed at the sky. Nothing seemed to tire them. He wondered if they could keep it up all night.

It. Did they know of *it*? Had Fenris been making inquiries? But quietly, as if hoping Loki would not overhear? Loki led them. He seemed more intelligent, perhaps benign, though immediately ridiculous. Fenris was an oaf, a noisy adolescent. There was something infuriatingly immature about both of them. Geeky. They were dorks. Compared to what he had encountered *out there*, he was not afraid of them physically. He analysed this instinct. Yes, he was more wary of their intentions, their motives for keeping him locked inside this room, than afraid of what they could do to him. He guessed, more than decided, that they were exuberant, delinquent, irresponsible, but harmless. And the old woman was an adult, responsible; she had fed him, retied the bandage, stroked his cheek. He remembered the sensation and shivered. Bad things didn't happen around grandmothers. He just had to relax and wait. The masks had given him a fright, that was all. But then, his well-being did not appear to be their priority. They were oblivious to the state of his broken head. *They were having a fucking party*. Had they really sent for help? He increasingly felt as if he were the victim of some elaborate practical joke. They were toying with him; they liked to know things that he did not. Pathetic.

But what to do? To do? To do?

The maelstrom of noise outside the house continued for so long, his exhaustion and fragility began to put him to sleep in spite of it.

FIFTY-TWO

Feet boomed up a staircase beyond the walls of his room; waking him. He sat up and made a feeble sound. The footsteps banged down the corridor outside.

Luke remained motionless on the bed, closed his eyes to a squint, hoping it might deter another visit.

It did not.

Fenris came in through the door, but left it wide open behind him; a long iron key dangled from the outside of the lock. Fenris was holding something in his hands. 'Luke! Wake up! You have slept for long enough, my friend. You are missing the party! Look. Look here.'

The bedding dipped sharply near his feet. As Fenris landed on his backside, the impact rolled Luke into the side of the box. He clutched his head. 'Careful!' The force of his own voice surprised him.

'Sorry,' Fenris said, automatically. 'I am sorry.'

'I think my skull is fractured.'

'Look here.' Fenris thrust a hand out clutching black-and-white photographs. His breath smelled vile, like spoiled milk, and vomit. Luke winced, drew away from the weaving drunken figure with the painted sweating face.

'The nausea. My headache. I think I have a fracture.' He was wasting his breath.

Fenris's eyes struggled to focus on him. 'Blood Frenzy,' he shrieked in an imitation of the screaming vocals on the recording still blasting outside the house. Luke winced; it hurt his ears, his head. He then tried to make himself seem oblivious to the open doorway behind Fenris, but it seemed to call to him. His thoughts fell over each other. Was there a town near the house? How far could he walk? Was that wise when so near the trees at night? Were these even the trees of the same forest they were lost inside, and had died inside?

'Look!' Fenris was getting annoyed at his failure to examine the photographs. Luke picked them up off the bedclothes.

Publicity shots of Fenris, Loki and one other man with incredibly long white-blond hair. Poses of shirtless figures holding swords, faces painted, grimacing at the camera. Some were taken of the three figures in the snow. Blackened wintry trees formed a skeletal backdrop to their posturing. In the winter shots they held their instruments. Loki played guitar; it looked like a banjo in his huge long-fingered hands. Fenris held drum sticks. This role seemed to make sense to Luke, as drumming would be the only thing to contain his fidgeting, his energy, and it also produced a lot of noise.

The third figure he had not seen at the house. He was slender, tall, and boyishly beautiful despite the white face-paint, in turn festooned with thin black cracks. His hair was lustrous, feminine, and his whole demeanour was somehow at odds with the other two musicians. He seemed to command a stillness about him the other two could only mimic. Was he the one who had gone for help?

They all wore leather trousers, big boots, studded belts. They liked bullets, tattoos, inverted crosses. There were over a dozen photographs, all featuring the same trio making themselves look as ominous, or evil, or hideous, or insane, or imperious as they could manage when shirtless with painted faces. Luke had seen similar before in *Kerrang!, Metal Hammer* – the magazines they stocked in the shop. He always flicked through them, but it wasn't his thing. He listened to and avidly collected classic rock, blues, outlaw country, folk, Americana. Always had done. Though he had not taken too much interest in the outré genre of heavy metal, he knew black metal was a Scandinavian thing. Didn't they burn some churches in the nineties? They were Satanic. It was an underground anti-authoritarian thing. He knew little else, but was pretty sure his ignorance would soon be corrected by Fenris. The thought made him feel more tired than he had imagined it was possible to be. And why they produced such music in the social utopia of Scandinavia puzzled him. Perhaps it was a protest to being the most spoiled people in Europe; an act of rebellion against having everything.

At the bottom of each photo the logo of Blood Frenzy was printed, as was Nordland Panzergrenadier Records, and a P.O. Box address in Oslo.

Fenris dropped a CD into Luke's lap. Then sat back, his arms crossed, his chin raised, his monstrous face grimacing. 'You have that in your store?'

The cover artwork featured a wintry northern landscape so dark it was hard to determine much definition. Gassy whitish mist or light trailed from a patch of water in the bottom left-hand corner of the photograph. Or was it a painting? The band's logo was red and inscribed like streak lightning at the top of the cover.

Luke turned the case over and saw one of the press shots

on the rear, featuring the three figures in the snow, holding broadswords in warrior poses. A track listing was stamped in Germanic writing down the left-hand side. He lacked the energy, interest and inclination to read the song titles. Feeling irritable, sullen, exhausted, he just shrugged and tossed the case back towards Fenris.

'You don't know!' Fenris lashed out and slapped Luke's face.

Luke jolted back and against the end of the bed like he had been electrocuted. They stared at each other. Fenris's blue eyes had narrowed, darkened. He looked psychotic. Luke swallowed. And then the figure was suddenly smiling again, as if pleased with Luke's reaction.

A bully. *A pissant little fuck*. 'Don't fucking touch me again.'

Fenris made a big deal of looking afraid. 'Or what will you do to me, Luke of London? Eh? Who work in the CD store, but do not know of the most evil band in the whole world! You must work in a faggot store. Sell music for pussies.' He laughed loudly at his own wit.

Luke thought of kicking Fenris in the face, with the heel of his foot, right into his dirty teeth. The disorientating throb of pain between his ears told him that maybe it was not the right moment. But he welcomed again the heat of anger building inside him; he'd had enough of this. 'We just don't get much demand for devil-worshipping horse shit.'

Fenris stopped laughing. Sat bolt upright. The energy of his body changed. Slowly, he moved off the bed, not once breaking his glare from Luke. The youth's addled face seemed to have reddened under the white paint. He had made Fenris so angry, the youth could barely breathe. When he managed to speak, his voice was low and mean. 'Devil? The devil? That what you think? Eh? We worship the devil? You don't know anything! We use the devil only because we hate the Christians. It is Odin who lives in us. It was Odin all along.'

He clenched both hands into fists. Closed his eyes. Gritted his teeth into a snarl. 'See how Christians poison us! We can only call things by their names. It is Odin, great Wotan, who mutters in our blood. What Christians say is evil is our religion. We are warriors. Wild, you know! We are open to nature. We feel no pity!'

'Sure. OK.' Luke did not know what else to say. His entire body tensed. He looked about for the wooden spoon.

And then Fenris gave it to him, speaking so quickly that Luke only seemed to hear bits of what the drunken youth jabbered at him. It would have all sounded ridiculous, had three of his friends not been killed in the forest. 'We have no pity for your friends. They were weak, they died. End of the story. Old Gods require blood sacrifice! They are, how you say?' He paused, sneering, for a few seconds to choose the word. 'Ruthless! Yes, they are ruthless!'

Luke slowly moved off the bed. Fenris was unstable, becoming hysterical, a maniac drunk; his whole body was trembling.

The youth turned his body and followed Luke with his cold blue eyes in that horribly painted face. 'We ride with Odin. He our guide. He lead us. He lead us through our blood. You cannot believe what is here. What lives *here*. You cannot believe it.'

'You'd be surprised what I now believe. But chill, yeah?'

Fenris was not to be calmed. 'Our blood whispers to burn the church, we burn it. Our blood says kill a faggot . . . a, a, a immigrant . . . a drug dealer. We kill them! Our blood says, come home. You are ready for the old one of the forest. God of . . . of . . . of your people. You come home. You are ready, because you have proven yourself to be true Oskerai! Who ride wild 'til Ragnarok comes. It is not some fucking devil! Some Christian shit! It is older Gods who speak to us.' Fenris clutched the knife handle at his belt.

Luke raised both hands, palm first. 'Sure. I get it. But I'm tired. I hurt. Please. Just calm the fuck down. Please.'

But the youth continued to sway towards him, blue eyes bulging in the cracked white face. 'We are Vikings. And now we rise. Through our blood, and through the soil of the forest, he speaks to us. Same with the Nazis. Wotan came back to them. Even Jung prove this.' Wild of face, delirious with adolescent passion for his idiot theory, he drew the knife from his belt. Luke's legs felt like they'd vanished. He shuffled his naked feet so he knew where they were.

'We do something no one else has done. Ever in the history!'

With the curved blade steely black, brandished and held aloft, Fenris snarled and jabbed it in the direction of the small window of the room. 'We shit on the Christian altars. No problem. Then we kill faggots like you! No problem. But it's not new. It's very much fun I can tell you, to be this evil. But it is not . . . not . . . Fuck it! The words, the words! Original! It is not original. But we will be the first leaders of black metal to summon a real God of old. Something you maybe have seen with your own eyes. And will see again, soon. We have prepared ourselves to meet a God. You better do the same, my friend.'

Luke edged away from the swaying figure, but the corner of the cabinet was soon pressing at his spine.

Fenris struggled to focus his eyes. 'In these woods is a real God! Not some Christian shit. Or some fucking devil. This place is sacred. Here there is real resurrection. It is Blood Frenzy who make music of Gods.'

When the tip of the knife was within a foot of his eyes, Luke swung the jug from behind his head, in an arc, and so quickly he surprised himself. And delivered its heavy wooden base upon the side of Fenris's skull.

There was a moment of surprise on the young man's face. And a terrible hollow-coconut sound echoed inside the room. The figure dropped the knife, took two steps backwards. His eyes closed. He suddenly looked like a child about to cry.

Luke swung the jug against the side of the man's head again. It did not break. But thudded, bounced off his skull. Fenris fell sideways, onto his knees. Luke raised the jug a third time.

But before he could strike again, something heavy and naked moved quickly into the room. He turned his head a fraction. Sucked in his breath.

The insane face of the mottled hare came at him so fast he gasped. Two chubby fists struck his face. At least three times, before he dropped the jug and managed to seize one of the girl's wrists. It was doughy in the palm of his rough hand. The hare's feet stamped and kicked at him. They whirled sideways, like a pair of drunks performing some ludicrous dance.

He shrieked as her nails raked down his cheek. He thought one of his eyes had been clawed out. Hot salty water blurred his entire vision. Or was it blood?

There was a long pause when nothing happened, and he was only able to detect a watery outline of the hare, swimming before his eyes. And then a small fist thumped down and into the open wound on his scalp.

FIFTY-THREE

Luke came to on a grubby floor, and wondered where he was. Looked up, at where the screaming voice so garbled with rage and grief was issuing from.

He saw tall Loki clutching the hare to his chest. Holding her back. Back from him.

Fenris was on his knees, moving groggily towards the door, moaning to himself.

The girl kept up her shrieking. It was like glass smashing inside his head. Luke tasted blood in his mouth. His head was cold, wet, opened. He touched his face. Then put his fingers in front of his squinting eyes. They were slick, bright red.

Nothing could stop the girl from screaming and kicking her small fat feet in his direction. Until Loki lifted her from the floor and heaved her away, towards the door. 'Let me cut him!' she screamed in English, directing her bristly face at Luke. 'Let me cut him.'

Loki shouted at her in Norwegian. But the girl was inconsolable. The glassy eyes of the hare seemed to fix on Luke, where he lay with a face all shiny and hot and wet. 'Let me cut him, Loki! Let me cut him up, Loki!'

'No! Then there will be nothing left. Think. Think. Think,' he repeated, though with his accent, it sounded like he was shouting, 'Sink, sink, sink.'

Fenris fell to his elbows, placed his head face down on the floor, and started a rhythmic moaning that made him sound like a child. His black hair puddled around his head. Luke stared at the man's ribs and the bony vertebrae under his blue-white skin. They were children, Luke thought. Kids. Damaged kids.

The kicking girl grew tired. She struggled less, then relaxed her body and started to sob. 'I want to. I want to,' she said.

'Not yet,' Loki said, and held her very tightly.

FIFTY-FOUR

If the hare had picked up Fenris's knife, he would be dead. He would have bled out, brightly and hopelessly on the dirty floor of this room. An image flashed into his imagination, of his dirty skin parted into long red mouths. He shut down his eyes and his disordered thoughts upon such a vision.

The argument still raged below. On the ground floor. Sporadically, Loki's voice rose out of necessity to force down the cries of the girl. For the first time in a while, Luke could not hear Fenris.

A chair scraped loudly across a floor, then toppled on to its side. Glass smashed. Upstairs in his little room, Luke flinched.

He used his forearm to dab at the blood trickling down his forehead. His head was hot and weightless, and there was a swelling behind his eyes. The actual gash didn't hurt so much any more. But it would do again. Soon. Endorphins had merely surged. Their good work was temporary. It always was.

The fight made him feel better. Stupidly so, because he had made things much worse for himself. Security would be tightened, grudges had formed, faces would have to be saved, revenge needed to be taken. Inevitable, predictable, childish; the consequences of being human. It was the way of things.

The ground rules were just being established between him and them. Every new grouping of people formed a hierarchy. And he was at the bottom of this one; a disempowered witness to their moronic sadism. That was his role.

'How? How?'

Below, the girl made a chesty groaning sound, like she had screamed and sobbed herself dry. Loki's voice rumbled. Still no sound from Fenris.

Luke sat down on the box bed and wished he had water to drink. Strangely, he also hoped he had not hurt Fenris badly. He took no pleasure in the look of animal pain he had caused.

At last his mind was really beginning to wake itself up. He welcomed this new urgency. Healing needed to be deferred, if that was at all possible. He needed to bite down on the pain and get the fuck out fast.

He had been taken from danger, from imminent mortal danger, but then enclosed in a stinking bed in an airless room in an old house, and left unaware of the location of the house. A person needs to know at least that to feel comfortable; needs to know where they are in the world. Ever since Hutch decided on taking the short cut, he was finished with not knowing precisely where he was. 'Fuck you, H.'

But when you have taken a person into your care, and you feed them, shelter them, but do not attend to what could be a serious head injury, and Sweden is a modern country with emergency services, hospitals, even helicopters when required, then . . .

Luke pulled his dirty fingers down his wet face, utterly confounded by the absurdity and the impossibility of the situation.

They would tell him nothing. Fenris evaded his questions. No useful information would be forthcoming from his hosts; he sensed that much. He was being kept here against his will. So escape should be his only focus. Because the masks, the music, the screaming, the fire down there in the dark grass: it was all leading to a terrible conclusion.

He'd tried not to think about that thing in the woods, of what killed his friends. Until now he had been too ill and hurt and tired to do so. But his dealings with it were not over. Of that he was certain.

They were here for *it* too. Blood Frenzy. And they had revealed their identities through the silly demoniac names that could be easily traced through the P.O. Box in Oslo and the name of the record company. And if there was any truth to Fenris's bragging, about what they had been up to, then his release from here was not imminent. They were on the run.

He thought of the freaky old woman. Wondered about her.

Slow heavy feet boomed up the stairs. Broke his thoughts apart and into a rout.

He tensed. Looked about for a weapon. The jug was still in the room, on its side, intact; incredibly intact. And the bucket. He went for the jug, gripped its worn handle. Images of Fenris's curved knife came into his mind and he shivered. He could not stop the shivers, or the trembling that took hold of his jaw.

'Luke? It is Loki.' No attempt was made by Loki to enter the room.

They were wary of him now. *That's good. Wary is good. They are just kids anyway. Fenris is a bull-shitter, a big mouth. They haven't killed anyone.*

Luke stood a few feet from the door and gave himself enough room to swing the jug. 'Yeah.'

'Good, you are listening.'

'All ears.'

'Of this I am very pleased, Luke. Because you need to listen very good. Yes?'

'Yes.'

'Tonight, you make a big mistake.'

'I do?'

'Yes you do, my friend, you do.'

'He came at me with a knife. What am I supposed to do?'

'If he wanted to kill you Luke, you would already be dead. You understand?'

'Not really.'

Loki sighed. 'Fenris has killed before. To him, killing is nothing. You see?'

Luke felt his skin go cold. Heat seemed to be draining away from his body through his own feet.

By an act of will, he forced the implications of what Loki had just said from his mind, and in much the same way that he had censored the vision of his knife-ruined flesh before. He had to keep holding himself all together or it was over. 'When it is me he threatens, it means something to me, Loki. You understand that?'

'He was not going to hurt you. He like you. Is glad you are here with us. He gets bored with me and Surtr. You see, me and Surtr are together and Fenris is the one left out. Yes?'

'Yes.'

'But now you have no friends here, Luke. You messed it up.'

'He was no friend, Loki. And I'm no fool.'

Loki guffawed. 'I never said you were, Luke. You want to survive. You fight. You are not weak. And I respect that. You are special. Which is why you survive and your friends die. Yes? Fenris was foolish to take his eye off you, that is all. But he learn a valuable lesson. I would prefer him not to know this lesson again, because now I have work to do. To be the peacemaker, yes?'

Luke stayed quiet. He found himself desperately trying not to like Loki.

'Are you still with me, Luke?'

'Yes!'

'Good. But please you are guest, so do not shout. OK?'

'OK.'

'Thank you.'

'My friends, Loki. Did you kill my friends?'

'No we did not, Luke. I cannot tell you precisely what happened to them, but soon I wish to find out—'

'What do you mean?'

'Luke! It is I who is speaking. So listen to me. Now you must be careful and . . . how they say? Sleep light. Because someone in this house, not far from your bed, they very much want to kill you.'

'You tell Fenris that I am sorry. I hit him because I thought he was going to hurt me. And I am very tired of being hurt, Loki. Can you understand that? My friends have been murdered and I want . . . I just want all of this to end.'

'I understand, Luke. And it will all end soon.'

This statement made him mad with hope until he realized that Loki was probably talking about a completely different ending to his story.

'But Fenris is not your problem,' the deep-voiced giant said into the door. 'He is mad at you, yes. He hoped you would be good company for him while you wait.'

'Wait for what?'

'I have not finished, Luke—'

'What, Loki? What am I waiting for? Eh? The police. Because that is who will be coming very soon.'

'I do not think so, Luke. Do not give yourself false hopes, my friend. You are far too important for us to give away to the police. And they are the last people we want to see. But I am sure they would like to meet us.' Loki laughed to himself. Disingenuous, but deep laughter. 'I tell you very soon, my friend. All in good times. But tonight's party was for a very good reason. As you will soon see. But you must be patient a little while longer, Luke. Until then, you must understand what it is I am saying about your behaviour as a guest in this house.'

'I am trying, Loki. I am trying very hard to understand why I am being kept here against my will.'

'Your will is strong, Luke. But please let me tell you the problem you have right now. Yes?'

'Yes. Yes. Yes. Tell me, Loki.'

'When I say you have a very big problem in this house, I do not lie, Luke. But it is not Fenris. He has a sore head, but he don't kill you. Your problem is Surtr, Luke.'

'You keep your mad bitch away from me. OK, Loki? How's that, mate?'

'I will try my best, Luke. But I must sleep also. And she is very absolutist.'

'I don't follow?'

'She likes to stab, Luke. To cut. She is a little crazy in her ideas. One time we got this guy and she . . . Well, let me make you imagine a man who tries to run with no toes on his feet. It was a very funny thing to see, I can tell you. And she never stop with his toes. All of him fits inside this . . . this . . . baggage. You know, the airport baggage?'

Luke thought he might be sick again. He needed to sit down. Tried to bring the strength back into his arms.

'I think you understand me, Luke. So I ask a favour from you. You do as we say. Which mean, no more fighting, my friend. I leave you to think on this.' His footsteps began to retreat down the corridor outside.

Luke moved to the door. 'I need water. Loki. Water.'

The loud footsteps returned to the other side of the door. 'I bring it.'

'Hot water. A bandage.'

'Not possible.'

'Some painkillers. Headache tablets.'

'Not possible.'

'Cigarettes, please.'

'Not possible.'

'Tell you what, call an ambulance. Right now.'

'Not possible,' Loki said, without a trace of humour.

Wincing, as even the minutiae of limited mobility seemed to make his swollen brain collide painfully against the insides of his skull, Luke moved his body across the bedding to the side of the bed. Slowly, he hooked his legs over and then stood upright. Even with his head supported by both hands, he felt unbalanced, seasick.

He gulped at more of the stale dusty water, straight from the jug. It trickled round each side of his mouth and spattered down his naked chest. Besides his damp underwear, they had removed all of his clothes. He felt too ill and anxious to explore the reasons why. But there were no medical supplies here, and *they* were not going to let him go. Those were the new facts. The new rules binding his life. *What was left of it.*

A terrible bolus of emotion suddenly came up from behind his sternum where it had been stored in his worn-out heart. It rushed, burning, through him. He knelt on the floor. Bent over, sobbed.

His throat was thick with an emotion that could have been loneliness, or sadness, or self-pity, or despair, or all of these things at once. He didn't know, but he thought anything, even death, was better than feeling this way.

He was hurting. So much. His head. He wanted it to stop. Would offer anything for a painkiller. Up and down his back, and around his calf muscles where thorns had curled and torn, the scratches shrieked with their own tiny voices. Even between his fingers there were cuts he could not recall the cause of.

He looked at the dirty swollen skin of his hands and fore-arms. And to think, he'd believed himself saved. His chest tightened and his skin pinpricked cold; the sensation felt horribly familiar.

Lying on the wooden floor, he curled into himself, held his broken head, and quietly wept until he was exhausted by the effort of producing tears.

FIFTY-FIVE

After the sobbing of Surtr finally ceased downstairs, Luke rested on top of the musty eiderdown and listened to the night. Dry blood stiffened and cracked upon his face. There were no electric lights inside the room. No power sockets. No electricity. So when the world outside went dark, so did the room, and the house around it. The coastal sounds of the trees swished near the house, but rose in deeper longer waves further out, stirred by the first strong wind he could remember since he'd arrived in Sweden.

He listened to the wind until a new commotion of footsteps came up the stairs. He assumed it was the youths and the old woman, rising to murder him. Luke tensed, stopped breathing.

Someone banged about in a room further down the corridor outside of his room – maybe two sets of feet – and then a door closed on those sounds. Other sets of feet shuffled and bumped downstairs, on the ground floor, but to destinations in other parts of the building.

He sucked in his breath, relaxed back into the mattress. His captors must have been going to their beds to sleep; some of them had gone into a room on this storey of the house. He sensed that it was a large building; it creaked and yawned like an old sailing ship, and he could hear the adjustments of its timbers in the distance. Sometimes he thought he could feel the floor under the bed moving too. He doubted the building was structurally safe.

Eventually, despite the headache and nausea, he fell into a coma of exhaustion.

To wake from a disorientating dream that involved him turning round and round and looking at a moon-white sky. Something had broken him from sleep. Noises. Above his room.

It must have been well after midnight. It was pitch-black outside and the sky through his little window had not yet begun to lighten for dawn.

But floorboards of a room directly above the ceiling of his room were creaking. And there was a faint bumping up there too. No scratching like the activity of mice or birds, but the shifting sounds of motion from a more substantial presence. Or presences.

Yes, he became sure that something, bigger than a dog or cat, was on the move upstairs, fumbling about. The pattern of movement brought to his imagination the image of several small children, blind and stumbling round the walls of an enclosed space, looking for a way out. He pushed the image from his thoughts. It was not the kind of thing he wanted to think about on his own in the dark.

Gingerly, he edged himself off the bed. The floor emitted a loud and lasting crack. Up above him all fell silent. He paused, held his breath and strained his ears for a few seconds. Then trod carefully upon the floor again. The silence of night amplified his movements as if through loud speakers.

He swore silently. The house was listening. The darkness was following him.

Nothing was moving above him now, but its presence still conveyed the sense that whoever it was had begun to listen intently to his movements.

He started to panic. Whimpered. He needed to act. To do something. Now.

At the window, he quickly moved his hands around the frame, then the glass. Could see nothing through it. The stars and moon were blotted out by cloud. The window was definitely too small to crawl through if he punched the glass out. His shoulders would not fit. The drop would snap an ankle anyway, maybe two. He shuddered. *No more pain. Please.*

Testing sections of the floor before he gave them his full weight, he moved unevenly across the room to the door. Pressed himself against it, felt its contours with the palms of his hands, turned its handle uselessly, implored it to have a flaw that would allow him to leave. But the door was solid. An old thing, not a moulding, no hardboard involved in its construction. He scratched at the thick hinges. He'd need a crowbar to get this bastard out of the frame.

On his hands and knees, he moved about the floor. Using the tips of his fingers, he picked at the spaces between the gappy floorboards, wanting to break through them with his bare hands. Puffs of cold air and dust came up at him, silent exhalations from the building's internal air currents. Beneath his hands, the floor was like the door: solid, ancient. He picked and pried, dirtied his already dirty knees. He gritted his teeth and silently called down curses upon the place.

Upright again, he then moved about the walls, shuffling his feet. The plaster was moist in places; powdery under the paintwork in other areas. He wondered if he might dig through the wall at one of these weak points with a shard of the broken jug or bucket. He was giving it serious thought when the activity above his head interrupted his considerations.

Voices.

Whispering voices.

Thump, bump, thump: the sounds of small bodies.

He moved into the middle of the room, at the foot of the bed, and something up there followed him. A pattering of babyish feet tracked across the ceiling to where he stood. Directly above him.

Luke moved towards the window. The little footsteps followed.

'Hello,' Luke said.

Silence.

Louder this time. 'Hello.'

No reply.

'Can you hear me?'

No one answered, but he was sure that a second tangible presence above him was attracted to the sound of his voice. Because another small form was now being dragged, or was dragging itself across the floor above. It could have been no bigger than a child, because the shuffling sound was so light, so delicate. It bore no weight, but merely scuffed at the old floorboards.

There was more whispering now too. Several papery voices were rustling up there. He could not make out a single word, but perhaps a note of optimism now defined their tone.

This summoned a third participant. Up there. From the far corner of his room, he heard another set of steps move across the ceiling, towards his position beside the window. But this figure was moving incredibly slowly, as if every step was a terrible effort. The sound of the footsteps was also hard, hollow and woody, as if this individual was wearing shoes with tipped heels, or was using crutches. It was more of a slow careful knocking than a skitter or dragging motion like the first two presences had made.

'I can hear you. English? Do you speak English?' he called out, softly.

The whispering intensified, then died away.

Silence.

This was going nowhere. Who did they have up there? Children? He thought of Fred and Rose West's house in Gloucester, of the entombed captives suffocated in the walls. Recalled bits of what he knew about the degradation of the victims of degenerate killers. Dahmer, Manson, the Green River Killer, Brady, Nilsen, the Night Prowler, and all of the stranglers and slashers with their hall of fame on cable television. He thought of their victims kept captive, toyed with, despatched, even fucked, often eaten. These thoughts made him feel so weak, he thought he should sit down.

Then he clenched his fists, ground his teeth. Wanted to bellow at the impossibility, the absurdity, the unfairness of it. There was simply no preparation in life for the determined madness of others.

Realizing he had either been holding his breath, or taking shallow breaths since hearing the movements above him, he greedily sucked the musty air of the room into his lungs. And shivered. It was so cold now. His feet were frozen; he wondered if they had gone blue. He became angry again because he had no clothes. Maybe his clothes were in a terrible state, or maybe his disrobement was a tactic.

He touched the tacky furrow that ran across the top of

his skull. It feels worse than it is, he told himself, but wasn't sure whether he believed this.

He made his way towards the vague outline of the box bed. A little rest and warm-up and he'd be in a better place to deal with this, with *them*. Tomorrow, he would have to make his play.

The thought made him sickly and strengthless again, and he vainly wished he had not struck Fenris. They'd be on their guard now. But he had to do something. Maybe dig at that plaster first. Yes, take a rest, then break that jug with the bucket, as quietly as possible inside the bedclothes. Start carving the plaster while Blood Frenzy slept off their moonshine and frolics. They were going to kill him anyway. Fucking up the wall was the least of his worries.

He sat down on the bed. Gaped into space. *Kill him anyway*. He wondered how it would feel to die. Maybe just darkness came after.

Up above his head all was quiet again, but he imagined that whoever was up there was now listening to his thoughts.

Luke lay back. The bed stank like a farm animal, but at least it was warm.

FIFTY-SIX

He stood at the window. The sky was white with moon. It filled the atmosphere like a planet about to bump into the earth. Stretching away forever before the house, the forest of so many tall black trees was still, but not silent. Strange cries issued in the distance, rising from down amongst the cold lightless spaces, beneath the canopy of great branches, that were like muscular arms raised to the luminous air in praise. Dark leaves upon the peaks of the tallest trees frosted in the falling brightness. Wondrous light, but not comforting light. Though he wished it were.

Behind him in the room, someone spoke to him in a tiny quick voice. A little person. What they said made sense to him, though he had never heard such things before in his life. He was not allowed to turn around.

And he felt an urge to go down there, to that whitish clearing beneath his window. Carved within the great ocean of never-ending trees, in this new world, was a circular flat space, carpeted with a soft pelt of shorn silvery grass. He felt euphoric before it, filled with a mad glee, but accepted it would be very hard to get out of the circle and the upright stones if he dared go down there. Down there to turn round and round, before the mouth of the dark stone chamber, while looking up at the white sky. He had done it before. Or had he? He wasn't sure.

And in the treeline the figures cavorted. They were children. They were angels. Tears filled his eyes. They were dancing. Or they were stalking around the edge of the clearing. Or maybe their skipping movements, before they dropped to all fours, were a combination of dancing and stalking. Sometimes they rose up on two hind legs and waved, or clawed their thin white arms at the sky.

It was hard to see the little white people clearly, because of the sudden darting of their pale child bodies into the shadows of the forest. They never remained still for long, and flitted about constantly. But the longer he watched the more he glimpsed of their pinkish eyes and their whippy tails, blood-purple like earth worms, before they withdrew to the endless darkness beneath the treetops.

Through the glass of the window he strained his ears to hear their voices too, as they called up to him. They cried out for him to come down and do the turning before the black stones, under the white glare of sky. But then he thought the sound they made was more like barking, or coughing, and not voices calling at all. And he was uncertain whether children should have such square yellow teeth in their wide mouths. Clutched in their tiny white fists were bones. Long bones from legs and arms.

Then he understood that they put the bones inside the stone chamber. It was the chamber that he was to go inside, to wait for another to come. From out there. Deep and far out there, among the forever of black trees, something approached.

Behind him, the tiny voice and the skitter of tiny fast feet on the wooden floor stopped.

And, suddenly, he was inside the stone walls of the old chamber of upright stones and he could smell the earthy pungency of the dirt floor inside it. And in the thin light he saw the bones. All of the bones. The bones strewn about the dirt floor. Some still wet and dark. Bones gathered amongst the stones.

He pitched from sleep and cried, 'Not in there. Not inside. Please.'

But the three figures about the bed all reached for him at the same time. Ashen faces cracked with black fissures, came in at him.

Fenris grinned. The whites of his eyes were incongruous and shocking within their black sockets. 'We have found your friend. Come and see, Luke.' His mouth was too red beyond the black lipstick, the tongue too visible, the teeth too yellow.

In his giant hands, Loki slapped Luke's forearms together. Luke tried to pull his hands apart, but Surtr worked faster with the nylon hoop. It must have been circling his wrists before he awoke, and now a strap was tugged and the loop *whizzed* smaller. His flesh purpled under the binding. The skin immediately itched.

He was pulled into a sitting position. Fenris yanked the eiderdown off his legs. Cold air rushed in and his body seemed frail, ungainly. Shame warmed through Luke.

'Up. Up,' Loki said.

Fenris smiled at him. 'Man, you stink.'

Luke rose to his knees. 'No. You're hurting . . . Stop.' And then the pain in his wrists silenced him as Surtr pulled the strap even tighter. Tears melted the vision of her moon-face and her spiteful lipless smile.

Fenris gripped his hands while Loki shovelled a huge hand under his right arm. Together, they pulled him upright, then off the bed and on to his feet. Fenris smiled right into his face. 'Big surprise for you today, Luke.'

Out of the room, then down a cramped wooden corridor they bumped and banged him. Surtr went first with wide bare feet padding across the wooden floors; her raised soles were as black as tar. Loki followed her, dipping his head to avoid smacking it against the ceiling and oil lantern; his bulk eclipsed the thin light in the narrow space. Close behind Luke, Fenris giggled. He felt the youth's hot breath inside his ear.

All of them were excited, pushy, shoving, impatient. He wanted to scream at them to leave him alone, but the idea that Dom was here shocked him mute. He was alive then. Impossibly alive. He thought his heart was breaking. 'Where did you find him? My friend?'

At the top of the stairs Loki turned his head, the long black hair swaying in an inky torrent. 'He found us.'

Luke could barely breathe, let alone speak. 'Is he all right?'

Fenris laughed and said, 'Very well.'

Loki frowned at Fenris, then turned away.

'Is my friend all right?' Luke demanded, his disorientation lessening, the pain in his wrists turning to warmth.

'These stairs are very old. They put you on your ass,' Loki said.

Fenris pushed Luke from behind. He skittered down the first three steps. Fell against the old walls, righted himself. It was like standing on the deck of a small boat, or walking through a moving train. His balance was shot. Whether it was because he had just woken, or because his hands were tied, or because of his head injury, he didn't know. And then he was at ground level, the floor solid beneath his naked soles. From the open front door, air fresh with damp and rain and earth engulfed him.

A cramped brownish hallway materialized. A murky kitchen led off it; inside he saw a black iron stove and chimney, an old wooden table with solid sides of plain board, chairs with rounded legs, peeling cabinets.

A bigger parlour, the walls dark with ancient timber and chaotic with antlers, skulls and blackened things, then came briefly into view through another doorway to his right. And then he was pushed from behind by Fenris again, and out through the open front door he went, and on to a sloping wooden porch.

The remains of the pyre from the night before blackened the grass. He could smell old smoke and wet ash.

To his left, the old woman stood on the porch. The sudden sight of her small body in the long dusty black dress, made him start. Tiny eyes glimmered in her collapsed expressionless face. The uneven ends of her short white hair were wispy in the day's grim light. She merely watched him. The youths ignored her.

Luke jerked away from Fenris and stumbled after Loki.

Desperately, Luke cast his eyes about. 'Dom. Mate. Dom!' He desperately wanted to see his friend, and needed to get a sense of the house he was imprisoned within, and essay the grounds, but he only succeeded in a bewildered stumbling into the grass paddock before the porch. And then his eyes caught sight of something up high, straight ahead, caught in a tree like a hapless parachutist gone all limp. He looked away and gasped.

Then whipped his head back to see the tatty figure in the treeline, strung up directly before the front door; the spot below his little window. In his eyes, the reds and yellows of raw meat, and the sudden white of bone, clashed with the backdrop of dark wintry green.

'We have summoned him wiv our music! See!' It was Fenris shouting behind Luke.

Luke dropped to his knees. Looked at the grass and at his bound hands. Peered back up.

Mackerel light silted down and through the tree branches. Dappled with shadow, Dom's face was perfectly still; white as candle wax across the unshaven cheeks either side of a thick bruised nose, but mired with dark blood around the mouth. His face seemed strangely expressionless, like he had been nonchalant about the circumstances of his final breath.

As if drunk and embracing the shoulders of friends on either side, Dom's pallid arms were stretched out and hooked between two tree limbs about eight feet from the ground. His torso and legs drooped, appearing weightless now that everything had been looted from out of his rib cage. The glimmer of the vertebrae, still moist, was worse than the beard of blood around the gaping mouth. He had been peeled from the waist to his heavy thighs. A side of meat in a butcher's window.

Luke's vision went hazy, insubstantial, then whited out. He fell onto his side and looked back at the house. Saw it for the first time. It was made from wood, stained black by age. Had a pointy dark roof. Small windows.

Two sets of thick-soled boots, embedded with silver rivets from toe to heel, came and stood too close to his eyes.

'Enough now. Just enough now,' Luke said, though he wasn't sure who he was talking to. 'Not Dom. Not my friend. No more.'

'We call to it, it come. Our music is raise magic,' Fenris said, excitedly. When these words finally assembled into a sentence inside his mind, the information confused Luke. Then he realized he could feel nothing. Nothing at all, as if every nerve had been stripped from out of his body like wiring torn from a wall cavity. When he realized Fenris was not talking about Dom, but about the thing that had brought his remains here, he closed his eyes.

'This is the most remote place in Scandinavia, Luke.' It was Loki speaking to him now. 'Where the oldest things can still be found, my friend. Here there are different rules. Different energies, you know.' Luke continued to stare at the house.

Then Fenris was talking again, quickly, near where Luke lay in the grass in his dirty underwear, wrists bound with a plastic loop from a DIY store. 'They kept it alive here. Kept it real.'

When he spoke next in his deep, softened voice, it was as if Loki was mollifying a confused child. 'Something is pushing to the surface of the world, Luke. And in us too. Something terrible. Destructive. I sense it in you also. It pulled you in, eh? And all of your friends. Us too. But, I am sorry to say, that sometimes the innocent are sacrificed.'

Fenris was babbling, breathless with glee. 'How do you think they have lived here? Lived for so long? No one fucks with them. They live as they please. It is the oldest forest in Europe. It is protected. That is why all this is still here.'

Loki's voice remained passive, unshocked, unaffected by the ruin of a father, a husband, a friend, a man, up in that tree. 'This is the land of our ancestors. Here Odin still rides. And you have to wake up and accept the wishes . . . the demands of something older and greater than you, Luke. That is all.'

He heard the voice of the old woman for the first time then. '*Det som en gang givits ar forsvunnet, det kommer att atertas.*'

Loki and Fenris stopped talking and turned to her. Luke looked at her wrinkled impassive face. Some thin grey teeth were visible inside her lipless mouth. '*Det som en gang givits ar forsvunnet, det kommer att atertas,*' she said again, as if simply stating a fact. Her voice was cracked with age, but the intonation was strangely melodic.

Loki crouched down, swept a curtain of hair over one shoulder and tilted his crudely painted face towards Luke. 'She says, what was once given, is missing. One will come to fetch it back.'

And then somehow Luke was on his feet, and the horizon of the forest was jumping in his eyes, and he was running on stiff awkward legs. Running away from it all.

Past the front of the house he went, then up the side of the building; a dark wooden wall rearing up on his right side, the forest blurring to his left. Behind the building a white pick-up truck with mud-plastered sides was parked before an overgrown orchard, the arrangement of the trees haphazard. Some of the tree branches hung heavy with dark-green fruit: cooking apples. A thin grassy track, grooved to clay in twin tyre tracks, travelled along the side of the sparse gathering of fruit trees, before vanishing round a bend.

Voices behind: Fenris whooped, then laughed like a jackal. Loki gave orders, his tone unhurried, methodical.

A glance over his shoulder. The girl ran after him. Ungainly, short legs pumping in tight black jeans; heavy bosom swinging in an oversized hooded top with something printed on the front. Her feet bare, white, thudding. Face round, excited.

Instinctively, Luke ran towards the clay track. It might lead somewhere. The ground would not be so uneven as the forest floor was bound to be. He could cut into the thick trees further down the track, drop and hide at ground level. The thought pushed him on, his exertions loud within his head. Every footfall jolted up his spine and seemed to widen the crack in his skull, which he would never believe was not there until he dared look into a mirror again. Not being able to pump his arms was slowing him down.

Eyes wild, teeth gritted, Fenris came at him from between the side of the truck and the shadowy rear of the house, looking to cut him off before he reached the track. A fat girl and a disturbed teenager with their faces painted like corpses, or demons, or whatever they thought they were, were coming for him.

Luke yanked at his wrist binding. Impotent fury welled up his throat. Even wearing big boots, Fenris was quick. Would have to be faced.

Luke stopped, turned. Thought of kicking him, heel first. The approach of the girl to his right, distracted him. Cheeks puffed, chest heaving, little hands balled into fists, her washed-out eyes widening: a high-pitched scream came out of her small mouth.

Fenris pulled up short. Grinned. Danced sideways. Backwards. Cried out something inarticulate, shrieky, triumphant.

A moment of indecision. Then Luke turned to the girl. She was almost upon him. He kicked everything he had into the gut of the rushing figure.

Her forward momentum knocked him off his back leg and he was falling. There was a look of surprise, then fear at being hurt, on her face, and she bowed away. The grassy turf came up too fast and slammed into Luke's shoulders from behind.

Fenris laughed. Clapped his hands against his thighs.

The girl was bent double, silent, winded.

Luke sat up quickly, swivelled his weight onto one buttock. Bent his left leg at the knee to propel himself upwards.

The toe of Fenris's boot struck him in the temple. Ice cracked inside his skull. Rivets opened his cheekbone. Red lights flared.

When his vision juddered back down and settled, he was looking at a dead grey sky and could not close his mouth or clench his jaw. His ear whistled and the side of his head thumped hot.

Again he tried to get up, but only succeeded in sitting before the girl's snatching chubby fingers were in his hair. Something had come loose inside her, unhinged: he could see it in her eyes. A belligerent keening sound, like sobbing but harder, came out of her.

Whatever had dried shut along the top of his head, came apart under his hair with a sticky-tape sound and his scalp flooded hot. The pain made him go white all over; it enveloped him like an immersion in cold water would. He withered into a faint.

She pulled him back down to the earth, flattened his shoulders against the cold grass. He broke from the faint, but thought he would be sick. Couldn't breathe. Thrust his hands upward, fingers locked like he was in prayer. His knuckles sank under her small flat chin. She made a sound like air escaping quickly from a cushion, until her mouth clamped shut on the sound.

Fenris stamped the corrugated sole of his big boot onto Luke's face.

Gristle popped. A streak of nose pain took the last of the strength from his limbs. The rubber sole twisted, rearranging the skin, and his features with it.

Luke knew the fight was over. He was done. Spent.

Surtr crowded out the light, dropped her heavy round knees onto his shoulders. Straddled his face. Through the delirium of pain, he caught her scent. She was yoghurty, sour-creamy, sebaceous. He was smelling her cunt through a nose he knew to be smashed flat.

Holding his hair, making rippy sounds, she yanked his head off the ground, then smashed it back down. Up again, then down.

Then her weight was gone. Suddenly lifted clean off him. And Luke rolled onto his side and choked the rust rush of blood from out of his throat. Spat loops of bloody saliva from his mouth. The sight of it frightened him. In what little of his mind was still working at its frantic scattering of thoughts, he visualized his face disfigured, his skull open, the organ inside grey and shivering at the open sky. He prodded at his wet face with his fingertips. The skin was tight. An egg-shaped lump, hard as bone, had already risen where he had been kicked in the temple. Merely touching it made him feel sick, so he stopped.

Loki held on to his girlfriend, his acolyte, tightly. Spoke

quickly and urgently into her disordered black hair. A smudge of her white face behind the fringe still peered intently at Luke, as if some urgent play had been disrupted by a parent.

Hung loosely over one of Loki's shoulders was the dark wood of a stock and the dull gleam of gunmetal. A hunting rifle. If Loki's white-faced devil hounds had not pulled him down, Loki would have shot him anyway. He was not leaving here. Luke lay back and closed his eyes on a grey world that did not seem to want him in it any more.

FIFTY-SEVEN

'Luke. I am having the hard time keeping you alive right now.' Loki's eyes were bright and blue and smiling in the beam of dusty light that fell through the little window. Loki was in a playful mood, a good mood. Grinning, he tossed his mane of black hair over one shoulder. He didn't seem so dour, so intensely serious now; it was as if the arrival of Luke's butchered friend had relieved the tension in the air. And he was drunk. Beside the closed door he had propped the rifle against the wall.

Luke had been lying still for hours before Loki's arrival. He could not breathe through his nose, which felt like it had swollen to four times its normal size, and his head was open like split fruit. Both of his eyes were swollen, one nearly shut. It felt puffy. He was covered in scores of hard red itching lumps from being bitten senseless by the bugs in the hideous bed. Scores of cuts and scratches covered his ankles and forearms, and he had not washed in a week. He stank. He was thirsty. He was hungry. He was broken. He realized he did not care about much any more.

And he hated himself for being relieved the giant was in a good mood. And he loathed himself for feeling some gratitude towards Loki too; since they dragged him out of the forest, Loki had now saved him from the other two twice.

But saved me for what?

He was tired of being helpless. Sick and tired of being sick and tired of this room, and of the stinking box bed in it, which would not dry and now reeked of his own ammonia. He had already been exhausted by his fear and pain and wretchedness before they even found him, and now the thin, indefatigable, but ultimately futile hope that had sustained him since he had awoken in this place was exhausting; the hope that somehow these young people would recognize some common humanity they shared with the dirty wounded man from the forest, and that upon recognizing that he was a good person, they would let him go. Its twin, the pathetic clawing infantile hope that help from the outside world would suddenly materialize way out here, was also exhausting. Hope was now more tiring than anything else. Its perpetual rise and fall through the terrible ache in his head, and its arrival and its disappearance while he passed in and out of consciousness, and while he moved from one strange world to awake in another crueller place, was more painful and more hateful to endure than the sadism of these adolescent bullies.

He supposed he was near the very end of himself.

At last. So at last he could stop caring. And before he could start dwelling on what he would miss in his life, and who might miss him back in the world, he now decided, quite calmly, that he just wanted it to end. And to end soon. Perhaps he could even hasten it. He smiled with broken lips.

'Your tattoos are a fucking contradiction, Loki.' His voice sounded thick, unrecognizable. Blood poured into his throat from the back of his nose and he coughed it onto his chest. Sat up. Spat his mouth empty. Looked at Loki and suddenly hated him so intensely and desperately, that when his loathing abated his mind was clear.

The giant paused in his expansive grinning. The morbid white face shook itself in mock surprise.

Luke continued. 'You despise Christianity. Am I right? Your lot set fire to those old wooden Stave churches. Because you hate God. You have a pentagram on your chest, another one on your shoulder, and an upside-down crucifix on your stomach, should anyone need further proof that you are a devil-worshipping badass motherfucker.'

Loki laughed, slapped his thighs, then swigged from his drinking horn.

Luke would not be silenced. 'Which all implies that you once believed in the devil. In Satan, Loki. But then you also have pagan tattoos. Heathen runes and shit like that. Old Norse runes all over your knuckles, Loki. A Thor's hammer, I see. Pre-Christian. A different belief system. So I'm guessing that you and Fenris are all about Odin these days. Yeah? Which implies you do not believe in the Christian God, or the devil any more. So vandalizing those churches was a waste of time? Places raised by a depth of belief, centuries ago, that I doubt you can even begin to understand, Loki. I've seen them in Norway with my friend Hutch, who was murdered by that atrocity you worship. Those churches are beautiful. Symbols of a more lasting devotion than your fads and your fashions, mate. Because now you're into something else. But these were places that once gave simple people comfort. It's your country's culture, it's your own history. Sorry to sound like your fucking mom, Loki, but you're a vandal. A wanker.'

'Luke, I tell you now—'

'So what do you believe in? What really is your fucking

point? Why am I here? Because from where I am sitting, I have stopped trying to figure you out. I have no more interest in trying to understand anything about you stupid fucking morons. I don't think you have a point, Loki. Any of you. You're just a bunch of little shits that have crossed too many lines. And now you're so damaged, you don't even make sense to yourselves. So come on. Do it. Get it over with, you big bastard wanker.'

Loki raised his large face to look at the ceiling and smiled. Nodded. 'Now this is just the attitude I am speaking with you about, Luke. That gets you in trouble here. But you know, I like your style. True, you are very er . . . misunderstanding my beliefs. Which is OK. As you are most probably the blind sheep, like everyone else. So I make allowances for you. Because you are asleep. But soon I think, you will be waking up.'

Loki rested his long back against the stained wall. He smiled, wistfully, which was immediately at odds with his painted-on grimace, then sighed. 'You know, Luke. I miss fighting the church. The Christians. At least real Christians have the balls to judge me. You are with us, or you are damned. We learn that from them. It is true. To be absolutist. Fascistic. I like their style.' He raised his two giant hands and shook his head, as if struck by a sudden revelation. 'And you are not wrong about some things. To think we burned the oldest churches. I try not to have regrets, Luke, but that is one. I should have torched the new American shit, eh? Scientology or something. It's even worse brainwashing for very unsophisticated people. But there are places where true and much older devotion exists, Luke. Like here.'

Loki eased his long body to the floor. Smiled wistfully. 'I

knew about it all my life, you know. I am from near this place. A bit south, in Norway. But close. This is still my true land. And I come back from the world to be here. To get away, you know? To come where there are no fucking Christians, no rules, no social democrats, or humanist bastards.' He spat, then swigged from his horn. Despite the many competing odours about him in the room, and the state of his nose, Luke could taste the unpleasant yeasty miasma of Loki's breath, even from where he was slumped inside the box bed.

'We have awoken, Luke. And we want our fellow Vikings to awake too, you know. We show them how. Up here. And with our music. It will be special, Luke. We are working on something very intense, my friend. It will have the voice of the older Gods in it. Arise. Arise it will say.'

He pointed the horn at Luke. 'Real magic, you know? That's why I come. I decide to show the others what real magic is. I brought only the fittest with me, you know? Who have proven themselves to me. Proved they were evil enough. That they were . . . *uncompromising*. A word I like when I learn it. They prove they could kill and burn. They who are of blood and soil.'

Loki suddenly laughed. 'Maybe too much, eh? Fenris! Not very smart, you think? He was already killing animals when I met him in Oslo, you know? No pets in his town, yeah. I say desecrate that grave, my friend. And he do it. So easy. Churches?' Loki made a sound of something exploding and shaped the flames in the air with his big hands. 'Kill a priest I once say when we are drunk.' Loki nodded, grinning, as if merely recounting some absurd and trivial exploit of rebellion. 'And he surely did.'

He straightened his face and adopted a more commanding

posture. 'To be a Viking, you must learn to be truly evil, Luke. Must be able to prove yourself in a blood frenzy. You know, you are very lucky. And I tell you this, because you are the first person to know this about us, who is still alive. Yes? OK, do not answer. But let me convince you.

'We have killed nine people. Including two priests.' Loki grinned, swigged again from his horn. 'Not bad, eh? Worst mass murderers that Norway ever has, and they still don't know it. That is the best part. They don't expect it to happen in Norway, but we are some of the first ones to wake, you know? Varg and Bard Faust, they were black-metal killers. Revolutionaries. They light the path for us to follow. But we go much further than them.

'And Odin is coming, my friend. Make no mistakes about this. There will be murder. There will be blood sacrifice. We will have our revenge. You will see. You will see.' He drank some more.

Sometime during Loki's confession, Luke lost what had been a sudden hot desire to goad the man. He didn't really know what he believed about the youths, or even knew to be true any more, but he now doubted that Loki was lying about what the group had done before they arrived here.

Luke started to laugh. He had to do something; it helped with the fear. Being afraid wasn't helping him. Hadn't done so for a long while. There was no time for fear now. Fear was useless to him; a repetitive survival instinct when survival was no longer a possibility. It was time for something else altogether.

Loki glared at him. This was not a reaction he expected, or wanted; Luke could see that. They wanted to be feared, and revered, as all morbid adolescents do.

'What happened, eh? Loki. What happened to that sweet little blond kid that you undoubtedly used to be? I bet you had one of those patterned jumpers too. With reindeers on the front.'

'Better not to make too much of the piss, Luke. You are on the very thin ice already, my good friend.'

'You were a healthy, educated, middle-class kid, Loki. Your country is the envy of the world. Because of your quality of life. What's your excuse? You were spoilt and bored and angry. And you went too far. Look at you now. An arsonist. Vandal. Kidnapper. A killer. And fuck knows what else.'

'Luke. Luke. Luke. Still you are the sheep. You are sleeping.'

'And your girlfriend was fucked up by something before you met her. She needs medicating, Loki. She's lost it, mate. I thought I'd been out with some high-maintenance nut jobs, but that fat bitch is in a different league. And maybe Fenris was too far gone too when you met him. Yeah, I think so. They were a couple of misfits who think you're some kind of messiah. Hardly candidates of the highest calibre for the revolution. What a sad and pointless tale it ultimately is.'

Loki shook his head, disappointed. 'Luke. You talk in your sleep.'

'Because I can't see the bigger picture, Loki. Because you, and Beavis and Buttmunch out there, have embraced sadism and the pitiless murder of innocent people. And I am a sleeping sheep because I fail to see the importance of it. I fail to understand the significance of your actions. Nor will I ever, Loki. When you finally kill me, I . . . Well, I will be dead and you will be a murderer. That's all there is to it. It's pointless. There is nothing magical or special about it. It's just sordid and wrong and rotten and all fucked up, like you and those dickheads who follow you around with their faces painted like ghosts.'

'Exactly! Now you have hit the nail with the hammer.' Loki grinned, then stood up and approached the bed. Luke could not help flinching, but hated himself for doing so.

Loki tilted the horn and poured a long draft of a foul-smelling liquid onto Luke's mouth. He tasted orange juice, and something like white spirit, or ethanol, and then he was choking.

Loki reclaimed his seat on the dusty floor. 'Good, yeah? I think so. Now, you are close to understanding that it is all part of the same thing. It does not matter if we hate Christians, or immigrants, or faggots. That shows we are serious, yes. But you have to look deeper, my friend. Wotan woke in us. And we answered his call. But at the start we were like, er . . . yes, like the children who want to do something, but don't know how they do it, so they do something else, yes?'

'No.'

Loki raised his hands in frustration at the limits of his second language. 'The devil is a good way to start, Luke. It is the start to be truly evil. To say fuck morals. I am evil. I am a Satanist. I desecrate. I burn. I kill. To separate us from the rest, the sheep. Then, we realize it was Odin who stirs in us. Great Wotan. Ancestral blood is boiling in us. We thought it was the devil, but it is not. It was Odin who wanted us to destroy the fucking Jewish religion and all the Christian bullshit that does not belong here. What has the Middle East got to do with Norway? Or Europe? So fuck it. Fuck the Muslims, fuck the Christians. We should have burned the mosques too. But that will come, I tell you this now. We are Vikings!

We have been tricked to sleep in our own ancestral land. But now we are waking. We go on the wild ride for Odin. We burn, we kill, so that we can wake. You see, we wake. It makes a . . . er . . . opening. A way in, for older things buried. To begin the new order. To signal other wild rides. You see? Ragnarok is coming, Luke. Soon. So we must begin to desecrate the world.'

'You're full of shit, Loki.'

For a long unnerving moment, Loki said nothing, but stared at the window. When he spoke again, the drunken oaf had retreated. The more reflective Loki had returned. 'I felt drawn out here, Luke. As you all did. For a very special reason. You cannot deny this. It was destiny.'

'We were on holiday, Loki. It had fuck all to do with Wotan or Odin.'

'No, you are wrong.' He turned his face to Luke. 'You were drawn into the forest at the same time as us. You came for the terrible ride. You just did not know it. But we are all here for the wild hunt. The true one. The oldest one of all. It needs witnesses. And sacrifice, Luke. So it pulls things in. As it once did. Of all the trails you could walk, you walk in this one. A big mistake, my friend.

'The Christians once stop the sacrifice and the wild rides up here. Long time ago. But the rides never really stop. What was once given up here, a long time ago, just had to be taken instead, you see? And the hunt used to happen at Yuletide, but this year it come early. Which is very bad for you and your friends, I think.'

Loki slapped his own chest. 'We come to this place where wild hunts have been seen. Real magic, you know. I know the stories from when I was a boy. Here they worship something that was in these woods before Christ.' He turned again to glare at Luke. 'We have nowhere else to go. We burn all our bridges, Luke. Some very angry people are looking for us. But that is destiny. Destiny brings us home. Destiny gave us no choice but to come here. To be true.'

Luke snorted, then winced because of the pain that dug behind his eyes. He prodded at the tears about his delicate, swollen eyes. 'It's not destiny. You're on the run. And you will be caught. Eventually. And my friends were killed by . . . something unnatural, I'll grant you that. But it's no God.'

Loki pointed at the floor. 'You are wrong, my friend. She knows. And she tells us that the old ride has started early. So we go out to see it. She lets us go to see something so old you cannot believe it. A God returning. That is when we find you. There is no one here to give sacrifice any more, Luke. So what is needed is taken now, you know? Just taken. Yeah? Like your friends. You and your friends started it early. But rites should be followed as they once were. She tells us. Something must be *given*, Luke. Again. To a true God of the North. That is how it once was. How it will be again now we are here. You see? She is too old, my friend. And that is where we come in. To *give*. Like others once gave. To be a part of something true. Old. Special. To give and be close to a God. The only one worthy of our loyalty. It is the . . . er . . . the gesture that counts. Like Christmas, it's all about giving.' Loki burst out laughing at his own joke. Luke said nothing.

'Like *you* will be given. Maybe tonight. We hope anyway. We get much closer. We have contact now. And you are wrong, because our God knows we are here. To do things as they were once done. No one but us would do these things.

No one is this uncompromising. And there is no one else up here to do it any more. It is all destiny, Luke. And what we needed to give, also came. *You.* You came and we came at the same time. A sign.'

Loki raised his hands to encompass the room, the house, the forest outside. 'These are the original settlers. The first people. But there were other things here before them. And the settlers paid a tax to the original occupants to remain here. To hunt, trade skins, live in the forest. Long ago. Give the God food and drink and they prosper. Give it animals to rip apart and the forest grows and protects. It is the way of the Old Ones. They have been pushed to the little places, Luke. To the corners. By Christians, and immigrants and social democrats.' Loki shakes his head, in bitter despair, then looks up. 'They call *it* by many names out here. In my family when I was a boy, they call it the Black Yule Goat. But that is not such a good name, I think. But in these woods is a God. A very real God. You can be sure of that. Christians call it a demon. But it is a God. Just not their God.' He shrugged. 'This place is sacred. Here there is resurrection. We come to make music of resurrection. To give a sacrifice and to receive blessings. To spread the message. To be in the presence of a God. As our ancestors once were. You, my friend, are privileged. You will see.'

'I've seen it.'

Loki nods his head. 'I envy you that, my friend. And we will see it too when it come to accept you. Soon. Now we have you, Luke. We have something to give. You see? As it should be. As it was. As Odin wish it. And to us it will come. She promise, Luke. She save you for this. It is the only reason you live a little longer. So you can be our tribute. Our tithe,

Luke. Our introduction to the old ways. You are our proof that we are true.'

'It's no God, Loki. You are wrong. The Christians were probably closer to the truth. Everything you have done has been for nothing. It's been pointless. Senseless. I've seen the temple. It's in ruins, mate. The old stones? Overgrown. No one to tend the cemetery. This is all forgotten, Loki. It's over. Died out. There's only that old woman left. And she can't have long, mate. And you're too bored and stupid to hang around here for long. So it's over. No more worshipping of some old wild, mad beast, or whatever it is. No more sacrifice. No more murder. This thing you call a God has no future.'

Loki's eyes were too wide, too bright for his big face. His lips were suddenly trembling with drunken emotion when confronted by Luke's repeated failure to understand, to acknowledge, *to believe*.

'And you'll be in prison, mate,' Luke continued. 'At least you'll be notorious. All that attention seeking will have paid off, eh? I only wish they had the death penalty here. I really do. Because all three of you, and that evil thing out there . . . you all need putting down. It's what you deserve.'

'You are wrong, Luke from London. I show you. I show you. So you know why it is that you must die here.'

FIFTY-EIGHT

They were coming for him again. All of them.

Outside his room, Fenris chattered, Surtr's bare feet scuffed the dusty floor, Loki's great boots boomed in all of the hollow places, and the tiny loud feet of the old woman led the strange procession of Blood Frenzy through the dark house.

Beside her proclamation outside the house that morning, Luke had not heard the old woman speak. But something had upset her now. For so mute a creature, she had certainly wanted to be heard downstairs in the confrontation preceding this noisy progress of his hosts towards his room.

She had admonished the youths, raised her aged voice and its peculiar singsong dialect to the dim rafters. He guessed, and he could not stop himself hoping, she was imploring them not to do something; like maybe kill him in what must be, he had come to believe, her home. But then he thought of her implacable little face and doubted his life was of any consequence to the diminutive creature. So, maybe she was in dispute with Loki about something else entirely. And whatever it was, it terrified Luke.

Her relationship to the youths was a curiosity. She was neither kin nor friend; but she may not have been in league with them either. During the confrontation he overheard downstairs, he was beginning to intuit, or even hope – though hope was a dangerous thing and he distrusted it greatly – that her role was that of a reluctant host, a compromised confederate at best. And maybe whatever Loki wanted to show Luke, and had threatened to share with him right now, their aged host was dead against him seeing it.

Since his attempt to escape that morning, his wrists, and now his ankles too, were bound with nylon zip-lock ties, so there would be no struggle this time. When he ran for the trees they took his final privilege of capacity from him.

The door of his room opened.

Luke kept his face blank, but watched the eyes of the old woman. She returned his stare. Her little mouth was tight, grim.

There were sheathed knifes at the waists of Loki and Fenris, but they came to him without the rifle. The plastic tie around his ankles was severed by Fenris so that he could walk.

He was pulled off the bed by his bound wrists and tugged from the room. Outside, they hauled him down the passageway to the right of his room, to lead him upwards and into the dark house, and not down and out of it.

At the end of the cramped passage, the old woman stood and blocked the bottom of a staircase that was so small and narrow, Luke imagined it had been built solely for the passage of children. In the amber light of the lamp that Loki carried, her embedded eyes glinted black with fury, and also with fear, like those of a mother afraid for her young.

Then the little old woman and her loud feet suddenly turned and clumped ahead of Loki, like she was suddenly eager to get up those stairs first. And now that she knew she could not stop the eager chattering mischief and insolent will of the youths, she seemed to move too swiftly for her years on those little loud feet. To Luke, the hidden haste of her limbs inside that old dress, its hem sweeping the stairs, and the sight of her little body topped by the tatty white head, scuttling upwards into shadow, was a vision as unwelcome and disconcerting as that of an unpleasant doll, suddenly come to life.

But up and into the smell of age Luke was pushed. Forced from behind by Fenris, he was squeezed into Loki's ungainly wake through the narrow dark staircase, its confines as hot as an unclean mouth. The attic had its own breath that came down dusty and tangy with roof spaces where old air collected under warped timbers, and was further thickened with a taint of petrified flesh. Luke recognized a smell sharpened by the long-ago desiccation of small bodies, of birds and rodents; their ruin now a lingering residue. It was the same odour he had discovered in the loft of a flat full of dead rats he once rented in West Hampstead.

His heart jumped inside his chest when he caught the scent, and his eyes burned from his inability to blink as he was pushed closer to the top of the staircase. Something was living up there; he had heard it in the night. And the fact that it was living up there in that terrible reek of dried-out decay, made him absolutely certain that he did not want to see it.

Loki struggled before him, his progress slowed to a squeezing and scraping of his length against the ancient timbers and the wooden planks and dry plaster that buckled between the uprights. Amber light, from the swaying oil lantern in Loki's hand, threw a warm glow downwards, between Loki's legs, and for moments Luke was able to see his feet on the little stairs that were so worn down and scuffed at their middle.

The girl stayed downstairs; her plump face unsmiling with alarm, or even fright; the washed-out blue eyes were magnified with awe at what Luke was being pushed towards by her collaborators. Up here was something she had clearly seen before, but did not want to witness again.

But up he went, reluctant, stumbling; pushed by Fenris and pulled by Loki to the threshold of the black space.

Inside, there was no light beyond the halo of Loki's lantern, which the giant suddenly shielded with one large hand. And then dimmed the flame inside the glass shade as though to protect sensitive eyes.

Not so much as a thin streak of murky daylight cut through a loose tile in the low roof above them. This was the peak of the house; the summit of all its mystery and horror. Walls and stairs and beams below in the old structure crookedly supported it, but also concealed what was up there; insulated it, preserved it and its continuing purpose. And Luke could now literally taste the impending revelation that he would rather be without. His terror was such that he could not even swallow. He tried and failed to rid his mind of the memories of what could still be found in these old places, out here among the oldest trees of Europe.

Loki and Fenris fell into a hushed reverence once they were inside the attic space.

A stinking hand curled around Luke's face and covered his mouth from behind to make sure he also observed a respectful quiet. Fenris. The slender dirty hand remained there, tight across his lips. A bony shoulder and chest pushed against his back and shunted him further into the darkness.

He peered down to see his naked feet, and at what they were scuffling across.

From somewhere to his left, amber light shone. Loki's old oil lantern had been placed on the floor. Loki crouched beside it, his shoulder hunched against the slope of the roof. Briefly, he looked into Luke's wild eyes and then turned his head, and raised the lantern to cast its meagre glow out there. So he could see. See it all.

The grubby light opened the space to Luke's eyes, which he wanted to shut and keep shut: the lamp illuminated a long rectangular loft with sloping sides that ran the length of the upper storey of the building. The ceiling was low as it sloped down from beneath a central beam that Luke could barely stand upright beneath; the furthest edge of the attic space remained in shadow. But to his left and right he could see plenty.

The terrible monument in the forest, the church, was not good enough for *them*. For some reason these dead had to be brought home and displayed here.

Small, thin bodies stood against the two side walls, or sat with their ankles crossed, their bony knees gleaming smooth. Hairless heads were bowed. Mouths hung open, giving their parchment faces the vacancy of the sleeping.

They were little people and their clothes had either blackened and adhered to their meagre frames, or their raiment was bleached of all but the dimmest colours and was now loose and dusty about the insubstantial shapes inside.

Some of the figures were belted together with rags, to keep their arms held at their sides. But then over there, were crude wooden boxes full of bones, the skulls bulbous upon the dusty sticks of collapsed limbs. Other occupants of the reliquary were reduced to mere cairns of bone and dust and dross upon the wooden floor. And there were other figures cramped into little chests, their remains mostly whole, their skin dark and leathery, their hairless heads propped upon the carved wooden sides of the ancient caskets. Another mottled figure had been crudely sown into what looked like silver birch bark, in which it sat and grinned at eternity over the rim.

Further in, as Luke was pushed forward by insistent Fenris, the heads of another half a dozen of the interned upright figures were yellowish. Lipless grimaces seemed poised to speak. Papery eyes were sightless, but seemingly raised in the murk as if anticipating the return of light. Their raiment was dark, their flesh tight on the bones beneath the petrified cloth, but not hardened, not fossilized yet. The lustre of their skins suggested a suppleness that Luke would rather not have noted.

At the end of the attic, he could see the old woman, but her face was inscrutable. She stood in partial shadow beside two small and huddled figures, draped in some kind of dusty black vestment or robe. They sat upon small wooden chairs. Ancient chairs. Children's chairs. Side by side, like a little king and queen interned in some airless tomb to honour their afterlife.

Luke recalled fragments of a recent dream. He thought of the sounds that came down to him through the ceiling in the night. The disintegration of even more of his sanity felt tangible. It slid with his reason into a rout of silent panic.

And then the whispering began. Behind him. Around him. Lilting up and down, up and down. No louder than the scratch of a rat's claws, but the faintest of choirs from the driest of mouths was still determined to be heard. Impossible.

'*Det som en gang givits ar forsvunnet, det kommer att atertas,*' said Loki from the corner.

'*Det som en gang givits ar forsvunnet, det kommer att atertas,*' repeated Fenris into his ear.

Luke thought, or he imagined because nothing that old can live, that he then saw movement upon those little chairs.

He strained his eyes in the dim light. There it was again. A twitch of one dry head. The gentle elevation of a pointed chin. A rustle of old paper. A sigh.

Fenris pushed him closer on legs he could barely feel.

The grubby silhouettes of a gaunt and wasted ancestry watched him from both sides. Like leaves disturbed by a barely perceptible draught, he then detected other suggestions of movement about him. In order to subdue a scream, he told himself the ghastly animation was merely caused by the surge and retraction of amber light from the moving lantern. But he could not turn his head and confirm this desperate hope that the subtle restlessness of the parched and the mummified upright figures, was nothing more than a trick of light, or a gust of air rising through the ancient timbers of the house. And soon such conjectures ceased, because the seated figures on their little thrones suddenly commanded all of his attention.

A small mouth opened to reveal toothless gums, thin as cartilage. After a flicker, an eyelid parted in its deep socket. A faint glimmer of a black eye shone in the lamplight.

The hand of the second little figure dropped from its armrest and into its dry lap; the fingers clattered as if they were holding dice. The head of the figure dipped, then rose, suggesting the figure was emerging from, or trying to keep itself from, a deep sleep. One of its thin feet moved, the bony foot clad in a pointed shoe, the leather creased and blackened by centuries.

They lived.

'These are the ancient ones,' Loki muttered.

Momentarily Luke's thoughts moved from rout to clarity. Their own dead and slowly dying were precious. The lives of strangers were meaningless; they were to be hunted and slaughtered like deer in the forest, then dumped in a rubbish-filled crypt of an abandoned church, while these brittle remains were stored here with reverence.

'The past and the present are the same thing here,' Loki whispered.

Fenris removed his hand from Luke's mouth. Luke shuddered, and made a sound like he was stepping into cold water. And suddenly he grasped that the old woman of the woods was defined by this closeness to her dead. They existed continuously. She lived with the dead. Kept alive a bond with the dreadful things of another time. The church and cemetery was a place of sacrifice, while the old servants of an old religion reposed here. It was despicable.

Luke groaned again as the impossible registered as reality. There was more shock than awe. As the air left his lungs, it sounded as if his life was leaving him too.

Such a reaction of despair seemed provocative in this place. He caught a suggestion of a dry mouth within a dry head, that had been pressed to the wall at his left, but was now gaping, or gulping towards, his presence. And then the body below the head, and the other two bodies flanking it, twitched ever so gently in their moorings, as if keen to be much closer to him in the musty darkness.

Luke dropped his eyes to the floor, to evade the signs of

their restlessness. But in the thin brownish light he saw that the legs of the upright figures resting against the walls ended in bone. In hooves. And that their murky lower limbs bent the wrong way at the knee. It was as if animal limbs had been stitched into their groins. Luke thought of the thin forelegs of another *thing* they had discovered in another blasphemous attic, and of the tiny black mummified hands fixed upon its bony wrists.

He whimpered. He mewled.

Luke pushed backwards against Fenris's pressing shoulder; he felt like he was being manoeuvred too close to the edge of a cliff, or within reach of a dangerous and cornered animal. Fenris dug his heels in, tried again to move Luke closer.

'Nay,' said the old woman.

'Nay, nay,' said Loki.

But Fenris would not be told and he pushed harder until Luke nearly toppled forward and fell. He thrust out one leg to keep his footing. His face skimmed closer to the seated figures on the little chairs.

Before him, a gasp. A sudden intake of breath inside a bone-dry chest. An audible creak, as the jaw widened in a little mottled face.

The second figure's head seemed to shake in a slight palsy, as if it were confused. Then an eye opened in what was mostly a skull papered with brown skin. The eye was bluish at its centre, milky at the edges. And wet.

Luke sucked in his breath.

The figure's mouth dropped open. A hint of tongue whisked inside; no bigger than the flick of a small fish's tail.

Both figures shifted on their chairs. More animate, their tiny movements progressed from vibrations to a sudden confused animation. He heard the scrape of old cloth, the click of bone in socket. They were afraid. Or was it excitement that made them move like that upon those small wooden chairs?

And then the old woman was standing before the two little seated figures; shielding them, and pushing Luke and Fenris backwards with her small hard brownish hands. Her black eyes were fixed on Fenris's face, over Luke's shoulder, and her eyes were filled with so much loathing it was hard to look too long into them.

One of her small arms then withdrew from Luke's belly that she pushed at; and suddenly that little hand moved behind her grubby apron, before returning with something extending from her tiny hand. Something thin and sharp and glinting within the tiny liver-spotted fist. Luke looked down and focused on the blackened steel of an old blade, an inch from his naked gut: narrow as a pencil, a museum piece, a relic whipped from a still life painted by a Dutch master. It prodded at him again.

There was commotion of heavy boots from somewhere behind him in the attic. And Loki's voice was suddenly loud all about them. Fenris began wheedling with Loki in Norwegian. Then he talked quickly and angrily at the elderly woman, who in turn bared her blackish gums and dark teeth and growled at Fenris like a small bear.

Luke was suddenly pulled away, backwards, to the entrance, his feet kicking and scuffling for balance on the old dusty floorboards. The lantern light leapt and retracted from behind him; it surged up and dropped down the underside of the ancient roof. And the amber light gave the impression that a row of the thin figures against the right wall, were all leaning forward at the same time as if eager for him to remain in there with them.

Then Luke was spun around above the opening to the attic staircase, and pushed at it by Loki; one huge hand cupping the back of his head. But Luke needed little encouragement and leapt down the stairs, skittering, stumbling, missing his footing, and crashing to his knees at the bottom.

He was talking, quickly, to himself; had not realized he was doing so.

Surtr stood before him, looking as frightened as he felt.

He tried to get up, but in his jittery panic fell forward onto his face. His forehead hit the floor, caught the tip of his swollen nose. Tiny broken bones moved within the inflamed tissue. His eyes turned over, white, and his stomach flopped inside out. He bleached into a faint for a few seconds, banged his mouth against wood, then woke and clasped his face with the imploring fingers of his bound and useless hands.

In the distance, up above him, there was shouting: Loki and Fenris. And another sound. One far more disconcerting. A deep, throaty growling that evolved into bleating. It didn't sound like a person. Didn't sound like it had come out of a human mouth at all. And it was then combined with a stream of words twisted enough in their anguish to inform the listener that hysteria was building within the speaker. It must have been the voice of the old woman.

FIFTY-NINE

'Now maybe you take us seriously, eh?' Loki stood over Luke, shaking his head in grave disappointment.

Luke looked up from the box bed through the one eye that remained open. Inside his mouth he could feel bits of teeth, like sand, from where he'd fallen onto his face. But, strangely, there was no tooth pain.

Fenris had been sent outside by Loki, to calm down. When they came down from the attic, Loki had bellowed at Fenris. He'd even cuffed him hard, outside of Luke's room, and then shoved him down the stairs. Surtr had meekly followed the petulant Fenris into the paddock outside. He could hear her now, outside his window, continuing Loki's admonition of sulky disobedient Fenris.

Leaning over the box bed, which Luke had crawled back to after falling down the attic stairs, Loki rebound Luke's ankles with a new nylon tie. And Luke did not resist, having had enough of fists and boots and shoving and yanking, but he had wondered if they found the little white loops here, in this place, or whether they had carried the ties with them, and had used them on other wrists and other ankles as they made their way north. The notion made him feel faint and nervous again. He thought he might hyperventilate.

A slight easing of the terrible nausea from his head wound

was now the only positive thing that he could identify within his reduced and wretched state.

Loki sat down on the end of the bed. The giant was breathing hard. He spoke with difficulty, was wheezy; it sounded like he had asthma, like Phil. Poor Phil.

'So now you know, Luke from London. Know that you are nothing. A worm compared to what is here.' He pointed one long finger at the ceiling. Then he looked at the little window, before checking the watch face between the two studded wristbands on his forearm. He looked back at Luke, his cold blue eyes alight with excitement inside their black sockets. 'She can call it, you know? We know she can. And she know we are fucking serious. She has promised to call it. For us. And for you, Luke. So tonight we try again.'

Loki screwed his face up into a demoniac scowl, and stuck his dark-red tongue out. Grinned. 'You are the lucky man. Tonight you meet a God, and you know the true meaning of a blood frenzy, Luke. You have been a great deal of trouble for me. But later, I think we will all be much happier people. Make peace with your dead God. Maybe you see your friends again soon, yes?'

Loki left him alone.

Luke continued to stare into space for a long time, unable to focus his eyes on anything around him. Up above him, in the attic, he occasionally heard the little loud feet of the old woman moving about up there; she still had not come down since the confrontation. That place was beloved to her. But Luke knew he'd rather die than ever see it again.

After a while she began to weep. Through her little sobs, she spoke in her old lilting language to those around her in the dusty darkness. And Luke did not know why, but he felt a great sympathy for her. Soon, his own tears cut across his cheeks.

The wind buffeted his little window and the clouds stifled the weak white sunlight. As the air dimmed about him, his thoughts lowered their own lights. And he wept for himself, and for his friends, and his heart's pouring seemed to flow into the great sadness that ran through the world and through all who were in it.

Maybe for short periods of time it seemed to him, inside that stinking bed, that some people were exempt from tragedy and pain, but these respites were short; in the scheme of things and in the length of eternity, respites were nothing but anomalies in a relentless flow of despair and pain and sadness and horror that surely would eventually sweep everyone away.

And for the first time since he had been at school, Luke prayed. The enormity of what existed in this place made him think in those terms. In the epic terms of gods and devils, and in the terms of magic and the great incomprehensible age that had swept through here and left such terrible things behind. It did him good to pray, and to cry and scour his damaged lumpy face with stinging brine; to dissolve some of the cold despair.

Outside, beneath his window, the music came roaring out of the old CD player and he could no longer hear the old woman above him. Intermittently, Fenris and Loki scraped their throats to reproduce black-metal vocals. They were drinking again; he could tell by the idiotic jackal giggle that Fenris produced when downing the moonshine. And so it all continued; it was dull in its predictability. Evil was, he decided, inevitable, relentless and predictable. Imaginative, he'd give it that much, but soulless.

He dabbed at his nostrils, carefully, with the back of one filthy hand. It was hopeless; he couldn't even wipe his own nose. It was gushing with snot and blood. He dropped his head back onto the grey pillow and closed his one good eye; the other had shut itself down. He lay still, in silence, on the reeking sheepskins and waited for the light to completely fade out, for the sky to darken. *To finally get this over with*.

And in the long hours in which he waited alone with his thoughts, he tormented himself briefly by replaying his attempts at escape. In his memory, once he'd hit Fenris with the jug, he should have beaten Surtr off before she struck his head wound. He should have been quicker and harder with her. He imagined himself doing it all over again, but successfully this time, and then running downstairs and finding one of the knives, or the rifle.

Or he should have just run straight into the woods after they showed poor Dom to him; he should not have aimed for the track beside the orchard. What had he been thinking? If he had gone into the woods maybe he could have hidden, then crawled away later. And the opportunity to dig through that wall was gone now too; he had fallen asleep and dreamed of his own death instead, and now his wrists and his ankles were tied. It was like this entire situation was part of some terrible destiny; like fate had drawn him here to be sacrificed. Like Loki had said.

'Piss off,' he murmured to himself.

But even if he had escaped from the house, and made it out there – what then?

He swore at himself. Sniffed. Winced.

This is how things were now. The thought settled heavily upon him, but at least acceptance brought the relief that comes with the final acknowledgement of a painful, decisive truth. When aspirations and pretension and effort can finally be set aside as the wastes of mental effort they usually are. No more yearnings or cravings or anxieties. It would all be over soon enough.

He had just been caught up in the way of the world; on one of its lunatic fringes perhaps, but had still been swept away by the true and deeper undertow of tragedy nonetheless. What happened to you eventually was just more extreme out here; that was the only difference to being ground down by increments in the other world he had failed at and had now departed for good. The possibilities for destruction here were not so different in any other place; they just took different forms. Nor was the intent for violence any different here; that was everywhere he had ever lived. Or the self-absorption, the pathological ambition, the spite and delight in the downfall of others – all of that was back home too. It led here eventually. It was building everywhere. It was in the blood. A few natural disasters, or the wrong people take charge, or a war gets out of hand and changes the colour of the sky, or the earth becomes irreparably poisoned and water and food run short . . . and skulls would be smashed, again. Over and over again. *Ragnarok*. This was the chaos Loki wanted. And he wanted it sooner rather than later, even if it was only around him to begin with, in his dismal, misguided, obsessive existence.

To think he'd always championed the outcast too; been a friend of the misfit, the underdog. He was the last person they should have been snuffing out. But losers just wanted to swap places with anyone above them in the hierarchy. It made his life seem even more hopeless.

'Fuck it.'

His own weaknesses and mistakes and defects seemed pitiful in comparison to Blood Frenzy. He couldn't even be bad properly. At least these guys really went for it. He wanted to laugh, but also acknowledged that he had probably lost his mind. *At last. About fucking time.* What good had it been anyway?

Maybe a terrible Karma had indeed led him here. Just so he could realize all of this now, the hard way. He grinned, and showed his own bloodied teeth to the dirty ceiling.

'I wanted it to stop out here. Just for a bit. To be with my friends for a few days. That was all,' Luke said out loud to God, to the things in the attic, to anyone who might be listening. He'd just wanted a break from the world he didn't get along with: his job, the dismal flat, the same nullifying disappointment every day, the getting older and the growing into it all. He had wanted a change and he had got one.

He smiled and then he sniggered. A bubble of blood popped on his lips. He suddenly felt mad, and wild, and free of the burden of himself.

The sound of big heavy feet outside. Loki. *Thank fuck*: Loki wouldn't kill him yet. He'd have a little more time to sort his head out before the end. He was beginning to interest himself; was finally in agreement with himself.

The door opened. Loki came through. He was sweating heavily, his make-up was tainting his sweat and dripping onto his beard and Satyricon T-Shirt. His hands were red.

'Loki. Your eyeliner's running, mate.'

The old woman followed the giant youth into the room. She carried a tray. Upon it stood another wooden jug, and a wooden bowl still steaming. The scent of meat and gravy hit the back of Luke's throat and made him gasp.

Loki grinned. 'More than eyeliner will be running from you soon, my friend. I look forward to seeing it. It will be quite a show. Maybe we film it too.'

'Bring on Ragnarok. Bring it! The things you can do with a life, Loki. And yet people like you can't wait to turn back the clock. Fucking savages. Barbarians.'

'Thank you, Luke. Now you begin to understand our Viking ways with foreigners who fuck with Odin.'

'You know, lying here with my face hanging off, I'm beginning to think that the end of the nuclear family was not a good thing. Because people like you might not have happened. There would have been no Blood Frenzy then, eh? I reckon you took it in the ass from an early age, Loki.'

'Mr psychologist, I think you are maybe full of shit.'

'You're nothing new, mate. Ragnarok, this time is it? Then a few hikers cop it. And some poor priest. You big shite, Loki.'

'Luke, I remind you, you are guest here.' Loki wagged a finger at Luke's face. 'I give you to an ancient one of the woods very soon. Maybe you tell it your theory. And it tear your fucking guts out while you do it. Throw you in a tree like an animal.' Loki grinned.

Luke laughed, until it hurt his nose, his split lips, his bruised cheekbone, and whatever had gone wrong with the top of his head. 'The most evil band in the world, eh? The serial murderers who summoned a demon. It's pretty rock and roll, Loki. I'll give you that. But it counts for shit. You are a fantasist. This is all a load of Dungeons and Dragons, mate. You're a cliché.'

'You are a dead man walking, Luke. Or one that is lying down.'

The old woman put the tray down beside the bed. Luke's mouth filled with saliva.

'Time for you to eat, Luke. And to stop talking.' Loki peered on to the plate and wrinkled his nose. 'I wish it was nicer for you, because it is your last meal, my friend.'

'You can stop this now.'

'Not possible.'

'Loki. At least let me run. Give me a chance out there.'

He grinned. 'Please eat. Do not make this hard for me. I am not a bastard like Fenris. I do not want to . . . erm . . . taunt you.'

'My friends had families. I want to see my dog again. That's it. I won't beg.'

Loki smiled. 'You eat. Then, we get you ready. I leave you alone now.' He walked towards the door, then paused, turned around. 'Hey Luke. If somehow you get off this bed, then crawl down the stairs, or something stupid like that, I let Surtr cut you like she want to. She is only a few seconds away from blood frenzy with you, Luke. So I make a deal with her. I tell her, if Luke run again before it is time for him, then, I tell her, you can cut off all his toes. You can totally fuck him up. And you know something, Luke? Luke?'

'What?'

'I am not joking.'

Loki left him alone with the old woman.

SIXTY

She prepared him with her small gentle hands. Luke watched those doll fingers cut the soiled disgrace of his underwear from his waist and legs, to reveal the tidemark of grime that rose to his hips. She cooed to him to reassure him when he flinched as the steel of the big old scissors was close to his genitals. The pads of her fingers were coarse and leathery, same as her face, but her touch was soft when she bathed his face and his swollen nose, and when she patted his crusting scalp.

She fed him with care and with precision, tucking the warm brown stew inside his swollen lips with the old wooden spoon. Then she held the back of his head, and let him gobble and snuffle at the stewed beets she held out to him. All about the cuts on his face and scalp, she dabbed a black mixture that smelled of rain and moss.

Her eyes were little obsidian flints set so deeply in that impossibly wrinkled hide of a face, and they were smiling all the time she worked about his body, trussed upon that reeking bed. But there was warmth inside her eyes too. It was genuine, he felt. But perhaps no more lasting than the affection shown to a favourite hen, or lamb, or piglet. He mattered as much as livestock. He was important, he was valued, but only for the sustenance of other older appetites.

Good times, old times she remembered. She was washing a corpse. Perhaps her own family had once been bathed and dressed too, but in readiness for the eternity of that loft, by other old women with gentle hands. She lived with the dead. Perhaps she had learned this ritual from those still-twitching ancestors upstairs, made from parchment and dust. And maybe she had prepared other poor wretches too, for that mighty and unnatural presence that governed these black woods. To be given. *Given*.

He began to breathe too quickly. Into his mind came the other attic he had seen out here, and with it the memory of a black face, long, and wet about the great pink bullock nostrils; he thought of worn but strong horns the length of swords. How long did it keep you alive out there in the wet darkness? 'Jesus. Jesus, Christ. Please.' He said, and tried to sit up.

She came closer, held him, gently touched his forehead, like he was a child having a nightmare.

He swallowed the panic. He welcomed her arms, and her quiet words that he could not understand. Her little body was so hard under that dusty black dress that stretched up to her wizened throat. But he welcomed her bosom and he sobbed into it.

The bones of men and beasts, the skeletons of forsaken homes, the forgotten places of worship, now bound them each to the other. He had come here living and warm but now must become *of* it. There was no other place for him in this world. Not any more.

Close to the upright stones, whose meanings and messages were mostly lost, and in the very soil of this lightless place, something was pursuing a purpose older than any living memory. He had sensed it, had tried to run from it, but was now overcome by it. The very idea of *it* caught the breath in his throat and slowed the blood cold in his veins.

'Oh God. Oh God.'

She smiled; she seemed to know and to acknowledge this great epiphany he was experiencing, that wracked his dismal little body and his frail mind upon that wretched bed of old skins and soiled hay.

The terrible will of this place demanded the renewal of old rites. Such things still existed up here. *Here.* Called by the oldest names, they came back to life. Tonight, for him. His life in the distant world, and even the distant world, meant nothing here. Nothing at all. This is how things were for him now.

A quiet voice came into his head and told him that thinking of what had been taken away from him would only make things worse.

This was a true wilderness and people went missing in it all the time. They died to celebrate what long lay hidden here, in its eternal retreat. It had come to the surface of the world early this year; broken its ancient slumber for the monotony of ritual and blood. They had woken it. It had slaughtered his friends, and enjoyed the hunt, the wild ride, but now it just wanted a gift; the provision of something wriggling, tied down. As it had once been surfeited by that ramshackle community above his head, it wanted to be remembered, and honoured. As all Gods do.

Luke gasped at the air. The panic covered him in a cold sweat. He shivered. The old woman cooed, she hugged him close, her little lamb.

'It's a secret,' he whispered to her.

She smiled. He smiled at her, his eyes begging; even this greasy old pillow over his face would be a mercy compared to what would soon come to him from out of those prehistoric trees. 'Please. End it.'

The old woman kept things going; she was part of a long line. She was in place, always; for the things that must be given, and taken away out there, into the eternal forest, into the darkness.

'God no. God no.'

He thought of all those brown bones in the crypt of that broken church: there was no escape. There were no deals to be made. And the very sense of the age of the place, and its size and its indifference to him, nearly extinguished him right there and then in that little bed. He wished it would, rather than making him just comprehend it.

'Please. I want to die now.'

It was like the rare flora and fauna, exempt from scrutiny and trespass, and nurtured by only those who understood.

'They don't care about you. They are using you.' He looked into her tiny black eyes. 'They'll destroy you too. You know it, don't you?'

Blood Frenzy were vandals; impatient, delinquent, angry. Misfits wanting to spit into the face of God, government, society, decency, and anything else that excluded them, or simply bored them. They were as unwelcome here as he was. The old woman was not afraid of them. She was merely tolerating them; he was sure of it. He entertained a lunatic hope that he and the old woman together could help the youths find their natural self-destructive conclusion. 'Let's get rid of them. You and me. I swear. I promise. I will not tell a soul about you . . . and your family.' He looked at her, then looked up at the ceiling.

She shushed him, she stroked his clammy forehead.

No matter the senseless age of what clung on, up here in the boreal wilderness, lit only by moon and sun and seen by so few, the last thing their startled eyes ever saw, Luke whispered to her that it would not begin the end of days that Loki craved. If they must see it as a God, then it was not a God with that kind of weight. He told her that his death was pointless.

But then maybe his life was anyway; it seemed oddly fitting that a damaged teenager's gruesome fantasy world should be the end of his floundering in this life.

And then he was staring at the ceiling and all of him felt as though it were rising from his very body. And in his awe and steadily growing comprehension at what existed out here, at this miraculous and dreadful thing, he suspected it was not long for this world either. What was extraordinary was how it had survived for so long. But its rule was over; it was endangered. An isolated God; all but forgotten and long demented. Branded a false God by the sign of the cross, its idolatry rotted in forgotten attics now, and about it false prophets and ragged messiahs gathered.

Eventually, and as the light dimmed, the waves of fear-induced madness exhausted themselves inside Luke, and slowly subsided from his tormented mind. He felt almost at peace. *Not long now.*

The old woman climbed off the bed. Her little feet knocked loudly against the old floor. She picked up what he thought had been a towel that she had laid upon the side table with the tray. But it was a smock. An old white gown, embroidered intricately with silvery thread around the high neckline; though stained horribly from the waistline to the hem. It had been laundered many times. Was washed out. But there were some stains that could not be removed, like where the aged fabric was black and stiff with old blood. She laid it with reverence across the foot of the bed.

Hearts torn out for the sun God in Mexico. Wretches ritually strangled and buried with their masters in ancient Britain. Simple people accused of witchcraft, pressed under stones and set alight in pyres of dry kindling. Commuters gassed in the Tokyo subway. Passengers flown through the side of buildings in jets full of fuel. *If only we could all stand up. All of us who have died unjustly for the Gods of the insane. There would be so many of us.*

Next, with a little sigh of love, from the bedside table she raised a garland of dry flowers that he was to wear like a crown when he died.

What had once been given, would soon be given again. One was coming to fetch it.

Outside his window, Fenris and Loki shouted to each other; their voices were tight, as if they were straining their bodies with some mighty exertion. And then the music started again and he could not hear the sound of their voices any more.

The old woman collected the gown and the crown of dead flowers. She leaned over him and, inexplicably, raised one gnarled and crooked finger to her lips, to bid him be silent even though he already was.

SIXTY-ONE

When she was gone, taking with her the tray and the plate and jug, the gown and the crown, Luke swung his legs over the side of the bed. Planted his bare feet on the floor, stood up, keeping his calves tight against the frame of the bed until he could establish whether it was possible to balance while moving with his ankles bound together.

It wasn't. When he tried to hop, he crashed to the floor, onto his shoulder. He spat and cursed into the wooden floorboards. Then waited for the sweats to stop and for the footsteps to bang up those old stairs and to rush to his room.

No one came. He wriggled his toes. They weren't coming off just yet. He grinned into the dust.

On his side, entirely naked, he shuffled across to the window. Then raised himself, by pushing the back of his shoulders up and against the wall. Eventually upright, and dirtied again, he turned himself about and peered out of the window.

Blood Frenzy had been busy. Another great pyre had been assembled about twenty feet from the treeline, and positioned much further away from the house than before. Surtr shoved smaller branches of kindling into the base of the structure. The red plastic can of fuel stood at her feet. And a hole had been dug a short distance from the pyre. Foundations, for the large cross that had been roughly cobbled together from two thick planks of aged wood.

Fenris and Loki began positioning the top of the cross inside this hole that had been cut into the turf. They were inserting the crucifix upside down.

Fenris called out to Surtr, who smiled back at him with her hideously painted face. She had added more blood around the nose and mouth than usual. She was also naked again, and her long black hair was lank about her creamy shoulders. She picked up a little silver digital camera from the grass and came across to take photos of Loki and Fenris, as they posed beside the inverted crucifix. It was all still a bit of a game to them. A lack of solemnity at his demise made Luke suddenly and briefly and absurdly angry.

And then he felt so weakened by the sight of that forlorn black cross, standing at a slight tilt under the low dark sky, that he sank to the floor and began to rock himself from side to side.

SIXTY-TWO

When *they* took him from the room, he was entirely naked save for the bindings at his wrists and ankles. *They* were clumsy and drunk; *they* were stupefying.

He did not struggle as Loki and Fenris squeezed him through the narrow passageway and down the cramped and unstable staircase, because he did not want them to drop him. Being three feet from the hard ground with no arms and legs at his disposal, to stick out and break a fall upon all of the sharp wooden edges and corners, made him nervous.

It was only when they took him outside, into the cold damp air, and under that sky dimming from grey to black, that he fought. Inside the little clearing of grass and within the pointy shadow of the old black house, he pulled his legs back suddenly using his hips, and broke them from Fenris's arms, which were supporting him like a heavy roll of carpet against his side. And then Luke twisted around within Loki's long white arms, so he was suddenly facing the earth before he was dropped to the moist grass.

He broke his fall with his knees, then tried to stand and fell immediately over, onto his side. In the cold wet grass, he paused to consider his next move.

Fenris issued his long thin laugh into the darkening air.

'Where will you go, Luke?' Loki said, wheezing but wistful.

The great fire cracked and spat and leapt out its orange tongues so high at the sky. Showers of sparks and porous sheets of leaf drifted up in hot draughts, twisted, and extinguished themselves in glowing red sparks.

The violent music played. The sound was dulled through the earth, but still enough of the cacophony spluttered and crackled out there and into the cold sunless forest, so that whatever crawled this terrible black earth, would know it was dealing with Blood Frenzy this night.

The rifle leant against the porch railing, perhaps as insurance in case Odin failed to discriminate between sacrifice and chosen one. In the shadows of the porch, sat upon a little wooden chair, the old woman watched Luke, her black eyes glinting at the end of the firelight that beat gently against her expressionless face.

To get him on that cross they'd have to cut the nylon from his wrists; and that would be his last chance. He heaved as much air into his lungs as he could and shuddered right down to his joints. Tried not to let urine stream down his legs. And failed; it spouted warm, like life, out of him, over him.

The dark crucifix looked thin, insubstantial. He wondered if it could hold his weight, and imagined the farce and banality of his own death upon an upside-down crucifix that would not stay upright.

'Oh God,' he said, and could not prevent himself making this exclamation of alarm, when he thought of long nails and a mallet; of Fenris's spindly tattooed arms swinging the hammer in the dying light.

But beside the crucifix, he saw coils of old fibrous rope, thin as a washing line, and prayed they were for his wrists and ankles.

Against the dimming trees, as the light drew back like a tide across the ancient roots and bracken of the forest, the sign of the inverted cross now looked too basic, and mock sinister; a prop in a bad horror film with no budget and a cast of overacting amateurs in face-paint. It was uninspiring and unimpressive, like a place or artefact that had acquired an undeserved cult status, and always disappointed whenever it was actually revealed. What a way to die. It should have been funny, but was just dismal and depressing instead.

'Now, Luke. You can run nowhere,' Loki said, his breathing returning to normal. 'We keep your feet tied. So there is no way you get away from this. If you struggle too much, we have to . . . er . . .'

'Knock you the fuck out!' Fenris shrieked.

'More or less,' Loki said in agreement. 'But what I can do for you is give you a last drink, my friend.'

The drinking horn was freed from behind Loki's silver bullet belt and then upended over his face. Luke welcomed its sour chemical burn inside his mouth and throat and stomach. He moved his chin to guide that brackish stream into his gullet. Then it made him want to throw up, before spreading a generous warmth through his gut. It made him dizzy too; like it was the first strong drink he had ever swallowed. It was neat alcohol cut with sweetened orange juice, and brewed in buckets by the desperate. He rolled onto his side and coughed some of it back out of his throat and mouth.

Blood Frenzy had also made a special effort tonight for a special occasion; it was not often they made the acquaintance of an ancient deity of the woods. Loki and Fenris had adorned themselves with a plethora of chains about their waists, and thickened their pale arms with studded armbands to their shoulders; their biceps bristled with actual nails. Each of them wore the band's own shirt, featuring the gloomy lake and spiky red writing. Their faces were freshly decorated and thickened with white paint. Eye sockets were blacked out and long imperious grimaces had been effected through their artificially downturned mouths. Only Surtr remained naked. She had no tattoos on her short plump body, but her labia were encrusted with silver piercings.

With the sole of his boot, Fenris rolled Luke onto his back. Loki grabbed Luke's ankles and pulled him across the wet grass, to the foot of their crucifix.

It may have looked insubstantial, but it took the total strength of both young men to lever the wooden cross back out of the hole and to then begin lowering it earthward; at least they knew enough to sink deep foundations.

Fenris caught his eye as he watched them slowly work the crucifix back towards the ground. 'Nice touch, eh? Old-school black metal!'

When the crucifix was no more than a few feet from the ground, they let it fall with a *whump* onto the grass beside him, ready for his binding to it. Then they used their hands to roll his body over and over, before Fenris seized his ankles and moved them to the foot of the long upright plank.

Loki called Surtr over. She padded across the grass to them. When she came closer Luke could see the white, red and black paint on her face had been perfected into a grin containing as much spite and cruelty as she had been able to fashion into her own features. Even without make-up, she didn't need much help looking hateful. Is this how she feels inside? he wondered hopelessly, and recalled what he had seen in her eyes when she attacked him; her closeness to him made him shrink inside.

What was wrong with them? All of them?

His stomach fell away at this reminder of their utter unfamiliarity to him; it was profound.

He hated them.

His ankles were lashed to the wooden cross, which was hard and splintery and untreated and felt horrid against his calves and heels. Surtr sat on his chest, facing him, pinned his arms under her buttocks; Loki pressed a huge boot against his throat. And they were swift, they were methodical. They were killers. *Killers*: the word repeated itself once inside Luke's mind and it made his whole body go cold.

And then a reel of all they were taking from him flashed up: he saw his mother's smiling face, his little dog, Monty, with his white head cocked to one side just before a walk, his sister, his father, pretty Charlotte in the beer garden, wearing her knee boots, her overbite too sexy to prevent him making a pass, his CD collection, the Billy Bookcase from IKEA with all of his paperbacks inside, stacked double, real ale in the Fitzroy Tavern . . . He stopped the film with one tremendous sob. Screwed his eyes shut. Then growled in defiance.

Once his ankles were fastened tightly to the rough wooden plank with the washing line, he could not move his feet or lower legs at all.

He could barely breathe with Surtr's weight upon his diaphragm either; the metal in her bare genitals was cold against his stomach. 'Your band stinks!' he shouted, when he realized that he would not be able to punch and thrash with his arms.

Surtr had pushed the heels of her little fat feet into his armpits, so when Loki reached behind Surtr's lower back and finally cut the nylon cord from Luke's wrists, it was easy for Fenris and Loki to take a wrist each and pull his arms apart and to drag the stinking smock over his head. Surtr removed her crushing weight from his chest and helped the boys bag him with the stinking gown; and they hooded him in the musty blood of the poor wretches who had died wrapped in that terrible cloth before him.

Loki and Fenris pulled each of his arms through the tight arm holes of the dress; stretched his arms wide apart and lifted his body onto the crucifix, with his hands pulled out to the ends of the cross beam. And when it came to tie his wrists off, the girl settled her considerable body weight through her knees, hard into his shoulders, which immediately flashed with pain at the point just prior to dislocation. Weak and dizzy and nauseous; he had no choice but to remain still for them.

He wanted to cry and beg and plead right then, but he screamed to control the pain and frustration instead.

Loki wrapped one of his wrists in rope. Fenris tied off the other wrist. Tight thin rope that burned and cut into his flesh, pinned him to that cross in the wet grass beneath a sky from which the last light was draining fast.

When Surtr clumsily removed her big knees off his shoulders, Luke understood there would be no last struggle; no final petulant fight to give them something to remember him by.

Fenris grinned, Loki frowned, and then they were straining with all their might and strength under the weight of the crucifix's long beam with Luke tied fast upon it. He shook and he struggled against the rough wood as he was raised from the ground. His little stinking white gown dropped down at the front towards his face, and his cock and balls felt horribly exposed to the night air. He felt like a baby, infantilized. There would be no dignity at the end. He hated them with such a black intensity, he could only hope that he might suffer a stroke and deny them his final screams, his abject terror at the very end.

Then he was upside down. Down his body, he looked at where he was skirted in the blood-ruined linen. Saw the black sky beyond his grimy toes. Dropped his head back to the wood. Looked at the grass so close to his face. Studded boots gathered near his eyes. The pressure of blood rushing downwards came into his head quickly. And upon his head they jammed that scratchy spiky crown of flowers, by shoving it upwards. They martyred him with that halo of dead petals.

And then they all began shrieking. They sang out their incomprehensible screechy lyrics. They drank from bone horns. They threw their thin arms at the sky he could see below the soles of his feet.

'You die on the cross of the false messiah, Luke! It is so exciting, you fucking Nazarene!' Fenris shrieked into his face.

Luke's face screwed up involuntarily. He thought he might break down. Then stopped himself. Then tried to get off. Stupidly, he just tried to get off the big upside-down crucifix. Then he sobbed. Then he shouted. Then lost his mind; saw it go, like a watery thing puffing into vapour, before there was just black and red colours and his own screams inside him. Good, because he did not want his mind. Did not want reason, or lucidity, or anything that would enable him to fully comprehend what soon would be coming for him from out of those dark trees, as he hung upside down upon that black cross.

'Your band fucking sucks!' he screamed at them again. And laughed like a maniac. 'You talentless fuckwits!' Some of the alcohol ran down from his gullet and into his mouth, stinging like battery acid. He spat it out, spat it at them.

The world of upside-down whirled about him; the fire dropped into the sky; the forever of trees clung to the soil with their roots to prevent themselves falling into that eternal canopy of cloudy darkness. He felt as if he were hanging over some great ocean, and could see no land in any direction, and was about to be dropped. If they cut him loose now he knew he would fall straight down and into the sky.

Fenris tried to out-scream him; he was getting to Fenris again. He knew it; skinny weasel-boy Fenris had unfinished business with him and didn't like any defiance from his victims.

'Hey Surtr,' he called out to the excitable figure, thumping herself around the fire with her face all painted like that. 'I'll be dead, but you'll still be fat and ugly. You look like a frog, you fat fuck! Your cunt is the worst thing I have ever smelled!' he screamed his throat raw.

And then Loki was restraining Fenris, who looked like a Bonobo monkey with a white face, driven mad by some experiment.

Luke screamed into the sky, the earth, the endless trees. He wanted to be mad and screaming when it came, low down and fast and eager. He called out to it. 'Come on you stinking fuck! Come on!' He would bite its face with the last of his life.

Soon he was fading, he was feeling faint, his head was swollen and hot and prickly.

Loki was calling to the old woman. He was angry with her. She seemed unconcerned, and sat silently on her little chair. Loki released Fenris, who stomped across to the porch and pointed at the tiny woman in her little chair. He screamed at her too. Clenched his hard white fists and shook them at her. Loki implored her. Then shouted at Fenris, who turned on him. There was some shoving between them. Then Surtr plodded across to the confrontation and screamed at Fenris.

The old woman stood up, and left the porch. She went back inside the house. Closed the door. Left them all outside arguing, with Luke upside down upon the cross.

Eventually their voices petered out. Loki muttered something to Surtr, who walked solemnly to the CD player and killed the music. Not even the fire seemed so fierce now. They were all just outside, getting cold in the damp and dark air. And the woods remained silent too. Like the old woman. Silent and old and indifferent.

Though the woods were not completely vacant. Luke's eyes bulged purple from the terrible pressure inside his head, and his vision darkened like the last of his sight was suddenly going out. But he saw their faces; the pale faces and pinkish eyes catching the flash of the fire as the little white people watched him. Watched him and then withdrew.

SIXTY-THREE

The moon is full and the forest outside his room has changed. It is larger than ever before; it covers the entire land to the cold seas on every shore. It is luminous. It is majestic. It is epochal. It is timeless. Before it, he feels smaller than he has ever felt.

The voices return from the space above him; whisperings he can understand.

'Look. Look,' they cry out to him. 'Look down.'

On the grass beneath the great moon-filled sky, he sees a figure dressed in white, crowned with flowers and propped upright in a cart full of bloodied fowl. The passenger is thrown about in its seat like a doll, or maybe it struggles.

Behind the cart, a ragged procession follows; in the places where the silvery light turns back the darkness, he sees the hunched, the loping, and the skipping thin figures in rags older than the crusades. They prance and caper alongside the cart, out to a place so old even the chorus in the attic tell him they have forgotten its true age. Perhaps this is the last of all the old places.

When the time comes will he call with them into the sky? they ask. Will he say the old names with them? When he hears the name he is to speak with them, he cannot breathe.

And from that cart, the figure in the white robe, wearing a crown of dead spring flowers upon its head, is taken down. The figure that is so suddenly *him*, and now he is amongst the stones. And upon the largest stones around him, his dead friends grimace silently in death. Naked and devoured down to their blood-blackened bones, they are tied to stones carved with forgotten poems. And upon a stone he too is mounted, between his friends, and what was once given will be given again.

From the trees he is watched by small, indistinct figures. They talk and make sounds that remind him of laughter. Their whispering voices fill his eyes and ears like flies.

He sees another place. And in it he can smell tallow and smoke and the reek of soiled straw. He is inside a dark barn, or a simple church; a plain structure of old timber that flickers with the reddish light of a fire.

In here, somewhere in the darkness, a woman groans in the agonies of childbirth. And he cannot prevent his legs from rushing across to where she lies even though his mind is screaming at him to run away.

Her cries are soon accompanied by the sound of newborn livestock. And he is standing amongst a group of small figures, about the shadowy straw-filled manger. And here is a thing, wet and mewling, that he cannot quite see, both of man and of another place, drawn out by its rear hooves from between pale lifeless thighs. It is brought out of the steaming, devastated womb of the dead mother and is clutched by the long fingers of those who witness a miracle.

Luke comes out of the dream with a cry. And looks about the dark room to try and see the faces of the people who are muttering at him so quickly. But the voices fade, retreat above him, back into the attic.

He stands again before the glowing white window of his little room, shaking from the dream of the birthing, and he looks down at the forest bathed in phosphorescent light. At the edge of the trees, small white figures, lightly haired and thin, gather and frolic. He blinks and they are gone too.

He turns around and the old woman comes towards him. Her tiny feet are no longer loud because they are bound in cloth. She offers him a knife. The long thin black one he has seen before.

The point of the blade seems to open a place inside himself that will not allow him to ever feel anything again but rage, or to remember anything but those moments of choking hatred, and to only think instinctively as the creatures of the forest think in order to prolong their lives and to evade the skilful predators.

The chorus above knock their little feet upon the floor of the attic. They bang the old timbers for blood.

He looks down at the old woman, but she is no longer before him in the room. The house cracks about him like an old hand closing its fingers; he stands alone amongst the splinters and the dust, holding the knife.

When the sun broke through the thin cloud, Luke awoke.

Again.

And sat up, gasping. But this time the air was colder and sharper around his naked body and he knew that this time he was really awake.

Luke adjusted his position upon the bed to ease the aches

in his ankles. He rubbed at his sore wrists. Widened his feet. The dreams let go of him.

His breath caught in his throat.

He was untied.

Startled mute and perfectly still by this realization, he stared at how the eiderdown had been turned down to the foot of the bed. Between his knees on the tatty sheepskins was a red Swiss Army knife; the main blade folded out. It was his knife.

Draped over the side of the bed was the blood-mired gown and the little crown of flowers.

SIXTY-FOUR

Naked, Luke squatted upon the floor of his room and watched the door. It was early. Outside his window the sun was bright and steely where it found fissures in the cloud cover. The rain had stopped.

He stilled the rushing of his thoughts; the chattery clutter that was eroding his advantage before he realized he had one. He tried instead to understand his new position in a world that was entirely a place of confusion, of terror, of the impossible and his bafflement before it.

The old woman; she came to him in a dream while he slept in the wretched bed, bound like a captive, like a sacrifice. But now he was free and within his hand was a knife. So she had really come in the night and cut his restraints and left him a weapon?

He gaped, he grinned.

They were so angry with the old lady last night, when she refused to call that thing out there, out from amongst the black trees. She disobeyed Loki; she refused to bring the demon, the God, to take him as he hung upon the cross. And now she wanted him to run, or to get rid of the youths from her home; he wasn't sure which, but he had good cause to do both.

The impossible idea of him living again, for more than just

ADAM NEVILL

a few hours, came back to him. It took his breath away, even his balance, and he had to steady himself by putting one hand against the dirty floorboards.

The awareness of his new circumstances shivered through him; it was a white electricity coursing under his skin. It made his eyelids jump and the nerves spark inside his muscles. He was as light as helium, as fast and jittery as a hare.

He could not remember ever feeling the same way before. There seemed to be no limit now to where his mind could reach or to where his limbs could carry him. He was strength. He was unbound.

And unsure he had ever been fully awake before right now, right here; naked and dirty and scarred and so reduced in this moment-by-moment existence. And he understood that he had given up long before this time. Had been drifting. Baffled. Inactive. Futile. His old self was flimsy, insubstantial. His old world grey. There had been hesitation at critical moments; so much self-doubt. He had languished, demoralized, for so long, forever. He understood this. The realizations came all at once and very quickly. His whole life until this moment was preposterous; and himself in that life absurd.

But now he wanted to live.

If he survived the next few minutes, every moment of his life would sing. Each word spoken would have meaning, every meal eaten and drink taken would be a gift: his salvation would be the living of life.

He smiled at himself. He was simply not about giving up. He received again a sense of what he loved, of who he no longer wanted to disappoint, of what he wanted to live for. It came back to him, but stronger, and clearer than ever. His memory rested on the image of his little dog, at home; the

368

small trusting figure, blinking snowy eyelids up at him in the mouth of his tiny dismal kitchen. He smiled and he cried silently at the same time.

He mattered again to himself. Watching his own end come closer and closer, while in constant fear, was abhorrent to him. He had arms and legs he could still move; senses that received and experienced the utter wonder of existence, moment by moment. He laughed, quietly, through his tears.

They thought they could take life away from him.

There were three of them. He thought of the sheath knives, the rifle. They were teenagers. Children even. Probably too young to go to prison. Could he hurt them if it came to it? This sudden stab of his conscience made him groan. This was no time or place for a conscience.

He rose and walked to the window of his room, and looked out at the upside-down cross, felled and flat upon the grass.

It was simply a world where one will dominated another. It was an uncompromising era. Insistent wills eroded him, dominated him, they always had done. Some even greater will, guiding all of the others who had tormented him in his life, had led him here for the final reckoning of himself; in a part of the world made by the damaged for the damaged, in the great age of the pathological. If he survived the morning, he swore he would fight it, them, whatever, forever.

He could defer to no one and nothing but his own survival now. It was an every man for himself world. He did not make it so; he had resisted it but was tired of being the victim. 'Victim,' he whispered the word. 'Victim.' Saying it was like sucking a battery. He victimized himself. And he would not have it any more. He would die here unless he killed them all. He was in the *now*; he knew what that meant.

Could he kill? he asked himself. His stomach turned over. Would he recognize himself after he did this thing? This was not some horror film; he would actually have to smash a knife through human skin into the density of a body.

He began to shake. Maybe he should just run, hide, run, hide, hope.

No. They would come after him.

He looked at the ceiling. He had to sow with salt the place where such things could still exist. He would need to go to the red, hot, unthinking place inside himself: the place he inhabited when he attacked the passenger on the train, and punched poor Dom off his feet. He needed to find the place inside himself that led to the smashings, the snappings, the middle fingers at drivers who did not stop for pedestrians on crossings, the grindings of his teeth to sand when he could not sleep and thought of the sociopaths he had worked with. The pathetic rage that destroyed his possessions and furniture, that turned itself against the inconsiderate and the rude in public, was always simmering in him, ready to boil. The gas needed to be turned up a notch. Right now. His life depended upon it happening. And he would need to stay inside that hot red place of instinct and rage until they or he were dead.

It was unthinkable; it was mandatory.

But it wouldn't come. In his thoughts and feelings he found it hard to change places with *them*. To suddenly be the one who was violent and determined.

He closed his eyes. Imagined their horrid painted faces; the triumphant smiles of these intense, committed, wilfully idiotic, cruel people. They were unfathomable. Why should they live, and he not? Why?

They deserved to die. He wanted them dead. He wanted their young but poisonous blood shed, and this wretched part of the world erased from the earth. Blood and soil. Yes, they were right. Ragnarok was coming down fast, but not in the way they anticipated. He'd give them their blood and soil.

He was naked so he put on the little stained gown. It smelled of rust. Then he crowned himself, as the old woman wished.

But if he overcame them . . . He remembered the terrible forest, and of what walked upon its floor. Luke shuddered. Closed his eyes against it all.

He crept towards the door. *One thing at a time.*

'One thing at a time, my friend,' said the part of him that had detached itself from all of the other voices inside him.

SIXTY-FIVE

The door to his room was unlocked. When he opened it, he expected someone with a painted face to suddenly come through it, grinning; or, at the very least, to be outside waiting for him in the shadows. But there was no one in the corridor.

He went out and into the dark house on careful feet. Pulled the door closed behind him, but paused when the old hinges began to groan. He left it ajar.

Listened as he had never listened before. Somewhere, something was dripping: a monotonous sound, ambient. There was a far-off creak in the roof, then a wooden floor-board moaned under his dirty feet. The old house was always shifting; the old spine trying to support the weight of its years.

At one end of the thin passage was the little door to the attic; to his left, at the other end, was the staircase they had been dragging him up and down for two days now. One other wooden door stood between him and the staircase leading to the ground floor. He remembered the pattern of footsteps at night: someone would be sleeping in that room, two of them.

Keeping his feet at the sides of the warped floor and his head low, he walked towards the top of the staircase. It was like moving below deck on an old ship. He was careful, but the floor creaked. Once, under the oil lantern, he nearly lost his balance.

Across from the bedroom door, he paused and listened so intensely it was like he was sending his consciousness inside that room to pad and paw about like a blind man.

Silence. Stillness.

At the top of the stairs he allowed himself to swallow, and to breathe again. His head began to hurt; a dull ache pushed behind his eyes.

Down he went, his skin goosing, like he was stepping into cold seawater. And the further he moved from his room, the more he fought the urge to speed up, to just flee. Inexplicably, his ankles hurt and quivered the tendons and muscles in his lower legs, threatening to pitch him over. He clenched his teeth. Why was his body trying to betray him?

Bottom of the staircase. Eyes and ears everywhere, seeking them out.

The old woman with the loud feet wouldn't let him run. She wanted a job done. And if he went straight for the trees, where would he then go? *It* would come; she could call *it*.

The truck. Keys. The truck.

Had she wanted him to get away, there would have been car keys along with the knife in his little bed that morning. But he could not just go into a bedroom and stab a sleeping body; the thought made him feel sick and faint. He leant against the wall of the little hall. Peered at the plain wood, either blemished with wood smoke or just blackened with a terrible age.

On the balls of his feet he slipped around another dusty oil lantern and passed into the parlour, into another era.

There were walls of dark wood, cloudy with ancient mould and damp near the bulgy ceiling. A gassy yellowish light came in through two small grimy windows facing the paddock. He smelled wet wood, dead smoke lingering.

Most of the walls were obscured by the dusty artefacts. Horse shoes. Animal bones. Another charnel house. Bones and remains from the forest. Skulls of martens or squirrels, antlers from red deer, the dinosaur face of a bear skull, the nightmare grimace of an elk; all sightless, desiccated.

The furniture was homemade, simple. Hunting materials lined the shelves in the heavy cabinet. The blackened head of a broad axe. A shield boss. Points of spears, arrow heads, knife blades. Other things of corroded iron that could have been hooks, or blades. He saw an oval brooch decorated with a leaping animal. And the sudden colour of glass beads; blue glass patterned with an undulating mosaic of red, white, yellow in a little brass dish. A rubble of round flat stones, worn like flints, maybe whetstones. Other implements, their purpose a mystery to him, all made from bone or stone and so old and bleached they resembled driftwood on a sea shore. His eyes scoured the floor, the walls, and the little table for the rifle.

Under his feet worn and mouldering pelts of deer covered dirty straw scattered about the dusty floorboards; the tattered remnants of the pelts were an unwelcome reminder of the trees and what hung from them.

Nothing of any use to him in the parlour; no clothes, no rifle. He turned on his heel, stepped across the hallway. Suddenly afraid of the darkness at the top of the staircase, he looked to his left as he crossed the passage. And came into the kitchen quickly.

And then there was Fenris. Inside the kitchen with him. A room bigger than Luke thought it could be. Long: the floor hard and cold with uneven tiles of slate. And upon the dark table Fenris lay inside a red sleeping bag, within the plain boards of a box bed. Beside the wooden box was a long wooden sheet, or lid; the tabletop for when the furniture wasn't being used as a bed. The pointy smeared face of Fenris peeked out of the covers; the blue eyes were wide open.

They looked down, took in the knife in Luke's hand, flicked back up to his face. Stared at him, almost doleful, in anticipation. Of what?

Fenris's studded boots stood empty, beside a wooden bench, along one side of the big box bed. Luke looked about the room again quickly: an iron range with black chimney, a dark-brown cabinet, some pots and wooden plates, a back door. And a tiny crib, hand carved, in which the old woman sat; in her dusty black dress beside the hearth, like a cat. She stared at him too, waiting. What did they want from him, these people?

And then he saw it; the rifle leaning against the wall beside the door he had come through. And Fenris saw him see it. The world then became a blur with a judder going through it as time passed too quickly.

Fenris swung his legs, then his whole body off the table, and stood up still inside his sleeping bag; it dropped in a scarlet ruffle about his knees. 'Good morning, Luke. Maybe you go back to London now, eh? Wearing your faggot dress. It look good on you.'

He slept in leather jeans and a T-shirt that advertised Bathory. In his hand was the sheath knife. It came into that slender feminine hand and the room and Luke's life so quickly he knew in a heartbeat that the youth could use it. Had used it. Relied upon it and slept with it like a lover.

Luke's heart dropped like a stone into a stomach that shimmered, then vanished. Only this far; only to get this far and *they* were there again, in his way.

He ran at Fenris, his own knife at his side. Then hesitated, one step away from Fenris, for a time shorter than a wristwatch could measure. He asked himself how it was done, the entering of a sharp point into a living human being. Even after all he had been through, it was simply not in him. But he had paused in that room long enough for Fenris to grin and thrust up a skinny white arm.

Luke flinched. Jerked to the side. Then his breath seized up inside him when he felt the opening of himself like wet pastry across his hip bone. A long sting followed the parting of his flesh under the gown. There was a hot flash down one thigh, and when he looked he was all red and drippy to the knee. He gouted, he gushed.

Fenris grinned, swivelled the knife about in his hand so it daggered down from his fist. Luke looked into the boy's hard blue eyes and felt too angry to breathe. He had not wanted this and because of his decency he would have to die in a dirty kitchen. 'Cunt,' he said, and spit came out of his mouth. It made Fenris blink. Then the boy's skinny tattooed arm was up in the air and coming down at him fast.

Luke walked under his elbow. Caught the girlish wrist in one hand, like he'd plucked a cricket ball whizzing through the air at second slip, and he had the ball in his hand before anyone had seen the actual catch. He punched his other hand up and into the skinny boy, blade out. His fist came to a stop as his thumb and knuckle indented the boy's flat stomach, and then he stepped away.

Fenris gasped. Looked down himself in surprise. Then screwed up his smeared face like he was going to cry, like he was so disappointed who something was over, or that he had been cheated.

Luke went for the gun. Around him all he could hear was Fenris's cries and his own breath, which was loud and hot and wet all over his own face. He was dizzy at the sight of the blood. It was all over his own leg, and coming out slippery between Fenris's long scarlet fingers where he clutched them at his soggy side.

The gun was heavy. Ungainly. Luke heaved it up and into his arms and nearly dropped it. His hands were shaking too much to hold it steady, or to get his finger inside the trigger guard.

Fenris howled. His face was fury and grief and panic now. The old woman looked on from her little wooden box, impassive, as if strangely bored with their behaviour.

Fenris stepped out of the sleeping bag and came at him. Luke forced a jittery finger inside the trigger guard. Put the end of the barrel in Fenris's direction.

Fenris did not stop.

Luke pulled the trigger. The trigger was unmovable. He tried to turn the rifle around to use the butt to strike Fenris, but the long barrel struck the wall behind his head. His own clumsiness and lack of coordination infuriated him; his arms felt like they were full of warm water.

He quickly swept the rifle to the side and parried Fenris's bony hand that came slashing at him with his hunting knife still gripped in it. The point of the knife whisked a slot across

Luke's bicep, then cut his chest above the nipple. It felt deep; seemed to wake him up. He kicked the heel of his right foot into Fenris's side, where it was wet.

The kid fell back, holding himself around the middle with both wet red hands. Luke ran sideways to the cabinets beside the window, to make room for himself, to get some air so that he could breathe. He looked down at the rifle; he had once fired a .22 rifle in the sea cadets; it had been a bolt action. He slid the bolt back and forth, hoping he was chambering a round. Pointed it at Fenris again, pulled the trigger. No movement from the trigger. 'Shit.'

He leaned the rifle against the wall. It immediately slid down the patchy plaster and clattered noisily against the floor.

Fenris was now leaning on the plain wooden box that he had been sleeping inside. He had dropped his knife so he could hold his wet side with both hands. He was crying now. Looking at the ceiling, he called out for Loki twice. Then moaned in anguish and horror at the sight of his own blood coming over his hands and around the handle of the Swiss Army knife that was still stuck inside him; the knife Luke had just kicked deeper.

Upstairs: footsteps. Loud, skittering, scuffing, hurried: coming through the ceiling.

Luke went to Fenris. Picked up the sheath knife from before the youth's skinny bare feet.

'Please Luke,' Fenris said.

Luke smashed it into the boy's throat. All the way through, until the finger guard of the handle stopped against the lump of his Adam's apple.

Luke stepped away, panting. 'I'm sorry. Shit. Shit.' He wanted this to stop now.

The Ritual

The old woman spoke in Swedish. She nodded her little white head in approval and her eyes smiled at him, over Fenris's shoulder.

There was a terrible wet choking sound coming from Fenris, and he could not keep still. He staggered about the kitchen, dripping, then tottered out of the room, as if there were someone who could help him outside.

Heavy boots banged through a tight corridor upstairs, then boomed on to the stairs. Loki.

Fenris turned left in the dim hallway and ran for the front door like he was sick and wanted air.

Luke picked up the rifle, stared at it. Saw the little steel lever above the trigger guard. Put the end of the barrel against the floor, reached down with a hand and slipped the steel lever away from the SAFETY position.

Big boots boomed against the bottom two steps of the staircase and then came banging down the cramped hall on the ground floor. Loki was trying to be calm, but was worried; Luke could hear it in his voice, as he called out in Norwegian to Fenris; who he must have been able to see out on the porch or in the grass paddock. Luke shouldered the weapon and pointed the barrel into the middle of the doorframe. The rifle was so heavy, so long; it was hard to keep it aloft and steady. It made his arms feel frail.

But as soon as he had the rifle's sights aimed at the doorway, Loki ducked into the kitchen, stooping at the waist so his head would miss the top of the frame. He did not see Luke until it was too late. Their eyes locked for a moment. Loki's were puffy with sleep, running with mascara, and twitchy with shock. Just as he frowned in confusion, Luke shot him.

The rifle bucked; not too hard. But the sound deafened him. It seemed to crack the slate floor, smash all the windows and roar like a jet too low to the earth. Loki disappeared from the door. Luke's ears whistled. The old lady cried out, afraid. Her little rough hands clouted her own ears. All was jittery around Luke; the world leapt in and out and nothing made sense in the ringing of his ears, in the impact of sending that bullet through a man.

Luke punched the bolt up, forward, back, and down. A brass shell dropped and bounced on to the slate stones; some smoke drifted from the end of the shell case. He was getting better. Not so clumsy. He could smell fireworks.

Loki was on all fours in the grubby hallway. Head down, hair covering his gasping face, his great back shuddering. Strangely, he too crawled at the front door which was wide open now.

Luke slipped on the floor. Looked down. His foot was wet with his own blood. He had slipped in the blood that was running down his leg from his hip. There was very little pain in his hip, but the sight of the blood made his vision go white. He stopped to be sick in the hallway, but nothing came out beside some phlegm. Mostly, it was just a big gassy burp. He looked over his shoulder at the stairs. But Surtr was not coming down yet. Up there it was silent.

Loki had reached the doorway and rolled onto his back, half on the porch, half in the hallway. They looked into each other's eyes. They were both panting, exhausted, and unable to speak for a while. He had not realized the barrel of the gun had been directed so low when he shot Loki, but he had gunned him somewhere through the pelvis, where Loki's big hands were now pressing into a dark wetness.

'Luke. Stop!' he commanded in his deep voice. Even covered in cracked white face-paint, Loki had never looked so pale.

Luke shook his head. Swallowed, but could not find his voice.

'Luke, no. I ask this of you.'

Then words rushed out of him. 'Where are the keys to the truck?'

Loki stayed quiet, but winced, screwed up his eyes against the pain.

'Keys, Loki?' He looked over his shoulder. Still no Surtr.

'Upstairs. In my jacket.'

'Where your fat bitch is? Nice try.'

Loki looked at him again; he was terrified, he had been telling Luke the truth about the whereabouts of the keys. Luke stared at the long figure down there, shivering in agony. The man couldn't have been older than twenty. Loki started to cry. Luke could not look him in the eye for long. He started to cry too; couldn't help himself. He felt a terrible grinding remorse for what he had just done to Fenris and Loki; he was about to shut down at any moment.

Luke stopped crying. Was suddenly angry with himself. Swallowed hard. 'My friends wanted to live, Loki. To see their children.' He cleared his throat; spat phlegm onto the floor. 'Mercy is a privilege out here. Not a right. You made it that way. You can die by your own rules.' Luke cleared his throat again and said, 'Fuck it.' He aimed the end of the rifle barrel at Loki's big face. 'Consequences, Loki.'

'No, Luke,' Loki said in a voice that was not so deep now. He raised a big hand and stretched it towards Luke, palm first. The palm was bright red and wet.

Luke shot him through his fingers. Banged Loki's big head down against the wooden deck of the porch. Behind his head was an instant wide swirl of murky liquid peppered with hard bits that Luke could not bring himself to look into. The sound of it coming out of Loki's head was the worst thing he had ever heard.

Luke punched the bolt up, forward, back, and down. Stepped over Loki, who still twitched and shivered down the length of his legs. Luke was not worried about him getting up again.

Luke sniffed; there was mucus all over his mouth and chin. With one forearm he wiped at his eyes, then at his mouth.

Fenris was lying on his side, still moving, about twenty feet from the house. Pulling himself along the ground with one arm, towards the trees. Just to get away. Luke followed him. There was a lot of blood in the grass.

Then Luke paused and turned around to look up at the windows of the house. The whitish balloon of Surtr's face peered down at him from the little window of the room where they had kept him captive. Her face was full of shock. They stared at each other and then she retreated away from the glass.

'Hey,' he said to Fenris. 'Hey.'

Fenris looked up at him, his eyes bulged from his smeared face. A horrible speckling of blood dotted his chin and the forearm beneath the hand that clutched at the handle of the hunting knife moving up and down in his throat.

Luke looked away, at the trees. He felt dizzy and sick and he just wanted to sit down on the grass, but could not bring himself to get any closer to the sounds Fenris was making.

'I could get the truck running. Put you in the back. Drive like a bastard to . . . Where, I don't fucking know, but that road must go somewhere, Fenris.'

Fenris propped himself up on one elbow. He gasped, he choked, his throat produced a horrible aerosol of blood, a mist as he pulled air in and out of himself from mouth, nose and throat.

Luke looked back at the house, wondering if there was a second gun. Nothing moved in the old black building, but Surtr would have to come down soon. From where he stood in the paddock, he could see through the open front door, and along the hallway to the far rear wall of the building. But still, nothing moved.

He looked down at Fenris again. He wanted, he needed, to speak. To make some sense of this to himself. It was like he was just doing things without thinking any of it through. He was operating on instinct now. But where did these instincts come from?

'It's too late for all that,' Luke said, surprising himself with his own voice that possessed an inappropriate strength. 'I don't think the world has enough time left for all that, Fenris. It's too late to understand, you know. Everything has just gone too far. You can't persuade any more, or re-educate. You think this, I think that.'

Fenris might not have been listening; he clawed towards Luke's leg.

'You kidnap, you murder. Can you expect any mercy? There are consequences. I told Loki the same thing. You never thought about them. Did you? Even if you were caught, you would still expect special treatment. That's what gets me the most. And you would get it. Fuck that shit, Fenris. Just fuck it.'

Fenris gobbled with his mouth at the air; he reached for Luke's leg again and convulsed. Luke shot him through his right eye from close range.

Luke turned and walked back to the house, paused on the porch. Stood beside Loki, to the left of the doorframe, and peered into the brownish hallway. Loki had stopped moving now, but was leaking all over the uneven planking. Luke regretted not asking Loki or Fenris where they had put his tobacco. He was light in the head, soul-buoyant. Wanted this finished, quick now.

'Surtr!'

No sound from upstairs in the dark house.

What to do. What to do. What to do.

Bullets. How many? There was a magazine before the trigger guard. But he wasn't sure how to detach it to check the ammunition, and if he did, he worried he would not be able to get the magazine back inside the rifle. These things were never simple. He would need a knife, a backup.

'Surtr! Loki's gone. Your friends. Gone. You hear me?'

Silence.

He hiked up the dress and looked at his hip; it was open like a mouth with no lips, and had soaked the hem of the dress with blood; new blood on old blood. He couldn't bear to look into it. The knife had gone down to muscle on his chest too, and peering below the neckline of the gown and seeing the wound so close made him faint and cold and nauseous. He bent double and dared to close his eyes. Breathed deep. Then straightened, stepped over Loki, and went back inside the kitchen.

He looked at the old woman; she looked at him. She had not moved from her little cradle beside the stove. And seemed expectant, dissatisfied with him; he had work to do, was not finished. *But how?* he wanted to ask her, though she spoke no English and could not answer him. He did not want to walk up that narrow staircase and go into the tiny rooms with their low ceilings; it was no place for a man with no blood left inside him and a rifle in his shaky white fingers. The girl could be up there waiting, moon-faced in the dark, with a knife in her pudgy little fist. *Bitch*.

And what was he to do with these wounds. He was about to point at his hip and show the old woman the new mouth, when she looked at the wall. The wall opposite the stove. And nodded her shrunken leathery head. Luke frowned. She nodded again, raised her top lip to flash her discoloured teeth in a little snarl.

Luke looked at the wall, and the moment he did he heard the door give a tiny moan from across the hallway. He shouldered the rifle. Surtr had come down the stairs silently on her flat round feet and was waiting inside the parlour. And she would have seen Loki too.

He swallowed. And moved slowly back to the entrance of the kitchen. Hesitated. Wondered if he should go into the parlour. Sutr could be just inside the doorway. Yes, the door had moved. He was sure he had not left it like that, pushed halfway back to the frame. Or maybe it had swung back of its own accord and she was still upstairs, hiding, waiting.

Holding his breath, he crouched and moved sideways down the hallway to the front door, stepped over Loki and sank himself down to the grass. Then stood up straight and peered at the little grimy windows of the parlour from the outside. Too dim.

Moving closer to the old brown glass, he placed one foot

on the sagging deck of the porch and Surtr came into focus so quickly he sucked in his breath and nearly yanked at the trigger.

Bent forward, she faced the floor of the parlour, which is why she could not see him at the window. She wore jeans and a black T-shirt. She was listening intently, pressed against the inside of the old parlour door; clinging and ready to swing around and into him had he walked back inside the room. Or she was poised to smash the door closed on the rifle as he went inside. Or maybe she would creep out and take him by surprise from behind as he passed that room to search for her. Clever. She wanted him. Always had done. No woman had desired him so much – desired him dead.

He boiled, sweated cold over his face. Gritted his teeth until they hurt and he raised the rifle at the window.

Fired.

In went the entire glass pane and up and onto her toes went Surtr, like she'd been electrocuted. For a split second she was all shaky black hair and big white eyes. Something smashed inside. She cried out.

Was she hit?

Up, forward, back, down with the bolt in the breech. When Luke looked up she had gone from the parlour, the door closed behind her.

Luke hobbled sideways across the paddock and looked down and into the hallway of the house from outside. Heard the bump bump bump of her feet, somewhere inside, in the dark, out of sight. But she could not have reached the stairs, so she must have run inside the kitchen. Luke continued to walk sideways, outside, across the face of the house, with the rifle raised. He'd shoot the bitch through the glass of the kitchen windows. An eagerness, verging on excitement, made him tingle all over and sweat heavy.

There she was, going out the tiny back door of the kitchen; he saw her through the dirty windows as he squinted along the gun barrel.

Luke ran, ungainly, sloppily, with his breath hoarse and infuriating in his ears, down the side of the house, the rifle raised. He was desperate to fire it again. But he made sure to come round the corner of the house carefully, and into the rear paddock before the orchard, looking everywhere and ready to go.

No one on the grass.

Movement out there: in the orchard, on the other side of the truck. Off she went, fast for a big girl, between the trees planted along the side of the rutted track.

The rifle sights swam, then moved before his eyes. His hands were overeager, shaky. He blinked sweat out of his eyes. Refocused. Had her sighted. Then she was gone from the sights again, changing her direction, dodging, her big thighs pumping.

When he finally had her shape in front of the rifle sights, as she moved between two black-limbed trees, he fired.

Too high. Or had he hit her? She had vanished.

Cordite seared his face, his eyes, throat and nose. His ears rang out their resistance like a drill.

But no, he had not hit her, because there she was, still on her feet and running across the track at the side of the orchard. By the time he had the rifle cocked again, she was gone, into the trees where the forest began, on the other side of the track.

Disappointed, he looked at the white truck. Went to it.

Through the passenger window, he saw sweet wrappers in the foot wells, a discarded book of maps written in Swedish. A right-hand drive. Opened the door. The smell of rubber, oil, wet metal, old cigarette smoke hit him. Scents of the old world; the world this vehicle could take him back to. It was filthy inside. Dirt was compacted into the mats and the seats; the floor of the cabin was bare metal. The rubber pads were gone from the pedals; upholstery was split on the long bench seat. A bright turquoise fishing lure hung from the rear-view mirror. In the flatbed an open bag of tools, empty red plastic fuel containers, a dozen crushed beer cans. It was not their vehicle. It had brought them here, but they had taken it from someone, somewhere else.

Luke put the gun down. Then leant inside the truck cabin and touched the steering column, put his finger tips on to the slot for the ignition key, hoping. Empty.

Keys, keys, fucking keys.

He decided there and then to just get the hell out, and fast. He turned and walked gingerly back towards the house, one hand clamped upon the movements of the new mouth in his hip.

Stopped. Turned around and went back for the gun that he had left on the grass. 'Fuck.' He wasn't thinking straight. Was dizzy with hunger and burning with thirst; faint from the excitement that kept draining out of him, before being suddenly invigorated back through him from his exhausted glands, over and over and over again. His thighs felt so heavy. Shadows flickered at the sides of his vision. He spat, carried on.

The old woman was gone when he arrived back inside the

kitchen. He called out. 'Hello. Hello.' But no one answered or came.

There were no taps, no sink; the house had never been plumbed. But he found six one-litre water bottles that had been reused to bring water to the house from the well he still had not seen. He uncapped one bottle; belted the warmish water inside him until a crippling stitch made him stop, bend over and gasp.

There was a pantry. Dark and brown and cool inside. A chunk of black bread he snapped from the hard loaf and crammed it to his mouth. Sucked it more than chewed it. Coarse against his tongue, it tasted of blood. There was a salted joint of meat in there; two sacks of beets; jars full of pickles and preserves lined four long shelves; dusty cooking apples; salt. Turnips, carrots, ancient coffee. But nothing to go. Blood Frenzy must have arrived empty-handed; these were her meagre provisions. They'd come to the end of the earth for this. Later, he could eat later. When he was gone.

Keys, keys, fucking keys.

He went up the stairs slowly, backwards, trying to keep the chewing mouth in his hip closed. He needed to wash it, bind it. At the top of the staircase, he turned himself around. Sent the barrel of the gun into the murk first and followed it with his body. He wondered if Surtr could have come back inside the house and crept up here. He dismissed the idea, but felt tense and brittle, like he would shatter at the first sound of her still being around.

Down the corridor. A peek into the first room. Two sleeping bags on the floor. One blue, one yellow. Loki and Surtr's room. Clothes strewn everywhere. Untidy, dirty, angry people. He went inside, looking for Loki's jacket. Then turned and gasped. Nearly shot from the hip, when he saw the three animal masks they had worn that first day. All three were lined up and staring from a wooden sawbuck table that looked as if the Vikings had made it. Did they bring the animal heads here, or had they come with the room?

A miasma of sweat and hair grease wafted off their clothing. In the mess on the floor he found a leather biker jacket. It was riddled with spikes around the shoulders; riveted with steel at the waistline and elbows. Celtic Frost, Satyricon, Gorgoroth, Behemoth, Ov Hell, Mayhem, Blood Frenzy, painted carefully in white paint on the back panel. Inside a pocket, a jingle-jangle. Six keys, attached to an inverted steel crucifix: what else?

For some reason Luke zipped the pocket closed after extracting the keys, then asked himself, 'Why?' Shook his head. It was like walking through treacle now. Was the house so hot? He could only remember being cold in here before. The building listed like a boat in a squall. The rifle was so heavy; the barrel banged against things. He swore at it. His face was burning, wet.

Back outside in the corridor, he glanced past his old room and at the little door that led to the attic staircase. Listened. A voice. He frowned. Moved down to the door, but it grew faint. He looked at the ceiling. Realized the voice was not coming from up there, but from outside. Someone was *singing*.

He went back into Loki and Surtr's room and peered down through the dirty glass of the window. Nothing out back in the orchard. He paused, listened again. It was coming from the other side of the house. Unable to bear going back inside the room they had kept him locked inside, he descended the stairs, breathless, dazed, his wounds burning but wet.

In the hallway, he raised the rifle butt to his shoulder and walked at the front door. The parlour door was still closed; the kitchen, he saw after a quick sweep with his jerky eyes, was empty. Back door was still open.

He stepped over Loki, looked outside.

The little old woman stood by the site of the second fire, just beyond the radius of scorched grass. A tiny figure dressed in black to her neck, facing the trees, indifferent to the motionless body of Fenris on her lawn. For such a small person, her voice carried. The wailing that came out of her was almost Arabic in intonation, but then Luke thought of North American Indians too. And whatever she sang lilted up and down in the singsong cadences of Swedish. She clapped out a beat with her little hands. What she sang was simple, repetitive, like a nursery rhyme. The same few lines, going up and down, over and over. He began to recognize one word. 'Moder.'

She called it out again, and again, at the end of the third line of the three-line verse: 'Moder.'

Mother.

'No,' he said to himself. 'Please no.'

The realization came quick and cold like the contents of a pail of freezing water thrown straight into his face. He swung his head like a tired horse, and knew that no man should be made to witness such things. Was he in hell? Had he died in that forest with his friends, and now this was an endless narrative of atrocity in an afterlife he stumbled about in?

He looped the keyring around his little finger, took aim with the rifle. 'Ma'am! I said no!'

She sang like a child, like a little girl, and raised her thin dusty arms into the air. She looked at the sky and called the old name.

When the time comes, will you sing with us?

He had suspected once or twice that she had been using him, but he had not dared acknowledge it. It seemed too improbable, too incongruous for such a small freakish lady who made stew and clomped about the hovel in her home-spun gown. But she had used him. Yes, to get the unwanted guests out of her house, to have her uninvited visitors bleed out on the lawn. They came and they invited themselves inside and made demands and would not leave. She was old and she wanted help ridding her home of the rodents. Fenris was a weasel and she wanted his neck wrung like a dish cloth; he had seen it in her black eyes. So she let him remain alive for a while, so Blood Frenzy thought they were in charge and that she was working for them, serving their purpose up here; but then she let the sacrifice be free to accomplish some chores for her. He'd survived the forest and Blood Frenzy because he had work to do for her; he was the angry one, the violent one. In the party of four that came through here to die, he was the man not so different to the youths with the painted faces, the man who could be useful, for a while. He had always felt his fate out here was predetermined. That he had a purpose. And this was it.

She'd played him from day one, but he was still to be given, and taken away out there, to the rocks and boughs and waters and the ways of prehistory. Now his job was done, the little old child was calling mother home. Because he was still a sacrifice. And he was even dressed for it. She had laid out the robe and crown for him to wear.

'God no.'

He aimed the shaky rifle sight between the shoulder blades of that tiny figure. And let the sights twitch and hover about the target.

All of these things should not be. He thought of Hutch, pale and bedraggled and naked and hanging between spruce branches. He remembered Dom's arms about his own shoulders not long before he too was opened and emptied like a rabbit by a hunter. He thought of poor Phil, all tatty and looted, the hood of his waterproof still up and keeping his pale face dry in death. And he remembered the sound of thin brown bodies, twitching in the darkness of an attic that should not exist. He bit down on horror. Clenched his jaw against the horror of it all. And squeezed the trigger.

Like a hand shoving her in the back, the little old lady made a surprised sound like all the air had been pushed out of her in one go. And up she went, off her feet, then came immediately straight down, onto her face. She never moved again. He'd shot out her tiny heart.

The world went silent and still. The whole forest held its breath. The sky paused in its gaseous swirling. The birds closed their beaks and the animals lay down their heads.

Luke walked across to her and looked down.

The hem of her dusty dress was hiked up to her bony knees. Unclothed, her legs were thin and covered in coarse white hair. The skin through the hair was pinkish. Her legs bent the wrong way at the knee joints. At the end of her goatish legs were little white hooves. Her tiny loud feet.

SIXTY-SIX

Luke rested on his shins, the rifle across his naked thighs, and closed his eyes. He knelt in the grass between Fenris and the old lady.

Could he get up again? He would have to; he needed clothes, more water. A bandage too, or anything soft and clean to wrap around his hip and plug his chest. He was sure the cuts were widening as he moved and breathed. His left arm was going stiff and he could barely raise it above his waist. He was slowing down, he was coming to a stop. He blew his lungs empty. A cigarette would probably kill him, but he would kill for one right now.

He turned his head and looked back at the house, at the peaked pointy roof. He wasn't finished here. He stood up, wincing. The giving and the taking had to stop. The door had to be closed. Loki had known about this place; others might do too. The barrier between the world and another much older place was much thinner here than elsewhere; things came and went. He understood that.

His friends had been slaughtered like game in season, like livestock. They had been hunted, swiftly despatched, field-dressed, and then displayed in the trees. An account had to be settled. For them. He'd do anything for them now.

Why had the old woman not called *it* home to clean out

her trespassers? Luke closed his eyes. His skin shivered. His head hurt as it wondered. There was no one to tell him anything. Not out here. He just guessed and flinched like a small animal.

Because of the rifle. And sheath knives. Because *it* could be hurt. She was protecting *it*. Her mother. And protecting the old family upstairs. It required an inside job and he was the man on the inside. *Maybe*.

But he did know that some species should become extinct. Luke opened his eyes.

Moder's rule and her pitiful congregation had to end. She was an isolated God; the last black goat of the woods. What he guessed was her youngest and most presentable daughter did her best to keep it all going up here. Maybe she was the girl left behind to look after mother. He did not know; he was guessing again. But it just all needed to stop. No more sons and fathers and friends should hang from trees. Not that, ever.

Luke walked back to the house; every muscle and sinew ached from a bruising so deep he doubted he could ever be fixed. The horizon of treetops juddered in his vision. Somehow the sky was all white now too, but he was grateful for the rain. It came down cold and hard. Was never far away up here. Just changed places with the snow. Over and over, forever.

He looked at Fenris. Reached down, gripped the sticky handle of the Swiss Army knife and yanked it out. Fenris sat up, head lolling, like Luke was leading him by a hand, then dropped back down to the blood and the soil. Luke stabbed the blade into the turf twice to clean it.

On the porch, he put down the rifle and the knife and

took off the little white dress. Dropped it over Loki's terrible face. But left the crown of dead flowers on his head; it seemed to be holding his thoughts together. And then he looked down the hallway to the staircase.

SIXTY-SEVEN

Through the door at the end of the corridor on the first storey, and up into the attic he went on feet so slow and clumsy they must have all heard him coming. Up there, in the warm dusty timeless darkness, they knew he was coming for them.

And into the lightless place at the top of the house, he crept and fumbled about, naked and bloodied as a newborn. He had no light; couldn't get it together enough downstairs to find an oil lantern and matches. But he went on memory to the places where he remembered the little figures to be sitting. And now he was up there, he found they were all too old and too weak to do anything but mutter.

The rain struck the roof and was amplified inside the attic space. Still, he could hear them all about him. Their voices were rustles, sometimes scratchy like the voices in old radios dimmed to a murmur. And they were not laughing now. They sounded confused, like elderly people who had awoken in beds and forgotten where they were.

He went in low, head down, ears cocked to their sounds. At the far end of the room, he knelt down. Laid the rifle upon the floor. Then fumbled his hands around the two little chairs, patting his shaking hands over their robes, dry as old bread, then over brittle limbs no thicker than woodwind instruments, until he found the first small head.

'You killed them amongst the stones,' he whispered. 'Yes, you showed me. Carried them out in wagons to die.'

He placed his finger atop the slowly moving skull, raised the knife up high, and then brought the blade down.

Through it went, through skin no stiffer than yellowing paper, and through an avian skull thin as eggshell, and into what remained of a living organ. Old magic may have kept it living, but new steel ended its long and miserable existence; a life that may well have begun when those great trees out there were mere saplings.

The other seated figure rustled in the darkness and tried to bite his fingers. He heard its dry jaw clacking.

'I saw your old house. I was there. You used to string them up over a basin. You showed me. Did you suckle your God on blood?'

The second figure was a woman, he sensed, though it was pitch-black in the attic, and they were so old when he had first seen them he could not really be sure. But he found himself amazed at just how accurate his instincts could be when he had nothing else to go on.

When his fingers found her in the dark, he heard her cartilage beak creak open again, then felt the snap of dry gums upon a finger joint. It did not hurt, but he had to stifle a scream all the same. She resisted to the last, like a dying insect with its stinger raised at a bird's sharp face.

He despatched the second fossil swiftly, struck it hard with the knife held like a dagger, and caved in half of its skull while throttling its wizened neck at the same time. He felt the head collapse to dust. Breathed some of it in, coughed, spat.

He stood up, and where they rattled and muttered against

the walls, on either side of the little throne room, he felt for their sharp-featured faces, their old dry heads, their desiccated grinning, and he punched the knife through them. Through them all. One by one. Broke every head to dust. Until nothing whispered or shook within its mooring any longer.

Once he had finished with them, he bent over and retrieved the rifle. And while turning his thoughts to finding clothes, far out in the woods he heard a sound so terrible, he lost his balance and sat his bare buttocks down in the hot darkness of the attic.

The dreadful bullock bark. The devil-dog yipping.

The wet sky, the aged trunks of sleeping trees, the cold unfeeling earth, functioned as an acoustic chamber, and within that space the oldest and most poignant sound of anguish pierced him, and every living thing within earshot, to the marrow. A mother's cry.

Moments later, he heard Surtr too. She unleashed a scream and he knew she had met a sudden and painful end in the claws or teeth of something much greater than herself. *Moder* was coming home now. Drawn by the loss of her own.

Luke scrabbled and half fell down the attic stairs. He ran into Loki and Surtr's old room and peered out at the trees. Little of the sun was showing itself, and seemed to grow afraid and moved back behind the low grey clouds.

Again, the bullock cough. He could not see her, but knew she was much closer now. Somewhere nearby, *Moder*'s black flanks were shuddering with emotion, and the yipping that came out of her trembled. She was crazed with rage. Blind. Intent.

Truck. Truck. Fucking truck.

Knife in one hand, rifle in the other, naked and begrimed, he ran down the stairs on skittish feet and staggered into the kitchen. Peered out through the window.

The tiny body of the old woman was gone from the grass.

He briefly thought of putting the rifle barrel inside his mouth and then a big toe inside the trigger guard.

The old black presence was invisible but immense; it reared up and covered the house, inflicted so much pressure upon his thoughts they hardened into diamonds of a terror that was total, mindless, pure and complete. He gaped, he pissed down his dirty legs. One arm started to shake so badly, the other had to come around and hold it steady. He made a groaning noise that just did not sound like anything that had ever come out of his mouth before.

Truck.

He shuddered across to the table, hyperventilating, shaking to the black soles of his Neanderthal feet.

Too many things; not enough hands. Rifle. Knife. Keys.

He put the keys into his mouth, bit down on all the screams that wanted to come out. His teeth oozed around the metal keyring like butter.

Rifle out before him, the stock banged hard into his shoulder, his saliva dripping all over the keyring, the knife in the palm of the hand that held the rifle barrel steady, he walked back into the silvery morning of the old world, naked.

SIXTY-EIGHT

It could move fast, he knew that. Though the last time it had cried out, the sound had been bellowed skyward from the other side of the building; what he thought of as the front. So he tried to reassure himself he could sneak away through the kitchen door in the rear; get to the truck, and go, while *it* still shrieked and paced about out front.

But he had taken no more than five steps through the grass, away from the back door, when he heard it again: to his front, to the right, where the forest resumed its oceanic immensity on the right-hand side of the orchard. It was as if it too was rushing for the truck now, keeping pace with his intentions. And it must have covered fifty yards in a mere matter of moments.

Down on one knee, Luke swung the sights of the rifle across the base of the treeline, anticipating the emergence of a long black shape pressed to the ground.

Nothing came; the trees remained still and dark in the falling rain. Would the weather mask his scent? he wondered, uselessly, because it had always known exactly where they were at any time. And *it* could see him now, he knew it.

Up on the balls of his feet, his breath too loud and unable to stop it wheezing in and out of his mouth like he was a tired old dog, he moved across to the truck. He could only see the white shape of the vehicle in his peripheral vision because not for a second did he take his eyes from the trees.

The haphazard and sparse plantation of fruit trees in the orchard, and the open gulley of the dirt track, would allow him to sight the rifle through their exposure, but he dearly wished the rear of the truck had not been so close to the treeline.

He decided to go inside the truck cabin through the driver-side door, with the rifle pointed at the forest until the last moment. There would be one shot, if that, if it chose to come at him from the trees as he entered the vehicle. Twenty feet, one bound.

Driver-side door open. Unwilling to even blink, he eased himself up and onto the broad bench before the steering wheel. Wound the passenger-side window right down, pulled his door closed and then rested the underside of the rifle barrel on the bottom of the passenger-side window frame. If the truck still functioned and moved him down the track, he'd be able to shoot from that side.

He placed the knife on the top of the plastic dashboard, took the keys from his mouth and tried to slip the ignition key into the slot on the steering column. His hands were shaking too much. One hand was dark black with his own blood from where it had clutched at his hip; the sight of it made him feel faint, sick again. On the third attempt he got the key into the slot.

Turned it. There was a click. Green lights glowed to indicate oil, temperature. Amber low-lights circled the speedometer clock and fuel gauge. He depressed the clutch with the sole of a dirty bare foot. The pedal was stiff. He turned the ignition key over again.

The cabin shook. The engine started immediately, impossibly. But there should be no fuel. Something should be wrong with the engine. Nothing should go right for him. That was the way of things.

He shut down the train of thought.

And the engine cut out. Cold. He turned the key again. The engine rocked into life. Sputtered out again. Luke checked the fuel gauge; about one tenth of a tank. They'd drained it for their stupid pyres. How far would that much petrol get him? *Far enough.*

Turning the key a third time, he worried about flooding the motor. The engine roared, then chugged into a shaky life. He depressed the accelerator pedal, kept the engine ticking over, idling with a bad cough. The truck was old, had been in the rain; how long would it take to warm up? Was there time for all that?

He looked back at the treeline, cursing himself for becoming distracted; it only took a moment to die out here. Phil had learned that the hard way.

Nothing moved.

The windshield was too blurry to see through. He found the switch for the wipers on the indicator column. Turned the wipers on, and the fog lights, and the hazard lights. 'Shit.' *No, leave them on.*

Handbrake off. Clutch down, into first gear. Right hand on the wheel. Left hand back to holding the rifle stock steady, the end of the barrel aimed through the passenger-side window, finger on the goddamn trigger.

The truck moved, under him, along the grass towards the

mouth of the thin track. He was revving too high. Eased back on the accelerator. It was disorientating; operating a vehicle, moving it with these tiny pressures of feet and legs. The last time he had driven had been a van five years before when he moved flat, from one dark corner of London to another.

The truck left the paddock and bumped along the track, the tyres seeming to find the grooves they had made coming in. This was too easy.

Eyes everywhere: to the treeline at the left side of the track, back across the bonnet, through the spindly trees of the orchard, then back again to the forest on his left. Nothing moving out there. Hope surged fiery through his chest. Stupidly, he burped. He needed air; opened the driver-side window.

He looked into the rear-view mirror for the first time. His vision swam. His face was smeared with blood from where he had wiped red sticky hands at sweat and tears; a dirty beard made him look Neolithic; his red-rimmed eyes were those of the witless; something like a crust on a Cornish pasty ran down his hairline, under the tiara of dead flowers, and ended within his left eyebrow; deep pale worry lines cracked the filth beside his eyes and mouth.

Past the orchard, the dark house almost vanishing from out of the rear-view mirror, and he realized he was chanting, 'Come on. Come on. Come on. Come on.'

He stopped speaking and cooled with dread at the sight of how the trees then leant in and curved over the muddy track up ahead. And once he was passed the orchard, the world went dark and he was in a natural tunnel; a funnel of dense foliage. It whipped, it scraped the sides of the truck. It came in through the open driver-side window and tried to slap an eye stinging shut. He drew the barrel of the gun back inside. Started winding up the windows. Was doing too much for his fragile coordination to cope with. With a jolt, the vehicle stalled.

'Shit fucker!' Getting angry now. The rifle butt was stuck on something, would not allow itself to be pulled into the truck cabin any further, which prevented him from winding the passenger-side window all the way shut. He had become a quivering thing of rushing thoughts in a thick heavy head, and was all big elbows and jerky feet; he hated himself, hated the trees, this land, everything. He believed in malign divine presences, supernatural forces of fate that kept him here, off balance and absurd in his mismanagement of everything. He was a bleeding farce.

'Stop! Stop it!' he told the dominant voice inside his mind. *You got this far. You did what you had to do to get this far.*

Took a breath. Looked down to his right. Slowly raised the rifle butt from out of a tear in the vinyl seat cushion. Wound the passenger-side window all the way up to shut and seal himself from the cold wet breath of the forest and the trees that were too unnervingly close. Took another big deep steadying lungful.

Restarted the engine. Out of instinct, he checked the rear-view mirror. Squinted. Had a long dark branch fallen across the back of the truck's flatbed? Yes, and now it felt like the rear wheels had lowered slightly, or sunk into the clay.

He caught his breath.

Yanked his head around.

Looked through the glass panel behind his head.

And saw the end of a black shape step off the rear of the vehicle.

405

And vanish into the trees.

But it had left something behind.

Luke looked into the flatbed. Surtr stared back at him. Pale-blue eyes wide in surprise, lipless mouth open, as if to say, *Remember me?*

Beneath her breasts, her rib cage had been torn asunder like a cardboard box. She had red-whitish flesh wings attached to an all too visible spinal column. She was all gone, down to her dark, sopping abdomen, but sat upright, her inert body resting against the tail gate of the truck. An inconceivable strength had done that to sinew, muscle and bone; literally torn her body wide open.

I'm still here, it was telling him. *Still with you, every inch of the way*.

Clumsily, he snatched up the rifle, but the dimensions of the cabin prevented him from moving the long firearm around. The engine cut out.

'Stop!' he cried at himself. What did it matter, which way the gun was pointing? The rifle was next to useless inside the cabin; could not be manoeuvred at all. What he needed was speed.

He turned the key over hard, so the starter motor squealed. The cabin shook as the engine came back to reluctant life again. He went from first to third gear in seconds and threw his feet from accelerator to brake, accelerator to brake, while tossing the steering wheel and the truck from side to side, down the track. Beneath the metal floor he felt the tyres grip and slip and fight to stay aiming straight ahead and away from this place.

He flushed hot and cold, twice nearly crashing the vehicle off the road and into the trees. No seatbelt. 'Stupid bastard!'

In his rear-view mirror, Surtr lolled and shook, bumped and banged, but would not take her eyes from him.

And then, suddenly, something moved behind her.

Only sporadically did the white-grey light break through the canopy of foliage over the rutted road, and shine steely through the tree branches that desired, and were designed, to smother the track into oblivion. But over the lolling pale head of his passenger in the rear, he saw something running quickly on all fours, behind the truck. But only briefly, for no more than a moment; no longer than it took him to say, 'Oh God.'

He checked the road in front of the bonnet, then looked into the mirror again. Behind the vehicle, a lanky darkness rose to full height and stepped away into the jumping shadows at the side of the track in the time it took to blink an eye. The figure had been at least twenty yards behind his rear bumper, but tall on those black legs, thin as stilts, that bent the wrong way at the knee joint.

He hurriedly turned the headlights on, then switched them to full beam; the sudden strobe of white light was an instant comfort inside the cocoon of rain-heavy leaves that now draped themselves across the windscreen like the flabby hands of protesters, attempting to slow down a diplomat's car driving through a crowd.

It had been running down the road behind him, was keeping up. A thing dark. Thin rear legs. No tail. A brief ripple of light across a flank tooled with muscle. 'Jesus fucking Christ!'

He was doing thirty miles an hour when he smacked his head against the steel underside of the cabin roof and was forced to brake, to slow down. One eye shut from the pain;

an old wound up there had reopened or just set fire to itself again.

Crawling, skidding; he spent more time looking into the rear-view mirror, than he did over the wet white bonnet.

Which is why he did an emergency stop when something darted across the front of the vehicle. His breastbone hit the steering wheel and set the horn blasting; his forehead banged, slapped, then pressed flat, against the cold inside of the windscreen.

For a while he did not know which way he was facing, until his senses landed safely and reorientated his spatial awareness. He pulled himself back hard into his seat.

As he lowered his eyes, he caught the last of something moving; close to the ground, slipping into the trees. It was a thing both lean and brawny.

Had he not stopped he would have hit it. 'Fuck!'

The engine had stalled again, and if it stalled once more he swore he would get out of the cabin and put a bullet through the bonnet of the spluttering shuddering mess of a truck.

He got it started again as the panic made his jaw shake as if he were suddenly freezing.

Were the rear wheels now stuck in a rut though? The truck would only now move in increments, as if the handbrake was still on. The engine whined and steamed. Then the whole vehicle jolted forward, almost pitching him off the road.

Something had been holding the truck again, from behind.

Luke glanced at the rear-view mirror. A black shape suddenly flared up, and reared away as if on long quivering stilts.

And then it was on the roof. Clambering and all about the

windows on every side. He heard himself scream. The dim light dimmed.

The banging of hammers upon the roof; the ricochets of bone feet on metal smarted inside his tender ears. A pink-teated underside of a great belly across the windscreen, black-haired and doggish. Hint of an amber eye the size of an apple to his right.

He looked at the eye.

Saw a great mouth opening instead. Black gums, and yellow canines the length of middle fingers. Breath condensed on the glass, then it was gone.

And so was he, with the accelerator plugged to the metal floor, and his thoughts reeling round and round in a terrible whirlpooling skull-wind, and the branches of trees grooved the side panels, and twigs scratched at the glass like they had claws of their own and wanted to shell him like an oyster.

Bang! Bang! Bang! The hooves of horses across a metal sheet, as something stamped upon the cabin roof again, then ran across the flatbed and vanished, taking poor Surtr with it, like her remains were the remnants of a disembowelled doll, held by one ankle.

Luke was still screaming when the truck veered from one side of the road to the other, entering the forest a few feet on either side of the track. A headlamp went smash. The bumper tore off, and the wheels went over it with a crumple he felt more than heard.

He stamped on the brake to regain control of the vehicle. The truck slid. Came to a jolting stop that put his forehead into the windscreen again.

He sat back, gaping. He'd got the vehicle wedged at an angle, diagonally across the track. Up ahead, the tunnel of overhanging forest narrowed, and completely shut off the light.

Reverse. First gear. Reverse. First gear . . . A ten-point turn before he stopped counting and began whimpering.

He thought of getting out and using the rifle. Then was certain, again, that he should just put the end of the barrel inside his mouth and end the delay of his demise. It was inevitable.

Fear and big white eyes inside a suit of dirty skin: that's all he was now.

His arms and legs were shaking. He watched his knee for no longer than a second but its palsy alarmed him. His hands and feet were all pins and needles, until he made his limbs work again by scrabbling for the knife between his legs where it had jumped from the dash. He gripped the knife handle between the palm of his right hand and the outside of the steering wheel. The blade was dull, thick with blood at its base. Its presence inside the cabin made him feel strength in the form of a thin wire of tension within the bones of his forearms.

Slowly, in first gear, he nudged the truck back onto the track and further into the shadows, into the greater darkness where daylight had no place and never had done. Driving fast was out of the question; this was second-gear driving all the way through. But *it* had not broken inside the vehicle. *Could not. Maybe.* He told himself he could tentatively wheel his way out of here, like a nervous motorist with a flat tyre in a safari park.

Minutes passed. How many he could not possibly know. But as each wheel turned one full rotation and he rolled forward and further along this hairline crack in the surface of the greatest forest of Europe, he promised himself that he would get out, and that this terrible black tunnel would end and that what stalked him through it could not possibly break into his shell of metal and . . .

He eased around a tight curve in first gear, and his one working headlight showed him a long stretch of narrow and straight track ahead. And the light also flashed upon what coiled and tensed down there on such long limbs.

Something tall and lean but shaggy about its haunches, was risen and poised; with bony arms, long as a stallion's forelegs, hanging before it. And the great shape of its head was raised as if to catch a scent or sound on the breeze. It was waiting. Waiting for him.

The terrible head-shape was so long, ragged. It pulled itself back into a centre of gravity, anchored in thighs springloaded to strike. A glimmer of headlight flashed across corneas amber-red.

He thought it was an impossibly tall man. For a moment. Or an ape, a large scrawny one, poised to pounce like a great cat. But then of it, and about it, as it lowered down upon great muscled haunches, and before it fled right at him, were the briefest features of other things that made Luke suffocate on a tongue he was sure he had swallowed in his terror.

A thick-haired face, black, with a wet bovine muzzle, made itself temporarily available for scrutiny. The almost human eyes filled his mind. Eyes curiously sentient. Eyes revealing a hideous intent. To merely see them made him whimper. But in the visible moments of its swift charge it seemed mostly goatish, that shape of a head upon the bullock neck; though the yellow teeth should have been in the mouth of something else, long extinct. And extending from all of this, were the greatest of horns, from another place altogether. And it was coming at him. And he was going at it.

The engine screamed at the end of first gear, for he had no presence of mind to go up to second. And he screamed over the engine, so loudly, until blood came up and into his mouth, and his vision blurred.

Then it was through the windscreen.

Poles of aged bone ploughed into the webbing glass. The steering wheel snapped in half. The top of a skull, broad as a small table, followed through. Glass cubes covered Luke like sugar crystals. He heard a sound like the puncturing of some giant ball, and on either side of his neck the horns kept on going and going through the rear of the seat and the sheet metal of the cabin behind his shoulders. Until his nostrils and teeth and eyes were pressed into oily bristles that tasted like old meat and shat-upon straw. Something snapped like plastic between his eyes. His already broken nose.

Billows of steamed-out breath, cankerous with dead shoals of fish and sulphurous with a pig's dung, infused the cabin, the world. And he was sick into it, onto it, that great matted skull. Just before it began the terrible thrashing of its head.

Luke was stuck fast into his seat. But the vehicle rocked like it had been T-boned at a junction by a speeding bus. Then two wheels were off the ground at the front. The rear wall of the cabin caved in and there was the grinding of great stones as those horns moved deeper into the steel of the cabin. The roof suddenly groaned like an old floor and then buckled like a paper bag. *It* was stuck; *it* was tearing the world apart to get out.

Against his stomach and groin, he felt a nose; as wet as seafood and contracting like a baby's heart in his navel. It was the worst sensation of all, in there, in the darkness, while smashed into his seat. Below the nose its mouth worried and busied and dripped. It was seeking something to pinch and tear like tracing paper between quick fingers.

A last moment of himself, an instinct, or maybe it was a spasm, a twitch, sent from the origins of his own species when they coughed out their last under rutting horns and snatching jaws, came to his right hand. The hand that held the Swiss Army knife.

His right arm had been hammered against a horn as the thing smashed itself through the windscreen. But he could bend that arm at the elbow, and he could grit his teeth, then part his jaws, and scream too. And he screamed out his last as he pressed his tiny blade into that great black throat.

A bellow from a mouth filling with liquid deafened him. He fell forward in his seat to the sound of two sword blades clashing.

And it was gone from his face, his chest, the cabin, from the bonnet. Wet damp air came in through the shattered windscreen to temper the abattoir stink all about him.

Silence.

And then coughing, out there, in the dark wet forever of trees. Coughing as if to clear a throat of a fine bone. Luke looked at his right hand; it was empty.

The engine had stalled. There was no steering wheel.

He closed his eyes. Then opened them. His mouth was wet. Blood. His nose was smashed.

He pushed the rifle out and onto the bonnet. Then followed it with his own naked body.

SIXTY-NINE

He never heard *it* cough again, or bark, or yip like a black-muzzled jackal. But he was not alone in those woods that arched over him, cut out the weak greyish sunlight, and dripped heavy fragrant raindrops onto him like the branches and limbs of the trees were the ceiling of a limestone cave, glittery, timeless, and dreadful.

No, he never heard *it* or saw *it* again. But other things kept pace with him.

He swallowed and swallowed to ease the terrible thirst in a throat scorched by cordite. He would be cold, then hot and sweaty; he saw things and heard the voices of people that were not there; he passed in and out of worlds. He walked. And he walked.

Out of sight, the white people scurried. They chattered like little monkeys. They leapt up at the corner of his heavy eyes; they were small and pale like naked children.

Twice in his delirium, he turned and knelt and fired the rifle into the trees at where he thought he had seen something small and pallid land on tiny feet and begin chittering. And then there would be silence. An awful silence loaded with anticipation and vague hopes. Before it began again: the prancing of little feet on the wet forest floor just out of sight, and the crying out of small mouths in the distant undergrowth.

She had quite a brood; so many young. *Moder* was hurt and her young were angry. If he fell and passed out with exhaustion, he knew they would take him from his own dreams and from the wet mud his feet slid about in. So he walked and he walked and he talked to himself to keep them from taking him.

It must have been early evening when he came to the end of the track and saw the sky in what felt like the first time in years. The track simply ended and when he turned and looked back at the great wall of trees, it was like he stood in a coastal cove, peninsulas on either side, and had passed out of a crack in the cliff face, or a well-hidden cave. He could no longer see the end of the track he had just walked for the best part of a day and evening, nor any break in the thickets of undergrowth, rising tangled to the height of a man.

He had come on to a rocky plane, windswept and misty with rain. Grey, moss green, and whitish stone, forever. Besides a scattering of small birch trees it was arid, desolate like the bottom of some great ocean that had been drained.

A great suffocating feeling of solitude came over him in the bleak stillness; he felt lonelier than he had ever been before in his memory, but also suffered a mad urge to wander farther, forever amongst the massive boulders. It looked uncannily familiar too, like he was back where he had started from, all that time ago. So long ago, with his three best friends all around him.

When he put some distance between himself and the edge

of the forest, he sat down and rested, yanking his head up whenever it dropped and he fell into a dark red sleep for seconds, or minutes, or even hours; he couldn't be sure. Eventually his shivering became too intense, so he staggered back onto his feet, shouldered the rifle and started walking even further away from the trees.

Beyond one of the great reaching crests of the forest, where the mighty trees thrust out together like a sweeping arm, he found another track: narrow, stony, overgrown, but offering the suggestion that someone with purpose had worn this thin line into the landscape of stone and grey reindeer moss. Someone that had also once walked away from the dreadful forest.

He didn't know which way was north or south, or where the track went, but the very sight of it made him weep and shudder down to his toes.

So into the darkness he shivered violently and he walked on legs like stumps and on feet he could not feel. Thin traces of moon and luminous cloud lit themselves up. He often stared at his hand before his eyes but could see nothing. The oblivion didn't last for long and the sky faded indigo, then dark blue, then pink, then white-grey.

For brief moments, his mind went clear and he felt warm. And he recalled things with so great a clarity, it took a conscious force of will to assure himself that he was not back at work, or in London, or talking to Hutch in a bar in Stockholm about books.

But in the repetitive, tedious delirium, in the tramp tramp tramping of his numb feet, in some incongruous moment of clarity, he decided that earning £863 a month after tax at the age of thirty-six did not matter any more. Nor did owing

NatWest Bank twenty-five grand in a loan for a business that had failed so long ago. It was irrelevant. The fact he disliked his job, and hated two of his colleagues, and was as poor as the poorest migrants around him at home in Finsbury Park, and that he dreaded Christmas because there were fewer and fewer places for him to go, and that he only owned three pairs of shoes, did not matter. And all of this fell from him. His eyes now looked at something that was beyond the horizon and so deeply inside himself at the same time. And he knew that what he now felt could never be truly revisited again. But that also did not matter. Enough of it would survive inside him, and live. And he knew the things that held him in place, and reflected an image of who he had once been back to himself, and that marshalled everyone else around him, and that those things a man should strive for and achieve in the old world were all now unimportant.

Even though he was crippled and caked in dross and stained with blood and his head was still crowned by the dead flowers, like they were holding irreparably damaged parts of his skull together, he felt light and giddy and unburdened. He was naked, and his head was bright with a whitish light even though the sky was grey and the rain fell upon him.

Nothing mattered at all but being here. Himself. There was still some life in him. His heart beat. Air passed in and out of his lungs. One foot followed another. Knowing how quickly and suddenly and unexpectedly life could end, how irrelevant life was anyway to this universe of earth and sky and age, how indifferent it was to all of the people still in it, those who would come to it and those who had already left it, he felt freed. Alone, but free. Freed of it all. Free of them, free of everything. At least for a while. And that's all anyone really had, he decided, a little while.

If you enjoyed *The Ritual*,
read on for an extract from

Under A Watchful Eye

By Adam Nevill

1
Many Communications
Must Remain in Doubt

He just appeared at the edge of Seb's vision.

Tall, dressed in dark clothing and exuding a faint impression of menace, the motionless figure was standing upon the red shoreline like an affront to the pink, blue and yellow doors of the pretty beach huts lining the promenade. The sudden, intense scrutiny gave Seb a start. Momentarily, even a blurred face suggested itself inside his mind, peering about, though his imagination must have been responsible for that.

Seb laid his coffee and notebook down, turned on the bench and squinted into the distance. He was sitting near the cliff edge on the headland south of the beach, and even on such a clear day he'd never make out the man's eyes at that range. But had they been in the same room, and had he been glared at by an unseemly stranger, Seb's discomfort would have been the same.

Fifty feet below where Seb was perched between Broadsands and Elberry Cove, the empty sea stretched to a vague horizon. The coastline curved north to Paignton and distant Torquay, the claret shores and grey cliffs reaching for Hope's Nose. His thoughts had been wandering out there, seeking the elusive impetus for what he was trying to write, but his reverie was obliterated by this abrupt intrusion.

Under closer observation, what became more surprising was that the figure didn't appear to be standing on the beach. He seemed to be positioned a few feet out from where the sand ended. The man must have been standing ankle-deep in the shallows, or was perched on a submerged rock. This created the impression that the man was standing *upon* the water. A curious trick of perspective for sure.

From his raised position, Seb could see only the far half of the beach, but no more. A few dogs raced about, darting in and out of the gentle surf, and a few people dawdled and chatted near their frantic pets. Still too cold for bathers in April and there were no pleasure craft out that morning, but the sparse crowd on the beach appeared oblivious to this lone sentinel standing so near to them. Or was he so unsightly that they pretended the man was invisible?

If Seb wasn't mistaken, a growing stillness had also been imposed by the solitary dark shape. The cries of the seabirds were gradually softening to silence inside his ears. And through the spreading quiescence the sea's chop rose as his absorption increased. Soon the running water no longer sounded like the sea at all.

Seb felt himself drawn outwards to be engulfed in a moment detached from the world. The breeze dropped. He became disoriented and slightly nauseous. Louder was the gush of the water's current. His mind cleared and was uncluttered for . . . he didn't know for how long exactly, but probably only for moments. And then, from far away and behind his head, or from deep within his mind, he heard a voice call his name.

Sebastian.

A train's steam whistle shrieked as if imitating the cry of

the dinosaurs whose grinning and collapsed remains embedded the coastline where the limestone and brick-red breccia sands crushed each other. Seb flinched, but even his gasp seemed to have originated from a mouth behind his shoulder.

Two miles distant, the train carrying holidaymakers chuffed slowly into sight on the opposing headland, making its way to the great viaducts built by Brunel. Clouds of steam billowed and unravelled into vanishing rags of vapour. A long line of carriages, painted chocolate and cream, followed the engine's slow, military determination.

Seb had lived in the bay for three years, but the train still summoned images of Agatha Christie's world: flappers and gents with pencil-thin moustaches who dressed for dinner. And he clawed at this nostalgia as if it were buoyant wreckage in deep water with no sight of land. He near begged the presence of the train to return him to the world that he had known only seconds before.

And it did. His fixation with whoever stood on the shore was severed.

When he returned his attention to the beach, and scanned its red length, the watching figure was no longer there either. *Gone.*

A few days passed and Seb had nearly forced a rational explanation for the disquieting experience: he was tired, maybe his sugar level was low, he had been mesmerized by the sun-flecked water.

But when he saw the man again he knew who it was.

2
This Coat is Too Tight

Seb had set out his laptop, coffee and water in preparation for the morning's work on the book that he was struggling to believe in, let alone write. The work in progress barely resembled his previous novels, never rose beyond an imitation of effect and a perfunctory progression of plot, peopled by undefined characters that were mere wraiths of what had been intended.

It had taken him six months to acknowledge that his imagination was failing. The energy at his core was mostly spent, or had leaked away during the writing of his previous novel, a book written with the needle of his inner reader's compass spinning wildly, in a blizzard of doubt and vain hope, without settling upon any specific direction regarding the book's quality. He'd remained unsure about the manuscript when he'd delivered to his publisher, as had been his increasingly restless and disheartened readers when it was published.

In the past, the cliff-side gardens in Goodrington, with their panoramic views of the bay, had always been a favourite place to write. Settled on the same bench, he'd worked on two other novels that were special to him. The gardens above the beach huts and promenade, at the north end of

Goodrington, were at their best in spring. And that morning, far below his feet, the sea remained dark on either side of a great strip of sunlight. A door in heaven might have cracked to release what glittered on the water like a million pieces of polished silver, cast all the way to a misted horizon far out at sea. To his right, the surf lapped the shoreline with a pleasing rhythm. *If you can't write here, you can't cut it anywhere.*

Goodrington and distant Brixham might have served as architectural models of coastal towns when sighted at such a remove. Built up the slopes of the hillsides, the white houses with their red roofs were arrayed like Lego structures. Tiny brushes of treetops sprouted from within the settlements and even a toy railway cut behind the seafront. Torbay, and the only place where he'd found peace with himself. But had the place and his comfortable lifestyle made him too content? Was penetrating the surface of the world to recreate its meanings, in unusual and interesting ways, dependent upon times of adversity? He did wonder.

He worried that a flabby self-indulgence had replaced his purpose. Maybe wishful thinking about his books had usurped his critical candour. He'd seen it happen to other writers. Perhaps naivety had swapped places with wisdom and imitation had overrun his trademark strangeness. He also feared that an indifference to the reader had taken hold during the good years. Writing this book had been homework and a chore from the start. But worst of all, he had become *incurious*.

The palms and the pink and red flowers in the heather sighed, ruffled by a cooling breeze. He inhaled the sweet fragrance of the gardens, placed the computer on his thighs and fired it up.

Long forgotten now, but the first sentence of a new chapter had come to him that morning while he showered. Perhaps the sentence would have invoked the restless urgency that had once driven his writing, near panting alongside him, a mad dog with foamy lips. This opening line might have been the beginning of a scene that would drill through the grey weight of a dull mind to produce a fracture. From a crack would burst the flood.

But Seb never tapped a single key. Way down below, the same solitary figure that he'd seen four days before made a second unwelcome appearance. No features were visible within that spot of bone-white flesh, capped in black, but he was closer.

Once more, Seb suffered the impression he'd caught the figure's eye and that they were staring at each other across the cliffs and sea. Again, the man wasn't standing on the dry sand, but seemed to be in the water. *Or on it?*

Small shapes of children frolicked on the sands of a low tide, a group of people walked dogs, others just meandered behind this sentinel of the shoreline, but none regarded him.

Shielding his eyes, Seb rose and walked to the railing.

The watcher raised his chin as if this distant vigilance had become confrontation.

The effects of another mute communication with the same stranger, and in less than a week, was far worse the second time. Quicker and deeper was Seb's absorption into that scrutiny. As if struck by a cold updraught of air, he shivered and wanted to shrink to make himself smaller and harder to see. Braced by his own dread, Seb clenched his fists upon the metal fence until his palms hurt.

The swish of the surf, a murmur of faraway traffic, and

the oddly clear voice of a boy on the beach faded, until all that he could hear was water running in the distance.

That was not the sea inside his ears, either. This time he was sure about that.

Seb slipped behind the hedgerow, a cover reinforced by a pine growing at a lower level in the gardens. Relief from that distant assiduity was immediate, then cut short by the mention of his name.

Sebastian.

His thoughts slid sideways, queasily. He then feared that his head was dropping to the pavement, or that the ground was rushing towards his face. Where were his feet?

His name had been called from an inner distance and one that took form inside his imagination as a grey and misted space at the edge of his mind. He sensed the drab emptiness was entirely without borders and reached much further than he was glimpsing.

Tasting hormones of terror in a dry mouth, he emerged from behind the shrubbery. Moving his legs was too conscious a manoeuvre.

The stranglehold of the moment abruptly passed and the figure was nowhere to be seen. Not on the water, the sands, the promenade, or in the park behind the beach.

Seb gathered up his things and jammed them inside his rucksack, managing to lose his hat in the process, which slipped down the back of the bench. He was too tense to regroup his wits but restrained himself from breaking into a run. Instead, he followed the serpentine path into Roundham Gardens, the beauty spot on the headland.

And that was the first time that he didn't linger to admire the blue expanse of the bay. Distant Torquay was ever a mosaic of white buildings, built over the hills and cliffs, an instant dreamy transport into the Mediterranean. But to hell with the view. Hurrying through a row of pines, their long trunks curved and harrowed for years by the wind, Seb made haste towards Paignton harbour.

Even if the man had been intent on engaging with him, scaling the cliff-side paths behind Seb would have been an impossible feat in the time it had taken Seb to get this far, but he still repeatedly glanced over his shoulder to make sure that he wasn't being followed.

Hatless and harried, as he moved out of the cliff-side gardens, his mind cast about for an explanation for the irrational sensation. He feared an early onset of dementia, and the worst kind of end that he had imagined for himself. Secondary terrors skimmed over schizophrenia and other hallucination-prone disorders of the mind.

Or had he actually seen a man standing in the water? *The same man twice?*

He was shaken enough to consider that there was something unnatural about the figure. Perhaps the impossible had been achieved during that strange possession of his mind upon the cliffs; he was even close to believing in the presence of the supernormal. The very subject that had made his name as a writer for so many years. The paranormal had allowed him to become that rarest of writers too: one with a good living. But, regarding the numinous, though he had curiosity and fascination in abundance, he had no faith. Uncharacteristically eager to immerse himself into a crowd, he ran from Paignton harbour to a place he rarely went: the Esplanade.

Unencumbered by family and a confirmed bachelor –

having thrown the towel in on *all that* by thirty-six, fourteen years gone now – the seafront and its attractions had never been designed for him. But the holidaymakers at the tail end of the Easter holiday did not share his reticence. It wasn't yet May, nor ten in the morning, but due to the warm spring there was already a large gathering of retirees, young families and groups of prospecting teenagers on the front.

Seb mingled amongst the beach blankets, windbreaks and small tents on the beach and hurried across the shoreline in the direction of Preston Sands. Cutting up and onto the Esplanade by the pier, he was engulfed by the fragrant haze of fried sugar and hotdog onions, then beset by the incessant jangle of the arcade's dark interior. As if he'd forded back across the river Styx and rejoined the living, the assault on his senses was joyous.

He picked up a polystyrene beaker of sweetened coffee to calm his nerves and moved past the shrieks and hurdy-gurdy jingles of the small fairground, pitched beside the adventure playground on the green. Feeling protected and even invigorated by the noise, the very electricity and energy that was relentlessly maintained by a giant pair of throaty speakers, Seb moved to the outskirts of the scene to where the strollers and the stream of cyclists thinned. He found a bench facing the sea and slumped upon it.

Tall white hotels lined up behind his seat. The Lodges, Houses and Palaces still clinging to their Victorian identities. Their cosy familiarity served as a strong arm placed about his shoulders.

Sipping his coffee, Seb made a call to Becky. Recent events had suddenly brought forward one of those times when his need for company, intimacy and affection exceeded his desire for solitude. He'd forgotten what it was like to be intimidated. Yet, in the cliff-side gardens, he'd felt more than merely intruded upon, he'd come away feeling threatened.

As if superimposing itself upon the new scene about Seb, the watcher on the shore's black shape continued to stain his thoughts while he fumbled with his phone. A sense that he was still within the figure's orbit would not abate.

Becky's voicemail picked up. Conscious of saying more than usual in a message to her, he also cringed at the note of desperation in his voice. 'Hi, it's me. The weather is just fantastic . . . and it's been a while, so I wondered if you fancied a trip to the seaside . . . Anyway, I'd love to see you again, soon . . . There's a great new seafood place just opened in Brixham—'

Seb cut off the hesitant stream of inducements because another now called for his attention. The figure in black stood at the pier's railing between a noodle bar and a seafood concession. And he was closer.

Getting closer.

He couldn't have been more than a hundred metres away now, which added an even greater intensity to Seb's discomfort at being observed, and not only from the outside.

On his phone a recorded message played inside his ear, offering a menu of playback, re-record or deletion. And he wished that at least two options were available for far more than a recorded message. He suddenly wanted to undo the beginning of his adult life, because the man standing on the pier, and staring right at him, was becoming horribly familiar.

Can't be . . .

Seb stood up, upsetting his rucksack and coffee cup.

Two cyclists, riding abreast of each other, whirred past, their heads elongated by helmets into the shape of alien skulls.

Seb trotted across the beach road and slipped between two parked cars to reach the promenade. He clutched at the railings.

His fear was joined by a compulsive curiosity about the stalker's identity. But more importantly, how had he moved from Goodrington's shoreline and around the headland to reach the pier? There had been no one behind Seb as he fled the cliff-side gardens. He'd looked back often enough. Of course, it could just be coincidence, two similarly dressed men in different places fixing him with their stare. But Seb was beyond even trying to convince himself of this.

As he tried to make sense of the man's relocation to the pier, he could not suppress a competing suspicion that the figure had known where Seb was running to. *To wait for you.* And again, his reason was overrun by the notion that the man had arrived at the pier by other means, and by a method and design that Seb couldn't even guess at.

But if this was to be a reunion, his memory began to reopen some of its darkest rooms in anticipation. Rooms with doors long closed and double-locked.

On the beach below Seb a frisbee was thrown badly. A mother, with broad tattoos on her lower legs, roared at her young. An elderly lady spoke to her spouse and said, 'But I don't want you to feel any pressure . . .' Gulls cried above the rinsing action of the waves upon the sand. And all of these sounds retreated to a distance found only in daydreams, or in echoes from the past.

Bewilderment and the swoop of vertigo made Seb press his

body against the railings to remain upright. An atmosphere of thinner air seemed to come into existence all around his body. He even feared that gravity was disappearing.

To the pier he looked beseechingly, his face pleading for a release and for that figure to make it all stop.

The man had vanished. He'd either sidestepped behind one of the little cabins at the side of the pier or had concealed himself within the crowd, *or even . . .*

Seb had no idea.

From an even shorter distance than before, he heard the sound of his name. *Sebastian.*

Again, the word might have appeared within the confines of his mind. It may also have issued from a range somewhere behind and slightly above his head. The only amelioration of his shock was provided by Seb's recognition of the voice. The speaker's face even appeared to him before quickly fading.

Could it be?

Seb turned about, and felt his vision drawn over the parked cars and to the man in black. He was now standing on the far side of the green within the shadow of the fir trees and behind a waist-high wall of breccia stone before the Hotel Connair.

He'd been on the pier mere seconds before. *Impossible.*

Seb could now make out the presence of lank hair and a baseball cap. A jaw covered by a black beard. The surrounding flesh issued an unhealthy pallor reminiscent of cream cheese, near-noisome at a glance.

The figure raised a long arm. The hand and wrist were as blanched as the face.

Seb moved hesitantly across the beach road. The world

looked as it usually did, though his vision twitched from shock. But the world was not the same. Where had sound gone? He might have been sleepwalking.

A car braked hard and Seb saw suppressed fury in an elderly face behind the windscreen that he'd nearly rolled across. He waved an apology to the driver and stumbled back to the bench where he'd left his bag.

The temporary suspension of the world ended. A universe of raw sound rushed like the sea into a cave and filled his ears.

A mournful chorus from the gulls upon their lamp-post perches.

The gritty bounce of a rubber ball on tarmac.

A car door slammed.

The grunt of a motorbike on the Esplanade Road . . .

The end of the episode left him shaken and as cold as a bather emerging into a crosswind.

The watcher behind the wall had vanished.

extracts reading groups
competitions books new
discounts extracts
competitions
books new
events books
extracts new books
interviews
events extracts events
discounts new books events
events new
discounts extracts discounts
www.panmacmillan.com
extracts events reading groups
competitions books extracts new
reading groups events reading groups